I JUST WANT TO BE YOURS

HEATHER GARVIN

Copyright © 2024 by Heather Garvin

All rights reserved.

No part of this book may be reproduced in any form or by any electronic or mechanical means, including information storage and retrieval systems, without written permission from the author, except for the use of brief quotations in a book review.

Ebook ASIN: B0CQNKTPS4

Paperback ISBN: 979-8-9885299-2-7

Cover Design: Sam Palencia at Ink and Laurel

Editor: Kristina Haahr

This is a work of fiction. Names, characters, businesses, events, and incidents are the product of the author's imagination.

author's note

I Just Want To Be Yours contains on page intimate scenes and is intended for mature audiences only.

playlist

Spotify: I Just Want To Be Yours

Like This - Jake Scott
In A Perfect World - Dean Lewis, Julia Michaels
the 1 - Taylor Swift
Tripping Over Air - Aidan Bissett
One For The Road - Arctic Monkeys
Hits Different - Taylor Swift
Blank Me - Hastings
Steal The Show - Lauv
Why'd You Only Call me When You're High? - Arctic Monkeys
Dancing With Our Hands Tied - Taylor Swift
Wildflower - Thomas Day
Parachute - Arden Jones
All That I'm Craving - Aidan Bissett
Hair toss, Arms Crossed - Mark Amber

To everyone who loves them
Thank you for giving me an excuse to continue their story

1
jackson

THE CHIME of my alarm sounds on the bedside table, and I let out a groan as I pull myself away from a very naked Margot to stop the noise. Soft light illuminates the room I've called home for the past couple of months, and I rub a hand over my face to try and wake myself up.

Her room almost looks the same as her dorm did. She has all the same posters, and her shelves are still lined with the journals and notebooks that make this room hers. The same boho sun theme runs throughout these four walls, but she had to get a new bedding set for her bigger bed. Gone are the orange sheets. She picked solid white with a burnt orange throw blanket instead.

If you ask me, the white theme looks way too clean for the things we've been doing in this room all summer. I can't keep my hands off her. American Thieves wrapped up our last tour in May, and I've been here, crashing at her new apartment, ever since.

Technically, I was supposed to stay with Matt at his apartment two doors down, but why would I stay on his couch when I can stay in Margot's bed? He found a roommate to replace me, but I hope Braden doesn't get too comfortable. I think the only reason Rae didn't move in with Matt this time around was for Margot's sake. But even with two different addresses, they still end up staying together most nights.

Margot stirs, reaching for me through the tangled sheets. Her eyes are still closed like she doesn't want to accept it's morning yet, and I turn back to face her again. I only get to look at her for a second before she buries her face in my chest, but I swear her face is the best thing to wake up to. My fingers absently run through her hair, and she doesn't tense when I do this anymore. I used to have to hold back with her in so many ways. Now, when I graze her skin with my fingertips, she relaxes.

The change happened so quickly, but it's been in the making for months. I left college with her still pushing me away, but when she came to that show in Chicago, it was like the switch had already flipped. Ever since she decided to give us a chance, those walls that once felt impenetrable are rubble at my feet.

I hate that I'll have to leave her again in a matter of days. American Thieves secured an opening spot for a band called Crooner Sins, and I'll be gone for another five months. My chest starts to ache, and I wrap my arms around her tighter. It will be different this time. This time, I'm leaving behind so much more.

Delicate fingers brush against my skin, and she presses a kiss to my neck that shoots straight to my groin. A low rumble leaves my throat because I know exactly what she's doing. This is payback for all the times I've tried to make her late for work. Today is the only day I need to be up and out of the house before her, and she's going to torture me for it.

Like she has the power to read my thoughts, she hooks her leg up and over my hip. God, she's perfect. She's warm and soft, and I have absolutely no self-control when she opens her legs for me. I tighten my grip on her, but the words, "I have to go," traitorously leave my lips.

Her eyes stay shut, but a gentle frown infiltrates the lines of her face as she shushes me into submission. Amusement lifts my lips because the feeling is mutual, but the band has a slot to play at a music festival this afternoon and we need to get there early if we want enough time to set up and scope the place out. We may have a 2:00 p.m. slot, but the headliners of the festival are big enough that just having the American Thieves name under theirs somewhere at the bottom of the lineup is a step in the right direction.

Margot's perfect mouth leaves a trail of sweet kisses along my neck and jaw, and I do my best to take a steadying breath. Damn it, she feels so good, and she knows it.

"Margot," I half scold, half plead, making no move to leave the bed. I can't. Especially when her fingers trail down my chest and wrap around my already hard cock. She pumps her hand, and I know I'm done for. Letting out a groan of surrender, I keep her leg hooked up and around me as I roll her on to her back and position myself over her. She still has her eyes closed, but there's a satisfied tilt to her lips now. She knows she's won. She *always* wins.

She's already wet when I slide into her, and her eyes fly open. Keeping her leg bent around me, she barely has time to look at me before I hit deep and her back arches against the mattress, her eyes rolling back.

I could never get sick of seeing her like this. Nothing beats her naked body on display in the glow of the soft morning light. Just watching the way her hips move to meet my thrusts could tip me over the edge. Margot would never give me the satisfaction of begging, but her body does it for her. It's the way her nails dig into my back and her wet heat clamps tightly around me every time I move into her. She needs this as much as I do.

Burying my face in her neck, I thrust into her harder. "You're going to make me late."

A soft moan leaves her lips. "Then you should probably hurry up and make me come."

I huff a laugh. I can't count the number of times I've kept her pinned to the bed when she was supposed to get ready. How could I not? Everything about this girl makes me do things outside of my control.

Sliding my hand up her leg, I grip the back of her thigh, pushing it up and resting it on my shoulder to give me a better angle. Fuck, she feels good. "I'll make you come, Red." She whimpers, and when my thumb finds her clit, her breath catches. I ease in and out of her while I add pressure where I know she wants it until her legs shake. If there's one thing I love about having so much time with Margot, it's learning what makes her tick. Sure, I know she has a thing about the toothpaste being put away, but I've also learned how to make her come so hard around my cock that she cries out without fail.

With one last brush of my thumb, she falls apart. She calls out my name and grips my hair at the roots while I pick up my pace and chase my own release. She's still pulsing and clenching when I let myself go, and I curse under my breath as I come inside her.

She's mine.

My lips brush against her neck and cheek as we both come down from our high, and she's panting, flushed, and bright-eyed when she looks up at me. "I thought you had to go."

I let out a groan and push into her one more time. I don't want to think about the fact that I'm probably late. All I want to think about is the fact that I'm the reason she looks like this. My lips find her ear, and I nip her skin before pulling out. "I'll get you back for this later."

A soft giggle leaves her lips. "I'm looking forward to it."

My mouth finds hers, and I kiss her more times than I

should before forcing myself to step away. I hope she's dressed by the time I get out of the shower, because I definitely can't risk going for round two.

After the fastest shower I've ever taken, I walk back into her bedroom to find her exactly where I left her, still tangled in the sheets. She watches as I get dressed, and I chuff a laugh. "You're staring."

Her lips twist. "So?"

Once I pull on my shirt, I lean over the bed and kiss her again. "Seeing you look at me like that is giving me too many ideas, and they all involve me being inside you one way or another."

She smiles sweetly. "Later. Have fun."

I kiss her one more time without thinking, grab my notebook and guitar case, and rush out the door.

2
margot

"MATT HAS OUR TICKETS, RIGHT?" I ask Rae as I adjust my high-waisted shorts and crop-top. She and I have been getting ready in our apartment for most of the morning. We'll be at the festival all day, and I'm buzzing to see Jackson on stage again. It's crazy to think I haven't seen him perform since the show in Chicago. The guys have mostly been working in the studio while he's been here, making music for the next album, but this music festival is their one show here at home before they're back on tour again.

For five months.

I freeze as I stare at myself in the mirror. It's hard for me to wrap my head around him being gone for that long. He's become a huge part of my everyday life, and I'm not ready for that to change.

"Yeah, he and Braden will meet us outside whenever we're ready." Rae walks over to share the mirror and adds another touch of mascara before she steps back and checks herself out. She looks incredible. Her blonde hair is curled, she has a cute bohemian headband, and she's wearing shorts like mine. Paired with her long flowing sleeves, she looks like she could rival Stevie Nicks. "What time does Jackson go on?"

I step back from the mirror, finally content with my look. "He said we should be at the side of the stage around 1:30 so he can make sure we're front and center before they play at two o'clock. He'll join us after his set."

"I can't believe your boyfriend is in a band," she says with a laugh and a shake of her head.

A smile stretches across my lips. "I can't believe my boyfriend is Jackson." When we first started dating while he was on tour, it was a little challenging, but not nearly as much as I thought. Maybe his bandmates being older is a good thing. They don't get too wild, and Jackson usually made a point to text me every night. But having him here feels like a wonderful alternate universe. We've been good—better than good. There's nothing like waking up and going to bed with your favorite person, and that's what he's become.

Grabbing her stuff, Rae chuckles. "Well, yeah. That, too."

She texts Matt to let him know we're ready, and by the time we make it out the front door, both guys are standing there, waiting for us.

Seeing Matt and Braden wearing khaki shorts and polo shirts doesn't exactly scream music festival or rock concert, but I don't think that's ever been their style, anyway.

"Holy shit," Matt says as he takes in his girlfriend. I can't blame him.

"You have our tickets, right?" Rae asks.

Matt rolls his eyes. "Yes, I have our tickets."

My mouth quirks. They're both used to being the responsible friend. Rae has always kept an eye out for me, and Matt has always kept track of Jackson.

Matt reaches for his back pocket and pulls out the four tickets Jackson gave us. Stuffing them back into his pocket he says, "Now can I appreciate how my girlfriend looks? Because .

. ." His eyes trail down her before finishing his sentence. "Damn."

Rae shakes her head, keeping her lips tight to hide her smile. "Margot looks 'damn,' too."

Matt's eyes never leave hers. "It's not my job to tell Margot how good she looks." His eyes quickly jump to me, so he can add, "No offense, Margot."

I laugh, loving how much he adores her. "None taken."

"Well, as someone who isn't dating either of you, you both look 'damn,'" Braden says.

When my eyes meet his, I grin in appreciation. I like Braden. He's a lot like Matt, who I adore, so it's easy to be around him. Really, Matt couldn't have asked for a better roommate. He might be lifelong best friends with Jackson, but he and Braden have more in common. And one thing's for sure, his apartment is much cleaner with Braden living there than his dorm ever was with Jackson.

Rae gives Braden a smile, too. "Thanks."

Matt nods toward the parking lot behind us. "Let's go watch Jackson shred it up." He starts playing air guitar, and Rae and I shake our heads.

"Do people really say that? 'Shred it up?'" She narrows her eyes at him playfully.

He pauses for only a second. "Of course they do. I just did, didn't I?"

Looking over at me, Rae sighs. "He's going to want to join a band again after this, isn't he?"

With a lingering smile on my lips, my eyes jump back to Matt who's still walking backward and playing air guitar for us. Leaning in closer to Rae, I say, "Even if he does, I think you're safe."

Matt points at me, but somehow still manages to hold his invisible guitar with one hand. "I heard that, Margot."

Rae calls back to him. "She would know. Her boyfriend is a real rock star."

My stomach flutters in excited anticipation at the sound of her words. She's right. Jackson isn't just some guy in a band anymore. American Thieves might not have headlined yet, but they're on track for it. With the tour they just finished in the spring, and now the other tour that starts at the end of summer, people are going to know American Thieves.

And Jackson thinks it all started with my blog.

That article has become my favorite thing I've written. It's pinned at the top of my site, and I still get hits on it every day. I haven't written about the band since then. My nerves were too all over the place to write about the Chicago show, but maybe today will give me new inspiration.

They couldn't have picked a more perfect day for a music festival. The sun warms my skin, but the heat isn't overbearing. The air moves with an unusual breeze for this time of year, and the sky is the brightest blue with scattered white clouds. Everything about the scene in front of me feels picturesque, like when you're remembering the past through rose-tinted glasses, but I've never felt more present.

Three stages make up the festival—a main stage and two smaller ones. As we walk through the rows of vendors selling everything from snacks to light-up bracelets, Rae and I have our arms linked while the guys follow.

Jackson said they're the second band to play at one of the smaller stages, and from here, it looks like the first band doesn't have much of an audience. It's mostly people cutting through, or groups of friends collected in front of the show randomly. A small group of people stand at the very front of the stage, singing along to every word as the band wraps up their set. The sight makes me smile.

"There he is," Rae says in my ear as she leans in close.

I stop scanning the scene to search near the side of the stage where Jackson casually leans against the bottom, and even though I just saw him this morning, a grin blossoms across my face. Sometimes I wonder if he knows how good he looks. Maybe that's part of the appeal—how effortless it is for him. His jeans and black T-shirt are probably something I've seen him wear countless times, but it doesn't matter. My boyfriend is really fucking hot.

I beam at him, and his smile widens. Letting go of Rae, I run up to him, and he laughs as he catches me in his arms.

"Excited for the show?" he asks as he smooths my hair back, letting his hand linger against my cheek.

"That must be it."

Letting out a breath of laughter, he presses a kiss to my forehead before turning to our friends. "I'm glad the tickets worked."

Matt cocks an eyebrow, the corners of his mouth turning upward. "Was there a chance they wouldn't?"

Jackson shrugs. "I don't know. The guy looked offended when I asked for them. We're one of the smallest bands here—he had definitely never heard of American Thieves."

Matt shakes his head disapprovingly. "He's never heard of you? And he calls himself a professional?"

Jackson stares at his friend with a halfcocked smirk. He shakes his head and mutters, "Fuck off."

Clapping a hand on Jackson's shoulder, Matt grins.

Rae's eyes skip to the stage in front of us before falling back on Jackson. "So, can we meet the band?" she asks with a pleading smile. "This is so cool," she adds with a laugh.

Jackson stares at her for a moment like he's trying to figure out if she's joking.

"She's serious," I say as Dave catches sight of me. His shoulder-length blond hair is tied up in a bun today, and he has a little more of a beard than the last time I saw him. He points excitedly and drops what he was doing to hop down from the stage.

"Look who it is!" he says as he pulls me from Jackson to wrap me in a bear hug. "You brought my favorite redhead!"

"Meet the band, Rae," I say with a laugh.

3
jackson

BY THE TIME Dave stops hugging Margot, the other guys have made their way over, everyone shaking hands and introducing themselves. I don't think I even realized my friends had never formally met the band. They've only been to one other show. Maybe I should have introduced them after? I don't think I thought about it. I was too hyped and hung up on wanting to kiss Margot outside the men's room after my first gig.

But as I stand here, watching my two worlds merge, it feels weird that it's taken this long.

The guys immediately strike up a conversation with Matt and Braden, thanking them for coming out, and Margot and Rae are all smiles. Margot laughs when Rae says something only loud enough for her to hear.

Her eyes meet mine. "What?" I ask.

Margot shakes her head, her cheeks flushing. "Nothing."

I study her, trying to figure out what they're not saying, but all I can focus on is the pretty shade of pink that warms her cheeks. My gaze wanders to her neck, then her collar bone, her perfect breasts. She always stops me when she walks into a room, but her outfit today hits different. If she looked like this when I had to leave this morning, I never would have made it. Her hair is down and straight, but every time she runs her hand through it, soft strands frame her face. It's taking all my self-control not to weave my fingers through it and crash my lips against hers.

She turns around to look at the stage while the last band tears down their equipment, and I fight back a groan. All I want to do is take a bite out of her ass in those shorts.

"You're just a cool boyfriend to have," Rae says with a laugh, filling me in on the conversation I had already forgotten about.

I cock an eyebrow. "Yeah?" I'm glad Rae thinks so because sometimes I'm not so sure. It's a feeling I've had since Margot and I started dating—like I'm bound to disappoint the girl who matters most.

Margot looks over her shoulder and locks eyes with me, but she just smiles and shakes her head, dismissing Rae's comment.

She never acts like I've let her down. By some stroke of dumb luck, she acts like she can't get enough of me.

Dave excuses himself from the conversation with the guys and pats me on the shoulder as he heads back to the stage. "We've got fifteen."

"That's my cue," I say to everyone before finally walking up to Margot and cradling her face in my hands. I kiss her slow and sweet until her lips pull into a smile against mine. "I'll see you after."

"Okay," she says, and she sounds breathless. She's still looking at me as she backs away to catch up with the rest of our friends.

It's only then that I take in the wider picture of my surroundings. A decent sized crowd has formed in front of the stage. My eyes widen, and I look back at Dave. Laughing, he catches my stare and mouths, "I know!"

Looking back at the crowd, I shake my head. We've played in front of large audiences before, but most of those people were there for Sidecar, not us. There's a chance these people are just camping out early so they can see the bigger bands up close tonight, but they could be here for us, too.

That's all it takes for the blood to course through my veins.

It's easy to spot my friends trying to work their way into the crowd. They'll never get to the front with how things are now. Jogging up to security standing at the bottom of the stage, I point to Margot. I saw Brady do this earlier for his girlfriend and hope I get the same results. Glancing down at his name tag, I say, "Hey, Mack." The guy looks at me, his long hair tucked under a backward baseball cap. "Jackson," I add as I hold out a hand.

He shakes it but looks like he doesn't know why some random kid is talking to him—which I guess is fair.

I point my thumb over my shoulder at the stage behind me. "I play guitar for American Thieves. Do you think you can let those four front and center?"

His eyes move from me to the direction I'm pointing. "Them?"

I nod. "Yeah, with the gorgeous redhead."

He lets out a laugh. "Yeah. All right."

I jog back to the side of the stage and call out, "Thanks, Mack!" over my shoulder.

"All good?" Dave asks once I reach him and the guys.

"Yeah." I grab my guitar and slip it over my head, securing the strap on my shoulder. "I figured we'd have an audience like the last band. Where did all these people come from?"

Dave looks out at the crowd with a slow shake of his head. "No idea. It's been a while since we've played a festival, but I'd say this is a good turn out for a midafternoon slot."

Marty comes up behind Dave and me, looping an arm

around each of us. "Uh, did we have this many fans last time we were home?"

"No," I say, not breaking my eyes away from the scene. Mack has gotten Margot's attention and waves her to the front while Rae, Matt, and Braden trail behind. Once they've secured their spots, Rae bounces on her heels and excitedly says something to Margot that makes her toss her head back in laughter.

She looks happy.

The corners of my mouth lift at the sight. I like seeing her happy.

Brady lets out a slow whistle. "Damn," he says as he looks at the still growing mass of people, lightly drumming his drumsticks against his thighs as he stands. "Let's give them one hell of a show."

Dave claps his hands together. "You don't have to tell me twice." Turning around, he reaches into a bag and pulls out a bottle of bourbon. "Ready?"

We all take a shot for luck before the show.

Dave swallows and blows out a breath before he shakes out his nerves and hits the stage. By the time we all take our places, he's already saying something into the mic about how, even though we only have an hour, we're going to party like we have all fucking night.

The crowd likes it. They cheer louder than they did when we first hit the stage.

Everyone's still cheering when I look up and spot Margot in the very front. Rae and Matt beam at Dave, clapping and cheering, but Margot's eyes are on me, a soft smile pulling at her lips. She blows me a kiss, and I have to look down at my guitar to hide my grin.

Because nothing beats having her at our shows.

Nothing.

4
margot

THE FAMILIAR DRUM beat of the first song starts, the vibration from the speakers reverberating in my chest. It's one of their biggest hits, and the crowd isn't disappointed. A roar erupts from the opening drums alone, and Dave pulls back from the mic to look at Marty with wide eyes. I catch the words "Fuck yeah!" on his lips, making me laugh.

Matt stands behind Rae with his arms around her as she and I sing along to the words we now know by heart. Braden stands next to Matt, bobbing his head along to the music. His dark blond hair looks incredibly neat given the current environment. Nothing about Braden says *rock and roll*—making him fit in about as much as Matt does. The two guys are probably the most clean-cut here.

Leaning in toward Rae, I yell over the sound of the music. "I think Braden needs a girlfriend!"

She throws her head back with a laugh. "Why?"

I shrug. "So, he's not a fifth wheel?"

She looks over at Braden as she considers what I've said. "Maybe." When she looks back at the stage, she leans in close and adds, "Yeah. I guess he'd probably have more fun with us if he were dating someone."

I nod.

Rae twists out of Matt's arms to invade Braden's personal space, and I rest my arms on the metal barricade in front of me. Jackson has his head down, lost in the music as always. He's focused, and precise, and it's sexy as hell.

I look over, surprised to find Braden looking at me as he leans in to listen to whatever Rae says in his ear. As soon as our eyes meet, he drops his gaze and focuses on hearing her over the music. She's on the tips of her toes, and when he pulls back to answer, his eyes jump to me again before he says something with a shake of his head.

I frown. The way he just looked at me felt heavy, like more than a brief glance in my direction. Trying to shake the feeling, I focus on the show again until Rae works her way back to me, and I lean toward her. "What did you ask him?"

"What his type is!" she yells over the music.

I let out a laugh, but it's forced. Why was he looking at me then? "And?"

She shrugs. "He says he doesn't have one." Before I can say anything else, she cups both hands around her mouth and cheers with the rest of the crowd at the end of the song.

And it takes everything in me not to glance over my shoulder at Braden again.

"There he is!" Matt cheers when Jackson and the rest of the band meet up with us after the show.

Jackson shakes his head at Matt but can't hide the subtle upturn of his lips. I know he loves this. He loves having us here.

Brady has his arm around a stunning brunette who quickly

gets introduced to us as his girlfriend, Kasey. I somehow make it through pleasantries, but after watching Jackson on stage for the last hour, he's all I can think about. He may have put on a fresh shirt, but sweat still glistens on his skin and the hair at the base of his neck is curled and flipped in the best way. Sometimes him being in the band feels like the biggest hurdle in our relationship, and other times—like right now—it feels like it's the sexiest thing about him.

His eyes land on me, and a slight crease between his brows form. I must look like I'm still drooling over him. Blinking back to reality, I quickly say, "You guys put on a great show."

Braden nods. "The crowd seemed to grow the longer you played, so I'd say that's a good sign."

Jackson tears his eyes away from me just long enough to throw Braden a "Thanks," but it only lasts a second. He's more interested in trying to read my thoughts.

Biting my bottom lip, I try to fight my grin. "A great sign," I agree.

Jackson laughs, his eyes never leaving mine. He knows I'm turned on. We still have the rest of the festival to enjoy, but all I want to do is take him home and have my way with him. I was worried that him going back on tour would make me withdraw and shut down, but ever since he told me he's leaving, all I want to do is jump him every chance I get.

"Which band should we see next?" Rae asks, and it helps to bring me back to the current moment.

I need to get a grip.

Dave points to the larger stage at the center of the festival. "Broken Ridge is great. They'll be next on the main stage."

Matt throws his arm around Rae. "Let's do it."

Jackson and I trail a few paces behind the band and our friends. He kisses the side of my hair, and I lean into him as we walk. His voice is low in my ear when he says, "You sure you don't want to find the van?"

Laughter warms my chest as I push him away from me. "I am not having sex with you in the van."

He grins, and I love seeing the amusement shining behind those eyes.

When he keeps looking at me, I add, "Really," to drive the point home.

Putting his hands in his pockets, he shrugs. "Offer's on the table, Red."

I roll my eyes and leave his side to catch up with Rae, hooking my arm through hers. When I look over my shoulder, Jackson's watching me with enough intensity to make my cheeks flush. He drags his thumb over his bottom lip as he shamelessly looks from my ass back up to my eyes, and that familiar heat settles deep within me.

"Behave," I mouth, playfully scolding him.

"No," he says loud enough for everyone to hear, a smirk toying at the corner of his mouth.

Rae looks back at him for the sudden outburst, but Jackson shrugs and points at me.

Rae nudges me and leans in to whisper in my ear. "Do you see the way he looks at you?"

Heat warms my chest and cheeks, and I nod. The way Jackson looks at me is one of my favorite things about him. He looks at me like I'm the only thing he sees.

Swallowing, my eyes dare to jump to Braden a few feet ahead of us. He's talking to Matt now, but I can't help thinking about how he had looked at me before.

I'm probably reading into it too much.

I'm sure it was nothing.

5
jackson

MUSIC FEELS SO FUCKING GOOD. The bass vibrates through my chest while the stage lights flash against the night sky. Everything about today has been so fucking good.

The edible Braden gave me a few hours ago might have something to do with that.

Margot and I split it, but Matt and Rae passed.

The ever-responsible duo.

I didn't have much of an opinion about Braden before today, but he's cool.

The song changes, and Margot changes the tempo of her hips along with it. She's been grinding her ass against me all day. Her hand holds the back of my neck as she leans her back against my chest, letting her hips continue their slow assault.

I can't wait to get her home.

Her hair is up after a long day in the heat, and I press my lips to her exposed neck. I swear I can feel her entire body hum happily before she melts into me more. Her fingers weave into my hair, tugging it at the roots while she dances against me. I wrap my arms around her, holding her close. Slipping my hand under her shirt, I drag it over her bare stomach and let out a low, guttural sound. She tilts her head back against my shoulder, giving me more access to her neck, and I kiss her just below her ear. I may not be able to hear her suck in a breath, but I can feel it. Just like I can feel her rapidly beating heart when she turns in my arms to face me. I feel the brush of her fingertips as she combs through my hair and the warmth of her mouth on mine.

I grip the back of her neck, my thumb tracing the soft curve of her jaw as I kiss her deeper. As soon as her tongue eases into my mouth, everything else fades away. I'm left with only Margot and the music, and I can't get enough.

This day has been fucking perfect. Even as I kiss her, she slips her fingers into the front of my pants, tugging me closer. When she lets go to turn back around, they lightly brush the bulge of my jeans, and I almost lose it.

Song after song, she finds new ways to keep me on edge, and I have a feeling she knows exactly what she's doing. I might have had to fight a hard-on with her all day, but I can't remember the last time I've had this much fun. I mean, we've been having a great time all summer, but there's something about being in this electric environment with her that makes this random Saturday feel like a cause for celebration.

By the end of the night, as we walk back to the parking lot with Matt, Rae, and Braden, I don't want it to end. Dave and the guys split after we watched a couple of sets together. I have no idea if they're still here, but I have a feeling they'll all wake up hungover tomorrow.

"You're good to drive?" Matt asks me after the show.

Tossing my keys in the air, I catch them. "Never been better." The edible has worn off, and the only high I'm still chasing is Margot in those fucking shorts.

Matt takes Rae's hand. "Good. I don't need you and Margot having sex in the back of my car."

Rae whacks him on the arm, and I squeeze my arm around Margot a little tighter. "You hear that? We can't have sex in his car anymore."

Margot's face heats, and she gapes at Matt. Choking back laughter she says, "We wouldn't—we've never."

Matt gives her a slow grin. "I know, Margot. Relax," he says with a laugh. Looking back at me, he flips me off. "See you at the apartment."

I return the gesture. "Don't wait up."

"Hey, thanks again for the ticket," Braden says as he walks backward with Matt and Rae.

"Thanks again for the drugs," I call back, and Margot hisses for me to be quiet. Braden laughs, though.

As one of the musicians in the festival, they had us park in the back with most of the other vendors. The guys drove the van, and I met them here since I knew I'd spend the rest of the day with Margot.

We walk, my arm around her shoulders and hers draped around my waist. I wish I could end every show like this. We'd drive home, and then I could make her come before falling asleep with my arms wrapped around her.

"There's no one back here," she whispers, pulling me closer.

"Yeah, well." I look over my shoulder at the festival that's still full of music and light. "I'd say the party is far from over."

With my car in sight, she turns and starts walking backward, pulling me by my shirt as she does. "For us too?" she says with a devilish glint in her eyes.

I let out a breath of laughter. "What do you want to do?"

She looks up as she ponders my question. "Hmm . . ." she says with a playful twist to her mouth. "I could think of something."

"I bet you could."

She grins, and something tightens in my chest. I don't know

if it's knowing that being here with her is temporary, or that she looks gorgeous under the subtle glow of the distant lights, but every part of me aches for this girl.

When her back hits the side of my car, she pulls me to her. Her mouth is on mine, full of heat, like she's been waiting for us to be alone all day. The kiss pulls a sound from my throat, and I want nothing more than to lose myself in her.

But I need to tell her. I need to say something of substance because if I don't, my chest might explode. "Margot," I say against her lips. "Get in the car."

She lets out a laugh as I step back and open the door for her. Once she's seated, I close the door and walk around to the driver's side. Looking back at the festival over the hood, I'm hit with a wave of mixed feelings. Part of me knowing I'll be onto bigger and better things soon, and another, louder part, knowing how much I'll miss this.

Once I'm in the car, I put the keys in the ignition and rub my hands over my face, trying to snap myself out of whatever funk this is.

"What's on your mind?" she asks, her voice soft. That's when I realize she's been watching me, carefully analyzing.

"I don't know." I lean my head back against the seat. Looking straight ahead, I rub my hands on my jeans. "I guess I just wish it could always be like this." I dismiss it with a laugh but keep my gaze forward. It's easier than looking at her. If I look at her, I'll feel everything twice as hard because she's the reason for all of it. "I don't think I'm ready for this summer to end."

She's quiet.

When I finally do look at her, she gives me an easy smile as she leans toward me over the center console. "But it's not over yet," she says simply. "And when it does end, you'll be living your dream again."

She's right, of course. All I've ever wanted was to

make a career out of music, and no one has ever supported me the way she does. She's selfless. Even though my dreams make things harder for her, she never lets me doubt them.

Before I can stop myself, I look her in the eyes and say, "Maybe my dreams are changing."

She sits up straight. "They're not."

A faint smile crosses my lips, but there's sadness behind it.

"They're not," she says again with more conviction.

My eyes search hers, the reflection of the lights dancing in the warm mahogany.

Taking my hand, she gives my fingers a light squeeze. "You can have more than one dream, you know."

Her words make me pause.

"Jackson," she says with a laugh. "You can want more than one thing."

God, I love her laugh. Reaching for her, my thumb brushes against her cheek. "What if I can't have the two things I want at the same time?"

She smiles, leaning into my touch, but there's a hint of reservation behind her eyes now. "Well," she says slowly, like she's choosing her words carefully. "Then you take turns."

My lips lift, but I can't shake it. I can't shake the feeling she's somehow getting the short end of the stick in all this, and I'm the one handing it to her. I want to tell her I'm sorry. I want to tell her how much she means to me. I want to tell her the thought of leaving her again has me dreading doing what I've always wanted.

But instead of saying any of those things, I say, "You're so beautiful," my voice barely a whisper as my thumb brushes over the freckles scattered across her cheek.

Her eyes widen, and I wonder if I've never said that to her? I think it every day. Hell, I think it every time she walks into a room. I must have told her, but by the way she's looking at me,

I know I haven't. That will be another thing for me to beat myself up over.

She climbs into my lap to straddle me, and I suck in a breath as I push the seat back. God, she feels good. Later. I'll beat myself up for it later. Before she can say another word, my hands are on her ass and my mouth is on hers.

"Margot," I groan, pulling her flush against me. I'm already hard, and after how much she's been teasing me all day, I don't have much more restraint. My tongue slips into her mouth gently, trying to make it last. And trying not to get my cock more excited than it should be. But she melts into me, and those damn hips are hellbent on making sure I feel just enough friction to make me snap.

My kiss turns hungry—starving—and I swallow her moans like they're the air I need to breathe. My mouth moves to her neck, to her collarbone, to her perfect breasts peeking out from the top of her shirt. Her head falls back, her eyes closing, as I worship every exposed part of her. One hand tightly grips the soft skin of her waist while I pull down her bra and take her nipple into my mouth. She gasps, her eyes flying open to look at me, and the heat behind that look is enough to make me groan. Her cheeks were already pink from the sun, but this blush creeps down her neck. Her lips part, and her eyes grow heavy with lust and surprise like she didn't think I'd be this wound up after eight hours of the game she played.

"Take your pants off, Red," I grit, before sucking another long pull on her exposed nipple. Her back arches, but her fingers are already unbuttoning the front of her shorts as fast as she can. While she works them down and tosses them to the other side of the car, I manage to unbutton my jeans and lower them enough to free myself from my briefs.

She doesn't waste time, hurrying to position herself over me. As soon as she lines me up to her entrance, I can feel how wet she is already.

She curses under her breath while she takes me in, and I let my head fall back against the headrest as I watch her. She moves slowly, every additional inch met with her warm, tight walls clenching around my cock. My fists tense as I fight the urge to slam into her, but there's something about letting her be in control that turns me on.

When she finally takes in all of me, I swear my eyes roll back in my head. We're both breathing hard, and when she lifts herself all the way just to lower herself again, I thrust up into her. She cries out, her grip on the back of my neck tightening.

But as much as *I* need this, she does, too.

I know by the way she bites my shoulder when I start to move.

I know by the way she knots her fingers in my hair and devours my neck.

And I know by the way she says my name like a prayer when she wants me to make her come.

6
margot

RAE DIPS her honey chipotle chicken tenders into the tiny cup of ranch before taking a bite. I can't believe it's already the middle of the week. The festival feels like it was just yesterday, and the way time is passing weighs my stomach with dread. It serves as a reminder that Jackson will be back on the road before I know it, and I'm not ready to say goodbye.

"Summer term sucks, but I've been loving these lunch dates," she says as she picks up a fry and pops it into her mouth.

I dip a chip into our shared queso. "Almost done at least."

She nods. "I can't believe summer is almost over." Her eyes jump up to meet mine. "How are you feeling about everything?"

"Fine," I lie. It's easier to lie than admit I'm scared. "We did it before when he was opening for Sidecar. I'm sure it will be okay."

The second part is less of a lie. I do know we'll be able to do it again, but this time, I really don't want to. I want to keep waking up to him, with his hair a mess and his arms wrapped around me as he buries his face in my neck. I want to get home from work and see him sitting on my couch with Matt. I want to keep having him be a part of my daily life.

"If anyone can do it, it's you two." She goes to take another bite but pauses. "I mean, you know he loves you. That much is obvious."

I blink, not sure how to respond to that.

Rae tilts her head. "You two have said it, right?"

"Um." I drop my gaze, pushing my fajita peppers around with my fork and trying not to choke on the way her question just made me feel. "No." I shake my head. "We haven't."

"Margot!" she says with a laugh. "How long have you two been together?"

A soft smile pulls at my lips. "Depends on which days you want to count."

She gives me an incredulous look. "You don't even know when your anniversary is?"

"Not really." I shrug, talking about this with her is hard. She and Matt are perfect. He knew he loved her so quickly and told her as soon as he felt it. But Jackson and I aren't Matt and Rae. We never have been. I know I can't compare us to them, but when I talk to her about things, it makes it hard not to.

Rae shakes her head. "Okay, let's think. You two got together the week after Thanksgiving, right?"

"Unofficially," I say with a nod. "But the show was in January, and then he didn't stop touring until May."

She does the math. "So, if you count since he's been home, it's been three months, but if you count since you two decided to be exclusive, it's been almost *seven?*"

"Yeah."

I know this. I've been running the numbers. Mostly out of curiosity. My ex, Chris, told me he loved me after a month, and I said it back even though I wasn't sure I felt the same. I'm not even sure he felt it to be honest. With Jackson, I *feel* loved, but for some reason, he hasn't said it. I think it's okay. I think feeling it is more important than saying it.

She sets down her fry and brushes the crumbs off her hands, giving me her full attention. "And if he doesn't say it before he leaves, he probably won't say it while he's gone . . ."

I swallow, sifting through my rice with my fork even though I have no intention of taking another bite. "Probably."

"Which means he might not say it until he comes back for the holidays?"

Letting out a breath, I set my fork onto my plate. "Or if I go visit him on tour, but it's fine. There's no rush."

Rae frowns as our server comes to the table. "One mini molten for you two?"

Rae's eyes jump from me to the tall blonde taking our order. "Make it the big one."

I'm about to disagree with her, but she gives me a look that lets me know she can see right through me, and she's right. This conversation calls for the bigger cake. "Okay. One regular molten," I agree with a nod.

"You've got it." Our server disappears into the back, and I brace myself for the way Rae is inevitably still looking at me.

"Rae, I prom—"

"Do you love him?"

I blink. "What?"

She rolls her eyes. "It's not a hard question." With a shrug, she asks again, "Do you love him?"

"Um . . ." I don't know how to answer her. It's not that I doubt my feelings for Jackson, but I'm also okay with the fact that we haven't said those three words yet. Our relationship doesn't feel like it's lacking anything. Most days I don't even think about how we haven't exchanged the phrase. I only think about it when the occasional prickling thought settles into the back of my mind—or when I'm talking to Rae, apparently. "I don't know."

She gives me a heavy-lidded stare. "You've been with him for over six months. You know." She throws her hands in the air. "Hell, *I* know you love him just by being around you two."

Our server sets the fudgy, chocolate cake with ice cream, Magic Shell, and a caramel drizzle in front of us. "Let's drop it," I say, even though I know there's no use.

Without looking at her, I take my spoon and dig in.

She doesn't do the same.

She's still just waiting for me to give her a better explanation.

I let out a groan and swallow my bite. "I don't want to talk about it. If I admit anything out loud, I'm going to think about it. I'm going to start overanalyzing why he hasn't said it. And I'm going to drive myself insane. So, let's just drop it, okay? I'm happy."

She looks like she's trying to solve a complex puzzle as she dips her spoon into the caramel drizzle. "You could say it first, you know."

I scoff and shove another bite of molten chocolate into my mouth. "I am definitely not saying it first."

I may have grown a lot when it comes to not bottling up what I'm feeling, but the thought of making *that* confession is still too terrifying. What if it makes me come on too strong? What if he gets freaked out? What if he doesn't say it back?

I'd rather not find out.

7
jackson

WE'VE BEEN in the studio for hours, and all I want to do is get home. Margot got off work over an hour ago, and I had to text her and tell her I have no idea what time I'll be done.

> MARGOT:
> No worries. We're making tacos. I'll save you some.

Slipping my phone back in my pocket, I wait for the latest direction from Dave. Now that our days in the studio are numbered, he's been on a rampage, making sure our next album is nothing short of perfect.

He's stressed. He's brought the band up from nothing, and he's basically done it all himself for the past seven years. Now that things are going well for us, he might be thrilled, but he's drowning.

We need a manager.

I give him credit for securing the two opening tours on his own, but if we're ever going to headline ourselves, we need someone who knows what they're doing. No one has mentioned it—not in front of me, anyway. I was hoping I wouldn't have to be the one to say something since I'm the newest member, but if this keeps up, I'll have to talk to Dave.

He's listening to what feels like our millionth attempt at the tenth track on the album, and when he rips the headphones off his ears and storms back in, I know we'll have to do it again. This has become the new routine, and I find it a little hard to believe we suddenly suck *that* much. Dave doesn't usually talk about his personal life. Hell, he's supposedly had the same girlfriend for years, but I've never met her. Part of me wants to just ask him what the hell is going on, because I don't think our music is the only thing getting him riled up.

"Fucking trash," he says with a shake of his head. "Marty, tighten your shit up or I'll have Jackson record both guitar tracks."

Rubbing my hand over my face, I try to suppress my groan. "Is that the only reason we haven't finished this song yet? He sounds fine to me." I casually lift my hand. "But honestly, I'll record whatever you want if it means we can all go home."

Marty glares at me as he gets his guitar ready again. "Shut up, puppy." He gives Dave a nod. "Take it from the top."

Even Dave looks disappointed by my response, but at this point, I'm too tired to care. "Take it from the top," he echoes, and I don't argue with him.

I just accept that it will be a long night and close my notebook in front of me. There's no way I can write lyrics—let alone good ones—with Dave like this. I can usually try to get a few thoughts down in between takes, but nothing about our time in the studio today has me feeling creative.

Take after endless take, we work on getting the song exactly how Dave wants it. He can't even give us the satisfaction of saying he likes it by the time we're done. He just nods with a reluctant, "Good enough," and all I want to do is shake him and ask him why the fuck he's avoiding going home, but that wouldn't help any of us. Instead, I tell him to have a good night and try to relax my grip on the steering wheel as I drive back to Margot.

When I finally get into Margot's apartment, it's almost midnight. I half expect her to be asleep, but she's curled up on the couch, rewatching *Ted Lasso*. The only light in the whole apartment comes from the small bulb over the stove and the glow from the TV. Rae must be with Matt unless she already went to bed.

"Hey," Margot says as she pushes herself up and gets to her feet. She sounds tired. As she walks toward the kitchen, she shakes her hair loose, and I wonder if she *was* just asleep. She's wearing lace-trim pink pajama shorts with a matching tank, and after the day I've had, the sight of her loosens something inside me that's been tightly coiled all day.

"Hey, I thought you'd be asleep." I give her a peck on the cheek and open the fridge for my leftovers. I'm starving.

She smiles, but there's a twinge of sadness behind it. "I'll have plenty of time to go to bed early after you leave."

Her comment is the heavy dose of reality I don't want.

Four days.

Four more days with her until I'm gone.

"How are you feeling about that?" I ask without thinking. We've talked about this, but that was weeks ago. I feel like we're in a good place now—a place I don't want to mess up.

She steps in front of me and reaches for the plate of leftovers in the fridge. With a light shrug of her shoulder, she says, "It is what it is."

As much as I'm disappointed by her answer, I can't disagree. There's nothing we can do about being long distance. We just have to give it our best shot and see how it goes. She's holding back, though. She's hiding what she's feeling, and that's the last thing I want.

The soft clank of her placing the dish in the microwave snaps me from my thoughts.

"Margot."

She looks over her shoulder at me as she shuts the door and pushes the button. "Jackson."

She's being playful because she doesn't want to talk about this. "How are you feeling about it?" I ask again.

She collapses a little as she turns and leans her back against the kitchen counter. "I don't know what you want me to say."

Running a hand over my face, I say, "Why don't we start with the truth."

A slight frown pulls at her lips while she considers me. "Rough day in the studio?"

I raise my eyebrows and blow out a breath. "Yeah." Keeping my attention fixed on her, I add, "But that's not why I'm asking you about this. We need to talk about it." The microwave beeps behind her, and I see the relief she gets from being able to turn away from me. When she hands me the plate, I thank her but don't eat.

I wait for her to answer.

We look at each other and she sighs. "I don't know how I feel about it."

I take a bite because the food smells amazing, and I haven't eaten since this morning. Plus, it gives her time to say more.

She takes a moment to think before speaking again. "I don't want you to think I'm not happy about your success. You know how much I want this for you."

"I know. I would never think that."

She nods but doesn't say anything else.

Before taking another bite, I prompt her. "But?"

She takes a breath, her eyes never leaving mine. "But I'm worried."

I know she is. It's the slight crease that forms between her brows as she absently chews on her bottom lip. It's always written plainly on her face, even though she tries to hide it by not saying any of those things out loud. I give her a leveling look. "About?"

She's rigid, like the thought of saying her deepest fears is paralyzing, and I wonder how long she's been holding onto them.

"Everything," she says as she releases a breath. "Drugs, alcohol, girls." The last word trails off and she drops her gaze.

There it is. The trifecta of vices associated with being in a rock band.

"Hey," I say, pulling her attention back to me. "You don't think I'd cheat on you, do you?"

"No." She shakes her head adamantly, but the way her eyes flick to meet mine at the last minute lets me know she's not as sure as she sounds.

I stand up straight. "Margot, I would never cheat on you."

She nods. "I know." But she looks down at her hands after, and my chest tightens. I don't know how to reassure her. I don't know how to take this fear away, because her fear has nothing to do with me and everything to do with the *lifestyle* she's imagining in her head.

"Dave has a girlfriend and Brady is practically married. The only one single in the band is Marty, and the only girls willing to give him the time of day have half a brain."

Peeking up at me through her lashes, she lets out a laugh. Some of the tension in my chest eases, but I know I need to say more.

"And I don't think the drinking and drugs will be an issue either. I mean, I might get drunk." I gesture toward her. "But that just means I'll probably blow up your phone with messages about how much I miss you."

Her smile broadens, and I start to relax.

I start to convince myself we'll be okay.

Because I need us to be okay.

Margot's smile slips, some of that insecurity seeping in through the cracks. "You're not worried?"

Setting down my plate, I reach for her. "Come here."

"No, it's okay. Eat. You're hungry."

"You're more important."

Her eyes lock on mine, and she takes a step before letting me pull her to me the rest of the way. She wraps her arms around my waist and presses her head against my chest. I hope she's not about to cry. Resting my chin on top of her head, I squeeze her to me. "You're more important than all of it, Margot. I'm not going to fuck this up."

She pulls back to look at me, and I'm relieved her eyes are dry. "Thanks," she says with a soft smile. Pointing to my plate on the counter, she adds, "Now eat."

A low chuckle rumbles from my chest as I take my plate and do as she says.

8
margot

MATT AND RAE stand in the doorway of Matt's apartment like proud parents while Jackson hugs them goodbye. I watch from the outdoor hallway, patiently waiting, and I can't believe the moment is already here.

Unless I go visit him while he's on tour, the next time I see him will be *December*. I don't think my brain can fully comprehend how many nights I'll suddenly be spending alone.

When he came home in May, it felt like we had all the time in the world. It felt silly to talk about when he would inevitably leave again. August was far away, and we were happy. But now that the moment is here, I can't help feeling like we're unprepared—like we should have created some sort of well thought out action plan for our relationship.

"I'll see you guys later," Jackson says with another wave at Matt and Rae before he puts his arm around me. I smile at the contact and hope he can't see the cracks forming behind it.

Neither of us says anything as we walk to his car in the parking lot. His stuff is already packed, and all that's left is the backpack he has slung over his shoulder. My heart drums in my chest, and my feet feel heavy with each step. How did we get here? How is it already time to say goodbye?

I thought I'd be ready—more confident—more . . . *something*.

But all I can think about is how his new beginning feels like our ending. Jackson deserves to give music his full attention. He's one of the most talented people I've ever known, and as much as I want to keep him to myself, it would be selfish to even ask. I'd snuff out the flame that burns inside of him, and I'd never forgive myself if that happened.

"Margot," Jackson says, giving my shoulders a squeeze.

"Hmm?" Registering the concerned look on his face, I'm going to assume it's not the first time he's tried to get my attention. "Sorry," I add, heat flaring in my cheeks.

I need to keep it together, just a little longer. Once he leaves, I can fall apart if I need to, but I can't let him see.

"Are you sure you have everything?" I don't know what else to say.

He lets go of me to put his backpack in the front seat, and despite the brutal August heat, I suddenly feel cold. "I think so."

"And Dave doesn't mind you leaving your car at his house?"

Jackson shakes his head. "Nope. That's what all the guys are doing."

"Okay," I say, racking my brain for another follow up question.

Once he closes the car door, he turns to face me, and how good he looks shouldn't be devastating, but it is. Because I'm going to miss every detail. I'm going to miss the way his hair always looks a little messy in the best way. I'm going to miss the spark of mischief behind those storm-like eyes. I'm going to miss the way his tongue darts out to wet his bottom lip before he kisses me. I'm going to miss the way he makes me laugh, and blush, and feel so incredibly happy.

"Did you figure out your schedule for the fall semester?"

I blink and suck in a breath, bringing myself back to the present. With a nod, I let a faint smile come to my lips. I'm glad I'm not the only one delaying this situation with random questions. "Yeah. I'll take classes on Tuesdays and Thursdays, and my internship is on Mondays, Wednesdays, and Fridays."

He lifts his eyebrows. "Busy week."

I force a laugh. "Well, there isn't much else I'll be doing." Immediately regretting what I've said, I fight the urge to grimace. If that doesn't scream pathetic, I don't know what does.

The corner of Jackson's mouth quirks as he brings a thumb to my cheek. "You'll still go out and have fun."

"I know," I say too quickly—even though it feels like a lie. I don't want to go out without him. He's the reason going out *is* fun. He's the reason I want to let loose. Without him, it won't be the same.

There's a trace of worry behind his eyes, and I can't take it. I can't take him pitying me. Leaving is hard for him, but nothing is worse than being left.

"We're both going to have lives while we're not together," I say with a little more conviction. "I'll try not to get into too much trouble."

He chuffs a laugh. "And if you do, call Matt." He pulls me to him. "Hell, even if I were here, you'd have to call Matt because I'd be getting into trouble with you."

My lips twist playfully. "You *are* a terrible influence."

He gives me a peck on the lips. "You love it."

I can't fight my grin. "Yeah," I say with a laugh. "I do."

He smiles, but it fades too soon. Something in his expression turns serious as he brushes his thumb over my cheek.

There's something he's not saying. I can feel the unsaid words hanging between us, and my mind betrays me, jumping back to the conversation I had with Rae. He wouldn't say he loves me *now*, would he? Because I don't want him to tell me he loves me just because he feels like he *should*—like he might as well get it over with now before he doesn't see me for who knows how long.

If he ever says those three words to me, I want it to be because he wants to—because *not* saying it makes him feel like he's going to explode. I want him to say it with absolute confidence, and I don't want our weird timeline to add pressure to it.

I study his face and wonder if I love him. For so long, I fought my feelings for Jackson. I was afraid of how vulnerable he made me, and admitting I love him only intensifies that.

But I think I do.

I think I love him.

We're both just looking at each other, his thumb absently tracing the line of my jaw as he rests his hand on the back of my neck.

His lips part, and I don't know if he's about to confess something or if he's just taking a breath, but I kiss him before he has the chance to do either.

I kiss him before he potentially tells me he loves me for the wrong reasons.

And I kiss him deep enough to make him forget he was about to say anything at all.

His hands move to my hair, and he takes control of the kiss. Every time he moves his lips over mine, I can feel my mind settling as the chaos turns to calm.

Breaking the kiss, he leans his forehead against mine. "Visit me."

"I'll try."

He shakes his head. "Margot, visit me."

I melt into him, my mind a blank slate. "Yeah. Okay."

A light smile touches the corners of his mouth. He knows I can't say no to him. Of course, I'll visit him. There's no way I'd make it to December. If I could afford it, I'd be going to every show. But I'll settle for a single weekend.

I have to.

9
jackson

PUTTING MY CAR IN PARK, I take in the scene in front of me. Dave and the guys are busy packing up the same van we toured in a few months ago, and just the thought of being on the road again has my adrenaline pumping.

I'm tempted to text Margot and tell her I miss her already, but I think that might be overkill.

I almost told her I loved her.

What the hell was I thinking? I've never said those words to anyone. I've never wanted to say them to anyone. And yet, those three words almost tumbled out of my dumb mouth.

But she kissed me.

Did she kiss me because she knew I was about to say something stupid? There's a good chance. I never thought about telling her I loved her until I was forced to say goodbye. I'm not sure why it never occurred to me before. We've been dating for a while, I guess. Does that mean I'm *supposed* to tell her I love her? Is she expecting it? The thought alone is enough to make the back of my neck sweat.

But she stopped it—maybe because she isn't ready. I've

been replaying that moment in my head the entire drive over here, and it's forced me to ask myself another question:

Do I love her?

"Fuck," I mutter to myself as I rub my hands over my face. When I look up, Dave and the guys are staring at me like they want to know why the hell I'm camped out in my car instead of helping.

I try to shake off the creeping panic. It works a little. My shoulders ease, and I force myself to abandon every thought that isn't about the band and packing up this damn van.

As soon as the car door opens, Marty opens his big mouth. "It's about time you showed up. Taking your sweet time kissing your girlfriend goodbye?"

I just shrug. "Don't worry, Marty. I'm sure you'll find someone who can love you one day."

The other guys in the group let out a laugh, but Marty flips me the bird.

The smile on Dave's face gives me a sense of relief. It's a real one. We finished the album just before our time in the studio was up, and he feels good about it—I think we all do. With it being my first album, I'm proud of every single song we recorded. I may not have written a ton of the lyrics, but I played on every track.

"You can put your stuff over here," Brady says as he waves me over. After touring in the van a few months ago, we at least know how to stuff it full of everything we need without playing a shitty game of Tetris.

Marty and Dave head back into the house, but Brady hangs back while I shove my backpack into its designated spot.

"He's in a better mood," I say casually over my shoulder. Brady and I might not be close, but we've always gotten along —enough for me to speak freely in front of him, anyway.

Which is more than I can say for Marty.

He chuckles. "Yeah. Lucky for us. He's still stressed,

though." I give him a questioning look over my shoulder, and he clarifies. "You know Dave. He's always thinking about the next step." He rubs a hand over his bald head. "Well, that and the breakup with Lynn."

I stop and sit back on my heels. "They broke up?" I don't know why it's a big deal to me. It's not like I ever met her.

Brady nods. The news is having more of an impact on me than it should. "It's about a year late if you ask me. She's great in her own right, but she's never loved the band as much as Dave needed her to. She stopped coming to shows, and it was like the more success we got, the more bitter she was about it all."

I nod, turning my attention back to what's in front of me, but I can't help wondering if the same thing could end up happening to Margot. Will there be a day when she doesn't want me to chase this anymore? Carefully, sliding my guitar case into its spot, I try to rid the thought and say, "Think he'll be okay? I'm all for planning ahead, but we haven't even started this tour yet."

"You don't have to tell me," Brady says with a huff. "He just wants to keep going while we have momentum. I can't blame him. The last thing any of us wants is to finish this tour with nothing else lined up."

Getting to my feet, I turn to face him. "What's he trying to line up?"

Brady shrugs. "Maybe more studio time. Maybe another opening tour. Maybe a headlining tour. Who knows?"

"A headlining tour?" I cock my brow. We're doing well right now, but I wouldn't say we're anywhere near headlining.

The side of Brady's mouth quirks, his dark beard concealing some of his amusement. "A small one."

Ducking out of the van, I let out a breath of laughter. "Right."

Brady leans against the van door. "It doesn't matter how

small it is. I still told him we need a manager. Or at the very least, a booking agent."

I stop in my tracks. "You did?" Before he can even answer, I add, "How did he take it?"

Brady runs a hand over his beard. "He didn't want to hear it, but he listened, and that's the first step."

The door to the garage opens, and out walks Dave and Marty with bottles of water.

"Well, I'm glad you said something. I was worried I'd have to be the one to tell him," I mutter to Brady before catching a bottle of water thrown my way. "He'll listen to you before he listens to me."

The van jolts over another bump in the road, and any hope I had for falling asleep is wiped away. It's Brady's turn to drive, but I'm tempted to swap places with him. There's no point in him forcing himself to stay awake while I just lie here, staring at the ceiling.

The first time on tour, I don't remember it being this uncomfortable. I mean, I'm not sure how it could be different now. It's still the same piece of plywood on top of our stuff, and we're all still lying in sleeping bags on top of it.

Turning my head, I look at the two guys next to me. Marty and Dave are both passed out, and I don't know how they adjust so quickly. Last night, I fell asleep in Margot's bed with her arms wrapped around me, and now I'm sleeping on a wooden platform in a sleeping bag next to two guys.

Reaching under my pillow for my phone, I dim the screen as much as I can and tap on Margot's name.

> **JACKSON:**
> Awake?

The three dots appear right away, and I check the time. It's after one in the morning. She should be asleep.

> **MARGOT:**
> Yeah. What's up?

> **JACKSON:**
> Why are you awake?

She starts typing again, but this time, she stops, and the dots reappear before her message finally comes in.

> **MARGOT:**
> Can't sleep.

I frown. Part of me wants to dig, but I have a feeling I know why she can't. So instead, I just type one word.

> **JACKSON:**
> Same.

> **MARGOT:**
> Because you miss me?

I smile at that.

> **JACKSON:**
> Margot, I'm sleeping in a van with three other guys. Of course, I miss you.

> **MARGOT:**
> I was looking at dates.

I expect her to say more, but when she doesn't, I send another text.

> **JACKSON:**
> To visit?

MARGOT:
Yeah.

Hope swells in my chest. Rolling over, I hold my phone in both hands, giving it my full attention.

> **JACKSON:**
> When?

She doesn't answer right away, so I pull up our tour schedule, knowing she's probably doing the same. It would have to be a date when we have two shows in the same state. If we need to drive overnight to get to the next venue, Margot and I won't get any time together.

A notification pops up at the top of my screen.

MARGOT:
I've always wanted to see New York City.

I swipe back to the list and check which date she's talking about. It looks like there's a weekend in October when we're booked for back-to-back shows in New York. It's perfect.

> **JACKSON:**
> Then NYC it is.

10
margot

MY EYES FLUTTER OPEN, and my first thought is that I'll see Jackson in New York. October may be two months away, but it's better than waiting for him to come back in December. Last night, I looked up everything I could find about Webster Hall and scoped out hotels in the surrounding area. I'll look into it more in the next few days. If anything, it will give me something to do while I wait for classes to start next week.

When I walk out of my bedroom, the apartment is quiet. Matt and Rae slept in separate apartments for the first time in a while last night. I think Rae figured I wouldn't want to be alone, but even though she was here when I went to sleep, lying alone in my bed still had the walls closing in on me.

I pad across the kitchen floor. The tile feels cool against the bottom of my feet, and when I pass the kitchen sink, I stop in my tracks. Jackson's coffee mug from yesterday morning is still in the sink, and it brings a faint frown to my lips.

This is ridiculous.

I shouldn't miss him this much already. I shouldn't see the Snoopy mug in the kitchen sink and have the memory of him making fun of me for owning it flash before my eyes. It's not like I won't ever see him again, and it's not like we haven't done this before.

But last time he left, I didn't know what it felt like to have him here. I had no idea what it would be like to wake up next to him, or to fall asleep with him in my bed. I didn't walk around taking note of his subtle glances and knowing exactly what each of them meant.

But now I *do* know how it feels to have those things.

Now I know how it feels to have him . . . and I miss it.

Rae's bedroom door opens, and I look over my shoulder to find her wearing an oversized Chicago Bears shirt and cotton shorts. "Morning." She rubs her hands over her face and squints against the soft morning light. "Are you making coffee?"

"Yeah." I refocus on what I came into the kitchen to do. Getting the machine ready, I add, "I'll make you one."

"Thanks." She pulls up a seat at the bar. Our apartment may not be big enough for a kitchen table, but it's modern and new on the inside. Rae and I loved enhancing the bright open concept with plants and natural oak furniture.

I can feel her eyes on me as I make the coffee, so I make a point to say, "I'm okay, you know."

"I know," she says a little too quickly. I look over my shoulder, and she relaxes into her seat. "I mean, it's not like you two broke up," she adds with a laugh.

She's right. I don't know why him not being here is hitting me so hard. I hand her a cup of hot coffee. "So, what's the plan today?" I ask, knowing there's a good chance she already has something in mind.

Bringing her mug to her lips, she pauses. "Braden is house-sitting for his cousin. I guess he has a boat he doesn't mind us using?" She tilts her chin up with a pleading smile like she already assumes I'll say no.

"Why are you looking at me like that?"

She holds her same position. "Because I don't want you to be sad."

Leaning against the kitchen counter, I laugh. "I'm not sad. I'm fine." When she still doesn't look convinced, I add, "I'd love to come."

She finally relaxes and lifts her mug to her lips. "Good."

"Margot, want anything?" Braden asks as he stands with the cooler open.

Tearing my eyes away from the soothing waves to look at him, I nod. "High Noon?"

He smiles, and I try my best to return the gesture.

It turns out Braden's cousin having a boat was only the tip of the iceberg. Braden's cousin is rich. There's no other way to put it. His modern contemporary home has access to the bay with its own private dock and an infinity pool. I figured we'd have to at least trailer the boat somewhere, but all Braden had to do was lower the electric lift, and we were ready to go.

Matt wanted to drive, so Braden hands me a drink and sits on the bench across from Rae and me.

"Thanks." I give him another small smile before popping the top and taking a sip. The bubbles in the seltzer dance across my tongue, the cold drink easing some of the summer heat. My hair whips in the wind as I look out over the water. The sun's reflection dances on the water's surface, and the palm trees look almost frozen in time as we zoom past them.

Before we left the apartment, I may have sent Jackson a sexy picture in my bikini. It was nothing crazy, but I've never sent him anything like it. He hasn't responded yet. It's Sunday, and I don't think they have a show tonight, but maybe it's his turn to drive the van.

Rae looks back at the impressive house behind us. "So, what does your cousin do for work?" When she looks at Braden again, she adds, "And are they hiring?"

He gives her a flash of white teeth as he rakes a hand through his blond hair. "Pharmaceutical sales I think?" He lets out a laugh. "Don't be fooled, though. He hates his job."

Rae lets out a sigh. "Well, I better love teaching because I can almost guarantee I'll never have an infinity pool to console me if I don't."

Braden looks back at Matt. "Hey!" he yells over the sound of the motor. "She wants an infinity pool!"

Matt gives a sharp nod in his LSU hat and Oakley sunglasses like he understands the mission he's been given.

Rae shakes her head, but amusement pulls at the corners of her mouth. "I don't think he realizes how high up he'll have to be at Disney to make that happen."

"Did he hear back from that guy who thinks he can get him an internship next year?" I ask, remembering something Matt mentioned a few weeks back. He loves the Happiest Place on Earth more than most people I know, and since his major is hospitality, it's practically a match made in heaven.

Rae nods before weighing her head back and forth. "Yeah, but I mean . . . it's Disney." When Braden and I glance at each other, she goes on to say, "Disney is huge, so the fact that his dad knows someone might help, but it might not. It's just too big of a company."

"Hey, Rae!" Matt calls out over the roar of the boat. "Can you get my phone out of your bag? I'm sick of Braden's shitty music."

Rae gets up at the same time Braden flips Matt the bird, and I have to laugh.

I would have never said anything, but he does listen to shitty music. Dating Jackson has definitely rubbed off on me. I know for a fact he'd have something to say about Braden playing America's Worst 40.

Braden's eyes widen playfully as he registers my reaction. "You hate it, too?"

To this, I just shrug. "My boyfriend is in a band."

"Right," he says with a laugh. "Hey, how's that going by the way?"

I blink. "Uh . . . he only left yesterday."

A nervous laugh leaves his lips. "No, I know. I just meant in general."

"Oh." It's been a while since I've had to come up with an answer for this question. Rae used to ask how I felt things were going with Jackson in the beginning. After he left for tour the first time and we technically decided to give things a shot, she'd ask if I had heard from him and how I was feeling about it all. But back then, it was so new, and I was still trying to figure things out. She hasn't asked that question in months. I think she stopped asking as soon as he was here for the summer. By then, she didn't have to check in with me. She could see exactly how things were going for herself, and when we're together, Jackson and I are undeniable. My phone buzzes in my lap, and I use it as an excuse to buy myself a little more time before answering. I don't know why, but I feel like I need to choose my words carefully around Braden.

> JACKSON:
>
> Jesus fucking Christ, Margot. Are you trying to get me to turn this van around?

I don't bother fighting my smile as I stare down at my phone. I just laugh and glance back at Braden. "It's good." I look back at my phone and shake my head, my bemused smile only growing. "It's really good."

11
jackson

WE'VE BEEN on the road for a couple of weeks, and it feels like a breath of fresh air every time we stop to stretch our legs or get out to play a show. I've been driving for a few hours now, and exit after exit, mile after fucking mile, it's all starting to look the same. I'm over it. I'm trying not to think about the fact that I still have an hour and a half left in my shift. My fingers reach for the dial, and I change the radio station, desperate to get away from the same used car lot ad I've heard at least six times. Unfortunately, there's no Bluetooth in the van. I'm not even sure this thing has an AUX-in socket.

If the guys were at least talking, it might not be so bad, but everyone is doing their own thing. Marty has headphones on while he bobs along to a song no one else can hear. Brady is asleep in the back, his open mouth on display in the rearview mirror. Dave sits next to me, but he's been staring at his phone with a look of determination for the past hour, and I know better than to interrupt that look. It's the look he gets when he's emailing contacts, researching venues, contacting studios. That look means he's almost in overload, and all it takes is a pebble in his shoe to make him explode.

I'd rather not be the pebble.

So instead, I sort through the crackle of country music stations and static until I end up back at the same fucking ad I was trying to escape. I don't even know if it's the same station or if Rip's Reliable Rides can afford to haunt me from every angle.

There's a loud clunk, and I sit up straight. My eyes immediately jump to the rearview mirror, checking to see if I ran over something, but the road behind me is clear.

"The fuck?" Dave mutters as he lifts his head and does a similar scan.

"I have no idea wh—"

The sound happens again, this time jolting Brady awake.

"Pull over," Dave says, pointing to the shoulder.

But before I can even put my foot on the break, it feels like the wheels lock. The steering and brakes are less responsive, and we end up skidding. I pump the brakes, hoping they fucking work, until we eventually slide to a stop on the side of the road just as the car behind us lays on their horn and swerves into the other lane to avoid slamming into us.

Marty rips his headphones from his ears and frantically looks around.

"Jesus Christ," Brady mutters from the back, and I nod, my heart pounding.

Dave pinches the bridge of his nose, his head falling forward.

"What the hell, Jackson?" Marty yells from behind me, and I swear I could hit him with the adrenaline already pumping through my veins.

"I didn't do anything!" I yell back. "If anything, I just saved your ass."

My eyes jump to Dave for some type of defense, but the beat of silence it takes for him to say something feels like an eternity. Eventually, he mutters, "The oil."

"What?" Brady asks.

Dave lifts his gaze but avoids looking at any of us. He stares straight out the windshield while he lets his head fall back against the seat. "I forgot to change the oil."

"You . . ." Brady shakes his head. "You forgot to change the oil?"

Dave says nothing, just closes his eyes like he wants to disappear, and it's all the confirmation I need.

"Fuck," I groan as I rub a hand over my face.

Brady leans forward. "How the hell did you forget to change the oil?"

Dave snaps, "Because I'm doing everything!"

"Well, clearly you fucking can't!" Brady says with an exasperated outstretched arm.

"I can fix it!" Dave says, avoiding our wide-eyed stares and getting out of the van. He pops the hood, blocking his view of the three of us.

"Fuck this," Brady mutters under his breath as he opens the door and gets out. I've never seen him like this. Hell, I've never even seen him mad. He leaves the van door open, so I can still hear him when he says, "What are you going to do? We need to talk about this before you go and make it worse!"

I can't see Dave, but I can hear him when he says, "Fuck off, Brady, it's fine."

There's no way I'm staying in this van alone with Marty. Getting out of the car, I ask, "What's wrong with it?" Even though I'm not sure I want to know the answer.

Brady crosses his arms, still glaring at Dave. "He's got too much on his plate. Now the fucking engine seized up."

I raise my eyebrows. Equally unsure of how to handle Brady when he's like this.

"This never would have happened if we had a manager," he continues. He points at Dave. "You know it. I know it." Looking at me, he says, "Hell, even he knows it."

There's no way he's dragging me into this. "Why don't we just focus on fixing the van?"

Dave has been glowering at the engine, but after letting out a frustrated, "Fuck!" he starts pacing.

Brady watches him with narrowed eyes. "You can't fix it. You'd be better off laying it to rest," he growls under his breath.

"Wait." I hold up both hands while my brain catches up. "It can't be fixed?" My eyes jump between the two guys in front of me. Dave runs both hands over his hair, smoothing it back while he looks like he's about to self-combust from panic, and Brady just looks like he wants to break something.

Marty finally walks up, but for once, he keeps his loud mouth shut. I wonder if he's ever seen Brady this mad or if he's just as shocked as I am.

Brady scoffs. "No. It can't be fixed."

Dave shoots him a glare but says nothing.

Running a hand over my head, I take a look at the engine like I might actually understand what any of it means. "So, we need a manager and something to tour in."

I can feel Dave's glare pierce through me, but I keep my eyes focused on the engine.

Marty finally catches up. "A manager?"

Ignoring him, Brady keeps his attention on Dave. "What about the guy from the festival?"

"What guy?" Dave grits, looking back at the engine. I'm pretty sure he has no idea what he's looking at either, but I don't blame him for not wanting to face Brady right now.

The look on Brady's face tells me that was definitely the wrong answer. "The one who wanted to manage us," he says through gritted teeth like it's taking everything in him not to strangle our lead singer. "The one you turned down, and the one who gave you his card and said to reach out if we ever changed our minds."

Lost, I shake my head. "There was a guy who wanted to manage us? Why the hell didn't I know about this?"

They all look at me with a flash of guilt, like the thought of clueing the puppy in on this decision had never occurred to them.

Dave's shoulders drop. "Listen, I'm sorry. You were off with Margot, and we weren't open to the idea, anyway. I didn't think it mattered."

"Some of us were open to the idea," Brady mutters, but Dave ignores him.

"Call him," I say, my voice coming out more resolute than I feel. They should have told me. I'm pissed they didn't fucking tell me, but right now, none of it matters. What matters is we're a band, headed for a gig, and we suddenly have no way to get there.

Dave blinks. "What?"

"Call him," I say again. "If he can find us a new van, tell him he can have the job. Maybe he can pull some strings."

Brady nods, finally looking more like himself. "I still have his number."

Marty takes a sip from his energy drink, not sharing an opinion one way or another.

I half expect Dave to turn on me, but he doesn't look nearly as angry as he did a few minutes ago. He's just staring at me with slumped shoulders and a set jaw, like he's torn between standing his ground and knowing it's a lost cause. He probably wants more of an explanation, but all I give him is a slight lift of my eyebrows.

Wiping a hand over his face, he shakes his head. "All right, fine. I'll call him."

Brady gapes at Dave, and even Marty has stopped drinking. "You're serious?" Brady asks. "That's all it takes? I've been trying to get you to call that guy for weeks!"

Dave rubs the back of his neck, and I know he feels like an

idiot right now. This is completely his fault, and usually nothing is his fault. Usually, we can blame everything on Marty.

"Yeah. Well, it looks like we don't have a choice." He shakes his head. "Let's just see what he says."

I pull out my phone, and Dave asks, "What are you doing?"

Glancing up at him, I say, "Looking for another van in case he doesn't pull through."

Because of all the things that could ruin this opportunity for us, I sure as hell won't let Dave and his ego be the reason we fail.

12
margot

MY BOSS, Karah, looks me up and down with mild concern. Her salt and peppered pixie cut and green pencil skirt makes her look like an elegantly aged Tinker Bell. "I know I asked you to stay on, but are you sure it's not too much with the semester starting?"

She's asked me this at least six times already, and every time, I assure her I can handle it. It's not like this is *Rolling Stone*. *Destination Tampa* is a small magazine with a dedicated group of local readers, mostly retirees who wouldn't know how to unsubscribe if they wanted to.

Not to mention, I could use the money. Jackson offered to pay for my trip to see him, but I want to do this myself. He has enough on his plate, and I know he doesn't have much money left over after pitching in for studio time.

"It's three days a week," I say with a reassuring smile. "I'm not exactly burning the midnight oil when I come here."

She purses her lips, still unconvinced. "But you've stacked your other two days with a full load of classes."

"Karah," I say with a tilt of my head. "If it gets to be too much, I'll let you know."

She points a finger at me playfully. "You better." Changing gears, she adds, "When will you have the small business feature done on that local bookstore?"

Glancing back at my computer, I say, "I was just going over my notes. I'll have it done by the end of the week."

"Great. We should be able to put it in this month's issue then. Have it to me by Monday."

"You've got it," I say with a grin.

She taps the door frame before waltzing away, and I'm left alone in my tiny office. Glancing out my one window at the rear parking lot, I see one of the pizza delivery drivers walk by. We're located in a plaza, crammed between a pizza place and a dental office, so my people watching is mostly limited to the delivery drivers who park in the back.

The office may be small, and the walls may be a dingy yellow color, but Karah and her team really make this place feel like a home. She's flexible, everyone has a positive energy, and this guy Derek always brings in his leftover culinary masterpieces. Seriously, the guy should be a chef, not an editor.

I've loved working here this summer, and I'm excited to stay on board as an "extended intern" as Sarah calls it.

My phone vibrates on my desk, and I look down to see a message from Rae.

> RAE:
> Braden said he'll bring home stuff for pasta tonight. Are you good with eating over there?"

> MARGOT:
> Is it that pesto pasta he makes?

Derek might not be the only culinary genius. Sometimes Braden makes dinners I'm convinced could draw a crowd.

RAE:
I think so. Do you want me to tell him that's what you want?

MARGOT:
... It wouldn't hurt.

She doesn't text back right away, so I give her time to relay my message and turn back to my computer.

The bookstore feature is my most recent project, and I'm still waiting for the owner to email back her responses to my questions. I'd rather wait until I have all the information before I start writing, so I look over the store's Instagram page, compiling a group of photos to send to the owner to approve for use.

I've scrolled back to the store's grand opening by the time I get another text from Rae.

RAE:
He says if you want pesto pasta, he'll make pesto pasta.

MARGOT:
Such a gentleman.

I stare at our texts. Even though I'm thrilled, I can't ignore the uneasy feeling in my gut. Braden is single, and even though I'm not, we're always together.

I quickly add another text.

MARGOT:
Tell him thanks.

If he sees me as anything more than a friend, he does a decent job of hiding it. He doesn't give me extra attention the way Keith did, and he's never said anything that oversteps a line. He and Jackson even get along well.

But it's a feeling I can't shake.

I open an email to the bookstore and attach the pictures I saved. Before clocking out for the day, I ask the owner what she thinks and for her approval to use the pictures in the feature.

As I gather my things, my phone vibrates again. This time, Jackson's name appears on the screen. He's sent me a picture. Swiping it open, I tap on the message to find an old RV staring back at me.

Another message from him pops up shortly after.

> **JACKSON:**
> Well, we can't have sex in the van. How about this thing instead?

Letting out a light laugh, I text him back.

> **MARGOT:**
> Is that your new home?

He answers right away.

> **JACKSON:**
> You're my home.

I stare at the words on the screen, reading and rereading. He's never said anything like that. It makes my heart thud in my chest, and I bite my thumbnail, unsure of what to say back.

> **JACKSON:**
> But we can still fuck in the RV.

The breath I was holding comes out in a gust of laughter, and I roll my eyes. I send him a text back as I walk out of the office.

> **MARGOT:**
> Not likely.
>
> Whose RV is it?

I give my phone my full attention as I wait for his next message.

JACKSON:
> Our new manager called in some favors. I think it belongs to a friend of a friend of a friend.
>
> Or something like that.

I blink when I read the words. A manager? Jackson had mentioned them needing one once or twice, but I had no idea it was actually in the works.

MARGOT:
> You guys have a manager now?

He's only been gone for a couple of weeks. Did they secure someone before he left?

JACKSON:
> Yeah, don't ask me how I feel about it yet. I haven't met the guy. But he's saving our asses, so he can't be all that bad.
>
> Dave accidentally murdered the van.

MARGOT:
> I have so many questions.

JACKSON:
> We all do. I'll fill you in as soon as I meet him. He should be here any minute.
>
> How are your classes?

A slight frown pulls at the corner of my lips when I look at the last message. It's such a mundane question. It's boring. Compared to his dynamic, ever-changing scenery, I'm stagnant. Okay, I'm not *really* stagnant. I'm doing things. I know that, but I still hate that he has to ask me how classes are going. I hate that such a boring question is so necessary for us now because I can't fill him in on how my life is going organically. I can't get home from work and tell him about what I'm working on, and for some reason, the things I'm working on just don't feel important enough to text him about throughout the day.

The sound of Karah's heels gracing the hallway with her delicate clicks pulls me from my thoughts and I quickly text him back saying classes are going well before turning my phone over and getting back to work.

My classes *are* going well.

But I don't want to fill Jackson in on my day-to-day life.

I want him to be in it.

13
jackson

HIS NAME IS BRIAN. Brian Marlow. I'm trying to take the fact that the manager for The Beatles had the same first name as a good sign. If only it were enough to make me stop sweating as I anxiously pick at the strings of my guitar.

I was the one who made this happen.

I told Dave to call him.

Well, so did Brady, but Dave only listened when I said it. And as much as I know we need a manager, if this guy ends up being a dick, it will feel like my fault.

Then again, he did secure an RV in a matter of hours, so he can't be all that bad. He even had someone drive it from North Carolina and drop it off at the gas station.

If that's not some sort of divine destiny, I don't know what is.

We moved all our stuff out of the van, organized it in the RV, and now we're parked outside Brian's hotel, waiting for him to fly in from Florida.

"At least we have some time to kill before the show in Richmond," Brady says as he walks around the perimeter of the RV behind Dave. I think it's safe to say he no longer trusts Dave's judgment when it comes to the condition of our vehicle.

"Who would have thought the puppy would be the one to talk some sense into Dave," Marty mutters playfully.

Dave claps a hand on my shoulder as I sit on the bottom step of the RV. "I have to admit, this might not be the worst idea."

Avoiding his gaze, I keep playing. "Don't mention it." I don't want to take credit for this—not yet. If this guy shows up wearing a button-down Hawaiian shirt and jorts, I'll never live it down. They've all met him, though. They would have seen if he had no business being in the music industry, right? Dave didn't say he wouldn't hire him because he didn't like him. He didn't want to hire him because he didn't want to hire *anyone*.

My knee bounces as I think of all the ways this could go wrong—all the ways this guy could disappoint me, and I haven't even met him yet.

"Think this is him?" Marty asks with a nod, and I hold my breath as my eyes track the black sedan pulling into the parking lot.

Dave takes a few steps forward as the car pulls up, and we all watch in anticipation. The car rolls to a stop, and it feels like it's happening in slow motion.

The rear door of the Uber opens, and I set my guitar aside with bated breath. I get to my feet, but my hands don't know what to do now that I'm not playing, so I shove them in my pockets.

Finally, the door opens enough for me to get a glimpse of this guy, and I feel like I can breathe again. He's wearing black slacks, a white button down, and a black tie. The guy wore a fucking *tie*. He grins as he steps out of the car, his hair a few shades lighter than mine, but a hell of a lot shorter. Everything about this guy is clean.

Maybe I didn't fuck up, because this guy screams professionalism.

He looks like he could take us to where we need to go.

He looks like a manager.

"Ah, good!" he says as he takes in the scene, holding a duffel bag by his side. "I'm glad to see the RV worked out."

Dave greets him with a firm handshake. "Nice to see you again. Thanks for saving our asses."

Brian gives a sharp nod with his single shake. "Thanks for giving me the opportunity."

Turning to the rest of us, Dave says, "Brian, you remember most of these guys, but you didn't meet Jackson at the festival." I wave, and I'm relieved to see Dave's in a better mood about all of this, but even with the smile plastered on his face, there's a hint of apprehension in his eyes when he adds, "We can take care of the paperwork inside and go from there."

We've been hanging out in Brian's hotel room for a few hours now. He talked to the front desk about letting us leave the RV parked out front for a while, and we've had our fair share of drinks. Dave agreed the contract Brian brought was pretty straightforward, and we've been celebrating ever since we signed our names on the dotted line.

Over the past few hours, Brian's tie has gotten steadily looser, and it's starting to feel like he's one of us. He's treated us to room service, boosted our egos, and now he wants to take us all out for the night. Scrolling on his phone, he says, "You guys know of any clubs around here?"

Dave sits on the floor, with his head leaning against the bed. "Nah, but Jackson is underage."

Brian lies sprawled out on his bed with an arm over his

head, but that doesn't stop him from lifting his head to look at me. "No shit?"

"No shit," I confirm. My age is what separates me from the band the most, and I can't wait for the day I can get into places with them. No one in the band treats me like I'm younger—except for Marty. But it doesn't matter how they see me, it matters how the law sees me, and to the law, I'm too young to get drunk with my band on a Thursday night after hiring our first manager.

He sits up on the bed. "Don't you have a fake?"

I shake my head. "Not yet. I'll get one." Up until now, I never felt like I needed one. I always hung out with my friends after our shows in Tampa, so I didn't care if the guys went out without me. When we were on tour earlier this year, the schedule was too tight for any of us to go out anyway. This is the first time I've wished I had a magic plastic card with a grainy photo and a fake name.

Brian rubs a hand over his jaw, mulling it over. "I mean, I can be persuasive, but I can't guarantee they'll let you in. The band isn't big enough for you to get in on clout alone."

"Don't worry about it." I get to my feet. "You guys go out." Snatching a half-finished bottle of bourbon off the windowsill, I add, "But I'm taking this with me."

They're all watching me, and I know they're trying to find a workaround. The only way around this is going somewhere that will let me in underage, and I doubt that's the type of place they want to spend their night.

"You're sure?" Dave eventually asks, and I hate that he feels sorry for me.

"Yup." I take a sip from the bottle. "It's been a while since I've bugged Margot, anyway. Maybe I'll give her a call."

Brady lets out a laugh. "Maybe you should leave the bottle here before you do."

My mouth quirks, but I shake my head. "See you assholes later."

I leave the room before anyone has a chance to call me back. I'm buzzed but coherent enough to tuck the small bottle into the back of my waistband before walking out of the hotel.

The RV feels bigger now that it's just me in it. It's old, but clean enough. There's a small couch with a fold-out table, a tiny kitchen area, a bathroom the size of a closet, and in the very back are two sets of bunk beds. Beyond that is one more sliding door to a fifth bed. The *primary suite* so to speak. I'm assuming Brian will spend his nights there and the band will take the bunks.

Bottle in hand, I collapse onto my new bed. There's nothing to it. The thin mattress makes the memory of my dorm bed feel like a luxurious dream, and if I roll over, I'll end up on the fucking floor.

But it's a space—*my* space.

It's at least ten steps above sleeping on a piece of plywood in a sleeping bag, sandwiched between two other guys, so I'll take it.

It only takes about thirty seconds for the silence to get to me. Grabbing my phone, I hit play on Spotify. Margot must have been the last one to pick the music on my phone because I immediately recognize the intro of "All Too Well" and groan. I check the song, and sure enough, it's the ten-minute version. That's just what I need right now. To be alone in an RV with a bottle of bourbon while Taylor Swift drowns me in my fucking feelings.

Taking a sip, I skip to the next song.

"Why'd You Only Call Me When You're High?" by Arctic Monkeys plays, and I'm much happier for it. It isn't until I lean back that it occurs to me how weird it is for an Arctic Monkeys song to follow "All Too Well."

Reaching for my phone again, I see that Margot has apparently made a complete playlist titled "For When You Miss Me." I scroll through the list and see it's mostly Taylor Swift's entire archive—only the ones that say (Taylor's Version) because if Margot is passionate about anything, it's supporting Taylor's best interests. Arctic Monkeys' AM album is sprinkled throughout, and she has "Landslide" in here at least seven times just to fuck with me.

Letting out a low laugh, I send her a text.

14
margot

MATT'S EYES roll back when he takes his first bite of pasta. "Dude, how are you single?"

Rae shakes her head with a laugh. "Can you not make that face when you eat?" She grabs a bowl from Braden, thanking him before she continues by saying, "And what does his pasta have to do with his dating life?"

Matt's eyes widen. "Rae, if I were into guys, and he made me this pasta, you'd never see me again."

She forces a laugh. "Did you hear that, Braden?" she calls over her shoulder where Braden and I are still standing in the kitchen. "You might be stealing my boyfriend."

Braden answers her while he scoops pasta into a bowl for me. "Don't worry Rae. Hoes before bros."

I watch their interaction with a smile teasing the corners of my lips. Rae shakes her head and mutters, "Oh my god. I can't with you two."

As Braden hands me a bowl, I say, "It *is* really good pasta."

The corner of his mouth pulls up as he looks down to make his own dish. "If only it helped me get the girl, right?"

"Invite her over for dinner. I'm sure it will do the trick," I say with a grin.

He gives me a small smile. "Yeah. Maybe."

"Can you two come sit down?" Matt asks with a mouthful. "The longer you stay in there, the worse it is that I didn't wait for you."

"Because rushing them to the table is so polite," Rae sasses with a light laugh.

Braden holds out his hand with the bowl. "After you."

I just say, "Thanks," and go to take a seat.

"Seriously, will you marry me?" Matt asks Braden as he slides into the chair next to him.

Braden moves his noodles around with his fork, a trace of laughter behind his words when he says, "Maybe one day."

Ignoring her boyfriend, Rae turns to me. "Did you book your flight?"

Her question brings a smile to my lips, and I take a bite. It could probably make my eyes roll back, but I try to rein it in. "I did."

"And he's taking care of the hotel, right?"

I nod. "Also already booked."

She raises her eyebrows. "Jackson does not play around when it comes to you, that's for sure."

Her comment brings on a new wave of flutters and a pang to my chest, the empty chair at the table suddenly feeling bigger than the rest.

"I'm just jealous you get to go to New York," Matt says, and I hadn't realized the guys were paying attention.

"We can go too, you know," Rae says to him. "We can go to the show with Margot and get our own hotel after."

Matt thinks about it long and hard before shaking his head. "Nah."

Rae lazily points her fork at him. "You just said you wanted to go."

"Yeah, but Jackson loves her way more than me. I probably won't even see the guy."

My heart gets stuck in my throat, and in a split second I've dissected all the possible meanings behind that sentence.

1. Matt is just assuming Jackson has said he loves me by now.
2. Jackson told Matt he loves me.
3. It means absolutely nothing.

My prize is probably waiting behind door number three, but that doesn't stop me from fixating on door number two.

Rae takes no notice of her boyfriend's words halting my world. She just stares at him and says, "I would be there, too."

He nods, not looking any more excited about it.

My phone buzzes on the table next to me, and I flip it over.

JACKSON:
What the hell is this playlist?

Another message comes in right after it.

JACKSON:
You put Landslide on here more than once.

In case you didn't know.

Laughter bubbles in my chest, and I have to fight a grin as I text him back.

MARGOT:
Miss me?

I set my phone down and take another bite of food. Matt and Rae are still contemplating their hypothetical trip to New York, but Braden's eyes are locked on me.

I stop chewing.

He blinks and clears his throat. "Uh, how's the pasta?"

I start to chew slowly. "Amazing," I say when it's safe to talk again.

He smiles and takes another bite. When he looks up again, he directs his attention to Matt and Rae, and I do the same until my phone vibrates again.

> **JACKSON:**
> You're so fucking beautiful, you know that?
>
> I don't say it enough.

I frown, my eyebrows pulling together as I look at the words on the screen. He's only told me that once before, and this time hits me just as hard even though it's over text. If anything, it hits me harder because it's so random.

Too random.

> **MARGOT:**
> Are you drunk?

I watch the three dots float across the screen.

> **JACKSON:**
> That's the conclusion you jump to?
>
> I can't just text my girlfriend and tell her how pretty she is?

> **MARGOT:**
> Am I right?

There's a pause before those three dots appear again.

> **JACKSON:**
> Maybe a little.
>
> I've been hanging out with a bottle of bourbon alone in an RV.

My lips twist as I try to fight my smile. When he told me he'd probably just end up texting me if he drank on tour, I figured he was joking. But this is actually making me really happy.

> **MARGOT:**
> You're alone?

Jackson is never alone. It's why we always text instead of talking on the phone.

> **JACKSON:**
> Yeah.

> **MARGOT:**
> Can I call you?

Before I realize what I'm doing, I shovel the rest of my pasta into my mouth.

> **JACKSON:**
> You can always call me.

"I have to go," I say as I stand up from the table. Pacing into the kitchen, I rinse my bowl before putting it in the dishwasher. "Thanks for dinner." I look at Rae. "Are you staying here tonight?"

She's watching me curiously. "I was planning on it. Do you want me to come home?"

I shake my head. "No, you're good. Have fun, I'll see you guys tomorrow!"

Before any of them can respond, I'm out the door and dialing Jackson's number.

15
jackson

MARGOT'S NAME pops up on the screen, and I answer. "This is a big step. I don't think you've ever called me."

The sound of her unlocking a door meshes with her breath of laughter. "Shut up."

"You called as soon as you found out I was alone. Are you planning on having your way with me?"

She laughs again, and it's the best fucking sound. Being on tour is a constant distraction. I still miss her, but there's always something to keep those thoughts at bay. I'll think about how much I wish I were still waking up next to her, but then I'll have to do a sound check. I'll wonder what she's doing, but then Dave will walk up and share some lyrics he's been working on. It's a blessing, really, having something to ground me when I start dreaming about being somewhere else. But hearing her voice? Hearing her laugh? I didn't realize how much I missed her until now.

"You'd love that, wouldn't you?"

"I would," I say, my mind already reeling. It sounds like she sets her keys down, and I can perfectly picture her walking through her apartment. I wish I were there. I wish I could touch her. Thanks to the bourbon, I blurt, "I miss you."

"I miss you too," she says with a smile in her voice, and it sounds like she's finally sat down somewhere. "Want to tell me why you're drunk and alone?"

Getting comfortable on my bunk, I say, "We were celebrating with our new manager, and I'm not old enough to keep the party going."

"Should I be judging this new manager for convincing the guys to leave you behind?"

My lips press together with amusement. She's the only one who's willing to get mad about shit on my behalf. "No. He's cool. I think my age just caught him off guard."

"Fine." After a moment, she adds, "Jackson, you have a *manager.*"

The excitement in her voice brings a smile to my lips, but it's quickly followed by a pang in my chest. I take another sip from the bottle. "I wish you were here. I wish I could bury my face in your neck and smell your hair."

Laughter bubbles out of her. "Smell my hair?"

"Your hair always smells like your strawberry shampoo. I miss it." I hesitate, but the words, "I miss you," tumble from my mouth again before I can stop them.

There's still a smile in her voice when she says, "How much have you had to drink?"

Don't I tell her I miss her when I'm sober? Rubbing my palm against my forehead, I try to remember, but nothing comes to mind. "Enough to make me say stupid shit, but not enough for me to fall over."

"You haven't said anything stupid," she says softly, and I wish I could kiss her.

"I just want to touch you," I rub my hand over my face. "Or see you . . . Fuck," I shake my head. "I don't know."

"What would you do if I were there?" she asks.

I pause with the bottle to my lips. "What?"

"What would you do," she says again, more slowly this time, "if I were there?"

My hand grips the bottle tighter. "Don't ask me that while I'm drunk."

She giggles, and the sound shoots straight to my groin. "That's exactly why I'm asking."

"Are you trying to get me hard, Margot?"

"Maybe," she says simply, sweetly—far more innocently than she is.

"Well, it's working," I mutter as I set the bottle down and readjust.

"Jackson," she says in a voice that makes the hairs on the back of my neck stand up. "What would you do?"

"You're serious?" I ask before tossing back more bourbon.

"Very," she says as she lets out a sigh. "I need this."

My jeans suddenly feel too tight, and I let out a groan. "Where are you?"

"On my bed."

"What are you wearing?"

She lets out a light laugh. "Nothing sexy. I'm still wearing the black skirt and white blouse I wore to work."

I know the exact outfit. I've seen her in it countless times, and I know how fucking gorgeous she looks. She looks gorgeous in everything. "No that's—" I swallow. "No, I can work with that." Just picturing her is making it harder to think straight. "I mean, I could work with anything when it comes to you, but that's . . . that's perfect." I down a little more bourbon before setting the bottle on the floor near my bunk. "You want to know what I'd do to you?"

"Please," she breathes, and somehow that one word has me more turned on than anything else she's said tonight.

I wipe my hand over my mouth. "Margot, are you touching yourself?"

"Not yet," she says in a voice that suddenly sounds shy. I know she gets herself off while I'm not there, but we've never done this together.

"I want you to touch yourself."

"Okay."

The image of her, in her black skirt, lying on her bed with her hand between her legs could probably get me off on its own. My thoughts are scattered as I think about all the things I'd like to do to her right now. There are too many.

"How does it feel?" I ask, my voice hoarse, and my mind still caught up in the visual she gave me.

She lets out a low hum. "Not as good as when you do it."

I stifle the groan those words threaten to pull from me as I lean back. "Fuck your hand like you fuck me, Red. I promise you know what you're doing."

"Jackson," she half scolds, half laughs.

"I'm serious. You never hold back with me, so don't hold back with yourself. I want to hear every sigh and moan that comes from your pretty mouth."

She sucks in a breath.

"If you were here, I'm not going to lie, I'd want to be selfish," I say, my voice low. "I'd want your mouth around my cock. I don't think I've ever told you how good your mouth feels, but it's so fucking good, Margot. And the sight of you?" I shake my head, my hand rubbing over my face. "Just seeing you look up at me while you slowly take me in is enough to make me want to come." A soft moan leaves her lips, and it gives me too much satisfaction. "You take me so well when I fuck your mouth, Margot. You're so fucking good. And when I come down your throat, I know you love it. I can see it in the way your eyes flutter shut as you swallow. I can feel it in the way you go back for more, sucking me dry." The sound that comes from her throat is enough to make my dick twitch. Unzipping my jeans, I reach into my pants and pull myself free. My eyes shut, and my head falls back as I wrap my hand around my cock and do my best to pretend it's Margot I'm feeling. "Admit it. Admit that you love it."

Her breath is tight and airy when she says, "I do. I love it."

"Love what?"

She lets out a soft moan. "I love when you come in my mouth."

Fuck me.

"Slip a finger inside you." I wish I could be the one to feel her, but knowing she's doing it herself does something to me in a completely different way.

"How do you make me so wet when you're not even here?" she breathes. Before I can say anything, she adds, "You know . . . I wish I could taste you now. I wish I could make you come while I do this."

I let out a groan, my hand pumping harder. There's something so soft and dream-like in her voice. I know she's getting lost in this. Fuck, I'm getting lost in this.

"I want you inside me," she says, her breath heavy with heat. "I want you to fill me until I can feel you everywhere."

Jesus Christ.

"Margot, have you put another finger in?"

"Mhm . . ." The sound comes out of her slow, laced in pleasure.

"Good girl," I rasp, knowing her eyes are squeezed shut. I know her lips are parted. I know she's rolling her hips in a way that could get me off in seconds. Moving my phone from the crook of my neck, I put it on speaker and set it on my bunk, so I can fucking focus. Her breathing quickens. "That's it. Fuck your hand like you fuck me."

Another moan leaves her lips. "Sometimes," she says, panting, "when you're inside me, it feels like there's nowhere for you to go." Her words come out choppy. "It feels like you couldn't possibly stretch me further . . . fuck me deeper . . . but you always do. You always fuck me so good, Jackson."

"Fuck," I hiss, my hand tightening around my cock. "If you keep talking like that, you're going to make me come."

"Tell me how you'd fuck me."

My balls throb, begging for release. "I'd bend you over and push that skirt up."

Another whimper.

"You'd be so fucking wet, and I'd take you from behind. I'd fuck you the way you want to be fucked, Red. Harder than I've ever fucked you before. Because you're mine."

"Oh, god," she says, and I know she's close.

My lower back tingles, but I grit my teeth. "You're mine. Say it."

She's breathing hard. "I'm yours," she says, quickly followed by the sweet sound of her coming undone. That's all it takes for my back to stiffen as my own release sends a shudder through my entire body. It's the hardest I've come since leaving, and just the sound of her ragged breaths slowly returning to normal has me wishing the band would leave me alone more often, so I can do this again and again.

16
margot

I'M ALREADY STARTING to reconsider my hectic schedule as I race around the apartment, getting ready for work. I stayed up too late finishing my essay for Women's Studies, and I may have overslept. I wanted this, though. I wanted a constant distraction so I wouldn't notice how much I miss him.

I still notice.

It doesn't matter if I'm alone or surrounded by people. I *always* notice.

I'm counting down the days until I'll be in New York. Every day, it's the first thought that pops into my mind.

As of today, it's thirty-two.

The past few days, we've tried to check in with each other at least once, but it's mostly over text. I can't stop thinking about what it was like to hear his voice on the phone the other night.

I want you to touch yourself.
Good girl.
Fuck your hand like you fuck me.
I shake my head clear of the thought.
Thirty-two days.

I reach for my keys as I race around the kitchen counter, but I'm too fast for my own good. The keys fall to the floor, and I bend down to get them, cursing under my breath. I cannot catch a break. Why does every little thing have to go wrong when I'm *already* running late?

In a feeble attempt to gather myself, I take a steadying breath before I open the door and leave my apartment. My hands shake from the nerves and adrenaline of trying to get to work on time, but I manage to lock the door and book it down the stairs to our parking lot below.

My chest heaves by the time I open my car door and throw myself into the seat. Missing the ignition with the key the first time has me craning my head around the steering wheel, but I get it on the second try.

No. No. No. No.

My car struggles for breath, gurgling and sputtering like it's drowning. I try again, but when the key turns over, the same terrible noise hits my ears.

Shit.

I don't have time for this. I don't have *money* for this. My head falls against the steering wheel. This isn't me. I am *prepared.* I don't oversleep. I don't show up late. I'm dependable and responsible and all the other "-ables," but right now, I'm struggling.

Sucking in a breath, I lift my head. Why the hell am I sitting here? I have Rae—and Matt! I have lifelines.

Scrambling out of my car, I rack my brain for the odds that Rae and Matt haven't left for the day. I run up the steps and down our hall until I'm panting at Matt's front door. There's a chance Rae may still be here, but I have no idea what Matt's schedule is like. All I know is he's usually home in the afternoon. My fist beats against the door as I glance down at my phone in my other hand. I will officially be late. There's no way I'll make it to work in eight minutes.

The door finally opens, but it's not Rae or Matt standing in front of me. It's Braden. His blond hair is a mess, his chest is bare, and he's wearing gray sweatpants, like he just rolled out of bed. Rubbing one eye, he squints at me with the other.

"Hey, Margot." His voice is rough with sleep.

"Uh, hey . . ." I push up on the tips of my toes to look past him. Has he always been this tall?

He looks over his shoulder and then back at me. "I think Rae and Matt already left if that's who you're looking for."

I drop on my heels. "Damn it."

His blue eyes start to clear, and he considers me, his head tilting. "Is there something you need?"

I glance in the direction of my woeful car again, wondering if there's another way. There isn't. I know there isn't. I'm stranded alone on this island with no one but him. Letting my eyes settle on him again, I finally take him in, and . . . damn. Does he always look like this, or is it just the magic of gray sweatpants? I stare longer than I should at his curved lines of clearly defined muscle. Does he go to the gym? He must.

Never mind. Not important.

Pointing in the direction of the parking lot, my shoulders drop. "My car won't start, and I'm"—I look down at my phone for the time again—"definitely not getting to work in the next four minutes."

"I'll take you." He leaves the door open and walks back into the apartment.

"What? Really?" I call after him, but I stay in the threshold like I don't spend half my time here. There's something about only Braden being home that makes this place feel off limits.

"Yeah, I just need to grab a shirt," he calls over his shoulder.

Relief washes over me, but so does something else—something I can't put my finger on. Like a nervous flutter and a flash of guilt. It disappears a moment later when he reappears wearing a white T-shirt with his sweatpants, and I let out a breath. "Thank you for doing this."

"No problem." He grabs his keys off the hook and gestures for me to take the lead down the stairs.

Braden's car sits parked a few spaces over from mine, and I pick up my pace and jump inside as soon as he unlocks it with the fob.

As he gets in, he matches my urgency even though he isn't late for anything. Without wasting time, he throws the car in reverse, backs out of the spot, and pulls out of our complex. Once we're on the main road, I text Karah to let her know I'm running a few minutes late. She doesn't respond. No dots appear, and I could really use a text of reassurance that this is okay. I don't live far from the office, but my heart still pounds in my chest every time we're forced to stop at a traffic light.

"Want me to take a look at your car while you're at work?"

His voice tears my attention away from the glowing text thread on my screen. "Are you good with cars?"

A smile pulls at his lips, his blue eyes sparkling. "Depends on what's wrong with it."

I nod. "Yeah, that would be—well, that would be amazing. Thank you."

"I can't make any promises. Don't thank me yet," he says with a warm smile.

I do my best to smile back, but as wonderful as this is, it feels . . . weird. Would Jackson mind? Why am I even thinking about what Jackson would think? This is harmless. This is an innocent ride to work because my car won't start. Just because Braden is attractive doesn't mean I have to feel guilty about him helping me.

"What time do you get off?"

I blink, trying to clear my thoughts. "Five. Why?"

He gives me a sideways glance. "Don't tell me you plan on walking home."

"Oh." I let out a laugh. "No. I'll text Rae and ask her to come get me."

With an eyebrow raised, he asks, "You're sure?"

"I am," I say with a nod. Grateful for an escape, I point up ahead on the right. "You can turn there. Near the pizza place."

His jaw drops. "You work next to Mimi's Pizza?"

He's acting like he just found out I've been harboring a pile of gold, and it brings a twinge of a smile to my lips. "I do."

"Margot." He shakes his head. "You've been holding out on me. I *love* Mimi's Pizza."

I can't help laughing. "Well, if you ever want me to bring something back for you, just let me know."

Braden turns into the parking lot and pulls up in front of the small office for *Destination Tampa*. "Oh, I could never ask you to do that." He tilts his head to the side. "But if you ever wanted to surprise me, I wouldn't hate it."

His grin widens as laughter bubbles out of me. "Okay."

I don't even realize how much lighter I feel until Braden's eyebrows shoot up and he nods to the office behind me. "Weren't you late or something?"

"Shit!" I frantically gather my things and notice the way he bites back a smile. I'm breathless by the time I get out of the car, standing with my arms full as I duck down to look at him. I'm out of breath when I say, "Thanks again."

"Leave your keys, and I'll take a look."

"Right." I rummage through my bag and hand him the keys. "Thanks," I say again.

He nods with that same tight-lipped smile as I close the door. But even with the separation, I can feel that last glance clinging to my skin, and I somehow know he's watching me through the rearview mirror as he drives away.

17
jackson

THE WINDSHIELD WIPERS of the RV give a steady, melancholy tempo while I sit on our small couch and play. My fingers pick at the strings, and a soft, slow melody fills my ears as rain pelts the windows and Brian's hushed voice makes his sixth phone call of the day. He's been nonstop ever since we hired him. Even though he's in the RV with us, he's still all business from 9:00 a.m. to 5:00 p.m. The only time he loosens up is after dinner when he downs a few beers and smokes a joint with the rest of us.

I don't even know what he does on those calls. Stuff for the band, I'm assuming, but he won't give us the details. Marty asked him what he was doing on the phone all day, and Brian's response was, "When I have something to tell you, I'll tell you."

So, I won't be asking him a damn thing. He's a cool guy. A little intense, but I think we're all glad he's here—just a little on edge with it, too. Like we suddenly have a father figure on board, and even though he's a *cool dad*, he's still the one we have to answer to.

My head snaps up when Brian shoots out from the back of the RV and points toward the windshield. He still has his phone balancing in the crook of his neck when he says, "Take the next exit."

Dave's eyebrows furrow in the rearview mirror. "But we still have half a tank."

"Take the next exit, Dave. We're picking someone up." Before any of us can say anything, he's retreating to the back of the RV with his phone pressed to his ear.

"What the hell?" Dave mutters from the driver's seat.

I look across from me where Marty and Brady are playing cards at a small foldout table. Both guys look as clueless as I feel. Why the hell are we stopping for someone? *Who?*

Setting down my guitar, I walk to the front of the RV and sit next to Dave while he drives. "Do you know what this is about?"

His bitter laugh bites the air around us. "Do I look like I know what this is about?"

"You look like you might kill Brian."

Dave grins, giving me a sideways glance. "We'll see, won't we?" Looking ahead at the road, he pulls off the highway and onto the exit ramp. He raises his voice when he says, "This might be easier if Brian would tell me where to go!"

Like clockwork, Brian briskly heads toward us from the back of the RV. He claps his hands together, and I give up my seat so he can direct Dave.

Brian pats me on the shoulder as we switch places. "Take this right," he tells Dave as he collapses into the seat.

We still have time before the next stop, but that doesn't make Dave any less annoyed about the prospect of another detour.

Brian continues to give Dave directions while my fingers pluck at the strings, but I'm barely playing. I'm distracted, counting the minutes we're wasting and reading the different street signs as we squeeze down the narrow city streets.

Dave takes another turn and grumbles under his breath, "I better be able to drive this thing out of here."

"You will. You will." Brian gives Dave a few reassuring pats on the back, and I bite back a smile at the way Dave's entire body tenses. He's over Brian's surprises, but in the past forty-eight hours, none of Brian's surprises have been bad. He's given us free beer, took us all out to dinner last night, and he supplied the RV we're all in, free of charge. If you ask me, I'll take whatever else he has hidden up his sleeve. "Stop here," Brian says as he leans forward and lays on the horn in front of a random apartment building.

Moments later, a girl bounds down the stairs holding a cardboard box and wearing a lime green backpack. She looks to be about my age, and once she runs up the RV steps to pop her head in, I see I'm right. Her bright green eyes bounce to each of us before she pulls back the hood of her rain jacket, revealing pink hair that she has up in a messy bun. A silver septum piercing rests just above her broad grin, a smile that I have no doubt could bring an army of men to their knees. She's pretty. She's not Margot. But she's pretty.

My hands stop playing as Brian stands to face the rest of us. "Everyone, this is Mya. She'll handle all the merchandise at the shows."

Mya props the box on her knee so she can wave.

"But we don't have any merch," Marty says, his dark eyebrows cinched as he stares at the girl.

"Well, this isn't the only box I have," Mya says with a laugh. She nods over her shoulder. "The rest is still inside."

Brian takes the box from her and opens the lid. Reaching in, he quickly tosses all of us a T-shirt. They're black with our band's logo printed on the front. It's the same . . . but also different. Like she took our band name and somehow made it better—sharper. Even though the colors are mostly made up of white, the design pops against the soft black material.

"Holy shit," Brady says as he lets out a slow whistle, and it feels like he stole the words out of my mouth. We have merch. We are officially a band with merchandise available for purchase at shows because there are people who would buy it. I try to let that sink in as my eyes trail from the T-shirt I'm holding up to the girl who supplied them.

Mya says, "I had to make those on my Cricut to hold us over, but when I order more from the printer, they'll probably look better."

I think we're all in shock, coming to the same realization that we have shirts, because none of us move until Mya says, "So . . . do you guys want to help with the other boxes or . . .?"

Her words are like a jolt of electricity through the RV, and we all jump to our feet. As we pass her, Brian calls out each of our names to introduce us. "Dave, Marty, Brady, and last but not least, Jackson."

Mya smiles at each of the guys as they pass, and when her green eyes land on me, she repeats my name with a nod like she approves.

Everything about this feels like a dream. This doesn't feel like my life. Maybe because, up until a few days ago, this *wasn't* my life. My life this summer revolved around Margot, which was amazing. But I can't lie. This feels pretty amazing, too.

18
margot

"STILL NOT TOO MUCH?" Karah's voice calls with a hint of amusement from somewhere as I storm through the front door.

I don't take the time to stop and look for her before ducking into my office, and even though I'm having my doubts about my overpacked schedule, I call back, "The perfect amount!"

Collapsing into my desk chair, I smooth my hair back and catch my breath. My inbox pings in front of me, and my heart plummets. It's a message from our editor. Derek's cooking may be magic, but getting an email from him is always a heavy dose of reality. It always means you'll have to do more. More work. More revisions. More *something*.

I click on the message and start to read, my jaw going slack. Staring at the screen, I blink a few times before coming to my senses and getting to my feet. The entire walk to Derek's office, my hands are clenched into fists at my sides.

I stop in his doorway. "Seriously, Derek?"

Karah's voice travels from her office. "I told you she wouldn't be happy about it."

I glare at the short, broad man with dark hair sitting behind the desk. "You thought I'd be *happy* about the fact that you're completely ditching my story and making me write a new one?"

He leans back in his computer chair, the plastic creaking beneath the strain of his weight. "Listen, the bookstore piece you wrote is good, but it's fluff."

I cross my arms. "Aren't most of our stories 'fluff?' Small businesses, local heroes, *Tampa's oldest dog?*"

He points a warning finger at me. "Don't you dare say anything about Bandit."

Pinching the bridge of my nose, I shake my head. "I'm just saying, a lot of our pieces follow a similar formula. Why interview the corporate white tie who owns most of the city?" That's what his email wanted. For me to abandon my article on the local bookstore, and instead, write an entire feature on some old, rich, white guy.

"Because he's paying us."

I arch an eyebrow. "I'm sorry, what?"

Derek holds both hands in the air. "He's paying for the space, and he wants it in next month's issue. So, the bookstore story will have to wait."

I grit my teeth, hating everything about this. That bookstore *needs* the publicity, and I'm pretty sure this guy doesn't. It's probably just some vanity project for him—which is fine, but not when it takes away from a business struggling to thrive. My lips press together as I try to think things over. "The bookstore will be in the October issue?"

He nods. "Definitely."

I'm still frustrated. We're only a few days away from finalizing next month's issue, so this is all last minute. I'll have to send over interview questions and write a whole piece on this guy when I have school work piling up as it is. "Fine," I finally say. "But the bookstore gets a center spread next month."

Derek frowns. "Margot, you know we can't—"

I walk over to his desk and take one of the homemade donuts he brought. "A center spread, Derek." I'm pushing it. I know I'm pushing it, but the faint smile pulling at his lips also tells me he doesn't really mind.

"You're killing me, you know that?"

"Thank you." I take a bite of the donut. On my way out, I raise it above my head and call out, "Delicious as always!"

His low laughter behind me is all the confirmation I need that what I did was okay. My summer internship may have been the perfect way for me to feel comfortable around everyone, but I'm still technically their newest employee. I don't think I'm in any position to bark orders at anyone, but it's not me who's being punished—it's the bookstore. If I have to step on a few toes to get them the visibility they need, so be it.

The donut is raised to my mouth as I prepare to take another bite, but I freeze when I see Karah standing in the doorway of her office. "You're looking pleased with yourself," she says with a smug, knowing smile.

I shrug, not sure if I'm about to be praised or scolded for the way I handled that. "Small victories."

She nods slowly, and as nice as she is, it's still unnerving. "It certainly seems that way."

I glance at my office door and wonder if I can be excused from this conversation. "Well," I say, rocking back on my heels. "Lots of work to do."

She shakes her head with a breath of laughter, and I duck into my office. I don't think I take a full breath until I'm sitting in front of my computer again. My hands shake slightly as I reach for the mouse, but I feel good. I stood up for something I knew was right, and now all I have to do is interview some sleazy rich guy and email the bookstore to let them know they'll be in the October issue with a full center spread instead.

My phone lights up on my desk in front of me, and I see a

notification from the American Thieves Instagram account. It's one of the few accounts I follow closely enough to set alerts for. I love seeing what Jackson's doing—especially on the days he's too busy to talk.

I swipe the screen open, and I'm met with a picture of the band wedged together on the couch of their RV, all holding up T-shirts for American Thieves. I notice Jackson first and smile. He's sitting with the rest of the band with a grin that somehow looks bashful and radiant at the same time. It looks like someone gave him a hard time for not smiling enough right before the picture was taken, and they caught him mid-laugh.

My chest aches. I miss him. I miss him so much but seeing him like this makes it worth it. This is what he's supposed to do. He's radiant when he's doing anything related to music, and as much as I'd love him to be sitting on *my* couch instead, I'd never forgive myself.

I scan across the image, taking note of Dave, Marty, Brady . . . my heart stutters. Tilting my head, I focus on a girl sitting on the armrest of the tiny blue couch. She's on the opposite end from Jackson. She's pretty. And by the looks of her pink hair and casual pose, she's *fun*. A feeling similar to panic rises within me, and I do my best to snuff it out. Jackson will be around a lot of new people while he's on the road—I *know* this. But he never mentioned a girl traveling in the RV with them . . . he never mentioned anyone other than his new manager.

I click on the caption and start scanning the words.

The crew is complete! Make sure you stop by and see Mya for all of your American Thieves merch! We're coming for you next, Asheville!

The photo was posted minutes ago and already has close to one hundred likes. This is becoming the new normal for them. They're getting more popular, and more people are starting to follow their journey.

Jackson said it was my article that made all this happen in the first place, which I find a little hard to believe. I think

American Thieves would have taken off with or without my help, but Jackson is always adamant I played a role in making his dreams come true. Maybe I did. Maybe it was my blog that put them in front of the right person.

My blog is the one thing I wish I left a little more time for in my new schedule. I still try to keep up with my posting schedule, but it's been difficult. I'm not exactly giving myself time to find new things to write about either. What am I supposed to say?

Try this new restaurant! I haven't eaten there, but the pictures on Google look great.

It doesn't work that way. Even the photo American Thieves just posted has me itching to write something. The photo would make a great headlining image for a blog post, but I'm not there. I didn't take it. I have no idea if someone actually had to make Jackson laugh right before snapping it.

I frown as I zoom in on the girl with pink hair, noticing her piercings and tattoos. She has a floral elbow piece, and even though I've never thought about getting a tattoo, I suddenly envy her. She looks like she fits in with his lifestyle, and part of me wishes I did, too.

19
jackson

THE GUYS ARE PLAYING cards inside the RV when I step outside to get some air. We're parked at a campsite with a couple of chairs positioned near a small fire pit that isn't lit. It would be way too fucking hot to sit by a fire right now. Taking a seat on the white plastic, I stare up at the sky. At school, I felt caged. I felt like everything was an inconvenience, getting in the way of what I wanted to do. But out here, in the middle of nowhere, I'm free. It's a type of calm I never had at USF.

The only thing missing is her.

I reach for my phone and contemplate calling Margot when I see she texted me a couple of hours ago.

> MARGOT:
> Just thinking about you.

The words tug at something deep, and a cross between a smile and a frown pulls at my lips. She's sent me those same four words a few times now, and they're becoming my favorite message. She usually sends them when one of us has had an extra busy day and we haven't had time to talk.

It's just past midnight, and I want to hear her voice more

than anything. I want to know how her day was and what she did. She has classes tomorrow, though. And with the way she packed her schedule, they start early.

My thumb hovers over her name, but I know I shouldn't call. I know she's already asleep, and the last thing I want is for her to be tired tomorrow because I kept her up. I've learned that one the hard way. It took me way too long to get back in her good graces after playing guitar before her first day of classes, and the last thing I want is for us to move backward.

"Hey."

I look up to find Mya ducking her head out of the back door. "Hey."

"Mind if I join you?"

I shake my head and gesture to the chair next to me. Disappointment washes over me. It has nothing to do with Mya. She's . . . nice. But even though I knew I wouldn't have called Margot, Mya's presence is another fleeting window of opportunity snatched away.

She must catch onto what I'm feeling because she cocks an eyebrow as she slowly takes a seat. "Did I interrupt something?"

I shake my head and turn my phone over in my lap. I'll text Margot in the morning.

"If you say so." She offers a shrug and plops into the plastic chair next to me before crossing her legs underneath her. That's when I notice the burning joint in her hand. She follows my gaze and then meets my stare again. "Want some?" she asks with an outstretched hand.

I've smoked more these past few days than I have in my entire life, but it helps to make the long hours on the road less boring. "Sure." I take it from her, and she grins in response. Bringing the joint to my lips, I take a hit before handing it back to her. "Thanks."

"Don't thank me." She lets out a huff as she reaches across

the space between us and retrieves the joint. "I stole it from Brian."

My laugh comes out as a cough. "That's what you call your uncle? Brian?"

She arches an eyebrow as she deeply inhales. "Technically, he and I are coworkers now," she says, her voice squeaky from holding the smoke in her lungs.

"Right." Without thinking, I turn over my phone to check for anything from Margot. I don't know why I do it. She's the last one who texted me, and I still haven't answered. It's just a compulsive tick at this point.

The gesture doesn't go unnoticed. Mya gives me a sideways glance. "Expecting to hear from someone?"

I shake my head. "Doubt it. I think she's asleep."

She nods slowly. "On tour with a girlfriend back home?" A hint of a smile pulls at her lips. "You're brave."

"Yeah." I reach for the joint again. "Brave or stupid."

She laughs and it's a light, airy sound. "For your sake, let's hope it's brave."

"What about you?" I nod in her direction. "Got a boyfriend?" A slow, knowing smile pulls at her lips, so I add, "Or girlfriend?"

She reaches for another smoke, and I pass it back to her. "Have had both. Currently have neither."

I lean back to look up at the stars. "Smart."

She takes another hit and follows my gaze. "Or a coward."

My head rolls to the side, and I know I'm starting to feel my high because I laugh. "You don't strike me as a coward."

"You, my friend, are too kind." Another puff of smoke enters and leaves her lips before she hands the joint back to me and says, "So, tell me about this girlfriend. Do you love her?"

I cough mid hit, and she bursts into laughter.

"Oh my god, you do," she says through her relentless laughter. "You love her so much."

"I . . ." My voice strains, and I cough again. "I don't know."

She snatches what's left of the joint from my fingertips with more force than before. "Liar."

I gape at her. "Hey, I wasn't done with that."

She holds it out of reach like I'm a little kid begging for a toy. "Not so fast. Friends don't lie."

"You're serious?"

Her eyes widen. "Do I look like I'm joking?" She leans her head back and does a slow pull on the joint like she's taunting me. "Everything about you screams lovesick, you know."

What the hell makes this girl think she has me pegged so easily? I've known her for all of what? Eight hours? I cross my arms. "Enlighten me."

She turns to face me in her chair. "Well, for one, you keep to yourself. You play your guitar. You come out here to . . . what? Stare at the stars?" She shakes her head. "And you didn't give me a second glance." She shrugs. "I knew you were either lovesick or heartbroken. I just didn't know which."

I force a laugh. "Maybe you're just not my type."

Rolling her eyes, she quips, "I'm everyone's type." Giving me a sideways glance, she adds, "If they're single." She tilts her head, considering her last words. "And sometimes if they're not."

I'm not sure I believe her. Even if I wasn't with Margot, I don't think I'd be interested. "Well, you don't lack confidence."

"I don't," she says with a determined shake of her head. "And neither should you. If you love your girlfriend, you should own it."

"Jesus." I rub a hand down my face. "Fine. I—" I trip on the words, my heart hammering in my chest as if I were saying it to Margot herself. Taking a sharp breath, I manage to get out, "I might love her." The words are out, and a flash of pure panic runs over me, turning my blood to ice. I've never told anyone I love Margot out loud. I have a feeling Matt and Rae know—hell, I have a feeling Margot knows. But just having the words leave my lips to this random ass girl, still leaves me feeling like my shields are cracked. Like someone knows my biggest weakness.

But Margot isn't a weakness. If anything, she's a strength.

"Might?" Mya's voice cuts through my spiraling thoughts.

My hands grip the plastic armrests, and as much as I want to stop my knee from bouncing, it has a mind of its own. Is she serious? My deepest confession wasn't good enough?

When I don't say anything, she rolls her eyes. "Words matter. You write lyrics, you should know that."

I scoff. "I suck at writing lyrics."

She sighs, leaning her head back against the plastic chair so she can gaze at the night sky. "Maybe you'd be better at it if you were honest about your feelings."

What game does she think she's playing? I just offered her something I've never told anyone. The anxiety I felt moments ago warms to a simmering annoyance, and I mutter. "I love her."

"What?" She holds her hand to her ear, leaning a little closer. "I missed that."

My hands grip the chair tightly enough to turn my knuckles white. "I said," I say through gritted teeth, making sure to raise my voice. "I love her."

Mya grins. "Yeah, obviously. Nice to see you finally catch up." Leaning over, she pats me on the knee. "See, look." Mya hums happily and she gently sets the joint back in my hands. "Our friendship is already doing wonders for you."

"Yeah," I say, unconvinced. I pinch my lips around the joint, sucking in like it will somehow tether me back to solid ground.

"Is there a reason you haven't told her yet?"

"What?"

"Well, I'm assuming by the complete freak-out you just had, you haven't told her yet. So, why?"

The joint still rests at my lips as I let out a breath of laughter. This girl is something else. "I've never said that to anyone, and now that I'm here"—I gesture to whatever the hell is around us—"I'd rather tell her in person."

"That's fair."

I cock an eyebrow. "Yeah? You're not going to give me more shit for that?"

The corner of her mouth lifts, and she tucks a strand of pink hair behind her ear. "I don't think anyone would give you shit for that."

I guess she's right, but I feel like shit for not telling Margot before I left. It's not like I didn't know then. I think I was overwhelmed with the band going on tour and spending every waking moment with her.

"I'll tell her next time I see her," I finally say with a nod.

Mya punches the air, like she somehow made this happen—and I guess she did. I smile and hand the joint back to her. "To new friendships."

Taking it from me, she winks. "And to love."

20
margot

JACKSON:
I'm always thinking about you.

A SMALL SMILE pulls at my lips as I stare at the text he sent just after one in the morning, but it doesn't ease the ache in my chest. I hate feeling so distant from him. Not so long ago, *he* was my alarm clock. I miss waking up to his hands—his *mouth*. It doesn't matter what sound I choose for my alarm on my phone. They're all obnoxious and cold compared to waking up next to him.

I'm up thirty minutes early, because even though Braden diagnosed my car with a dead battery, I didn't have time to run out and get one yesterday. I'll have to Uber to class this morning, so I want to give myself some extra time.

Before dragging myself out of bed, I send Jackson a quick text.

MARGOT:
I hope you have a great show tonight.

I add a heart emoji and press send. I wish I could surprise

him like I did his last tour, but there's too much going on between work and classes.

After a quick shower, I style my hair and throw on yoga pants and a T-shirt for class. Grabbing my keys off the hook, I head out the door and hurry down the front steps as I open the Uber app on my phone. There are drivers all over this city. I should be able to catch a ride without a problem.

A car hood in front of me slams as my feet hit the pavement, and I look up to find Braden standing next to my car. He casually rests his elbow on the hood as he crosses his ankles, leaning against it with a pleased smile curling at his lips.

"What are you doing out here so early?" I ask with a tilt of my head. He's barefoot in nothing but sweatpants, and I try not to look at the muscles that shape his torso.

"I figured you'd want to drive yourself this morning," he says as he tosses me the keys.

I blink, my eyes jumping from the keys to him. "You fixed my car?"

He lets out a low laugh. "Don't give me that much credit. It was only the battery."

Sure, maybe a battery doesn't take a lot of mechanical skill, but he still *fixed my car.* I'm frozen in place, not sure if I should scold him or thank him.

I should thank him. I should definitely thank him, but this feels like . . . a lot.

My feet are still stuck. "You drove to the store and picked up a battery this morning?"

He nods.

"And then you came here and installed that battery all so I could leave on time?"

Another chuckle leaves his lips. "I saw how stressed you were yesterday morning. I figured for everyone's sake, we should avoid a repeat." I let out a breath of laughter and fidget with the keys in my hand. I'm still not sure how I feel about him doing this, but before I can debate whether I should feel guilty about something I didn't ask him to do, he adds, "You owe me for the battery, but you can pay me whenever."

My head snaps up, and I smile a little more easily. "Of course. I'll Venmo you."

We both stand there, staring at each other as his smile slowly grows. "And you're welcome."

"Oh my, god! Thank you! So much—really. This . . ." I let my eyes wander to my car behind him, the engine purring. "This helps a lot. Thank you."

He grins. "Anything you need."

And just like that, the new but familiar feeling of guilt creeps into my chest again. If he were Matt or anyone else, I'd probably wrap my arms around him in a bear hug and squeal with appreciation.

But he's Braden.

And doing that—or anything else with him—feels like . . . too much.

By the end of the day, my brain is fried. I usually hate when the apartment is empty, but I'm grateful for the quiet as I collapse onto the couch. I managed to pour myself a glass of white wine at some point and accidentally leave it on the counter. It was from one of the bottles Braden supplied for us, and I let out an audible groan when I see it taunting me in all its sparkling glory.

My head rolls against the back of the couch, and I stare at the glass of Pinot Grigio, debating how badly I want it. I consider leaving it and curling up to fall asleep under the cozy throw blanket, but my phone does a dance on the same counter a few inches away, and I'd hate to have no wine *and* a missed call.

I push myself up from the couch and let my legs drag me into the kitchen. It isn't until I see Jackson's name that I suddenly feel awake. Those letters on the screen are enough to send a bolt of energy down my spine.

"Hey," I say, sounding out of breath after lunging for the phone.

"Hey." His voice is rich, and deep, and *God* do I miss him. Just the sound of that one word makes my entire body warm.

My eyes dart to the time on the stove. "Doesn't your show start—"

"Soon. Yeah."

I take the glass of wine in one hand and walk back to the couch. "And you're calling me?"

"Margot, you're my girlfriend. Of course, I'm calling you."

My cheeks flare as soon as the word *girlfriend* falls from his lips. This is ridiculous. I know I'm his girlfriend. We've been together for months, but when he was here, things between us were . . . effortless.

Easy.

Now that he's gone, there's a disconnect. The titles we never had to rely on while we were together are one of the few things connecting us while we're apart.

"It's nice to hear your voice." I don't think Jackson and I have gone a whole day without sending some type of text message to one another, but neither of us are fans of long text conversations. Our texts are always short and sweet. I thought the next time I got him on the phone, the floodgates would open. I imagined gushing about all the things I've wanted to say to him over the past few days, but now that he's on the other end, my mind draws a blank. It's like there are too many things, and I can't decide which is the most important. Eventually, I land on, "How are you feeling?"

"About what?" he asks, but before I can answer, he adds, "The show? How my life has completely changed these past few weeks? Or how I constantly have to fight the urge to catch the next flight to Florida just so I can spend another night in your bed?"

That last one hits me right in the chest. "All of the above."

"Well," he says with a trace of a smile in his voice. "I'm nervous for the show. This place is fucking huge, and the only thing keeping me from you is the lack of funds in my bank account."

I let out a light laugh at that last part because I feel the same, but that's not the part that caught my attention. "You never get nervous." I set my wine on the coffee table and sit up straight.

"Of course I get nervous. I just . . ." He pauses. "I don't know. I guess I hide it well."

My heart cracks under the strain in his voice. "Jackson, you're so talented, and the band always sounds phenomenal. The only one who should be nervous tonight is the headlining band because they're going to have to follow you." He's quiet, and I wonder if I said the wrong thing. I wait for what feels like forever, but I can't take him being quiet like this. He should be excited . . . celebrating. "Jackson?"

"Thanks, Margot." His voice is tight. Controlled. The sound of it brings a frown to my lips. He's holding something back.

21
jackson

THE SOUND of her voice eases some of the restlessness I've been battling since we got here. Playing smaller venues is fine, but tonight we're playing our first arena, and Crooner Sins sold out. Margot was there the first time I took the stage with American Thieves. She surprised me the first night we opened for Sidecar earlier this year. The music festival this summer practically revolved around my time with her. Margot has been there for all of it. Tonight feels like a milestone she'll miss, and I'm trying not to let it get to me.

She laughs on the other end of the phone, and my chest tightens at the sound. "Don't thank me. Own it. You'll be great tonight."

God, what I would give to see the way her nose crinkles when she laughs. I miss her so much it hurts. "Twenty-two days."

"The torturous countdown," she says with a sigh. "Hey, I saw the band's post yesterday. It looks like you got a new member?"

There's a hint of caution in her voice, and I close my eyes.

Of course. I might not be particularly attracted to Mya, but I'm not blind. She's pretty, and she's on tour with us.

"That's Mya," I say, hoping I can ease whatever thoughts are making her voice come out slow and hesitant. "She's our manager's niece, and she is in no way anything for you to worry about."

"Who said I was worried?"

I rest my fist against the wall and kick at one of the red bricks near my feet. "She's cool. A little prying, but I think you'd like her."

Her voice is soft when she says, "I bet I would."

Even though she sounds pleasant, something feels off—like she's treading the fine line between being unhappy with the circumstances and unhappy with me.

The metal door opens a few feet away, and Brady sticks his head out. "Hey! We've been looking for you."

"What's up?" I ask, covering the mic so I don't yell in Margot's ear.

Brady grins. "Mya sold out of shirts."

"How the hell . . ." I blink, understanding what this means. "She *what?*"

Brady just nods enthusiastically. "Sold out. Not a single one left. She's already working on where she can have more printed before the next show."

"Shit," I mutter with a bewildered shake of my head.

"Jackson, that's amazing!" Margot says in my ear, and in the shock of the moment, I had almost forgotten I was on the phone with her.

"Once you're done, we'll take a shot." Brady nods to me on the phone, and I give him a silent thumbs up.

"Do you know how many shirts she started with?" Margot asks, and she's back to sounding lighter again.

"I have no idea." I run a hand through my hair. "There

had to have been"—I think back to when Mya had us help her load up the RV—"at least eight boxes."

"And she *sold out?*" Margot asks, her shock mirroring my own.

I let out a bewildered laugh. "Seems like it."

"Jackson, are you famous?" I can hear the smile in her voice.

The question catches me off guard. "I—no. I don't think so."

The concept of fame is weird to me. People knowing who you are when you don't know them. People feeling connected to you when you've never even seen their face. There's something to be said for the way music can forge such a connection, but it's still fucking weird to think about. Letting out a sigh, I look up at the darkening sky. "I kind of hope not."

"What do you mean?"

I glance around, but I'm completely alone. There's some guy throwing trash into a dumpster about fifty feet away, but there's no way they'd be able to hear me. It's not even like I want to say anything bad. I just don't want to come across as an ungrateful asshole. "The potential fame is probably the one part of this I don't love." I lean my head against the brick wall. "I want the band to be successful, and I want people to love our music, but I kind of wish I could keep my head down and just play."

She's quiet on the other end. We haven't talked about this. I try to be positive about everything when it comes to the band because I asked for this. When Dave was being a dick in the studio and making us stay there all day, sure, I was frustrated. But being stuck in a studio with three other guys who look like they want to murder each other is still better than writing an essay about the way technology has shaped society in the past one hundred years or some shit.

"But I can't," I add to fill the space. "Because if I act the wrong way or do the wrong thing, it could mean losing a fan." I shake my head. "It's too much pressure. I'm bound to disappoint someone."

"You won't," she says, her voice soft.

I scoff. "Margot, I disappoint everyone. My parents, Matt, you."

The last word is barely out of my mouth when she says, "You do not disappoint me—or Matt for that matter. I don't even think you disappoint your mom." She takes in a breath like she's choosing her next words carefully. "As for your dad . . . I don't think you've disappointed him any more than he's disappointed you. You both want different things, but at the end of the day, it's your life Jackson, and you only get one."

How does she do that? How does she always know how to spin things to make it so different than how it is in my head? I could tell her I love her. It's right there, on the tip of my tongue. Ever since I admitted it out loud to Mya, the thought, the feeling—the fucking declaration—has grown into something too big to hold onto.

But I can't. Not yet. Not like this. So instead, I blow out a breath, and say, "Thanks." Running a hand through my hair, I add, "You know how your blog made all this possible?"

Margot snorts. "I still find that hard to believe, but sure."

I could roll my eyes. It doesn't matter how many times I tell her, or how many times Dave tells her. She doesn't think her blog was the big reason we got our break. I think she wants me to feel like I did this on my own, but a lot more than that goes into it. Sure, it's hard work, but it's also luck. And in my case, some of my luck came from her and that post.

Ignoring her comment, I make my point. "All I can think about is how easy it would be for someone to undo that. One article, one viral video on a bad day, one blog post. That's all it would take for people to turn their backs on us and write us off."

"Jackson, you can't walk around determined to be on your best behavior all the time. That's exhausting. You're not the Prince of England, you're a *rockstar*. Your fans want the real you. If you're genuine and authentic, they'll love you. It would be impossible for them not to."

I hope she's right. "The Prince of England thing doesn't do it for you?"

She laughs on the other end of the phone, and I wish I could bottle that sound. "No," she says, the smile still evident in her voice. "I like you messy and uncensored." There's a pause before she adds, "Why would you think you've disappointed me?"

I close my eyes, wishing I would have kept my mouth shut. "Because I'm not there." It's an oversimplified answer, but I can't get into this with her right now. I can't confess all the ways I feel like I'm coming up short before I take the stage.

"Jackson, you're touring the country doing what you love. That could never disappoint me. If anything, it's inspiring."

She's too good. Too supportive. Too understanding. It all feels like a debt I'm determined to pay back, and I don't even know where to start. How do I pay her back for something that feels priceless? She's giving me what no one else ever has, and part of me knows I'll never be able to tip the scales.

"Hey," she says when I haven't said anything. Her voice is soft and sweet, and the vice in my chest loosens at the sound of it.

I clear my throat as I blink back to reality. "Sorry."

"Don't be," she says lightly. "Go play your show and enjoy every minute of it knowing you're doing exactly what you should be doing. You're doing exactly what we all want you to do."

I know she's excluding my parents from that statement, but

I don't care. I don't need my parents' approval when I have Margot in my corner. She makes their absence feel small.

"I—thank you." I scratch the side of my head as I glance at the door to the venue, knowing my time is probably up. "You make everything better."

There's another pause, and I wonder if she'll comment on how I've never said anything like that. I've felt it. I've thought it. But I've never said it. I'm trying to be better about that.

She doesn't, though. Eventually, she just says, "So do you," and the newfound thickness in her voice has my own throat bobbing as I swallow.

We say our goodbyes, but even after she's hung up the call, I stare down at my phone for a long moment before slipping it back into my pocket. So much was left unsaid between us. I definitely held back on my end, and I wonder if she held back on hers. Is she looking at her phone wishing she would have said more the same way I am?

Maybe I'll never know.

Blowing out a breath, I walk to the metal door and yank it open. The energy has shifted since I stepped outside. There's an electric current in the air from everyone gearing up for the show.

Marty comes out of nowhere, hooking an arm around my shoulder. "It's about time you decided to join us!" He pulls me to where the other guys are standing backstage with Brian and Mya.

Dave has a bottle of Patron in hand, and he raises it when he sees me. "Did you hear Mya got rid of all our shirts? I hope that gorgeous girlfriend of yours knows what a fucking rockstar you are!"

Marty finally releases me, and I run a hand through my hair. "Yeah," I say with a breath of laughter. "I think she knows."

My eyes dart to Mya, and she beams at me with a wink.

I JUST WANT TO BE YOURS

Dave pours us shots in plastic cups, and we all raise them before shooting them back. The tequila warms my throat on the way down. When I spoke to Margot, it felt like I was with her. She has this way of pulling me from whatever I'm in and consuming my every thought. I like the feeling of getting lost in her, but now it's time to get lost in the music.

22
margot

I TRIED to stay up for Jackson. I wanted to hear how his show went, but I ended up falling asleep on the couch. When I woke up at 3:00 a.m. to the glow of the TV and still no sign of Rae or Matt, I dragged myself to my bedroom.

Our conversation lingers in the back of my mind. How could he think he disappoints me? And Matt? The guy is his biggest cheerleader. By the end of the call, I think he knew it was all in his head, but I can't help wondering how long he's felt that way.

I thought I would have heard from him by morning, but as I squint at the screen, my eyes still heavy with sleep, there are no new messages. Jackson may not have texted me last night, but a notification for American Thieves stares back at me. I unlock my phone and tap on it.

My heart sinks in my chest as soon as the picture loads. It looks like they posted it after the show. A large group of people stand backstage. It's the members of the headlining band and everyone on the American Thieves crew.

My eyes immediately jump to where Jackson stands in the photo. Sweat glistens on his skin making the ends of his hair curl at his neck. One of his arms is around Brady and the other around Mya. The sight feels like a blow to the chest, and there suddenly isn't enough air in the room. Sitting up, I zoom in, noticing where her hand rests around his waist and the way his arm casually falls over her shoulder as they stand side by side.

And even though it's stupid—so incredibly stupid—I have to fight the sinking feeling in my gut. The longer I look at the photo, the harder it is to keep it at bay. My jealousy isn't warranted. I know it isn't. But it's *loud*. It's screaming at me, taunting me, and a harmless picture has put a heavy strain on my heart in a matter of minutes.

A tear slides down my cheek, and I curse as I wipe it away.

I wonder if I'd still feel like this if he had texted me? Maybe it's hitting me harder because I haven't heard from him. Maybe hearing from him—knowing he's thinking of me—would have made me see this picture for exactly what it is.

A backstage photo with the band.

He told me I'd like her, and maybe I would, but all I can think about is *why* he thinks I'd like her. Is it because he likes her, too?

How much?

This is ridiculous. Turning my phone over, I leave it on the bed and head into the kitchen. As I round the corner, I see someone standing in front of my open refrigerator, and my legs lock. My heart stops, and for a fraction of a second, I let myself imagine how it would feel to have Jackson surprise me like this.

I know it's not him. The sandy blonde hair poking out above the fridge door tells me it's Braden, but for one fleeting moment I let myself pretend. Hope soars into my chest only to come crashing down because I can remember so clearly when it *was* Jackson here in the mornings, and the ache that feeling knocks into my chest is enough to steal the air from my lungs.

My eyes burn with the threat of fresh tears, and I frantically try to blink them away when Braden pulls back to look at me around the fridge door. "Hey. Sorry if I woke you. We're out of milk, and Matt said—" He pauses and slowly shuts the fridge. "Hey, are you okay?"

I quickly wipe the corner of my eye with the back of my hand to stop anything from falling. "Yeah," I say with my best smile. "Sorry. I just woke up."

He nods but doesn't take his eyes off me, and his frown deepens. "Did something happen?"

God, why does he have to sound so genuine? Just the fact that he cares threatens to bring new tears to the surface. "No, of course not." I wave him off and walk to the Keurig, so I can turn my back to him without making it obvious. As I reach overhead for a mug, there's no sound of him opening the fridge again, and I can feel him studying me. Doing my best to sound upbeat, I ask, "Think we'll all order pizza tonight since it's Friday?"

Only then does the refrigerator open again, and I let out a breath as I relax my shoulders. "Probably not. I think Matt and Rae are going out tonight."

"Oh." I meant to say it happily, but even I hear the sulkiness in my voice. My schedule doesn't match up with Rae's lately, and I miss her. It's bad enough that Jackson is gone, but if I have to stay in this apartment alone with my thoughts, I might lose it. I know she's not busy on purpose. If anything, I'm the busy one. I'm gone all day, and when I come home at night, I usually don't have the energy to do anything. She and Matt are allowed to make plans for a Friday night. It's exactly what they should do.

"Yeah," Braden says behind me. He finally gets the milk and starts walking toward the door. "I'll bring this back later."

Looking over at him, I flash him a small smile. "Keep it."

We share almost everything, anyway. Sometimes it feels like we should have just rented a place that could fit all of us.

He gives me a wave without saying more, and I wait for the front door to open and close. As soon as I'm alone again, I choke back a sob like that performance just took everything out of me. I hate feeling fake. It's never been something I'm good at, but the last thing I want to do is talk to Braden about anything.

That, and the quiet of the apartment feels like a punishment. How lonely and pathetic must I be if just the sheer absence of noise is enough to tip me over the edge?

With my coffee in hand, I wipe my traitorous eyes and head back into my bedroom to start getting ready for work. I'm hoping Mr. Richie Rich has emailed me back his responses to my interview questions. The sooner I can get that article finished, the sooner I can pour my heart and soul into the two-page spread for the bookstore.

My phone lights up on my bed, and I walk over. Setting my coffee down on my dresser, I tuck one leg under me as I sit and get my phone off the blanket.

JACKSON:
Remind me to never drink Patron again.

I should be happy, but all I can think about is the fact that he was drunk while he was hanging out with another girl, and I'm back to spiraling. Does he think she's pretty? I'm sure he does. He'd be crazy not to. Cute button nose, pink hair pulled back in short French braids, trendy overalls and tattoos . . . that's what she looked like last night, anyway.

Swallowing the burning questions bubbling inside of me, I type a response.

MARGOT:
Rough night?

Those three dots appear, and his response comes sooner than I thought it would.

> **JACKSON:**
> Great night. The only thing missing was you.

Some of the tension in my chest eases, and a faint smile pulls at the corner of my mouth. Turning on the shower, I quickly text back what I know we're both thinking.

> **MARGOT:**
> 21 days.

23
jackson

THE COUCH in the RV becomes Mya's makeshift bed every night, but as soon as she's up, she stashes her blankets and pillows somewhere to turn it back into a couch for everyone. It's a good thing she wakes up earlier than the rest of us. Coming out here feels like a good way to clear my head before I'm around the guys for the rest of the day.

I take a seat on the tiny blue couch and send Margot a quick text to ask her what she's doing today. I barely have time to hit the send button when my phone gets snatched out of my hand by Mya skipping past. "Good morning, Lover Boy," she says in a sing-song voice.

I sigh. "Why do you have my phone?" I swear, there's something about living with someone inside an RV that makes a week of knowing them feel like years. Mya has already become the little sister I never wanted. A very annoying and pushy but surprisingly cool little sister.

She innocently sways back and forth while shamelessly reading my conversation with Margot, her eyes going wide. "Is she coming?"

Leaning forward, I snatch my phone back from her grip. "That's the plan."

"So, I get to meet her?"

She's looking at me like she's six and I just promised to take her to the North Pole. "Uh, yeah. I don't see why not." I tuck my phone into my pocket where it's safe from prying eyes.

"When?" She's practically bouncing on her toes.

I let out a laugh. She looks the way I feel when I think about seeing Margot, but I have no idea what warrants this type of excitement from her. "The show in New York City on October twelfth."

With one more hop, she spins and collapses on the couch next to me. "Oh, I love this."

My eyebrow lifts. "You do?"

She nods before leaning back against the cushion with a whimsical look like she's watching a movie in her head. "You know," she says before looking over at me. "New York is very romantic."

"Really?" I say flatly with a huff. I've never been, but when I think of any big city, my first thought goes to alleys that smell like piss.

She sits up straight, turning to face me with fresh light in those green eyes. "So romantic! It's basically our Paris."

I cock an eyebrow. "Have you been to Paris?" Her lips twist into a smile, and I roll my eyes. "Have you even been to New York?"

She waves off my question. "That's beside the point." Staring at me with more determination, she adds, "The point is, New York would be a *great* place to tell Margot how much you love her."

"Whoa!" Marty pops up out of fucking nowhere. "Is the puppy in love?"

Rubbing my hands over my face, I get to my feet. "Fuck off, Marty. It's too early for your shit."

I'm met with Marty's cackle of laughter and the sound of Dave pulling the curtain open on his bunk. He sticks his head out, his blond hair a mess. "Marty, we all know Jackson's got it bad. It's nothing new."

I run my hand through my hair as my eyes search the RV for a place to hide. Walking to the back, I grab my guitar. "Marty, when's the last time you got laid? I can't remember."

To my satisfaction, Marty's laughter stops short, but it's quickly replaced by Dave's howl. I ignore Marty's glare as I head back to the front of the RV and sit on the couch with my guitar.

"Sorry," Mya mouths with a grimace, and I'm surprised by how genuine she looks. I honestly don't care if she talks to me about Margot. I like Mya. I already feel more comfortable with her than I ever have with Marty.

Dave braces his arm overhead and looks down at me while my fingers pick at the strings. "So, what's your plan with Margot?"

"He's going to tell her he loves her," Mya pipes up next to me.

My fingers halt on the guitar, and I look over at her with wide eyes.

She gasps before squeaking, "Sorry!" again.

Bracing myself, I bring my attention back to Dave standing in front of me. His eyes are still on Mya, his eyebrows raised. "Oh, yeah?" Looking back at me, he grins. "Nice."

"I'm getting a hotel that night," I say flatly, knowing that's the answer he was actually looking for.

Everything with Margot has felt fleeting lately. Our calls, our texts, the time I get to spend with her. None of it is enough. They're all just tiny glimpses into what we had when we were together all the time. Holding onto her is starting to feel a lot like holding onto water.

"Good," Dave says, pulling me from my thoughts. "I don't think one more person in here would be a good idea."

He's right. When we first got the RV it felt like a ton of room, but with the added people on board, it's already cramped like the van. It's crazy how as soon as you achieve something, you want the next thing. I guess that's the curse of this business: never being satisfied. I'm already imagining how much better things would be with a tour bus.

"Yeah, don't worry. I rented a room walking distance from the venue once we get there."

Dave nods. "How long will she be here?"

"Just the one night." It will be too short of a trip. Even saying the words out loud leaves an ache in my chest. I know it won't be enough.

"Nice. You'll have a good chunk of time with her then." He claps a hand on my shoulder, his words contradict everything I'm thinking. Luckily, he doesn't wait for me to respond and heads toward the front of the bus. It's his turn to drive and give Brady a break.

Mya makes sure to keep her voice down for once when she says, "Are you going to plan something special for when you tell her?"

My fingers go back to picking at the strings. My first reaction is to say, *no*. I haven't planned anything outside of getting us a room, but something nags at me from the pit of my stomach, and instead, I ask, "Like what?"

"Jackson, you'll be in *New York City!*" Her sharp whisper is enough to pause my playing again.

"So? You heard how much time I'll have with her right? I'll be lucky if I get to tell her backstage."

Mya pins me with an unwavering stare. "Don't you dare."

I let out a breath of laughter. "By the time we get out of the show Saturday night, everything worth seeing will be closed." What does she expect me to do? Break into the Empire State Building?

Mya pulls her feet up and rests her chin on her knees. "No, that won't work." Her lips pout as she thinks. "You're right, a lot of sightseeing things will be closed, but still, it's the city that never sleeps." Before I can even open my mouth to agree with her, she lifts her head. "Times Square!"

"You want me to tell Margot I love her in the middle of Times Square?" Even saying the words out loud have my heart rate spiking.

"Well, it's better than *telling her backstage.*" She deepens her voice to mimic me, and I narrow my eyes.

I didn't think Margot would care where or how I told her. I almost told her standing near my car for Christ's sake. But what the hell do I know? I'm no expert on long-term relationships, and Mya is looking at me like I should understand the gravity of this situation more than I do.

"Okay. I'll figure something out," I say, just wanting this conversation to end. Margot hasn't said anything about wanting me to tell her a certain way. Hell, I don't even know if she feels the same. I think she does . . . When she looks at me, I think she does. The bottom line is that she deserves it. If Margot needs me to make a big deal out of this, I will. I'll do whatever it takes to keep her.

24
margot

MY FEET DRAG up the steps to my apartment, and I hope Rae is home. Even though my day was busy and full of distractions, that image of Jackson standing next to his beautiful new traveling companion has been gnawing at me all day.

Even if they're just friends and he's not attracted to her at all, she's still there. She's the one celebrating his successes. She's the one telling him they had a great show at the end of the night. She's the one waking up with him and doing it all the next day.

I figured there would be groupies eventually. But for there to be a girl on the bus who looks like *that?* Yeah, I didn't think this through.

I want Rae to be home so I can get her take on things. I'll show her the picture and see what she thinks. She'll talk me down, and I'll feel better.

But when I reach the top of the stairs, there's someone standing outside my door with his back leaning against the wall. He looks up when he sees me and flashes a beautiful smile.

"Braden?" The shock of seeing him works some type of magic, and I feel less like a zombie.

He holds up a container in one hand, and a six-pack in the other. "You looked a little down this morning, so I made you pesto pasta." He glances at the bottles in his other hand. "I didn't make the beer, but you looked like you could use that, too."

I freeze at the top of the stairs. "You made it for me?" Blinking, I add, "The pasta, I mean."

He grins. "Yes. That part I made."

My stomach rumbles. Now that I think about it, I didn't eat lunch. My eyes jump to the container again. "That was really thoughtful. I hope it wasn't too much trouble."

His eyebrows furrow. "Are you kidding? I could make this stuff in my sleep at this point."

Walking toward him, I laugh. It's the first time I've laughed today, and it feels like something inside me cracks open at the force of it. "You do make it a lot." Pulling out my key, I unlock the door.

"Well, you seem to like it a lot."

My eyes flick up to meet his, and the way he's looking at me is enough for me to look away. I open the door and step inside, determined to lighten whatever made that look so heavy. "Didn't want to use the spare key?" I ask as I set my bag on the kitchen counter.

Braden stretches the back of his neck, and I can't help noticing the way his striking blue eyes are accentuated even more by the color of his cobalt shirt. "You looked a little surprised to see me this morning. I didn't want to scare you."

I let my hair down, loosening the strands as I massage my scalp. "Yeah, sorry. I was a little off my game."

"And now?"

My movements stop as I consider him. He's putting too much weight into his stare again, and my pulse quickens. "Still a little off." I look around the apartment to shake off some of what I'm feeling. "No Rae and Matt?"

Braden gets two bowls out of the cabinet overhead, and just the fact that he's moving helps to make things feel less . . . serious? "They'll be here soon, but they said we can go ahead and get started."

Relief floods through me. Rae and Matt will make this less . . . whatever it is. I don't know why being alone with Braden leaves me restless. He's never been anything but nice. He's always been respectful, too. Something about him leaves me guessing, though. It's like he never says what he's really thinking, and I'm too afraid to know what thoughts lie beneath those blue eyes. "Sounds good to me," I say with my best smile. "I'm starving."

He flashes me a smile before turning back to our bowls and spooning pasta into each of them. The silence that falls between us makes my entire body constrict, so as soon as he walks toward me with a bowl in hand, I ask, "How was your day?"

He raises a beer before answering, and I nod. As he opens the bottle for me, he says, "My day was good. Classes were fine, and I have a little time before I have to head to work."

He sets down the beer in front of me, and I thank him. "You work nights? Why did I not know that?"

Braden shrugs as he sits on the barstool. He clinks his beer with mine and we take a sip. "I think there's a lot you don't know about me."

He's right, of course. I haven't spent a lot of time *trying* to get to know Braden. Anything I do know about him are little crumbs I've picked up through Rae and Matt. "You're probably right," I say with a light laugh. "Where do you work?"

"I'm a barback at Fields."

I blink. I've heard the name, but I've never been. I don't know why I find him working in a bar setting so surprising. He certainly fits the mold of being the hot guy behind the bar. Even if he isn't the one serving the drinks, I'm sure the girls at Fields notice him. I tilt my head a little. "You must meet a lot of people there." Now that I think about it, I've never seen Braden bring home anyone. I've never seen him date. He's never invited anyone to hang out with us. All I've ever seen Braden do is provide alcohol, cook pesto pasta, and occasionally get stoned.

He shrugs. "A few."

My eyes narrow. "Why don't you have a girlfriend?"

He gives me a sideways glance.

"Or boyfriend?"

With a breath of laughter, he shakes his head. "Girlfriend, Margot."

Something tingles in the back of my mind at the sound of him saying my name, but I brush it off and jump to my next question. "You go out. You even work at a bar. I'm sure there are plenty of girls who would want to date you."

He gives me an unconcerned nod and goes back to eating. "And there are a lot of guys who would want to date you."

"But I'm with Jackson," I blurt, my spine going rigid.

He gives me a small smile. "Of course, you are." He casually shifts his attention back to his food. "I'm just saying, you have your reasons, and I have mine. I'm not looking for anything right now."

A forkful of pasta hovers over my bowl, but I can't bring myself to take a bite. I can't bring myself to do anything.

"He's the reason you were upset this morning, wasn't he."

I swallow. His words don't even come out sounding like a question. He says them like he already knows he's right. But was Jackson really the reason I was upset? Indirectly, maybe. But he didn't do anything wrong. My feelings were just a product of having a boyfriend in a rock band. "I . . . I don't know."

He nods, looking down at his bowl and moving his noodles around with his fork.

The door swings open, making me jump. Rae walks in first, followed by Matt. She beams and then breaks into laughter when she sees what we're eating. "Seriously? Again?"

Braden's eyes dart to me, staying a beat too long before he shrugs and says, "Margot likes it."

Matt has already grabbed a bowl and reaches over Rae to scoop some of the food into it. "I'm with Margot. I could eat this stuff forever."

Matt continues to fill his bowl, but Rae's eyes dart between Braden and me. I just stare down at my pasta.

25
jackson

WE'VE JUST FINISHED an amazing set when I collapse into a folding chair next to Mya at the merch table. The place is packed with people watching Crooner Sins, and the energy rumbling through the crowd could keep me wired all night.

We're not playing huge stadiums. Most of the venues are all standing room only, dimly lit, and have an untamed pulse that makes me relish in the chaos. Something almost always goes wrong. The venue staff can hardly point fingers at who was supposed to take care of what, but these are the venues I love the most. I love being so close to the overcharged energy from the crowd being drunk on cheap beer and great music. Hell, even Marty has fun at these places, usually disappearing into the crowd after our set and trying to use what little clout we have as a way to get a girl to talk to him.

I love it here. I love the organic movement from the crowd that comes from no one having a ticketed seat. I love having Mya inside the venue selling merchandise while Brian is perched on the side of the stage. And I love how even if we're all split up, like we are now, it still feels like we have a finger on each other. Dave and Brady are at the bar having a beer, Brian stands in the back, surveying the night, and Marty is . . . being Marty.

"You did great tonight!" Mya moves her chair closer to mine to be heard over the live performance and roaring crowd. The line for merch died down as soon as the headlining band started, so she won't have a line for a bit.

I grin, happily taking the compliment. Tonight was flawless. It was one of those sets that *felt* perfect. The crowd was chanting every word, the guys were in a great mood, and all the staff here actually knew what to do with us when we arrived.

"How were sales tonight?"

Her eyes widen mischievously. "Want to see?"

She must take my puzzled look as a yes, because before I can answer, she quickly pulls the cash box from a small holder fastened to the underside of the table. Tilting it my way, she opens the small, metal box, and I nearly choke at the stack of twenties.

Sitting up straight, I lean toward the box, my eyes jumping from it to her a few times before I manage to sputter, "Holy shit."

Mya doesn't bother hiding her excitement. "Right? We're only taking cash right now because I haven't gotten the card reader yet, but I ordered twice as much as last time and I'm almost sold out!" Shaking her head in awe, she closes the box and puts it back where it belongs. "I'm probably going to have to pick up a second cash box for nights like this."

I chuff a laugh and lean back in my chair again. "I'm glad you ordered more stuff than I told you to."

She gives me a leveling look. "I always order more than you tell me to. You're terrible at inventory."

Her disappointment only makes my smile grow. "How did you get so good at this, anyway?"

She grins at the compliment. "Well, let's see. I've been to . .

." She looks up, like she's doing the math in her head before her green eyes settle back on me. "Over one hundred shows in the past three years."

My eyebrows shoot up, and she laughs.

"Every weekend," she says with a reassuring nod. "There's a small venue near my apartment that always has great bands most people have never heard of. I actually saw American Thieves play there when you opened for Sidecar."

I don't bother hiding my surprise. "No shit?"

"No shit," she confirms. "When Brian got into the business, I think I asked him a million questions. His last band was good, but not really my vibe. When he signed with you guys, I begged him to let me come work for him."

"You did?"

"Yup," she says with a sharp nod. "I told him to give me three shows. If I couldn't make a profit in three shows, I'd catch a ride back home."

My eyes fall to where she secured the cashbox. "Well, you've certainly done that."

"Even with your lousy inventory help." She gives me a playful sideways glance.

"I just find this . . ."—I gesture toward the room around us—"a little hard to believe."

"Well, believe it." She gets to her feet and greets a fan who wants to buy one of our shirts, so I smile at the girl. I'm still not sure if anyone would recognize my face or if they just know the band name. Sometimes I think people assume I'm Mya's lazy assistant. When the girl quickly smiles but then gives her full attention back to Mya, I pull out my phone to let Mya work her magic. I swear half the reason we run out of inventory all the time is because she ends up selling people more things than they came for. I don't think anyone can say no to her.

As soon as my phone screen lights up, I check for Margot's name, but there's nothing. I think she tries to give me space on the nights she knows we have a show. It's like she thinks she'll take away from my experience, but she wouldn't. Having a text from her, telling me about her day or some random remark made by someone at the paper would only make this better. Maybe I should tell her when I see her. Maybe she needs to hear it.

I contemplate sending her a text on the off chance she's still awake, but my thumbs hover over the keys. What would I tell her? That I can't wait to see her? That I wish she were here? That Brian has been interviewing drivers for the RV, but Mya doesn't think he'll ever hire anyone because he's such a picky bastard?

Redundant.

Redundant.

And . . . not important.

"Um, excuse me?"

I look up to find the girl Mya was just helping, now holding a T-shirt, hat, and band photo we all scrambled to take last week when Mya insisted we needed one for the table. She's staring at me with wide, brown eyes, her shoulder-length hair swaying from side to side as she shifts on her feet.

"Sorry," she says as soon as my eyes meet hers. "Um, you're Jackson Phillips, right?"

I blink. She's acting . . . *nervous*. And it's because of me? Planting my feet firmly on the ground, I lean forward in the chair and give her my full attention. "Uh, yeah. What's up?"

She smiles, relief flooding through her features like she was afraid I might be an asshole. "Sorry to bother you, but can you sign this?" She holds out the band photo.

I look down at the photo and then back at her. "You want me to sign it?"

"Of course, she does," Mya says with a laugh as she jams a Sharpie into my hand. "She was just telling me how much she *loves* American Thieves."

My eyes jump from Mya to the girl, only snapping out of my shock when Mya widens her eyes at me. People have asked for my autograph before, but they were all local. That was at home. Here, we're just the warm-up band. We're the ones killing time until they can see who they really bought tickets for.

"Right," I say, doing my best to hide my shock. "I'd be happy to." Taking the photo from her, I set it down in front of me. It's a black and white image Mya took on her phone, but it looks good. It might even be able to pass for a professional photo with the way she edited it. I scrawl my name in the sky near where I'm standing and hand it back to the girl. "Here you go."

"Thank you!" She does a quick hop on her toes before clutching the photo to her chest with the rest of her items. Turning on her heels she disappears back into the crowd.

"Look who's getting *famous*." Mya playfully pushes my shoulder, and I swat her hand away with a laugh.

Famous.

The thought is ridiculous. I'm in this to play music in front of an audience of people like we did earlier tonight. The thought of celebrity sends a spike of anxiety through me.

"Looks like you're not the only one getting attention tonight." Mya sits in her chair, and I realize I've been zoning out with my fist pressed against my lips.

Lifting my head, I follow her gaze. At first, I have no idea what she's talking about. Then, I see it. Marty has some blonde pressed up against the back wall of the club.

"Jesus," I mutter with a shake of my head. Fucking Marty. He's going to gloat about this for weeks, I can already feel it. I figured Dave would be the one we'd have to worry about on tour with him being newly single, but as far as I know, he's been focused on the music and nothing else.

"You know, I'm kind of impressed." Mya tilts her head, her

eyes never leaving Marty and his latest conquest. "I didn't think Marty had game, but she looks close."

I cock an eyebrow. "Close? From making out?"

Mya gives me a sideways glance, amusement glittering in her green eyes. "Um, open your eyes, Lover Boy. He's hand-fucking her." She shakes her head before standing to help another customer, but I don't look to see who walks up to the table this time.

This time, my eyes are fixed on Marty.

His mouth is on the girl's neck, and I just know he'll leave a mark. He's devouring her, and the movement of his hand under her shirt suggests he's rolling and pinching her nipple with as much enthusiasm. His other hand—the one I didn't pay attention to before—is slipped into the front of her unzipped jeans. It's hard to see with the way his body covers hers, but there's no mistaking it now. I have no idea how I missed it the first time.

Mya's right. The girl is close. She looks like she's telling him what to do. It only takes a few more moments for her eyes to roll back. Marty covers her mouth with his and hardly waits for her to come down from her high before he pulls her toward the bathrooms.

"Don't look so horrified." Mya laughs. She's been watching me. "You're a rockstar. That's what rockstars do."

With a shake of my head, I say, "The only horrifying thing about that is the fact that it's Marty."

"Fair," she says as she grabs an item for a customer, handing it to them and taking their payment. Over her shoulder she adds, "By the looks of this line, you could have your fair share of fun, too."

The pull between my brows quickly turns to surprise when I see the line she's talking about. Close to two dozen women stand with their friends in front of the merch table. "What the hell . . ."

Mya multitasks, accommodating the next customer as she talks to me. "Notice how they're not looking at the merchandise? They're looking at *you*." She laughs. "That girl must have told her friends the hot guitarist from American Thieves was hanging out near the table. Looks like word got around."

I blink, taking in the scene in front of me with fresh eyes. She's right. The girls are giggling and pointing at me as they talk to their friends. My eyes wander to the girl with short black hair at the very front of the table as Mya hands her a keychain. She's already looking my way, and when our eyes meet, her cheeks flare and she drops her gaze to the ground.

What the hell is going on?

26
margot

RAE EYES my small duffle suspiciously. "You're sure you have everything?"

I nod and set it next to our front door. "I've only had multiple weeks to make multiple lists of everything I'll need." Even though I never lost the first list, making repeat lists of things to pack made me feel like I was getting closer to this day. It helped me feel like I was at least doing something to prep for the trip I wanted to go on so badly. I probably have at least a dozen in my notebook by now. All decorated with the same items in different orders.

She's still eyeing my bag like it might belong to Mary Poppins, so I laugh. "I'm only gone for a day. You're literally picking me up tomorrow."

Lifting her eyes from the bag to me, she gives me a faint smile. "Excited to see him?"

Just the indirect mention of *him* has my toes curling in my Timberlands. "You have no idea." The words rush out of me like a secret I've been holding for far too long.

"Nervous?" she asks before quickly adding, "Not that you should be. It's just been a while since you've seen him."

Resting my arms over the back of one of our kitchen barstools, I pick absently at the sleeve of my sweater that's too warm for Florida but will give me an added layer when I land in New York. "Yes."

I am nervous. I hate that I am. I want to see Jackson more than anything, but a small part of me can't help wondering if things will be different. What if we don't have that same spark we had this summer? What if we can't find things to talk about after being apart for so long? What if he's realized he needs to be single while he's on tour?

Okay, that last one might be a stretch. I don't think he'd actually break up with me, but what if I'm wrong? What if he wants to do it in person, so he's just been nice enough to keep me content until he can see me face to face?

"You're spiraling."

My eyes jump to meet Rae's, and I give a tiny nod.

Sympathy coats her features. "Don't." Walking over to me, she takes both my hands, stopping me from fidgeting with my sleeve. "He *loves* you, Margot." I open my mouth to correct her, but she cuts me off. "And I don't care if he hasn't said it yet. I know he loves you, and you should know it, too."

My lips twist. I want to contradict her. I want to lay out all the times he *could* have told me if that were the case, but relaxing my shoulders, I just say a quiet, "Thank you."

She gives my hands a squeeze before letting go to grab her keys off the counter. With a shrug and a coy smile, she says, "And if he doesn't, I'm sure Braden wouldn't mind having a shot."

"Rae!"

Laughter bursts from my best friend. "Have you seen the way he looks at you?"

Rubbing my arm, I grimace. "I might have noticed."

"It's bad."

I wince, rubbing my palm over my forehead. "Is it?"

She snorts. "I mean, he doesn't look at *me* that way."

Leaning my head back, I let out a groan. "I can't worry about Braden right now. He knows I'm with Jackson." Straightening, I shake my head. "Which is why I need you to drive me to the airport." I give her my best pleading smile, and it only makes her laugh more.

"Come on." She nods toward the door. "Let's get you to your rockstar."

JFK is busier than any airport I've ever seen. If this were the closest airport to me, I'd probably rethink traveling. My flight wasn't bad, but as I watch the masses of people surround the baggage claim like ants to a crumb, I'm grateful for only having my small duffel.

I still have a bit of a walk ahead of me, but I go ahead and text Jackson.

> MARGOT:
> Just landed.

Before I can tuck my phone in my back pocket, a message comes through.

> JACKSON:
> I'm here. Can't wait to see you.

My lips lift at the sight of those words. I don't know why I was stressing earlier. We're fine. We're more than fine. I don't know how I'm so sure all of a sudden. It's not like he's reassured me in any real way, but there's something about being in the same place as him that just makes doubting our relationship seem silly.

I wasn't feeling us drifting apart. I was feeling the physical distance between us. I was feeling the lack of warmth that comes with the person you love being miles away.

Love.

Damn that word. It keeps popping up when I least expect it, and it stops me in my tracks every time. I take a steadying breath and try to force out all thoughts of "love" on my exhale. I think it works. Until I breathe in, and it occurs to me that he might say it while I'm here. He could say it tonight or tomorrow. He could even say it when he sees me *right now.*

Sweat prickles at my hairline, and I force another steadying breath since the first one worked so well.

Damn.

Damn.

Damn.

Get ahold of yourself, Margot.

My shoulder knocks into something, and I stagger back as a pair of firm hands steady me.

"Pissed off already?" a voice says with a laugh.

"No, I—" My embarrassment wanes under the realization that I know that voice. I know that voice, and I know that amused tone all too well. I lift my gaze to find Jackson smiling at me with a faint line between his brows. He looks amazing. His hair is a little longer, but I already knew that from pictures. He's filled out some, but in a good way. Like he's been working out. Has he been working out? I'll have to ask him when I remember how to speak. For right now, those gray-blue eyes have me lost. I could drink in those stormy waters for an eternity. If I'm ever lost at sea in Jackson's eyes, please no one save me.

"What's got you all fired up, Red?" His thumb brushes my cheek, the proof of concern only evident in the way his eyes aren't matching his smile.

I blink. "Nothing!" Dropping my bag, I shake my head and throw my arms around his neck. "Oh, my god. Nothing."

He squeezes me tightly, a laugh rumbling in his chest. He smells like the soap he used when he'd fog up my bathroom with steam, and I breathe him in. I've missed that smell. He kisses the side of my head, and it's like something inside me cracks open. Finally, being here with him is too much for me to take in. I'm overwhelmed with the feeling of finally being at the home I've always wanted, and by the time he pulls back to look at me, my eyes are wet.

He frowns. "Seriously, did something happen?" He looks past me to the countless people carrying out their travel plans.

I laugh as I wipe a rogue tear. "No. I'm sorry, I'm just . . . I've missed you."

Jackson grins, and if I thought I was cracked open before, seeing him happy completely destroys me in the best way. "Me too."

Then his mouth is on mine. It's an overdue kiss full of heat and longing. It's a kiss that somehow steals the air from my lungs and gives me breath. It's a kiss that grounds me and leaves me thoughtless. All I can focus on is the way he's never kissed me this hungrily in public, and all I can think about is how little I care if people stare.

27
jackson

AS MARGOT and I go from the AirTrain to the subway, I go over tonight's plan in my head on a constant loop. Well, it's Mya's plan, but I've done a decent job following her instructions and setting up everything. After the show tonight, we'll go see Times Square lit up, we'll eat at one of the restaurants open late in Hell's Kitchen, and we'll catch a late-night comedy show. It might not be the perfect date, but it's the best I could do with the little time we have.

Mya insists I should *let Margot see New York* and *tell her I love her in the middle of the city that never sleeps.* The whole thing is starting to feel like a lot of pressure. This is why I never wanted to date someone. There are too many expectations. Too many things you're supposed to make a big deal about, and I hate feeling like I'm going to let people down.

But Margot isn't just anyone.

I watch the way her mouth moves as she carries on about the paper. She's so animated when she's talking about her passion. It's adorable. She's in the middle of explaining all the trials and tribulations of a local bookstore when I lean over and kiss her, cutting her off mid-sentence.

Margot smiles against my lips, and I drink up the breath of laughter that tumbles from her. She expects it to be a quick kiss. She expects me to pull away and let her get back to her story, and maybe that was my plan originally, but she tastes too damn good. With my hand gently clasped around her throat, I pull her in to kiss her deeper, and she melts in the seat next to me. Margot's default setting might leave her rigid, but the way she softens and opens every part of herself for me makes me feel like I hold a sacred key, and seeing her this way is the treasure she keeps locked away.

When we finally do break the kiss, I relish in the sight of her. Pupils blown, cheeks flushed, chest rising and falling in shallow breaths.

I did that to her.

Margot clears her throat, and another flush of pink flares underneath the surface of her skin. "So, are we meeting up with the band or—"

"The hotel," I answer quickly, my voice rough. "We're definitely going to the hotel."

I booked us the nicest room I could afford in New York City, which isn't saying much. If the four walls had arms, they could easily high-five each other. The room gives the word *small* a whole new meaning, but I'm not sure Margot cares or notices. Hell, the only reason I notice is because it took fewer steps than I expected to walk her back to the bed, my lips never leaving hers.

I drop her duffle to the floor with a soft thud as I gently lay her back onto the white comforter. Margot looks up at me with bright eyes. Her lips are swollen and red from how much I've been kissing her, and her rosy complexion makes her absolutely stunning. I wish I could capture a picture of this turned on, blushing version of Margot. This version of her rarely shines through text. The version of her who's panting and wanting.

And mine.

My lips press against the sweet skin of her neck, and I murmur her name. Her breath catches like I knew it would, and it brings a faint smile to my lips.

Working my way down her body, I lift her sweater and kiss her between her perfect breasts, her name leaving my lips again. There's a tiny arch of her back this time, her eyes jumping to the ceiling like she's saying a silent prayer, but I'm the one who's worshiping right now.

Slipping down her pants, I groan at the sight of the already damp cotton of her underwear. We've both waited so long for this.

"Margot," I say again, but this time the awe is evident in my voice. She's so fucking ready for me, and I don't know what the hell I did to get this lucky.

She goes to clamp her thighs shut with a whimper, but I pry them back open. I'm not sure if she's embarrassed, or if she's just trying to ease the ache, but I'm just getting started. With a hand firmly on either thigh to keep her spread for me, I lower my face between her legs and run my tongue over the damp cotton in one, slow, savoring stroke. The familiar sweet smell and taste of her floods through me, and I groan out her name one more time.

Not patient enough to actually pull her underwear off, I move the fabric aside until she's glistening and bare before me. I'd love nothing more than to devour her, but with another slow stroke of my tongue, I savor her.

She cries out the first time I suck on her clit, and it sends a ripple of pleasure through me. "Fuck, I've missed this."

She nods, her breath coming in short pants. "Me, too."

"Is this what you thought of?" I dip inside her, fucking her with my tongue. "When you got yourself off all those nights?"

Her hips buck in response, and I move to hold her down again. "Among other things," she says sweetly—*playfully*.

Sucking hard on her clit, she cries out again. "Well, I promise to give you plenty to think about until I come home for the holidays."

"Please," she breathes, all signs of playfulness gone. The only thing I hear is *need*.

After a few more teasing strokes of my tongue, I increase my pace. Margot's legs shake, and her hands grip my hair so tight it hurts, but I relish in the pain. She tastes like a fucking dream, and I'll take the pain if it means I get to bury my face between her legs a little longer.

She comes fast and hard. The cracked sound of her crying out is something I've dreamed of hearing for months. The way her body tightens and breaks apart is what I've thought about for weeks. And seeing it all finally come to light has me cursing the fact that she'll only be here for a single day.

I collapse onto the bed next to her as she comes down from her high, and as soon as the haze clears, she turns her head to look at me. There's a soft smile tugging at the corners of her mouth as she catches her breath, but the way she's eyeing me goes deeper than the surface. Something about the way her steady gaze bounces between my eyes lets me know she's searching for something. I'm not sure what it is, but I hope she finds it.

Running my hand through her hair, the familiar urge to tell her I love her has my chest tightening. I wish I would have said it months ago. I probably felt it but was too stupid to act on it, and now that it's been left unsaid, those three words feel a lot heavier than they should.

Tonight.

I'll tell her tonight.

Margot blinks, her eyes clearing. She pushes herself up and straddles me, kissing my neck and chest as she grinds against my briefs. I suck in a breath, my body shuddering when her tongue grazes over my nipple. With expert proficiency, she pulls down my briefs, and I wonder if I imagined the look in her eyes. She doesn't seem deep in thought now. Hell, she doesn't seem to be thinking at all. She's following whatever she's feeling, and when she lowers herself onto my cock, I stop thinking, too.

Fuck, she feels good.

Margot gasps when I thrust up into her, unable to control myself. I've waited over two months to be with her again, and she feels better than I remember. Everything about her is better than I remember. Digging my grip into her ass, I grind against her, hitting deep inside her every time.

Margot cries out, but she rides me so fucking well. She lets her head fall back, her eyes closed. Long red strands of her hair cascade over her shoulders and down her back. She's completely lost in the moment—completely lost in *me*. Her hips roll with each of my movements, and she meets my thrust perfectly.

Every.

Fucking.

Time.

"Touch yourself," I say, my voice rough.

Margot's eyes fly open, but they're full of lust and heat.

"Show me what I've been missing. Show me what you do when I'm gone." I thrust up into her, and the moan I get as a reward has me dying to do it again.

Margot's perfect hand slowly slides down to her clit. As soon as she makes contact, she clenches around my dick, and I let out a groan.

I thought she'd be embarrassed. I thought she'd close her eyes or look away, but she doesn't. She keeps those gorgeous honey eyes trained on me as she lets her fingers get to work. I physically ache with how badly I want to fill her right now.

Watching her bring herself closer to the edge for a second time is one of the hottest things I've ever seen.

"I always think about you," she says with another savory roll of her hips, testing my restraint.

"Fuck." I breathe out the word as I tighten my grip on her.

Margot stays flush against me, her hips rolling so fucking good, and so fucking deep like she always does when she wants to make me come.

Fuck me.

My voice comes out gritty as I trust into her. "You want me to fill you up, don't you?"

She whimpers, her eyes squeezing shut as she nods.

"That's it. Come for me, Red. Show me how bad you want it."

By the time my last word leaves my lips, she's already pulsing around my cock. Her body locks, her hands bracing on my chest while she rides out the prettiest orgasm I've ever seen. Just seeing her this way sends me free falling over the edge. I thrust into her once, twice, and then I'm done for. I lose control and give her all of me, cursing her name while I spill into her.

Grabbing the back of her neck, I pull her lips to mine. She chokes out another moan as another wave of pleasure goes through her, and I kiss her like I can't get enough. Because I can't.

28
margot

JACKSON KEEPS his arm around my shoulder as we head into the venue from the back entrance. The band's sound check is about to start, and I have no idea why I'm nervous. It's not like I'll be the person on stage tonight. There's something about seeing what Jackson's life is like first-hand that has my heart racing. This is his world now—his world without me for the most part.

As soon as the heavy door shuts behind us, my eyes adjust to the backstage lighting. Before I can fully see Dave in the distance, I hear him.

"There's my favorite redhead!"

Jackson lets out a huff of laughter next to me, but I pull out of his grip to run up to Dave and give him a hug. He's definitely my favorite member of the band. There's something about Dave's energy that's contagious. It's a gift I know has worked its magic on their fans, and I think it's why they draw a crowd so easily. Everyone is a moth to Dave's flame.

Wrapping me in his arms, he briefly lifts me off my toes before setting me back down and releasing me. "How was the flight?"

"Fine," I answer with a grin.

Brady walks up with his drumsticks lightly thumping on his legs, and I rush over to give him a hug, too.

"Margot!" he cheers as he gives me a tight squeeze.

Marty catches my eye and gives me a wave that I return over Brady's shoulder. I don't exactly have a hugging relationship with Marty. Jackson may be the youngest member of the band, but I think Marty has the most growing up to do. Plus, Jackson is still on the fence about him, and that's enough for me to want to keep my distance.

Once Brady lets go of me, Jackson is back to having his arm around my shoulder. I love being close to him. Especially in a setting like this. The way he stays by my side backstage warms something inside of me. Turning me slightly, Jackson nods to a clean-cut man in a suit. "Brian, I'd like you to meet—"

"Margot, I take it?" the man says with a gentle smile as he holds out a hand for me to shake. "It's nice to finally meet you."

"Where's Mya?" Jackson asks, looking around. My heart stutters at the name. I think out of everyone, she's the one I'm most nervous to meet.

Brian steps toward Jackson. "She's setting up out front." Looking back at me, he adds, "I think she plans on putting you to work tonight."

Jackson scoffs. "Margot will be backstage."

"I don't mind helping," I offer, even though I'm not sure what exactly I'm signing up for. Walking back over to Jackson, I wrap my arms around his waist and look up at him. "Might as well make myself useful, right?"

He hesitates, scratching the side of his head before he says, "Uh, yeah. Sure. Whatever you want to do."

There's an edge to each word as it leaves his lips. Is he

nervous? What could be so bad about me spending time with Mya during the show? He said I'd like her, right?

He must sense my scrutiny because he looks at me and gives me a smile that doesn't fully reach his eyes. "Come on, I'll introduce you."

"See you guys in a bit," I say to the rest of the band and Brian as Jackson takes my hand and leads me to the front of the venue. We occasionally pass staff walking with different cables and equipment, so his sound check must be soon.

"Oh my god!" The words echo throughout the mostly empty venue as soon as we open the black metal door. It's easy to spot the source when there are only a handful of people in the large open space, and one of them has pink hair and is headed straight for us.

"She might be a little excited," Jackson mutters under his breath, and I let out a light laugh.

We meet in the middle, closer to the stage than the table she was setting up since she practically ran to us. Her pink hair is down in shoulder-length waves, and she's wearing jeans with a black American Thieves oversized pullover that I desperately need now that I've seen it. It's not one I've seen on the band's Instagram yet.

She's beautiful and looks like the last person you'd want to fuck with at the same time. I kind of envy her for it. It's a delicate balance that she pulls off flawlessly with tattoos, a nose ring, and sparkling green eyes.

"This is probably going to sound creepy, but I don't care. I've heard so much about you and thank God you're here because I am long overdue for some feminine energy."

Jackson shakes his head. "Margot, this is Mya. She handles all our merchandise. And Mya, this is . . . Well, you know who this is."

"Do you design everything?" I ask as I marvel over the design she's wearing. It has their logo in its usual font, but flowers and vines wrap around the letters giving it a more feminine touch.

"Yeah!" Taking note of my stare, she stretches the sweatshirt so I can see the design better. "Like it? It's a brand new one I plan on rolling out tonight."

"I love it. I was actually just thinking I should buy one."

On stage, the other guys in the band emerge for the sound check, and Jackson kisses the side of my head. "Get anything you want." Looking at Mya, he adds, "I'll cover whatever she picks." His eyes dart between the two of us with a shred of uncertainty and the uneasy pit in my stomach returns. "I'll be back as soon as we're done," he reassures me.

"She's in good hands!" Mya hollers after him. With a shake of his head, he faces forward and jogs toward the stage to meet up with the other guys.

I'm mesmerized watching him get his guitar and take the stage as he slings the strap over his head and gets positioned. It feels like it's been so long since I've seen him in his element like this. The last time was at the festival before he left, and even then, it wasn't the same as seeing him in a venue like this. They may be opening for Crooner Sins now, but they'll be headlining their own tour soon enough. I can feel it.

"Come on," Mya says, pulling me toward her half set up table. "You're going to love this stuff."

I have no doubt I will. It's safe to say I've become one of American Thieves' biggest fans, so regardless of what the designs looked like, I'd still probably want it all.

When we make it to the table, I take in the items she already has displayed. There are a few T-shirts, both long and short sleeve, the pullover sweater she's wearing, a hat, a group photo of the band with everyone's autographs, and then individual photos of band members with their respective signatures.

Picking up the picture of Jackson, I take a closer look. It's a black and white photo I've never seen, but he's gorgeous in it. The shot is candid. He's relaxed as he holds his guitar and looks off to the side with a genuine smile that was probably taken mid-laugh.

The corners of my mouth lift at the sight, and I look up to find Mya watching me carefully.

"He's thriving," she says with a smile of her own. With a laugh, she adds, "He misses you like hell, but he's made for this."

"I know," I agree, not feeling offended in the slightest. Anyone who knows Jackson knows he belongs on stage with a guitar.

"I'd never tell the other guys, but I have to order almost double the photos of Jackson. He's gained a lot of admirers, and it's only getting worse." She laughs. "Or better, depending on how you look at it." She shrugs. "It's great for business."

"Somehow, I'm not surprised," I say with a laugh. The memory of going to his gig alone last year flashes before my eyes, and I remember the group of girls that surrounded him even then. Carly, in her teal dress, slipping him her number.

Fuck Carly.

The way he kissed me then is something I'll never forget.

"That's why I came up with these new designs. Most of the newer fans are women and girls fawning over the guitarist. We'll see how it goes tonight with sales, though."

Picking up the pullover off the table, I hug it to my chest. "I guess that means I should get mine before they're gone?"

Mya grins. "Consider it a uniform. We've got work to do."

29
jackson

THE SOUND CHECK GOES SMOOTHLY, and I hop off the stage to find Margot exactly where I left her.

Except she's different now.

She's looser. Her head falls back as she laughs at something Mya says. She's settled in now, and she's comfortable here. Seeing her wearing our logo on her perfect chest, being around the people I've spent every waking hour with, and knowing she fits right in, has my head spinning.

"Hey," I say as I walk up. "It looks great over here."

Margot looks over her shoulder at me while she helps Mya pin a shirt to the pop-up wall behind them. "Hey." I swear, between her smile, the way her pullover has lifted to show a sliver of her lower back, and the way her ass looks in those jeans, I could drop dead right here.

"Lover Boy, you're staring." Mya has a hand on her hip as she appraises me with a lifted brow.

I don't even look at her. "She's mine. I'm allowed to stare."

Mya lazily looks over at Margot, unimpressed. "See?"

Lowering back onto her heels, Margot just laughs with a shake of her head.

My eyes jump between her and Mya, and before I know it my finger follows. "What is this?" I lock on Mya. "I knew you were going to talk shit."

She feigns a gasp. "I would never."

Margot giggles, and my attention snaps back to her. "She was talking shit, wasn't she?"

Looking over at Mya first, Margot quickly shakes her head before dishing out a similar acting performance. "No, not at all. We were talking about, um, keychains."

I cock an eyebrow. "Keychains."

Margot nods innocently, but her lips press like she's trying to hold in a laugh. "With big, red hearts and your name on them. Mya thinks they'd sell really well."

Mya busts out with a laugh, and I level with both of them. "I'm not sure how I feel about this alliance," I mutter, gesturing at the two girls in front of me.

Hooking an arm around Margot's shoulder, Mya shrugs unapologetically. "I wish I could say I was sorry."

Margot smiles sweetly at me. "You did say I'd like her."

She's right. I knew they'd hit it off, but knowing the secrets I've told Mya has me second guessing whether or not their newfound friendship is a good idea. "Maybe you shouldn't."

Ignoring my comment, Margot tilts her head. "You didn't mention anything about becoming so . . . popular."

"Because it's nothing." Why would I tell her a good chunk of our fans have noticed me and it's not for my music? Why make her worry for no reason? Girls was one of the things included in her holy trinity of rock and roll, and I'm pretty sure she's less concerned about drinking and drugs.

"I wouldn't say it's *nothing*." Mya chimes in as she gets back to work. "He's not allowed to hang out here with me anymore. He was becoming too much of *a distraction*."

"Oh, no." The words come out bubbled with laughter as Margot eyes me with mock pity.

"You." I point a finger at her. "Don't start."

She grins and leans across the table to kiss me. It's a short kiss. A sweet kiss. But damn if it doesn't make me want more.

"I talked to Dave about heading out early after our set."

Mya shimmies. "For the big date!"

I glare at her. How am I supposed to leave Margot alone with this girl for the better part of an hour?

"A date?" Margot asks, not bothering to mask her interest.

"Why do you sound so surprised?"

She blinks. "I don't think we've ever been on a date." She opens her mouth to say more but shakes her head instead. Shifting her feet, she finally asks, "Like a real one?"

What is she talking about? We've been on lots of dates. We've been seeing each other for months. But as I try to think of a time I've taken Margot out on a traditional date, I come up empty. How have we never done that? How have I never looked at this gorgeous girl and told her I'll pick her up at eight—or whatever the hell people say when they plan dates?

Mya pretends to refold one of the shirts on the table, but I can feel her eyes watching Margot and me closely.

Fuck, I want to apologize. I want to tell her right here that from now on we can go on as many dates as she wants. Wherever. Whenever.

But all I can do is swallow. "Yeah," I say with a nod. "A real one."

Margot smiles, but it isn't the open grin I've come to love. It's a sweet, small one that doesn't hide the appraising pinch of her brows.

She's looking at me like I just suggested we hop on a train and ride across the country. Who knew trying to be a good boyfriend would be so out of character for me?

Mya breaks whatever silent conversation Margot and I are failing to have. "Well, doors are about to open, Lover Boy. And you're too pretty for the public."

"Yeah, yeah." I wave her off but keep my attention on Margot. "You're okay?"

Mya puts her arm around Margot's shoulder. "She's in good hands. Don't you worry."

"I'm fine," Margot assures me, and I'm relieved to see a more genuine smile from her this time.

"I'll come back here after the show. Just stay here with Mya," I say as I walk backward toward the stage.

"Yes," Margot says with a laugh. "I'll be here."

My smile naturally widens at the sound of her laugh, and she blows me a kiss.

"Shit," I mutter before changing gears and jogging back up to her. Leaning over the table, I grip the back of her neck and pull her mouth to mine. It's a slow kiss. It's one that hopefully tells her I'm sorry for not being the type of boyfriend who takes her on dates. One that lets her know how glad I am that she's here, and how much I'm looking forward to spending the night with her. When I break the kiss, I say, "I wanted the real thing."

Margot laughs again and playfully pushes me away. "Get out of here," she says with a grin.

My feet bounce against the floor as I back up again, feeling lighter than I did the first time. "Don't talk shit, Mya!"

Mya wiggles her fingers in my direction. "Wouldn't dream of it, Lover Boy."

With a breath of laughter, I shake my head and turn toward the stage.

It's showtime.

30
margot

I'LL NEVER UNDERSTAND how Mya usually does this on her own. We've been nonstop since the doors opened, and even with the two of us, there's still always someone waiting in line. The place is packed, the excitement in the air palpable, and even though American Thieves haven't performed yet, we're completely sold out of Mya's new floral design and the other products are starting to dwindle.

I've only gone to a few concerts, but I've never purchased merchandise for the opening band. I thought maybe Mya would get a few sales *after* their performance if new fans wanted to get a keepsake. I couldn't have been more wrong. The band is due to go on any minute now, but there's been a constant flow of customers who already know exactly who American Thieves are.

I even overheard one girl ask Mya if it's true the band sometimes hangs out with fans after they perform, and it nearly stopped me in my tracks.

Then her friend said she adores Dave Lutz and would *scream* if she met him.

Then the first girl said she likes Dave, but she would *literally drop dead* if she saw Jackson Phillips.

That *did* make me stop in my tracks.

I couldn't move. I just stared at the girl, assuming maybe I'd heard her wrong. She was talking about Jackson?

My Jackson?

Mya had to subtly bump me with her hip to snap me out of it. "Yup, Jackson's a cutie," she said to the girl as she handed over a band T-shirt and sent her on her way.

Being here is a lot like I expected it to be, but *more*. More fans. More fawning girls. This venue is bigger than anywhere he played back home. Everything has escalated.

Which is good.

So, *so*, good.

I only get to see Jackson behind the scenes, but if the rest of the guys in the band work as hard as he does, they deserve all the success in the world.

There's a deafening roar from the crowd, and I look up to find the guys taking the stage. Jackson smiles at Dave and the guys as he gets into his usual spot, and Dave grins at the crowd the way he always does.

"I know you're here to see Crooner Sins," he says into the mic. "But we're American Thieves, and we're going to hang with you guys for a little while!"

The crowd cheers, and I can't help smiling. It feels like it's been so long since I've seen Dave greet the crowd.

Or Marty clapping him on the shoulder as he walks by to plug in his guitar.

Or Brady gently tapping his drumsticks in preparation for the big solo he'll jump into as soon as Dave is done with his speech.

Or Jackson. It's been so long since I've seen Jackson doing what he loves—being a part of something bigger than himself.

How could I have missed so much? They may not have

gone from street corners to stadiums, but this still feels like a huge step.

A huge step I haven't been a part of.

The song starts, and I blink back to the present. My spiraling thoughts dissipate as soon as Jackson starts to play. His fingers expertly move along the strings as he gets lost in the music, and the sight brings a smile to my lips the same way it always does.

"They're really great!" Mya yells over the music as she sits in one of the folding chairs behind the table and gestures for me to do the same.

I nod enthusiastically, my eyes jumping from the chair back to the stage. I'm not sure I want to sit. I don't want to miss this. If this is the only time I'll see Jackson while he's on tour, I want to watch every second of the set. I want to be in the crowd and feel everyone sing along to the songs I know by heart.

But Mya has been wonderful, and it's great having someone to spend time with while he's up on that stage. I can sit for a little while.

"So, what do you think of all this?" Mya asks when I take a seat next to her.

"Um." I raise my eyebrows as I take in the scene in front of me. From the back of the room, I may not be a part of things, but being a spectator has its perks too. From here, I can see the full impact the band has on *everyone*, not just me. "It's a lot," I finally answer with a laugh.

Mya smiles, and there's a warmness to it that makes me feel like she cares. I might have only met her an hour ago, but that one look is enough for me to know she cares about Jackson and me. "Did you go on his last tour with him?"

I raise an eyebrow at her. "And sleep in the van?" With a shake of my head, I laugh again. "No, but I went to one of his shows. Kind of like this, but also not at all like this."

"The van! I was never in it, but I've seen pictures." She

makes a gagging face before frantically shaking her head. "I can't believe I forgot about the van. Forget I asked."

"Yeah. Your uncle really saved the day with that RV."

She rolls her eyes. "He should have just gotten them a tour bus. At the rate they're going, they'll need one soon, and they can probably afford it." She points to herself. "Plus, I can only sleep on a couch-bed for so long."

I'm not sure why it hadn't occurred to me where she sleeps before this conversation, but I don't bother hiding my surprise. "You sleep on the couch?"

Pressing her lips together in a firm line, she gives a deliberate nod. "Yup." She waves a hand in the air like she's trying to get rid of her animosity. "I mean, I don't mind. It's worth it if it means I get to live this."

Sleeping on an RV couch would be rough, but I think part of me envies her—just a little bit. My teeth sink into my bottom lip as I watch my boyfriend on stage.

Mya's delicate hand touches my arm. "Hey, are you okay?"

I blink. "Yeah," I say with my best smile. "I'm sure touring with the band is a great experience."

She huffs. "It's certainly something. You'll know all about it one day."

My eyes wander back to Jackson as he takes the mic, ready to sing the one song he does vocals for. The crowd roars, and he rubs a hand over his head, looking as humble as ever. At the sight of him up there, in front of his adoring fans, something in my chest aches. It's an ache for something I already have, but still want—like a longing for how things used to be, even though I'm currently living it.

"Yeah," I say, my eyes never leaving Jackson. "Maybe."

But even though Mya seems confident, I'm not so sure.

31
jackson

WE FINISH our set with our most popular song off the new album, and the crowd goes crazy for it. The whole place pulses with a steady rhythm, and the crowd goes wild even after we stop playing. That's one of my favorite parts of the night. That final applause before we leave the stage always sinks its teeth into me. There's something about the roaring energy that reverberates off each and every molecule under my skin, making my entire body buzz with new energy.

Tonight, I don't soak it up the way I usually do, though. Because as I scan the back of the room to check for Margot and Mya, all I see is a petite girl with pink hair at the table. At first, I think maybe it's the lights. Maybe I just can't see Margot under the glare. But the longer I look, the more my anxiety sets in. Where did she go? Why would she leave Mya?

My thoughts race as I scan the crowd, but I don't see any sign of her. It isn't until I turn to exit the stage with the guys, that I spot the gorgeous redhead standing on the side of the stage, waiting for me. Everything in me relaxes at the sight of her. She tilts her head against one of the rafters with a smile that makes me feel better than any applause.

Holding the neck of my guitar in one hand, I wrap my free arm around Margot's shoulders to pull her to me and kiss the side of her head. "Why didn't you stay with Mya?"

She looks up at me, wrapping her arm around my waist. "And miss out on having the best seat in the house?" She shakes her head. "Once things calmed down, she said she didn't need my help anymore, so I came to enjoy the view."

I let out a huff. "The view."

Margot points over her shoulder toward the merch table. "Do you want me to tell you how many Jackson photos we sold tonight?"

I grimace. "Please don't."

Those photos are probably my least favorite thing Mya has come up with, but I can't say anything because she sells them like candy. Thinking about all the people who have that random ass picture of me somewhere with my chicken scratch signature near my head feels equal parts awesome and fucking weird.

"Did you have fun?" I ask to change the subject.

She smiles up at me, and it packs a bigger punch than I expected. I knew having her here would feel incredible. But now that it's happening, it's so much better than I thought it would be. And the fact that she's only here for a short time feels like a bucket of ice water hanging in the balance. I know it will crash into me and wake me up in a matter of hours, but I wish this could never end. I wish *this* were my reality when I walked off stage every night.

"Of course! You're right, Mya is awesome."

I'm grateful Mya was on her best behavior. The last thing I need is for her to scare Margot away with one of her games of Twenty Questions or telling her how *lovesick* I am while she's away. "She's something."

"I'm going to head back that way. She might get a rush of people now that your set is done. Meet me by the table?"

I kiss her forehead. "Yeah, just give me a few minutes to pack up."

Margot releases me and leans around me to call out to the guys. "Great show tonight!"

A chorus of "Thanks, Margot," rings out behind me, but I can't take my eyes off her. I can't believe she came all this way just to see me. She's not bothered by the fact that I can't spend a ton of time with her alone. She isn't trying to rush out of here now that our set is finished. She's like the perfect missing piece to this crazy puzzle, and I love her even more for it.

She turns on her heels and heads back for the table, and I blink when I feel Dave clasp a hand on my shoulder.

"She's a good one," Dave says. "Don't fuck it up."

I look over my shoulder and lift a brow at him.

"Speaking from experience. You know, since I fucked my shit up with Lynn."

"Yeah . . . want to tell me what happened there?"

Dave rubs the back of his neck, his shoulder length blonde hair damp with sweat like my own. "I wish I knew. I think she thought the band was winding down, and when it started picking up . . . it just went against her expectations, I guess."

This is the most he's opened up about his breakup since we've been on the road, so I try to tread carefully. "She wanted a white picket fence?"

He lets out a huff of laughter. "Exactly." Lifting his gaze, he quickly adds, "And I want that, too. Eventually. But to pass up on all this? I just couldn't bring myself to do it, and she didn't want to wait around more than she already has. I get it. We're not as young as we used to be, but you've got to go when the lightning strikes, you know?"

I don't know. Not really. Settling down feels like some distant, far-off place that I may or may not go. Sometimes I forget that as long as I've wanted this, Dave has wanted it longer. Hell, all the guys have. I lucked out. My band got picked up to go on tour after mere weeks, but these guys have been waiting for this same chance for *years*.

Reading through my hesitation, Dave laughs. "You and Margot are lucky. You're both young. You've got nothing tying you down or holding you back. You haven't built a life yet—in a good way. You've got nothing but time and freedom."

"I guess I never thought of it like that." Balancing the tour and my relationship with Margot feels hard, but hearing Dave talk about it makes it sound like we have the perfect setup. Maybe we do. Maybe it isn't a bad thing that Margot and I got together right before I left. Maybe it was perfect timing.

32
margot

MYA'S FACE floods with relief as soon as I'm back at the table. "Margot! Thank God!"

I slip through a gap in the line and make my way around the side of the table. "What's up? Everything okay?" I do a quick scan of the scene to see if anything stands out, but the line is nowhere near as busy as it was when we were both working.

She frantically waves me over before handing a guy his T-shirt with an award-winning smile. In the time it takes for customers to swap places, Mya leans in and says, "The cash box is missing. I thought I put it in that box to hide it under the shirts, but now that box is empty and it's not there."

My eyes widen before looking at the cashbox she just put money into.

"This is the second one," she quickly adds with panic rising in her voice.

"Okay," I say with a nod. "We'll find it. It will be okay."

She nods too, but her green eyes are almost glassy like she's trying to hold back tears.

Starting with the box at the end, I rifle through its contents, hoping to feel the cool metal against my fingertips, but there's nothing but shirts and more shirts.

There's no way someone could have rifled through the boxes without either of us noticing. We're practically backed up against the wall. Someone would literally have to step over boxes just to get to most of them.

With each box I check, my anxiety spikes. Even if the money is locked up, I don't think it would be too difficult for someone to break it open. We have two tables set up perpendicular to each other, basically making an L shape that would bar anyone from coming in on one side. I'm assuming this is how Mya sets up for all the shows, and I don't think she's ever had an issue with missing merchandise or cash boxes before, but what do I know?

A hand on my back makes me jump, but I look up to find Jackson's storm-like eyes scrutinizing me with a slight crease of worry as he crouches down next to me. "What are you doing?"

I'm kneeling by one of the final boxes and digging through it. "Mya can't find the cash box."

Resting his elbow on his knee, he looks over at Mya who's still handling customers like nothing is amiss.

"The other one," I clarify.

Jackson's eyes jump back to me. "Was it full?"

I shrug. I haven't been the one handling money all night, but if she moved to the second box, I'd say there's probably a decent amount of cash in the first. "Full enough?"

"Fuck." The word bites the air around us as it leaves Jackson's lips. "Brian will give her so much shit for this." He moves to the box next to me and rummages through the various pullovers and hoodies.

We finish checking each box, but there's no sign of it. There aren't many other places to look either. Unless we decide to scour the entire venue.

"Let's check the bathrooms." Jackson takes my hand. "I

doubt anyone would try to break it open here, but you never know."

"Okay." Reaching out, I gently tap Mya.

As soon as she looks over, her face goes from a customer service smile to anxious in an instant. "Any luck?"

I shake my head. "We'll keep looking."

She bites her bottom lip and nods before looking at the next customer and flipping the switch. She beams up at him and even laughs when he says something that probably wasn't funny.

As it turns out, checking the bathrooms is easier said than done. Jackson gets stopped four times on the way there. Each time it happened, he looked at me like I was a lifeline. I could see how torn he was. Stuck between wanting to tell them he had more important things to do and not wanting to let down his fans. When he'd stop to take a picture with someone, his eyes always found mine for a fraction of a second—checking to see what I thought of all this. I don't think he's used to this much attention yet. I'm certainly not used to seeing him get it.

But I put on my best smile because he can read me too well for his own good. I nodded encouragingly when someone asked for him to sign their ticket. I squeezed his hand reassuringly before letting go so he could take a picture with a group of girls. I even pulled him back when an eager fan called out to him, but he didn't hear it.

Of course, he's overwhelmed. It's overwhelming for me, too. Not in the same way it is for Jackson. I get that. But even being in close proximity to him feels like getting sucked into a vacuum.

The other band hasn't taken the stage yet, so it looks like everyone is using this time for a quick bathroom break. The men's room miraculously doesn't have a line, but the line for the women's restroom runs along the narrow hallway.

"Damn," Jackson mutters as he takes in the scene. "Okay,

I'll go check the men's, and then I'll come wait with you. Try not to do anything that will start a riot."

I smile sweetly at him. "Me?"

He scoffs. "You don't fool me, Red."

I know he's referring to the cats. I'm pretty sure he got angry texts for the better part of a month. A soft smile brushes my lips at the memory as I watch him walk away and into the men's room.

"Was that Jackson Phillips?"

I look at the girls in front of me to find almost *every* woman in line craning their neck to get a better look at me.

My mouth opens but the pressure of their combined stares makes it impossible to say anything. Am I supposed to lie? Would confirming it's him essentially start a riot? But at the same time, these women *know*. They already know, without a doubt, that Jackson Phillips just went into the men's restroom, and that I was the one who walked over here with him. "Um, I think so?"

I sound so stupid.

"How do you know him? Are you his girlfriend?" The girl closest to me stares with wide eyes, and I feel like the intensity behind her expression doesn't match the question she asked. She's looking at me more like she just asked if I was a foreign spy sent here to destroy us all.

"Oh, please don't tell me he has a girlfriend!" One girl further down practically wails, and I jolt, startled by her outburst.

What the hell am I supposed to say? Jackson never told me how to handle something like this, and I didn't realize he was well-known enough for me to ask beforehand. Damn my famous boyfriend for not telling me he was *actually becoming famous*.

Jackson exits the bathroom, and I suddenly know how every fairytale princess has felt when the knight in shining armor shows up to save her. He may be wearing a somewhat wrinkled T-shirt and nothing about him shines or gleams, but I feel like I can breathe again.

It takes him half a second to spot me still in line, and another half a second to read through the pure panic in my gaze. When he slowly looks at the other women standing in front of me, he must put the pieces together because he walks up to me, grabs my hand, and says something about how, "It's probably not in the bathroom."

He quickly pulls me away from the line, but not before I hear the immediate chatter break out. I have no idea what they're saying, but I have a feeling I'm not their favorite person right now.

33
jackson

CROONER SINS IS HALFWAY through their set, and we still haven't found this damn cash box. I'm trying not to think about the time I have with Margot dwindling down. I'm trying not to think about what it would have felt like to walk through this city with her. Or the fact that the comedy show I bought tickets to started twenty minutes ago. Or how, if we would have left on time, I would have told her I loved her already.

It would have been done.

I wouldn't have this crushing weight on my chest with the anticipation of saying those three words. I'd be past this milestone that feels like it's been slowly trying to suffocate me for months. I'd be able to breathe again.

But instead, we're all sitting with Mya at her table, not sure where else to look but unwilling to give up just yet.

Brian knows. He's been angry-pacing off to the side for the past thirty minutes—which if you ask me, is probably the least helpful thing he could do at a time like this. Not that what I'm doing is any better. I've been sitting in this plastic chair next to Margot, anxiously patting a rhythm on the inside of her knee. I feel like fucking Brady with his constant drumming, but I can't stop.

There aren't any customers now that everything has settled, and people are enjoying the main show. It's good because we can all talk freely about what the hell we're supposed to do now, but at the same time, it sucks because Mya doesn't have to hide how upset she is. This girl is always bright light and fucking pink clouds, but right now, she's confused, embarrassed, and angry with herself, and I can see it all too clearly.

Looking over at Margot, I mouth the word "sorry." It isn't the first time I've done it tonight, but I have to say it again. This is supposed to be our one night together, and instead of having fun, we're sitting here, staring at a problem we can't fix. Honestly, Margot and I don't need to be here. We're not helping anything. We've already looked everywhere we could think to look. But leaving makes me feel like an asshole, so we'll sit here until the band figures out what they want to do even though Mya has tried to get me to leave at least five times. She's the only one who knows how important tonight is to me. Hell, she's the one who made me build it up into something bigger.

Margot gives me a small smile and rubs my back in response. She doesn't mind. I know she doesn't. But she isn't the one who planned an entire night for us.

Mya does this every night without a hitch. Why does tonight have to be the night that something goes astray? I swear, sometimes it feels like the universe is giving us a chance on a silver platter, and other times like it's doing everything in its power to ruin things.

"I don't understand," Mya mutters as she rakes her hands through her pink hair. "I do this all the time. It's never an issue. I always put the first cash box into one of the boxes when it starts to get full. I would have done the same thing tonight—I know it."

Brian stops and wipes a hand over his mouth. "But do you remember specifically putting it into the box tonight?"

Mya frowns. "I . . . I don't know? I think so?"

Brian scoffs and the ice behind it makes me feel even more for Mya. I think he's harder on her because they're family. I've never seen him act this way toward any of the guys in the band.

"It's possible someone saw her put it in the box and then took it. They'd have to be sneaky, though. We were both sitting right here all night." Margot looks at Brian as she talks, and there's a familiar edge to her voice. I haven't heard it in a while, but I know when she wants to scold someone for acting like an idiot—because, for a long time, that idiot was me.

I should probably get her out of here. As soon as the headlining band finishes their set, we won't be able to sit out here as easily, anyway. I attract attention, but so does Dave. He might be older than me, but he's a good-looking guy, and I think the fans are starting to suspect he's single.

"Hey!" A petite woman with dark hair says, and I brace myself for the fake smile I'll have to muster if she's a fan. When I look over my shoulder, I see her black pants and polo with the venue's logo on it. She works here. And she's holding a small metal box in her hands.

Mya jumps to her feet. "Where did you get that?"

The woman grimaces. "Were you looking for it? I'm sorry." She points to the second merch table. "It was just sitting here, and you were with a customer. I didn't want anyone to take it, so I picked it up. I was going to give it to you once you were done." She points over her shoulder with a nervous laugh. "Then everyone and their mother needed something back there, so I tucked it behind the bar for safekeeping. I'm sorry! I should have gotten it to you sooner."

"No! Are you kidding?" Mya practically jumps with joy. "Someone could have taken it. Thank you!"

The woman smiles, but it's uneasy as her eyes dart to everyone else in the band. I think we're all just dumbfounded that the fucking box is back. "Right. Well, have a nice night." She gives a quick wave before scurrying off to do whatever it is she does.

"I'm so glad it was safe the whole time!" Margot beams up at Mya.

Mya opens the cash box and checks its contents. Her eyes widen like she's registering how big of a bullet we just dodged. "Yeah, no kidding."

Brian crosses his arms. With a cocked eyebrow, he says, "So you did leave it on the table."

Mya's smile fades, and Dave gets to his feet. "Aw, come on Brian. Give the girl a break. It was an honest mistake. We've all made them."

Brian pinches the bridge of his nose and huffs in disbelief. "It's a domino effect. She loses that money, there goes the budget for inventory at the next show."

I can practically see Dave's hackles rise. "We've got the money, Brian. Relax. Even if she lost it, the band can afford to have some T-shirts made."

"It won't happen again," Mya chimes in with a set to her brow as she looks at her uncle similarly to how Dave is looking at him. "I was excited to have Margot here. It probably just threw me off."

"I'm sure it was just a fluke," I say to Brian. What's the guy going to do? Fire his niece after one mistake? She's been incredible the entire time we've been on tour.

Plus, if Brian is as picky as she says, we'd never find a replacement.

Mya nods. "Definitely just a fluke." Turning to me, she adds, "Now can you *please go?* Don't let me ruin your night."

I could tell her my plan is already pretty much ruined, but I don't want to make her feel bad. I turn to Margot. "Ready?"

She gives me a dazzling smile before looking around at everyone. "Will I see you before I fly out tomorrow?"

Dave lets out a laugh. "I'm not sure Jackson wants to share you more than he already has."

Margot looks back at me, the corner of her mouth teasing. "Will I?"

Getting to my feet, I shake my head. "Nope. You're mine after this, Red." She doesn't fly out until tomorrow afternoon, but I have a feeling we won't be getting out of bed early. I nod toward the guys. "Say your goodbyes."

Margot jumps to her feet and heads straight for Dave first. She wraps her arms around his neck, and he squeezes her hard enough to lift her off her toes. After, she quickly hugs Brady with less enthusiasm, waves to Brian and Marty before stopping in front of Mya.

"Have fun tonight," Mya says with a wiggle of her shoulders.

"We will," Margot says with a laugh. "It was great meeting you."

The two girls hug, and I wait patiently, itching to be alone with her again.

And determined to find a way to salvage this night.

34
margot

IT MIGHT BE AFTER TEN, but the streets are busy in the city that never sleeps. New York has this bustling energy, not unlike Chicago, but still unique in its own right. My body buzzes with anticipation, but I'm not sure if it has more to do with being in one of the greatest cities in the world, or if it has everything to do with finally being here with *him*.

Jackson puts his arm around me as we head down the sidewalk, and I welcome the added warmth. I can't remember the last time I've felt this good. Probably this summer if I had to guess. Being here with him makes me feel more like myself than I've felt in weeks. It's funny how you don't even realize you aren't running on full until you are. Before coming here, I thought I was fine. Of course, I missed Jackson, but I was used to it. Being without him was just a part of my life as much as anything else.

But now that I'm here, my heart is full, my cheeks hurt from how much I've smiled tonight, and my mind is perfectly at ease. I was nervous about meeting the girl he's on tour with, and I was nervous things between Jackson and me might feel different, but both those fears have dissolved. Mya is wonderful, and Jackson and I have picked up exactly where we left off.

"So, you bought tickets for us to watch a comedy show?" I ask as we walk.

Jackson lets out a breath of laughter. "Yeah, but it's probably ending soon."

Pressing my lips together, I narrow my eyes at him. "You don't strike me as the type of person who would enjoy watching stand up."

That bashful smile pulls at his lips as he absently scratches the side of his head. "Yeah. I honestly didn't care about going."

We stop at a crosswalk and wait for the cars to pass. "Why buy tickets then?"

He looks at me, still holding me close, and I swear there's a storm brewing behind those gray-blue eyes. I just don't know what's causing it. "I wanted to do something for you."

"And what about me screams *comedy show?*" Jackson rolls his eyes, and I giggle. The light tells us it's okay to cross, so we hurry to the next street. "Is it how funny I am? When you think of me, you think of stage-worthy humor?"

"Yeah, Red. That must be it," he mutters with a laugh. Once we're on the other side of the street, he stops, and there's a seriousness to his features I wasn't expecting. "Look, I just . . ." He takes a breath. "I wanted to do something a boyfriend would do. I wanted to take you out, and the comedy show was one of the only things starting at a time we could make."

The corner of my mouth lifts.

"It's not funny," he says, even though his expression starts to match my own.

"I didn't say it was funny."

He sobers slightly, eyeing me with uncertainty. "Listen, I know I'm not a typical boyfriend. I just wanted to do something the way I'm supposed to do it for once."

Taking a step closer to him, I grab his jacket with both hands and pull him toward me. "Want to know what I think?"

The uncertainty in his expression still lingers, but he says, "Sure."

Seeing him vulnerable melts something inside of me, and I push up on my toes. I kiss him, and when I pull back, I whisper, "Typical boyfriends are overrated." Jackson laughs but looks away, so I pull him closer again to bring his attention back to me. "And do you know what I really want?"

He gives a slight nod in my direction. "What do you really want?"

My smile warms. "New York pizza."

There's a huff of what might be considered laughter as he reaches into his jacket pocket and pulls out his phone. He unlocks it and types something before handing it to me. "Take your pick."

On the small screen is a list of all the nearby pizza places, and my stomach growls just looking at some of the pictures on Google. One picture in particular stands out to me, and I quickly swipe through some of the raving reviews before pulling it up on the map. Turning the phone back to Jackson, I say, "This one."

Jackson takes his phone back from me and zooms in on the map before glancing up at the street name closest to us. "All right. Let's get you your pizza."

Taking my hand, he leads us down the sidewalk. I love the feeling of his hand in mine. I've missed the rough feel of his fingers, callused from playing. There's always been a familiarity with Jackson. I've always been able to be myself with him more than anyone—even if that wasn't always a good thing. I've never had to filter the things I say, or water down my emotions. I've always just been able to lean into whatever I'm feeling, good or bad.

There's an ease to being around him, but I don't think I've

ever been able to pinpoint the feeling until now. Because as I walk these busy New York streets with him, I'm struck with the sudden realization that Jackson feels like home.

It's one thing to feel at home with a person when your literal bed is in the next room and you're surrounded by your friends. But I feel at home with him *now*. More than I do at my apartment in Tampa, and a lot more than I do at my parents' house in Indiana.

My thumb runs along the back of his hand as we walk, and I get the sudden urge to stop him and kiss him. The alarming rush of emotion that comes over me feels like it needs an outlet. It feels like it's about to burst out of me. I don't know how I got to this point of needing him the way I do, but it's thrilling and terrifying all at once. It makes me feel desperate and totally at ease. Secure and completely out of control.

Unable to resist, I lightly squeeze his hand, and Jackson looks at me with a slight lift to his lips. His eyes search mine the way they always do, but he won't find anything worth hiding. Lifting our clasped hands to his lips, he kisses the back of mine.

It's a small gesture—probably something he's done a million times before, but my heart swells like it's the first, and I hope that this overwhelming, borderline uncomfortable, wonderful feeling lasts.

35
jackson

THE SMALL PIZZA shop is busy the same way everything still open in this city is busy. The sign on the door says they're open until two, so we have plenty of time to get Margot as much pizza as she wants. Holding the door for her, she smiles sweetly and says a soft "Thanks" as she walks past.

I follow, and my hand finds the small of her back. Her eyes are fixed on the menu board on the far wall, and I love how seriously she takes her ordering decision. There's a slight crease to her brow as she mutters the different options with total concentration.

Giving me a sideways glance, she says, "I'm not on the menu, Jackson."

My eyebrow kicks up. "Aren't you, though?"

She dismisses with a shake of her head. "Not *here*. Figure out what pizza you want and stop staring at me."

My amusement grows. "I thought you liked it when I stare at you."

A huff of disbelief leaves her lips, but it doesn't hide the slight upturn of her mouth. "Pick your pizza."

I shrug. "I'll have whatever you're having."

This makes her look at me. "What if you don't like it?"

"I like everything."

Her eyebrows crease. "You don't like onions."

"That's not true."

She balks at me. "Jackson, you pick them out of everything."

"Margot, I eat onions all the time."

"Should we order something to find out?" There's a knowing glint in her eye, and I don't trust it.

"Give me your best shot," I say with a nod toward the register at the front.

Margot, looking far too pleased with herself, heads to the counter and orders one of their specialty pizzas with a mess of toppings—one of them being onions. Reaching from behind her, I hand the guy my card. We each get a drink and find a small table in the corner of the dimly lit shop.

Margot secures our order number into the thin metal stand on the table. "So, should we bet on this? Because I like my odds."

"Bet on what?"

She appraises me with a playful upturn of her lips. "How much you like onions."

"What do you want?" I love seeing this spark in her when she tries to challenge me.

Margot tilts her head, her long, red hair falling to the side. "If I win . . ." She looks around the pizza shop like inspiration might be hiding in the parmesan. "You have to show me the lyrics you've been writing."

My body stiffens, but I try to shake it off. "What lyrics?"

She gapes at me, and I know I'm caught. "Jackson, you always have that notebook with your guitar. You'd bring it to practices, to shows, and you never left it behind unattended."

I narrow my eyes at her. "Because you would have snooped if I had, wouldn't you?"

Her grin broadens, and I smile at the unabashed way she confirms I'm right. "I just want to see," she says, softening. "I'm sure they're great."

There are two very good reasons why I haven't shared my half-baked ideas with her.

1. They're terrible and most of them I haven't even shown Dave because they suck.
2. Almost all of them are me confessing my feelings for her, and I figure I should probably tell her I love her before she figures it out from a shitty line I wrote.

By the way her smile widens, I'd say Margot knows she has me backed into a fucking corner. My mouth has gone dry, so I clear my throat. "And if I win?"

"You pick. That's sort of the idea."

Her snarky tone snaps me from my panic, and I lean back in my chair. If there's one thing that will make Margot sweat, it's breaking the rules. "If I win, we're going skinny dipping."

She tenses. "Where?"

I shrug. "I'm pretty sure our hotel has a pool somewhere." When we checked in earlier, I was a little too busy trying to rush us into the room to look around and notice, but I think I remember seeing something about it when I booked a few weeks ago.

Her eyes narrow, and I wonder if she'll scold me for coming up with such an idea. Instead, she reaches her hand across the table. "Fine."

Leaning forward, I extend my own hand. "Then it's a deal, Red."

Her delicate fingers wrap around mine, and that familiar pulse of electricity shoots through me. I thought it would have gone away by now, or at least faded. But if anything, I think it's grown.

"I can't believe we spent all that time looking for a cash box that wasn't actually lost," Margot says with a laugh as she pulls her hand away.

I blink, coming back to reality. "Yeah. Well, that's Mya for you." I shake my head, regretting my statement. "I shouldn't say that. She's usually on top of her shit."

"I really like her."

This makes me look at her more seriously. "Yeah?"

Margot nods. "You were right. I didn't think you would be, but you were."

Our pizza arrives and the corner of my mouth kicks up as I put a slice on a plate for her. "I'm right about a lot of things."

"Some things," she corrects.

"Eat your pizza, Red."

She grins and takes a bite. As soon as she starts to chew, her eyes roll back. "I get it," she says with a nod. "I always thought Chicago had the best pizza, but I get what they say about New York."

I put a slice onto my own plate. "I'm glad you approve."

She considers me. "Have you ever been here?"

"To New York?" I shake my head. "No, the only traveling we did when I was a kid was for my dad's company trips, and those were always to some tropical island that wasn't much different from Florida." Something in her sobers, and I know what she's going to ask before she even says it, so I add, "I haven't talked to him."

She frowns. "So, it's been . . ."

"Almost a year," I say with a nod. The last time I talked to my dad was when I went home for Christmas. It wasn't as bad as Thanksgiving, but the entire visit was tense. He let me know more than once that he wanted nothing to do with me *throwing my life away.* Margot is still staring at me, and I know she's torn between knowing my dad is an asshole and feeling like she should encourage me to have some type of relationship with him. She's figured out how to follow her dreams and still talk to her parents, so she thinks I should, too. Looking at her with more conviction, I say, "Margot, he's waiting for me to fail, and I have no intention of failing."

She holds my stare for another beat before giving a soft nod. "Okay."

There's a sadness in her that lingers, and my anger toward my dad spikes at the sight, like he's somehow to blame even though he's a thousand miles away. I nudge her with my foot under the table. "Besides, I only get to be around family when the band takes a break from touring, and I'd much rather see you than sit at his depressing kitchen table. You're my family now." I said it casually, but Margot's eyes widen just enough to make me want to backtrack. With a shrug, I add, "And Matt. I guess you can throw Rae in there too, but I draw the line at Braden."

Her shock melts into laughter, and I can't help smiling at the sound as I take my first bite.

36
margot

"LOOK at the onions on your plate!" I point an accusatory finger like he's spilled actual blood in the middle of this New York City pizza shop. To be honest, I wasn't *that* certain of my theory. The amount of time Jackson and I have spent in the same state as a couple isn't much, and it's not like we cook with onions daily. There was really only one instance when Braden cooked some type of casserole, and Jackson ate around them.

Jackson doesn't talk about himself much. Sure, he talks about the things he wants—mostly music and me—but he doesn't share the little details. But those are the details I soak up like a damn sponge.

Apparently, it comes in handy when you want to place a bet.

Jackson glances down at his plate. "What? They probably just fell off."

My eyes narrow. "Jackson, there's no way *only* onions fell off your pizza. Plus, I saw you pick them off."

The corner of his mouth kicks up when I say his name, but he seems unfazed about the bet. I hope he doesn't think I forgot. Or maybe he thinks I won't cash in. But I refuse to believe his lyrics are "trash," as he so often puts it. I want to see them for myself. I want to know what he was scribbling in that notebook all summer. Already excited for my prize, I sit up a little straighter and lift my chin. "I win."

Jackson doesn't react or look disappointed in the slightest, and it takes some of the fun out of winning. At least let me gloat.

He pushes his plate aside. "All right. Maybe I don't love onions, but I didn't pick them all off."

I laugh. "You picked off enough."

He holds my gaze like he's debating whether to fight me on this. When he finally looks away, he lets out a sigh. "Fine. You win."

I grin, but he cuts me off when he leans forward and points at me.

In a low voice, he says, "But I want you naked as soon as we're in that hotel room. Skinny dipping or not."

"And you'll let me look at your lyrics?"

He scratches the side of his head and drops his gaze. "Some of them."

My lips twist. I love seeing him squirm. It's such a rare thing that I only feel a little bad about being the cause of his discomfort.

"The good ones," I tease.

"Good might be a stretch." Stacking our plates in a neat pile on the table, he nods toward the exit. "Come on, let's get out of here."

On the walk back to our hotel, Jackson asks at least six times if there's anything I'd like to see before we head in for the night.

"Are you sure you don't want to go to Times Square?"

Make that seven.

With an incredulous look, I say, "Would you stop? You're acting like Times Square is going to disappear by morning."

He scratches the side of his head. "I just figured you'd want to see as much as you can while you're here."

Stepping in front of him, I cut him off, stopping him in his tracks. "I'm not here to see New York, okay? I'm here to see you."

His eyes search mine the way they always do when he thinks I might be putting up a front. It breaks my heart a little that he thinks he has to cram in special dates and sight-seeing just to make my trip worth it. He would be the highlight of my trip regardless of what we did.

When he doesn't say anything right away, I add, "We can plan a trip when you have a break from touring. We'll come back together and see everything this city has to offer."

"You're sure?"

I shake my head, a bemused smile pulling at my lips. "Would you stop doing that?"

A slight crease forms between his brows. "Doing what?"

"Doubting me," I answer simply. "I know what I want, Jackson. If I wanted to go to Times Square, I'd tell you."

A slow, easy smile stretches across his face. "Oh, I could never doubt you, Red." He tucks a strand of hair behind my ear, his fingers trailing down my neck. "You're one of the few things I'm sure of."

My entire body tingles at his touch until a familiar heat settles between my thighs. I don't know how he does it. All it takes is a brush of his fingertips and I'm ready to jump him. He's so close to me and breathing in his familiar scent has my head spinning. How does he smell this good even after a show?

When I'm quiet, there's a flicker of amusement behind those eyes. He takes a step closer, forcing me to look up at him. His hand still tracing lazy circles, like at any moment he might wrap that hand around my neck and pull my lips to his.

I fight the urge to press my thighs together.

"Tell me what you want," he says, his voice low.

My brain struggles to keep up with what he's doing to my body. With a small disbelieving huff, I ask, "What?"

Cradling my face in both hands, he gently kisses my lips, and my legs go weak, the heat between my thighs intensifying. "You said you know what you want, so what is it?" Another slow kiss lingers on my lips until he murmurs against my mouth, "Tell me."

My voice comes out barely above a whisper. "You're impossible."

His low chuckle sends a tingle down my spine. His thumbs brush over my cheeks, his hands still holding me in place. "It's okay if you don't want to say it. I think I have a pretty good idea." He gives me one more chaste kiss before stepping back, a taunting smirk playing at the corner of his mouth.

"You," I say with a shake of my head, my lips twisting as I fight my smile. Instead of finishing my sentence, I turn and start walking. "Unbelievable."

His footsteps speed up, and I yelp as he wraps his arms around me from behind. "Know where you're going, Red?" he says in my ear.

It's hard to keep the laughter out of my voice, but I manage to say, "You're frustrating."

"Good." He kisses my cheek from over my shoulder. "It will give me something to redeem myself for later."

My entire body warms, and I'd love to know how he plans on doing that.

Stopping me, he spins me around.

"What?" My voice comes out more alarmed than it should, my body still on edge from thoughts of him redeeming himself.

He points over his shoulder with his thumb, and amusement shines in his eyes. "The hotel is back there."

Craning around him, I see the entrance to our hotel a few feet back. "I was distracted."

"Because I distract you," he says it like it's an accomplishment, and I get the urge to roll my eyes again.

"You . . ." But I can't argue his point. He *does* distract me. Always. It doesn't matter if he's thousands of miles away or standing right in front of me, Jackson Phillips is the best kind of distraction. Instead of finishing my sentence, I push up on my toes and kiss him. Jackson wraps his arms around me, deepening the kiss, his mouth warm and soft on mine. It isn't the same as when he kissed me earlier today. This kiss is slow and packed with feeling, and I do everything I can to memorize this moment.

I'm breathless by the time we break the kiss, and grasping his hand, I pull him toward the hotel. The sound of his low laughter warming my soul.

37
jackson

MARGOT LEADS me through the desolate lobby of the hotel, but when she starts walking the wrong way, I tighten my grip on her hand. She looks over her shoulder at me and shakes her head. Keeping her voice low, she says, "I want to see the pool."

You'd think she just said something a lot dirtier with the way those words grabbed my dick's attention. "But I lost the bet."

She raises a mischievous brow. "Maybe I want to add to my prize."

This time my hand tightens around hers for a completely different reason. Sometimes I feel like I know Margot better than anyone, but then there are times—like right now—that she takes me completely by surprise. I've never seen her this bold.

Catching up to her plan, I blink the shock away and hurry after her. "You're serious?"

She shrugs innocently. "We'll see."

The pool is tucked away in the back of the hotel, and the dim glowing coach lights make me wonder if the area will be locked. Everything around us is quiet, and I get the feeling we aren't supposed to be back here this late. Margot glances at me, suddenly looking less brave, but even though there's no one around, the door is unlocked.

Her eyes widen, some of that excitement and mischief returning. "This is nice!" she says in a loud whisper, and I follow in behind her as she takes in the space.

Stone pavers surround the pool, giving it an outdoor feel even though it's not. The only sound is the gentle flow of water from two small fountains, and there's something about finally being alone with Margot—really alone—that puts my mind at ease.

I thought she'd want to go to Times Square. I thought she'd want to explore, and I thought I'd be able to tell her I love her under the glow of the city lights. But she'd rather be with me in this hotel, and I didn't know it was possible, but I think I might love her more for it.

Keeping my distance, I let her take everything in. She marvels at the soft lighting, and the beautiful fountains, and before I know it, she's slipping off her shoes and dipping her toes in the water.

Glancing up at me, she smiles. "It's warm."

My eyebrows lift. "Yeah? Want to go in?"

She beams brighter. "Yes." Her face falls and she looks around with a crease forming between her brow. "Do you think there are cameras?"

I huff out a laugh. "Yes."

Her eyes widen and lock on me.

"We're at a hotel in New York City, of course there are cameras. At least one, anyway." I look up and nod to a small black dome on a metal arm. It's the only one I see. "There."

She follows my gaze, her arms dropping at her sides like all her fun has been ruined.

I walk over to the camera, and as I do, I pull my black T-shirt over my head. I stop just underneath it and look back at Margot. "What do you say, Red? Want to go for a swim?"

The apprehension wanes from her expression the longer she looks at me. "Have you been working out?"

Looking down at my shirt, I double up the material as I let out a breath of laughter. "A little." It turns out boredom is a great motivator, and nothing is more boring than spending hours in an RV as you drive from city to city. When my eyes meet hers again, I raise my eyebrows and hold up the shirt to remind her of my question.

She's biting her bottom lip as she shamelessly takes me in, and just that look could make me hard. With one last glance at the camera, she nods. "Yeah. Let's go for a swim."

An easy smile pulls at the corner of my mouth as I toss my shirt over the lens, blocking its view. "Margot Reid, breaking all the rules."

"To be fair, you're a terrible influence."

When I turn to face her, she carefully grasps the bottom hem of her shirt on each side before slowly lifting it over her head. I drink in every sliver of skin as she reveals more of herself inch by inch. I should walk toward her. I should lessen the distance between us. Hell, I should fucking *say* something. But I'm mesmerized by her. I'm completely in a trance as she slowly unbuttons her jeans and gently shimmies them down her thighs, her eyes never leaving mine.

She's just in her underwear now. Light pink cotton panties and a matching bra. Reaching behind her back, she unclasps her bra and lets it slide down her arms. Her ivory skin in the glow of the coach lights is fucking perfection. Those pink, taut nipples are perked and begging to be sucked, and my cock throbs against the strain of my pants at the thought.

"Jackson?"

I blink, darting my gaze up to meet hers. I hadn't realized I was committing the curves of her breasts to memory. "Right.

Sorry," I rasp as I take a step toward her, then another. Halfway there, I remember I still have my fucking pants on, and practically hop on one leg to kick off my shoes and get out of my damn jeans. By the time I'm standing in front of her, I'm in nothing but my briefs. My hands grip her, and my thumb brushes over the pebbled skin of her nipple, making her gasp. That's all it takes for me to lose it. I mean, other than the fact that I've been dying to be inside her again all night. I swallow the sound, and without wasting time, I lift her up. She wraps her legs around my hips, her muffled squeal getting buried in my neck. I carry her down the steps and lower her into the water.

But I refuse to let go.

If anything, I grip her tighter, my cock pressed against the soft cotton of her panties. I should have taken my boxers off before scooping her into my arms, but even with the added layer, Margot stills and lets out a breathy sigh near my ear that sends me spiraling.

My mouth finds hers again in a rush of need and heat. I should slow things down, but I can't. I can't control myself around her right now. It's been too long, I'm too fucking hard, and I love her too damn much. My lips crash against hers with a hunger I haven't felt in months, and when she sucks in a breath, I take full advantage. My tongue claims every part of that gasp, until she melts into me. She completely surrenders, opening for me to kiss her deeper, and every time my tongue meshes with hers, I slip further into oblivion.

"Jackson," Margot pants.

I move to kissing her neck, my hand palming her perfect breast beneath the water. "Hmm?" It's the only response I'll give myself time for.

"We should probably slow down." But even as the words leave her lips, her legs fall open, and she grinds against my cock like she's begging to be fucked.

As much as I hate it, I know she's right. We aren't even technically skinny dipping yet, and I already want to carry her back to our room and have my way with her. She just feels so fucking good. Running my hands down her body, I lift her on to the edge of the pool and stand in the shallow water so I can keep kissing her.

Margot gasps at the sudden loss of warmth, her skin breaking out into an elaborate pattern of goosebumps to compliment her freckles. Pulling back, I kiss her collarbone, her shoulder, trying to hold myself together as I do. The pebbled skin of her nipples calls my name, and I take one into my mouth. My teeth gently bite down, and she cries out before I run my tongue over the sting and suck.

Hooking my fingers into the sides of her cotton underwear, Margot's words come out in a rush. "What are you doing?"

Releasing her nipple from my mouth, I look up at her. "Slowing things down," I say as I gently maneuver the pink cotton down her body. Once I slip them over her ankles, I wring them out and set them onto the brick pavers. "See, we're officially skinny dipping." I lift her leg slightly and kiss the inside of her knee.

A laugh floats from her lips, but she's looking at the ceiling like it's taking everything for her to control herself, too. "I think I'm supposed to be in the water for that."

Kissing the inside of her thigh, I murmur, "Semantics," against her skin, unconcerned. "You're naked by a pool, and you're mine. Let me enjoy this."

A faint smile flutters across her lips. "Don't think I've forgotten about my actual prize. I want lyrics, Phillips."

Everything in me tenses, but she's right. She won the bet, and if lyrics is what she wants, lyrics is what she'll get.

38
margot

JACKSON STANDS AGAIN, the water only kissing his hips. His eyes are everywhere but on mine. He takes in my body without reservation and without shame. Every dip of his gaze is another caress, and even though he isn't touching me, I feel him everywhere. There's a hunger behind those storm-like eyes, and just knowing I'm wanted by him is enough to make me ache.

"Jackson," I plead. If he doesn't touch me again soon, I might pass out.

His eyes flick up to meet mine. "You're beautiful, Margot." His voice is low, like it's a secret he's been keeping.

It's the third time he's ever said that to me, and my entire chest warms. Jackson's gaze momentarily slips, and I know he's taking in my physical reaction. I know my chest, neck, and cheeks are flushed just from those three words. My breath comes in short pants, and it isn't until he closes the space between us that I feel my heart rate calm and spike all at once. He casually drapes his arms over my thighs as he stands between my legs, his thumbs tracing small circles on my lower back.

He presses a kiss between my breasts, and I finally inhale a full breath. Lifting a hand, he pushes some of my wet hair away from my shoulder, his fingers grazing my skin. Another kiss, and he murmurs, "Somehow, when she's not here, I'm the one who feels miles away."

My breathing halts.

Jackson presses a warm kiss to my neck, and I suck in a breath at the contact. "Someone, catch me. I've fallen for her icy stare."

Moving to the other side of my neck, his fingers graze down my breast, down my stomach, and over to my hip where he lazily traces circles, and I have to suppress a shiver. "She's unstoppable," he says against my skin, his warm breath teasing my flesh. "She's a force I never saw coming, but I'm so lucky to have been in her way."

I'm afraid to move—afraid to stop whatever this is—but at the same time, I need more of him. He's being too gentle, too teasing, and combined with the words leaving his lips, I'm done for. Slowly, he runs his hands back up my waist until he's palming my breasts, and I let out a soft moan. He presses a kiss between them. "If loving her is playing with fire, I'm begging to be burned."

My lungs lock. Did he just say what I think he did? My heart hammers in my chest. Was that a confession or a lyric? Are they all about me? Is this how he feels? He doesn't look at me. Instead, he kisses lower and lower until he gently lifts me closer to the edge of the pool. So many questions swarm in my head, and I want to ask him all of them. I want to know how deep these lyrics go. I want to hear more of them—all of them.

But before I can remember how to speak, Jackson lowers himself and buries his face between my legs, his eyes only flicking up to meet mine a moment before he leans in to part me with his tongue. My head falls back, a throaty moan leaving my lips. I choke on a sob when another flick of his tongue sends me reeling. He sucks hard on my clit, and I yelp at the sudden mix of pain and pleasure. Then he follows with gentle strokes that make it hard for me to hold myself upright. I swear, the way he uses his tongue shouldn't be allowed. It isn't fair. He flattens his tongue against me, and I feel like I'm on the verge of blacking out.

Heat coils in my core and my legs start to shake. How am I this close already?

His tongue slows to teasing strokes, and I'm desperate for more. Propping myself up with one hand, I use the other to grip his hair, and he groans. "We're slowing down, Margot."

I don't want slow. I'm panting and needy, and the fact that he's keeping my orgasm just out of reach has me reeling. Pressing my heel into his back, I try to bring him closer, and he lets out a low laugh against my center. "Let me take my time."

"Why?" The word comes out breathless.

"I've missed the way you taste." Jackson grips me tighter, his tongue working slow and deep up my center, his next words dragging out of him like a groan. "Fuck, I love the way you taste."

A whimper leaves my throat.

The sound brings a slight lift to his lips before he goes back for more. Moving one of his hands between my legs, he slowly pushes into me with two fingers, and I desperately clench around them. Finally, he gives me more. His fingers curl deep inside me while his tongue delivers dangerous strokes to my clit. The combination is too much, and I lose it. I come hard, and through every pulsing current of electricity, he savors me.

I've barely come down from my orgasm when Jackson hoists himself out of the water and pulls me to my feet. I'm still dazed when he picks me up. I feverishly kiss his neck. I don't care where he's taking me. He can have me anywhere he wants.

Droplets of water fall from his hair as he lays me down on one of the large luxury loungers inside a decorative cabana, and before I have a chance to think, his mouth is on mine. There's a new hunger in the way he's kissing me, and it's making my mind a blank slate. His hands are greedy as he rakes from my breasts, to my waist, to my ass, and as soon as he straightens and frees himself from his briefs, I can feel him at my entrance, hard and ready. My legs open wider, my body begging him to ease the empty ache, and he doesn't take his time. With one quick thrust, he's inside me, thick and dominating. The air rushes from my lungs, and my body tries to catch up, my walls tensing then relaxing around him. My head falls back as my hips tilt to take him in deeper because he feels so good. It isn't until Jackson is rooted deep inside me that he takes a breath, like fucking me is the fix he needed.

Leaning forward, he kisses me gently while he thrusts into me hard. The contradiction has my head swimming. Taking my chin between his thumb and forefinger, he's gentle but firm as he forces me to look at him. His eyes are dark, the gray and blue almost completely swallowed by black.

"You're mine."

Panting, I give a faint nod. "I'm yours."

That's all it takes for his mouth to crash into mine. He fucks me like I'm his for the taking, and I am. There's something about seeing him use my body this way that turns me on. There's something carnal about the way he's taking me. Each hit has me clinging to the cushion, and with every hard thrust, my hips open to him, begging for more.

"Say it again," he commands through heated breaths.

It's hard to find my voice. It ends up coming out shaky and cracked. "I'm yours."

He picks up his pace, angling my hips in such a way that my eyes cross. I'm going to come if he keeps this up. "Jackson," I plead, and he answers by slamming into me harder. I tighten around him like a vice a second before I fall apart. I cry out on the lounger beneath him, and he covers my mouth with his hand a second before he stiffens, pouring his release into me. I clench around him as I ride out the aftershocks of my second orgasm and take a little too much pleasure in the shiver that runs through him. I love that I'm the only one who gets this side of him.

I love that he's mine.

39
jackson

I PANICKED. As soon I said that last lyric, I knew I shared too much. We're back in the room and she hasn't brought it up again, but I know she won't forget. I had her again in the shower when we got back here, and now she's still in the bathroom. My knee bounces as I sit on the side of the bed and wait for her. I don't know how long I can keep this up. I can't just fuck her every time I'm afraid she'll bring up my feelings for her, but I was supposed to do this right. I was supposed to make a big deal of this, and I'm failing.

My fingers rake through my damp hair, and I force out a breath. I need to get a grip. How can I want to tell her something more than anything, but every time I have the chance to do it, it's paralyzing?

"Hey, you okay?"

I lift my head to find her eyeing me cautiously with her towel scrunched in her hair. She's wearing one of my T-shirts I left behind at her apartment, and my eyes snag on where the hem ends halfway up her thigh. It takes literally nothing for this girl to turn me on.

Slamming the door shut on everything I was feeling thirty seconds ago, I give her my best smile. "Yeah. Tired?"

She weighs her head from side to side. "Yes and no." Taking a seat, she turns to face me and hugs the towel to her chest. "I don't want this to end." Heat blushes her cheeks like she just admitted one of her deepest secrets, and I brush my thumb over the pink, skating across a pattern of freckles I could probably draw with my eyes closed at this point.

I know how she feels. One night isn't enough after we've waited months to be around each other again. It sucks. It's probably the only part of touring I don't like, and the fact that I can't fix it pisses me off.

Dropping my hand, I try not to let her see everything I'm feeling. "Have you talked to your parents about staying in Florida over the holidays?"

She nods. "Yeah. They didn't love it, but I told them Rae will spend Christmas with Matt's family, so we'll fly back for Thanksgiving instead. This way I don't have to travel alone, and I'll be able to see you when you come home."

The corner of my mouth twitches. "I'd just fly to Indiana when the tour wraps up, if you were there." I've never met Margot's parents. I don't even know if she's told them about me. Hell, I haven't told mine about her, but I haven't told them about anything. I think talking to her mom stresses her out, but she talks to her dad sometimes. I wonder if he knows I exist.

Her eyes widen at my offer. "You would?"

Is it surprising? I figured it would be obvious. She's the one person I want to see when I come home. Of course, I'd go to where she is. I let myself fall back on the bed with a huff of a laugh. Resting an arm above my head, I ask, "Why do you think I wouldn't?"

Margot's cheeks flare again, and I hate to see it. I hate to see her holding back anything. We're supposed to be past this

—we *are* past it. She doesn't hold back her feelings like she used to. Not with me.

She turns to look at me more, abandoning the towel in her hand so she can brush her fingertips under my shirt and up my side. My cock twitches at the contact, and I try to stay focused on whatever she's about to say.

"I didn't think you'd want to be around my parents."

My immediate reaction is to emphasize how much *I don't* want to be around her parents. I want to be around *her.* But something in the way this conversation has her nervous gives me the common sense to take this a little more seriously. "Do they know about me?"

"Somewhat." Lying down on me, she crosses her arms on my chest and props her chin up to look at me. "They know I'm seeing someone, but they don't know you're . . . you."

A smile pulls at the corner of my mouth as I run the backs of my knuckles over her cheek. "A college drop-out who's in a band?"

"Stop." She playfully swats at me. "You're more than that, and you know it."

"Maybe, but that's how my parents see me, so I figured yours would feel the same." A frown settles on her beautiful face, and I force a laugh. "Come on, don't look at me like that."

She blinks, her features softening. "Sorry. It's bullshit, though."

I cock an eyebrow.

"I mean, my parents don't know any better. They might think of you that way at first, but that's not who you are. Anyone with eyes can see it, and your parents should know that better than anyone."

Something in my chest aches, but I push the feeling away. At the same time, Margot crawls up my body so her face is over mine, and it's like the feeling never even happened.

"They should know you're smart." She kisses the side of my neck, and my lungs remember how to work the moment her lips touch my skin. "And kind." Her lips press another kiss. "And hardworking." She moves to the other side of my neck and leaves a kiss there. "They should know you're talented." Her mouth moves up to my jawline where her lips tease my skin with another light kiss. "And driven." She leaves a gentle kiss on my cheek, but I turn my head and catch her lips with mine. No one has ever seen me the way she does. I'm not sure I deserve it. Reaching for her, I weave my fingers through her hair and kiss her deeper. She opens for me, letting my tongue find hers. She indulges me for a moment, but it ends too quickly. Pulling back, she's a little breathless when she says, "You care about other people, too. So many people in your position could be selfish, but even though you're chasing your dreams, you care about the people you left behind."

My eyes search hers, but there's no resentment in them. I hate that I'm leaving her behind. I hate that she feels left at all. Brushing a stray hair from her forehead, I let my hand cup the side of her face and love the way she leans into it now. "I don't know if I deserve you."

She looks at me a little more sharply. "You deserve everything." She rests her chin on the backs of her hands again. "You deserve to be on that stage, *and* have a family who supports you, *and* a girlfriend who lo—wants to see you happy." The second part of her sentence comes out rushed, but she quickly centers herself on top of me and presses her mouth to mine. I groan and slip my hand under the hem of her T-shirt only to be met with her bare hip. She's not wearing anything underneath and despite it being the middle of the night, I feel a surge of energy at the discovery. I'm dying to be inside her again, but I have a feeling she needs to hear what I'm about to say.

"You deserve to be happy, too." My fingertips graze the

bare skin of her hip, and it takes everything in me not to bury myself between her legs for the fourth time tonight. "Whatever you want, I want you to have it."

"I do have what I want." She palms me outside my briefs, and I groan as I pull away from her. I need her to understand this. I need her to listen.

Confusion etches her features, and she sits up. I'm grateful the motion puts her a few feet away from me because the only way I can have this conversation with her is if she can keep her hands off me for five minutes.

I sit up too, my elbows resting on my bent knees. "I don't want you to ever put your dreams on hold for mine. Everything you care about—your classes, career, your blog—they're important, okay?"

She frowns. "I know they're important." She tilts her head. "Jackson, what's this about?"

I blow out a breath, my hand reaching up to rub the back of my neck. "I just hate that you're having to bend so much for the things I want right now. I'm sorry this isn't ideal." She moves to crawl toward me on the bed, and I hold up a hand. "Stay over there, Red."

She pauses. She's on her fucking hands and knees, frozen in place with her bare ass exposed now that my T-shirt has ridden up.

"Sit," I command. I can't think straight with her in that position, and the fact that she does as I say only has my dick straining more against my briefs.

"Are you sure you're okay?" Her words come out with careful consideration.

"I'm fine." I wipe my hand over my mouth as I look at her. "But everything you do turns me on, and I want to get this off my chest before I fuck you into this mattress."

Her cheeks flare, and she puts her hands in her lap. "Okay," she says a little breathless. "I'll be good."

I rub my hand over my face and crack a smile. "Jesus Christ."

When I look at her again, the corners of her lips are pressed like she's fighting a smile. She knows exactly what she's doing. "Go ahead," she says with a reassuring nod. "Get it off your chest."

I can't tell if she's mocking me, and my eyes narrow a little before I give in and say, "There's a lot of focus on me in the band right now, but I don't want you to ever feel like you ever have to put your dreams on hold for mine, okay?"

Now that I've said it, it doesn't feel as big as it did in my head. Maybe it's because I'm still turned on, or because she just had me laughing, or maybe it's just because in my head things always feel bigger than they actually are. Maybe it's because she makes everything a little less overwhelming.

She waits for a beat, a faint smile playing at the corner of her mouth. "Am I allowed to speak now?"

I huff a laugh. "Since when do you ask me for permission to do anything?"

Her smile grows, and she crawls toward me again. This time settling between my legs and holding my face in her hands. "I don't mind bending. I know it's hard for you to believe, but I'm genuinely excited for you." I open my mouth to say something, but she cuts me off. "And I know my dreams are important, too. I still have all those things you listed. I'm still doing all of them."

"You haven't posted on your blog as much lately."

She blinks before letting go of my face and dropping back on her heels. "You still read my blog?"

"Of course I do. Where else would I know to find the best place to buy vinyl records in Ybor?"

She still looks surprised, those big, brown eyes blinking before she pushes herself up on her knees again and drapes her arms around my neck. She's taller than me like this, and I have to look up at her. Without thinking, my hands find her bare thighs and move up to cup her perfect ass.

"Post on your blog more, Margot."

She nods, her breath catching when my hands move up her hips and waist until setting under the curves of her breasts. "Okay," she breathes.

She kisses me, and it feels different than all the other times we've kissed tonight. The kiss feels like she's thanking me, but I haven't done anything. If anything, I should be the one thanking her. Gently pushing me back on the bed, she never breaks the kiss. Not until she softly says, "I promise to always go after the things I want, but right now, I just want you."

In the next kiss I flip her onto her back and hold myself over her, letting my hips settle against hers. "You have me, Margot. You always have."

40
margot

MY EYES FLUTTER OPEN, and I've never been so disappointed to see sunlight peeking through the curtains. Jackson's leg heavily rests over mine as he sleeps on his stomach beside me, and I take a moment to just look at him. His hair is a mess, but it somehow suits him. His back is exposed, and I fight the urge to run my fingertips over the muscles of his shoulders.

I woke up this way for weeks when he stayed with me over the summer, but I don't think I ever fully appreciated it. I thought I did. But after spending the last couple of months without him, I know how much better this is. The difference between waking up in my bed alone and waking up *here* is stark. I know he's safe. I know how his night was. I know he had a great show. I don't have to wonder or worry about anything at all. It's probably the first time I've woken up and not felt the immediate need to check my phone in case there are any messages from him or any posts on the band's social media.

Carefully reaching for my phone, I tap the screen to check the time and do a double take.

10:37 a.m.

I blink. It has to be wrong. There's no way we slept so late. I mean, sure, we *did* stay up half the night. But even with that, I figured we'd wake up around ten at the latest. I figured we'd have time to lie in bed together and grab some breakfast before my flight at one, but I need to get to the airport . . . soon. Really soon. JFK is no joke, and if I don't want to miss my flight, I need to get there *now*.

"Shit," I mutter under my breath, and Jackson stirs next to me. He reaches for me, but my heart is already racing with adrenaline, and I'm ready to grab my stuff and go. Jackson rolls onto his side and pulls me in so my back is against his chest, the length of him pressing against my ass.

Damn mornings.

But even though I *know* I need to get to the airport, I ache to stay here with him.

Jackson's mouth is hot on my neck, and he works his expert fingers over my exposed hip and between my legs. I gasp when he finds my clit, and my back instinctively arches, making my ass grind against him. The low, guttural sound from his throat has me wanting to forget about my flight altogether.

I used to wake up this way all the time. This was once our norm. He'd work his magic, knowing it's almost impossible for me to say no to him, and I'd be left scrambling to get ready for work on time. He loved it. He loved watching me frantically try to piece myself together after he just made me fall apart. I could tell by the way he used to watch me dash around the room with a subtle lift to those perfect lips of his. But this is different. I can't just be late to my flight—I'll miss it.

"Jackson," I pant, already growing slick between my legs.

"Mm?" He follows by devouring my neck with more vigor, his free hand moving up to palm my breast.

The combination has me arching against him more—the same way I'm sure he knew it would. "Jackson," I try again, but my conviction wanes with every passing second.

Flipping me onto my back, he holds himself over me, his mouth moving to my collarbone while he grips and gropes me everywhere. My body is putty in his hands, molding and shaping. My muscles are always looser around him. Even with the added stress of knowing we need to get to the airport, my legs still easily fall open with the slightest touch.

"Say what you need to say, Margot," he croons against my skin. The head of him rubs against my clit, and I can already feel myself slipping.

It would be so easy to stay in this bed with him but doing that would derail everything. I have work tomorrow. I have an essay I still need to write. With my heart racing for more reasons than one, I blurt, "My flight!" The words come out cracked and desperate.

Jackson finally pulls back to look at me. "What about your flight?"

You'd think I'd be used to having his undivided attention by now, but my thoughts still scramble. I'm breathless and wildly aware of how hard he is against me, but I manage to say, "We overslept."

He blinks, his eyes clearing before he reaches for my phone, flipping it over to see the time. He stares at the screen a beat longer before letting out a groan and giving me a peck on the lips. "Okay. Let's get you to the airport."

My stomach sinks. It shouldn't. That's exactly what I needed him to say, but I'm left wishing he would have said something different. Jackson is my reckless streak. He's the one I throw caution to the wind with. Maybe that's why I let myself imagine what it would feel like to have him say *fuck it* for half a second. Maybe that's why I secretly wish he wanted me to ignore my responsibilities, so I could be persuaded.

It's ridiculous.

Trying to rid the feeling, I move from underneath him and start to gather my things. Jackson lies on the bed, staring at the ceiling for a moment before he looks over at me. I can feel his eyes on me as I walk to the nightstand and unplug my phone charger.

"Margot."

I look up, still leaning over.

"I need you to put on pants." His eyes trail to my ass, and I'm suddenly aware of the position I'm in.

"Right. Sorry." I huff a laugh and carry my clothes into the bathroom, leaving him to rub both hands over his face.

Shutting the door behind me, I stare at myself in the mirror and take a steadying breath. I should rush to get ready. I should be haphazardly throwing my things into a bag and scrambling to get out of here as fast as I can, but for whatever reason, I can't make myself move faster. I just stand and look at myself in the mirror, realizing I haven't really looked at myself in months. Physically, nothing has changed for the most part. My auburn hair is still long, my body still slender. But something behind my eyes makes me pause. I've changed—I'm *still* changing. I'm not sure how fast or slow, but everything I've done this past year has shaped me into a better version of myself. I'm more confident in who I am, I'm more sure of my actions, and I'm not as afraid as I used to be.

And he's a huge part of that.

I hear Jackson rustling in the room and my gaze jumps to the door behind me in the reflection of the mirror. With one last glance at my own eyes shining back at me, I get dressed and gather my things. I can do this. I can go without seeing him again for months. I love being around him, but I can stand on my own two feet. I'm not the same girl I was when we met. I'm not weak. When I get home, I'm going to make a better effort to be more involved in my life *there*. Because I miss this version of me. I miss not feeling hollow.

41
jackson

WE'RE ALREADY BACK at JFK, and it feels like we were just here. Well, I guess we were. When I picked her up yesterday, the possibilities felt endless.

Now she's anxiously looking over her shoulder at the line, and I know she needs to go. It took everything in me not to drag her back to that bed this morning, but she gets stressed about things like being late. And as much as I'd secretly love for her to miss her flight and stay longer, I can't be the reason it happens.

"Okay," she says, bringing her attention back to me. She takes a deep breath, her eyes searching mine. "I guess this is it."

I nod. "Go. Don't miss your flight."

She frowns, and I somehow feel like I've said the wrong thing. "Yeah. Okay. I'll um—"

"December."

She finally smiles. It's a small one, and it fades quicker than I'd like, but she nods. "December."

Kissing her, I want to memorize everything about this moment. The way she melts against me. The way she pushes up on her toes to kiss me deeper. The way I don't want to let go.

When I force myself to pull away, I rest my forehead against hers. "Text me when you're at the gate."

"Okay." Her voice comes out sounding more like a whisper, and I notice the way her delicate fingers grip the front of my jacket like it's her lifeline—I try to commit that to memory, too.

"And text me when you land."

She lets out a light laugh. "Okay."

"Text me for anything. I don't care if it's early or late, or if you think I'm busy. Text me."

She takes a small step back, and I think a piece of me goes with her. "I should go." She points over her shoulder with her thumb.

"You should."

But she doesn't walk away. Her smile gets a little bigger, and she says, "December," one more time before kissing me.

Then she does pull back.

She does turn away from me.

And she walks deeper into the airport, following the signs for where she needs to go. Just before she turns out of sight, she looks over her shoulder to find me still standing here, still hating the distance between us with every step she takes. She tilts her head in mild surprise like she thought I'd be out that door as soon as she turned around. I give her a small wave and point for her to keep going. She waves back before laughing to herself and walking around the bend. Disappearing from my sight.

Then I'm just standing there.

Staring at nothing.

Letting out a breath, I rock back on my heels. I can't leave. Not yet, anyway. I don't think she'll miss her flight, but I want to be here if she does. Looking around, I spot a metal bench by the window and take a seat, leaning my head back against the glass.

I can't believe she's gone. Our big trip—the one that was supposed to make all the waiting worth it—flew by, and now we're back to waiting again. Two months isn't that long. I know that. I know a lot of people wait a lot longer to see the people they love.

Fuck.

Leaning forward, I rub my hands over my face and let my knees shake out some of the panic lodged in my chest.

I didn't tell her. It was the one thing I was supposed to do, and I didn't even tell her. Part of me actually considers running through the airport like one of those idiots in the movies, but I stay where I am. I rest my elbows on my knees and clench my fists. I look in the direction she disappeared and rest my chin on the backs of my knuckles, but I don't move.

Why can't I do this? Why can't I do what countless people do every day? Why is the thought of telling her just as paralyzing as the thought of not telling her?

I can't remember the last time I've said that to *anyone*. I've definitely never said it to someone I've dated, but I don't think I've said it to anyone else in years. My mom? Maybe? I can't remember a specific time recently, but I'm sure there was one. Definitely not my dad. I don't think he's told me he loved me since I was six or seven. Matt has told me he loves me more than my dad has over the years, but do I ever say it back?

My thoughts are giving me a headache. They're too loud, and they don't matter. All that matters is that I fucked up again. I was supposed to make some big deal out of telling her, and instead, I didn't tell her at all.

Mya is never going to let me live this one down. Part of me doesn't even want to go see the band after this because I know Mya will be eagerly waiting to hear all about my big, romantic gesture. She'll want to know every detail, and I have absolutely nothing to tell her.

I don't know how long I sit there, contemplating my every move over the past twenty-four hours, but eventually Margot texts me to tell me she made it to her gate in time.

With no other reason to sit here, I get to my feet. I might not want to hear what Mya has to say about this, but the band is waiting, and at some point, I'm going to have to face the music.

Everyone stayed in a nearby hotel last night since Albany is only a few hours away and we didn't have to drive through the night. It's nice to have a break from sleeping in the RV. We can't afford to do it all the time, but Brian handles most of the budgeting. A few weeks ago, he sat us all down and asked us what our goals were. Ever since, he's been rejecting any ridiculous requests we have like some kind of top security bank.

When I get dropped off at the front entrance of the hotel, I spot the RV in the parking lot and head that way instead of going inside. Dave texted me earlier saying they were about to check out and grab lunch from somewhere inside. Brian must have been feeling generous. The place they stayed in looks just as nice as the one I stayed with Margot. Maybe he wanted to give everyone in the band a reason to celebrate. I'm just glad we didn't end up at the same place.

Imagining Margot by the edge of that pool already feels like a far-off dream, and now I'm awake, trying to cling to the pieces before they fade away.

"Hey, man." I lift my head at the sound of Dave's familiar voice. He's leaning against the RV with his phone in his hand.

I nod as I walk up to him. "Hey." He looks better than I've

seen him in weeks. Lighter maybe, like he isn't carrying as much on his shoulders.

"Margot on her way back home?"

Standing next to him with my back against the RV, I nod again. "Yup."

He holds up his phone. "I was just talking to Lynn."

My eyebrows lift. "Oh yeah?"

Dave nods, a tight-lipped smile forming. "Yeah. I think we're going to try to work things out."

"That's great." I know Dave has missed her more than he's let on. He's barely looked at another girl since we've been on tour, and he hasn't been himself. "What changed?"

Dave shrugs as he slips his phone in his pocket. "Nothing really. We still have a lot to figure out, but after seeing you with Margot last night, I realized I wasn't ready to take the easy way out. Balancing Lynn and the band will be tough, but I think it's worth it."

"It is." I'm surprised seeing Margot with me had any effect on him. I figured they all looked at us like a couple of crazy kids who have no idea what we're getting into. They wouldn't be wrong. But the fact that Dave was somehow inspired by what Margot and I have feels pretty good.

Dave lets out a laugh. "I'm surprised you let her get on that plane. With the way you were looking at her last night, I figured you'd find a way to take her with us."

My lips twitch. I'd love to have Margot come on tour, but she has her own life. "She wants to finish school and build a career."

Dave takes a better look at me. "You've asked her?"

I shake my head. "It would just give her something else to stress about." Leaning in a little closer, I add, "Plus, I don't think I want her around Marty more than she needs to be."

Dave lets out a bellow before clapping me on the shoulder. "Aw, come on. He'd behave."

I cock an eyebrow, and it only makes him laugh more.

"All right. I get it."

Why would Dave ask about Margot going on tour? We've only been together a few months. Dave and Brady were with their girlfriends for years. Before I can stop myself, I ask, "Did you ask Lynn to go on tour?"

Dave sobers slightly. "Yeah. Of course." He looks up like he's trying to remember. "We've had that talk . . ." He blows out a breath. "Shit. I don't even know how many times at this point."

"She said no?"

He lets out a low chuckle. "Every time."

"But why?"

He shifts his weight. "She already has a great job doing something she loves. It would be too much of a sacrifice for her." He looks up at the RV next to us. "Plus, there's the whole living arrangement. I'd love to fly back and spend a few days with her between shows, but we're not earning enough for frequent flights yet."

"So, why did you think I'd invite Margot?"

A rueful smile pulls at the corner of his mouth. "Jackson," he says with a hint of amusement, and I don't think he's ever said my name so deliberately. "You and Margot are *young.* I know it might not feel like it, but she's as detached as she's ever going to be. She hasn't built her career yet. You two can afford to be wild and free in a way the rest of us can't." He lets out a low laugh. "Now is the time for you two to make reckless decisions and challenge the impossible."

I huff, but I'm not buying everything he's selling. He didn't hear the way Margot talks about her internship. He didn't see the spark in her eyes when she broke down her strategy for covering the small bookstore in town. Her career might be new, but that doesn't make it less important.

Instead of arguing with him, I lightly bump my knuckles against the side of the RV. "And the living arrangement?"

He shrugs. "You two are used to those shitty dorm beds."

A breath of laughter leaves my lips.

Pointing back at the hotel, he says, "Listen, I have to get the others, but we're pretty much ready to hit the road. Want to come?"

"I'm good. Do me a favor and make sure Marty at least showers before he starts bragging about what he did last night."

"On it." Dave gives a two-finger salute before turning on his heels and heading back toward the hotel.

And I'm left to wonder what it would feel like if I were standing here with Margot instead of standing here alone.

42
margot

THE COOL AIR and bustle of New York gets quickly traded for heat, humidity, and palm trees. I'm surprised to see Rae's Jeep Liberty already waiting front and center, and I pick up my pace. Opening the door and sliding inside, I toss my bag in the back. "Thanks for picking me up."

She grins. "Of course. How was it?"

"Great," I say a little breathless as I buckle my seatbelt, but my smile is genuine. Every second I spent with Jackson this weekend just made me wish we had more time. There's still so much we could have seen and done . . . or talked about. I feel like even though I told him about my job and my life, I still could have talked to him about so much more. There just wasn't enough time.

Well, I guess we *could* have talked more, but we chose to do . . . other things.

I don't regret a second of that either. My memory jumps to us at the pool, and I can already feel my face flushing. I can't believe we did that—I can't believe *I* did that. Having sex out in the open like that was thrilling and reckless, and I never thought I'd be so willing to break the rules.

But with Jackson, I *do* break rules. With him, I hardly think about what we were doing and where we were doing it. All I can see is him.

"What did you guys do?"

I blink, hoping my expression doesn't betray me, but Rae laughs.

"You two didn't leave the room, did you?"

A slow smile creeps across my lips as I bite my thumb. "We did a little."

Rae gives me a rueful smile. "I should have known." With a shake of her head, she looks over her shoulder before pulling away from the curb.

"Okay, so we may have done a lot of *that*, but we were long overdue. Honestly, the trip was perfect. Too short. But perfect."

She glances at me. "I figured it would be. You look good by the way—happy."

"I am." I smile, and it's probably the most genuine one I've given her in weeks.

As we drive toward our apartment, I tell her all about Jackson's show. I tell her how the crowds are getting bigger, and how people are recognizing him even when he's not on stage. I tell her about Mya and the missing cashbox, and how Jackson's plans didn't work out, but I didn't mind.

As Rae drives, she laughs and gasps at all the right times, and something about this drive back home feels nostalgic. Something about it feels like when we used to drive around together in high school and gush about all the boys we thought were cute.

Rae shakes her head. "He wanted to take you to a comedy show? Jackson?"

I shrug. "He just wanted to plan something I think."

"I mean, I guess. I'd understand if he wanted to take you to see a band or something. Times Square I guess makes a little more sense but still."

"Yeah. He was really set on that one, but I'll see it when I'm there longer than twenty-four hours."

Rae gives me a sideways glance. "Did he tell you he loves you?"

The words hit me like a punch to the gut, and my cheeks warm. I shake my head. "No, not directly." Even though my answer is true, it feels incomplete. The lyrics he shared have been echoing in the back of my mind ever since he murmured them against my skin.

Maybe they're just lyrics, but I think they mean something more—I *hope* they mean something more.

The crease between Rae's eyes deepens. "Do you think he was planning to? Maybe that's why he worked so hard to plan a date?"

I pause, letting her words sink in. Could that have been the reason he wanted to go so badly? I guess it could have been, but it doesn't make sense as to why he would have decided not to say it at all. "I don't think so? I wouldn't care where he tells me." I let out a laugh. "He could have told me as we were walking into the pizza shop, and I would have been happy about it."

Rae raises a brow. "Yeah, but does *he* know that?"

When I stare at her blankly, she waves her hand in the air. "I'm not saying you should have told him, but think about it. Jackson has never had a serious girlfriend, right?"

I nod.

"So, he's probably never done this before. Maybe he thinks it needs to be a certain way."

I let out a light laugh. "That doesn't sound like Jackson at all."

Rae joins me with an amused smile. "No, it doesn't." She shrugs. "I don't know. Maybe I'm wrong."

"Maybe," I add lightly before looking out the window as we pull into our apartment. It doesn't matter if she's wrong or right. Even if Jackson *was* planning to tell me with some big romantic gesture in the middle of Times Square, he didn't. Something held him back, and that's okay. He's always been the one who can communicate what he wants or how he feels. If he's not ready to love me, I can respect that.

My phone vibrates in my lap, and I look down to see a message from Jackson. In my rush to get to Rae, I didn't text him from the airport.

JACKSON:
Everything okay?

MARGOT:
Yeah. Sorry, with Rae now. We just pulled into the apartment.

The three dots appear right away.

JACKSON:
I miss you.

MARGOT:
Already?

JACKSON:
Too much.

Rae parks her Jeep, but I can't stop looking at his last message. It warms my chest in a way that only he can. It's okay if he doesn't want to say those three words. I feel pretty loved anyway.

MARGOT:
I miss you too.

43
jackson

"YOU DIDN'T TELL HER?" Mya practically yells even though she's sitting right fucking next to me on the small couch in the RV.

"Would you keep your voice down?"

Dave pokes his head out of his bunk in the back. "Tell who what?"

Mya looks back at me, and I hope she can see how much I don't want her to talk about this anymore, but she looks personally offended by this whole situation. The longer she looks at me, the more I see it. She jumps to her feet, crossing her arms as she walks over to Dave. "Jackson didn't tell Margot he loves her."

I'm too tired to deal with this. Rubbing both hands over my face, I stay where I am. There's no point trying to beat Mya at her own game.

Dave tilts his head. "Like today?"

Mya looks back at me, disappointment seeping from her every pore. "Like ever."

Dave sits up on the edge of his bed. "Wait." He does a little math on his fingers before looking up again. "Haven't you been dating her for almost a year?"

"Almost," I answer dryly. When he says it like that it sounds pretty bad. "But we've been apart for most of it."

He balks at me. "But you've never broken up, right?"

I shake my head, hating the thought. "No. Nothing like that."

Marty hops down from his bunk, and I wish he were driving. I wish he was doing just about anything to keep himself busy and away from this conversation. "Better be careful, puppy. There are a lot of guys who would have no problem telling that girl anything she wants to hear."

Staying put, I flip him off. Something about the way he just said that makes me think he'd be one of them, and I don't need to be any closer to him than I already am.

Dave holds up a hand in warning to Marty. "Easy." Looking back at me, he says, "If you're not feeling it, why go through all the work of trying to keep her?"

Mya jumps in. "He *is* feeling it. He's just scared."

Marty laughs, and I shoot him a look before glaring at Mya again. "I'm not scared. I had it planned, but someone lost the cashbox, and everything got fucked."

Her eyes widen and soften, realization sinking in.

"Yeah." I pointedly confirm what I know she's thinking. "You told me I had to make it a big deal, so I tried. I had it all planned, and then the night fell apart."

A low chuckle leaves Dave's throat. "You don't have to make it a big deal. I told Lynn I loved her for the first time when she took me to get stitches in my hand after dating for two months. It was probably the least romantic way I could have done it. I think I still had blood on my shirt."

"Yeah, and I told a girl I loved her just last night. Well, one of them, anyway—the younger one," Marty chimes in.

Mya rolls her eyes. "Gross."

Ignoring what Marty said, I keep my eyes locked on Dave. "Seriously?"

He laughs again. "Yeah. Who the hell told you it had to be special?"

My eyes jump to Mya, and her cheeks flush with what I'm assuming is guilt. "I still think you should try to make a big deal of it, but if I knew your alternative was not saying it at all, I would have told you that was stupid."

"Thanks," I mutter.

Dave looks back and forth between Mya and me with a bemused smile pulling at his lips. "Listen, if you want to make a big thing of it, fine. But you don't have to. If you want to say it, just blurt it out next time you see her. I'm sure she'd be happy to hear it."

I try to imagine doing just that, and my knee bounces at the thought.

Unfortunately, Marty is the one who notices and laughs. "Lord help us if he ever decides to propose."

I scoff and get to my feet. "Don't get ahead of yourself, Marty." When I pass Mya on the way to my bunk I ask, "Want to smoke?" I need something to get rid of the regret I'm feeling. I should have just told Margot. In my gut, I think I knew that, but the whole thing has turned into a massive block for me. Next time I see her, maybe I should just do what Dave suggested and blurt it out. Maybe holding this in is what's making it feel like I have a bomb strapped to my chest.

Mya looks surprised by my offer, but quickly agrees. "Yeah. Of course."

Dave runs a hand through his hair. "I'd join you, but it's my turn to drive. Brian and Brady have been up there long enough."

Marty opens his mouth to say something, but Dave cuts him off.

"You're coming with me. Jackson already looks like he wants to kick your ass."

I let out a huff but keep my mouth shut because Dave is right. Marty always gets under my skin, but Marty talking about Margot has me feeling more on edge than I have in weeks. I can't remember the last time I've gotten into a fight. Elementary school maybe? But the thought of causing Marty pain and wiping that smug look off his face is starting to get more appealing.

Marty looks me up and down. "Nah, we're fine. Aren't we Jackson?"

Rocking back on my heels, I stuff my hands in the pocket of my hoodie so he can't see how tightly my fists are clenched. "We're fine," I say with a sharp nod.

Dave's wary eyes jump between the two of us. "Either way, you're coming with me."

Thankfully, Marty doesn't fight him this time. As soon as he and Dave are at the front of the RV, I take a hard seat on the edge of my bed.

Mya quickly sits down next to me. "I'm sorry I ruined your night." She reaches beneath the bunk for the box where we keep our weed and expertly rolls a joint as she continues. "I feel so bad. The whole cashbox thing. I'm so sorry, Jackson."

Taking the joint from her, I shake my head as I put it in my mouth and light the end. "Don't be. You didn't ruin anything." She's still looking at me with wide, worried eyes, and my exhale comes out as a choked laugh. Offering her the joint, I shake my head. "Don't look at me like that. We had a great time." She doesn't look completely convinced, so I add, "Plus, you were right. I was scared."

Her face relaxes. "Really?"

"Fucking terrified."

She narrows her eyes at me playfully as she lifts the joint to her lips. "I knew it." Once she's taken a hit, she hands it back to me.

"Not anymore, though."

"No?"

I shake my head. After hearing Dave's story, I think he's right. Margot wouldn't give a shit how I tell her. Maybe Mya needs a grand gesture from someone, but I don't think Margot does. Hell, I don't even think she'd like that, and all it took was Dave to talk some sense into me. My voice comes out muffled as I get ready to take another hit. "Nah. Fuck it."

44
margot

MY EYES BURN into the paper calendar on my desk in my office. Taking off the sheet for October was bittersweet. Just two weeks ago, I was visiting Jackson. I had been counting down the days, doodling, and writing notes to myself just to get to the day I'd see him. I liked seeing that written excitement as a reminder even after the trip was over.

Now we're officially in November, and there are no fun plans. No doodles. No notes. Just scheduled work meetings and deadlines penciled in. There won't be anything Jackson related on my calendar until next month, and it already makes me wish I could skip ahead to the day I can peel off the November sheet.

Then he'll be home. His tour will have ended, and even though his manager has talked about a headlining tour, there's nothing officially on the books yet. Maybe he'll be home for a longer stretch of time than he was in the summer. Maybe they'll go back into the studio and take their time with it since they have more money to work with.

All things I should ask him, but all things I'm the tiniest bit afraid to know the answer to. There's a chance he'll have to go back on the road right away, and I want to hold on to this naïve hope a little while longer.

Derek stops at my door and knocks on the frame. "I'm heading out, but there are a few cookies left in the break room if you want to take them home for your roommates."

I get to my feet. My workday is done, too. I should probably get home and stop staring at this calendar. "Are you sure?" I ask as I pick up my cardigan from the back of my chair and slip it on.

He pats his stomach. "I certainly don't need them."

I laugh. "I'm sure my roommates would love that. Thank you." I technically only have one roommate, but I think I talk about Matt and Braden enough for Derek to assume they must live with me.

He nods before giving a wave. "See you Monday, kid."

"Enjoy your weekend!" I call after him as I gather my things.

Leaving my office, I turn to head into the break room, but stop short when I almost run into Karah. "Sorry. Hey," I say, taking a step back.

"Oh, Margot. I've been meaning to talk to you." She smiles, but there's a chill behind it. "I saw your latest submission, and it needs some work."

"For the bookstore?"

She nods.

"Derek approved that already." I falter as I point my thumb over my shoulder like Derek might still be behind me somewhere.

She nods solemnly. "I know. It's just—well, I don't think it's your best work. It just didn't grab me, and if we're going to give it as much space as you insist, it needs to be . . . better."

"Better?"

"I'm afraid so."

I blink. "Oh. Um, sure. When do you need it by?"

She grimaces, but it doesn't come across genuine. "Well, it was supposed to be finalized today."

"It was finalized today."

She raises an eyebrow.

"Right. I'll just get it done now. I still have . . ." I check the time on my phone. "Ten minutes left in my shift."

"Just make sure it gets done." She beams with a catlike grin. "I'll lock up behind me since you'll be here alone, and you just do the same when you leave."

Ever since I stood up for my story on the bookstore, being around Karah has felt like a double-edged sword. She may have commended me for my actions that night, but ever since, it's felt like the opposite.

"Okay. Thanks." I give her the best smile I can muster before stepping around her to go into the break room. I need one of those cookies.

"Oh, and Margot?"

Stopping, I slowly turn on my heels. "Yeah?"

"Don't bury your voice." She winks before turning and heading toward the front doors.

I stare after her, unsure of what that even means, but I have no interest in asking her to explain further. With a small nod, I give a tight-lipped smile and head into the break room. I stand, staring at the beautifully plated cookies for a moment and wishing Derek were still here so I could ask him what the hell I'm supposed to do now.

I wait for the sound of Karah closing and locking the front door to snatch the cookies off the table and march back into my office. My fingers punch the keys as I type in my password to log back into my computer. I pull up the story on the bookstore and glare at it. How is this not my best work? This is the story I've been most passionate about for weeks. Karah saw the original and seemed fine with it. Once I learned it would get more page space, I had to add to it.

Reaching for my phone, I debate texting Jackson. We've been texting more since New York. I think the trip is what we needed to fall back into a sense of normalcy. I thought I would feel distant from him now that we're apart again, but I haven't. He's always within reach with a push of a button. I just wasn't utilizing it enough before.

It's a Friday night, though. I don't even have to look up the tour dates to know he's probably doing sound checks and warming up with the band. Plus, if I don't want to be here all night, I need to work on this. Calling him will only delay the weekend at this point.

Instead, I unlock my phone and text Rae.

MARGOT:
Working late tonight.

The three dots appear right away.

RAE:
Noooo. On a Friday? That shouldn't be allowed.

MARGOT:
I know! I'll tell you about it later.

She likes the message, and I turn my phone face down so I can get to work. I scan over the words I carefully curated, trying to figure out what *my voice* even is, so I can know if I've lost it somewhere along the way.

I'm not sure how long I've been working, but I'm completely lost in what I'm doing. My fingers type away at the keys as I try to insert more of myself into my work, but I still don't fully understand what she meant, and it's making this a slow process.

A knock on the front door jolts me from my thoughts, and I stare in that direction even though I can't see the actual door from here. I'd have to turn down a small hallway to get to it, but I'm suddenly gripped by panic. Reaching for my phone, I turn it over to check the time. Who the hell would try to get into this office right now?

The knock sounds again. It's slow, not aggressive, but that somehow makes it more eerie. My heart races because I *know* I shouldn't answer that door. I've seen enough crime documentaries to know that. But at the same time, all the lights are still on in the office. If I even walk out there to get a better look, whoever it is will likely see me.

Maybe it's Derek? Maybe Karah told him she wanted me to stay late to redo the story and he plans on offering some help? As nice as he is, I think that would be a little too generous, even for him.

The knock sounds again, but this time it's accompanied by a voice. "Margot?"

45
jackson

IT'S AFTER THE SHOW, and Brian insisted on buying us all drinks. He's in rare form tonight. He keeps smiling and throwing his arm around anyone's shoulder who will let him—he even kissed Dave on the cheek at one point. Usually, Brian sits in the corner, wears his suits, and makes sure none of us get too out of line. Tonight, he's a different man, and I can't figure out what the hell he's celebrating.

Sure, we had a great set, but we do most nights. The place was sold out, but that's not new either. Everything about tonight's show holds up to how our shows have gone for most of the tour. The only thing different is the fact that it was Brian who suggested we hit the bar down the street and not Marty.

It's a nice place—definitely nicer than any bar I would have walked into on my own. The guys seem to feel right at home, but I'm just pissed no one asked to see my fake now that I finally have one. Maybe we're starting to be well-known enough for them to not want to risk turning us away. If we all left, I have a feeling most of the people here would do the same. The bar probably figures letting me drink is worth the risk at this point.

I'm still standing at the bar, watching Brian live like a king in a booth toward the back, when Mya brushes past me. Catching her by the elbow, I pull her closer so she can hear me over the music. "What the hell is up with your uncle tonight?"

She looks over her shoulder to spot Brian before she looks back at me. "He's having fun." Placing both hands on my chest, she adds, "Maybe you should try it." She gives me another playful pout as a dismissal before sliding up to the bar next to me and ordering her next drink.

She's right. I probably shouldn't be unsettled by it. Maybe Brian's just excited that so much of the tour has gone well so far. He's entitled to enjoy a night out as much as the rest of us. Hell, he may have earned it the most out of all of us.

Grabbing my whiskey from the bar, I head toward the back where most of the band sits with our suspiciously happy manager. Marty is the only one missing, but that's nothing new. I don't even have to look for him to know he's finding the next girl willing to fuck in the bathroom.

When I approach the table, the three guys cheer. It only takes a second for me to spot the array of shot glasses in front of each of them.

Sliding into the booth, I nod to the mess of scattered glasses on the table. "You know it's not a race, right?"

"You want one?" Brian sits up straight like he's ready to flag someone down and order more.

Lifting my cup, I shake my head. "I'm all right."

Brady eyes my whiskey. "Did they card you?"

"Nope." I set down my glass. "Fucking waste."

Dave's laugh still manages to carry throughout the bar. "Aw, don't let it get you down. I'm sure there will be plenty of opportunities for you to use your fake."

Brian studies me as I take a sip of my drink, and I pause. "What?"

"You're too sober." Looking at the other two guys, he reiterates. "He's too sober."

Brady laughs as Brian's hand shoots into the air, signaling to someone he'd like another round.

I smile. "Someone should keep an eye on us now that you've loosened your tie."

Mya slides into the booth next to me. "Damn, this place is packed."

"Hey, Mya, want to make sure no one fucks up tonight?" Brian yells across the table over the music.

Mya's eyes narrow. "You mean do *your* job?" She holds his stare as she brings her drink to her lips. "No."

Dave snorts a laugh. "If you think about it, the only one who might need watching is Marty." He points to me first. "He's head over heels for Margot, I'm trying to get back in Lynn's good graces, and Brady will probably propose as soon as this tour is done." He shakes his head. "I can guarantee you that pissing off any of those women is ten times more terrifying than the threat of bad press."

Brady lifts his beer. "I'll drink to that."

Dave gives Brian a knowing look that has him cursing under his breath. "Let me go find that horny son of a bitch."

Brady steps aside to make room, and a tall brunette sets four shots on the table. Before he leaves, Brian points to the shots and then points at me. "Three of those are for you." Grabbing the fourth, he mutters, "I'm taking this one."

"You do that." I toss the first shot back, and grimace. "Tequila?" I shake it off before downing the second. "Gross."

Mya reaches past me to pick up the third. "Then you won't mind if I take this one." She downs it like a machine, but quickly chases it with whatever pink drink she's sipping through a straw.

By the time Brian comes back after finding Marty, I've somehow let Dave talk me into taking another shot, Mya left us and is now flirting with some girl at the bar, and Brady has been talking to any fan who stops by the table. The way he can talk to people he doesn't know might be even more impressive while he's buzzed.

I've just been drinking.

Well, that, and I texted Margot to let her know I'm thinking of her. I'm always fucking thinking of her.

"Well, I think he'll keep his dick in his pants until he's in private," Brian says with a huff as he collapses in the booth. You'd think the guy had just run a marathon hunting down our bass player.

"Did you tell him public bathrooms aren't private?" I ask as I take another sip of my drink.

Brian stares at me. "Do I need to?"

I shrug. "Wouldn't hurt considering his track record."

I figured everyone knew about Marty's quickies, but based on the way Brian lets out a sigh and says, "Goddamn it," I guess I was wrong.

When he goes to get up again, I motion for Brian to sit back down. "Let him have his fun. It's not like we're at the venue." It feels weird to defend Marty, but I don't want to be the reason he gets scolded.

Brian considers my point before fully sitting again. "I guess that's fair."

Dave leans in closer to me. "We'll just leave out the fact that he told a few of the staff from the venue to join us here."

I shake my head and take another sip. "Of course he did."

When I'm brought another whiskey, I start to sip slower. I'm feeling it, and the last thing I need is for someone to get a kick out of me stumbling.

Someone jumps into the booth next to me, and I look up to find Mya peering at me innocently as she rests her elbows on the table.

"How are you feeling? Drunk? Happy? Agreeable?"

My eyes narrow. "Why?"

Taking in a deep breath, she casually turns one of the empty shot glasses on the table in front of her. "There may be a girl at the bar who loves the band, and she may have asked me to introduce you."

I look over my shoulder to find the girl at the bar already staring at me. I lift my drink to her before turning back to Mya. "I thought you were flirting with her."

"Oh, I was. I'm hoping this will score me some points. Help a girl out."

I let out a breath of laughter. "I'll do my best."

Mya pats me on the shoulder like I've passed some type of test. "Try not to scare her away before I get back from the bathroom." She gets out of the booth, and I follow her lead.

"Better be quick." Meeting fans is fun, but I usually like when we do it as a group. I'm not like Brady. I can't make small talk the way he can.

By the time I get to my feet, Mya has already disappeared. The girl at the bar has long, blonde hair, and she's wearing a black leather jacket. She's pretty, and there's an edge to her that makes it clear why she'd be Mya's type. Gesturing toward the drink in her hand, I say, "That looks a lot like whiskey."

She smiles and brings the glass to her lips. "Bourbon."

"Good for you." The only other girl I've known to drink dark liquor is Margot. She only did it at that house party we went to, and she might have only done it to spite me at the time, but I swear the whiskey somehow tasted sweeter knowing her lips had touched the bottle before mine.

She nods, looking pleased with herself before taking another sip. "Thanks for coming over here and meeting me. I've been a huge fan for a while. I actually came to the show tonight to see you guys more than Crooner Sins."

It isn't the first time someone told me something similar, but it still surprises me when I hear it. Crooner Sins feels lightyears ahead of us, but maybe it's just because I didn't join the band that long ago. To me, the work still feels the same. The cities and venues are different, the crowds are bigger, but we're still the same group of guys playing the same songs each night. Half the time we aren't even aware of people discovering our music until moments like this when we're blind-sided by someone knowing who we are or knowing the words to one of our songs. "Yeah?" I ask, my eyebrows shooting up. "That means a lot. Thanks."

The girl holds out her hand. "Tarah."

"Jackson."

When I shake her hand, she gives me a funny look. "I know."

I crack a smile and take another sip of my drink. "Right." Looking around her, I ask, "Did you come to the show alone?"

She shakes her head. "No. My friends are around here somewhere. But can I tell you something?" She wraps her fingers around my bicep, her thumb grazing over my skin. Leaning in close, she playfully whispers in my ear, "I'm kind of glad they wandered off."

"Annoyed with them already?"

She cocks an eyebrow, and amusement flickers in her features. "No . . . I'm glad they aren't here so I can talk to you alone."

Red warning flags slowly raise in the back of my mind, and I look over my shoulder to see if Mya is coming back from the bathroom yet, but she's nowhere in sight. Looking back at the girl, I say, "Weren't you hitting it off with Mya? She's great." I sound fucking stupid, but I have no idea what else to say.

Her lips lift. "She is great, but I just met her tonight. I've had my eye on you for a very long time."

My eyebrows shoot up. "Really? That's uh . . . bold." What the hell do I say to that? I've had fans flirt with me, but there was always some type of barrier. There was always a barricade, or a merch table. Hell, even Mya can be a great diversion when I need her.

I go to take another sip of my drink, but Tarah takes it from my hand and sets it on the bar behind me. She lets out a light laugh. "That's not bold." Her hands run from my chest to my abs. "But I can be." She hooks her fingers into the front of my jeans and leans into me. "Say the word, and I'll show you bold."

46
margot

OPENING the front door to the office, I poke my head out and look around. "Braden, what are you doing here?" I half expected to see Matt and Rae with him. But it's just him.

Raising the pizza box in his hands, he shrugs. "We ordered from Mimi's and Matt sent me to pick it up. I remembered you work next door and thought you might be hungry."

I blink. I'm starving. I've already eaten four of Derek's cookies while I've been working, but the smell of the pizza has my stomach growling. "Aren't Rae and Matt waiting for you to bring it back to the apartment?"

"Yeah, but they won't mind if I feed you first." He huffs a laugh. "Rae would probably rip me a new one if I didn't."

"Probably," I agree with a light laugh of my own. Opening the door further, I gesture for him to come inside. "I think there are paper plates in the break room. I'll grab a slice and you can head back." Looking over my shoulder, I add, "Thanks, by the way."

"No problem." Braden looks around the office as he follows. "They really have you working this late?"

My sigh is barely audible. "Unfortunately. I should have been done by now, but I'm a little stuck."

Braden follows me into the break room and sets the pizza box on the small round table in the middle.

"How so?"

"I don't know." I shake my head as I grab a plate from the cabinet. "My boss more or less told me I was losing my voice in this latest piece. I think I've fixed most of it, but something about it still isn't sitting right." I shrug. "Maybe I've read it too many times."

He opens the pizza box, so I can grab a slice. "Yeah, if you stepped away from it a bit, I'm sure it would be clear, but I'm assuming you don't have time to do that."

"Exactly."

"Want me to take a look?" He points to the door of the break room even though he doesn't know where my office is.

"Really?"

He closes the box of pizza now that I have my slice and shrugs. "Why not? I might not be able to help, but I'm happy to try."

I hold his stare as a mild dose of panic travels through my veins. Plenty of people read my work after something has been published, but the idea of sitting and watching him read something I've written, when I *know* it's not good enough yet, has me second guessing his offer.

But maybe he can help.

"Sure," I say before I can talk myself out of it.

"Yeah?" Braden doesn't bother hiding his surprise.

"Yeah, that would be great. As long as you don't mind."

He genuinely smiles, and it's like something inside me warms. His blue eyes, so different from Jackson's, have a little more spark in them now. Picking up the pizza, he gestures toward the door. "Lead the way."

So, I do. I let him follow me through the hall to my tiny

office in the back. I sit in front of my computer so I can wake everything up and minimize some of my other windows.

"You've been holding out on me."

I look around my monitor so I can see him. "What?"

He nods to the corner of my desk. "You have cookies."

Letting out a light laugh, I nod. "They're from my coworker. They're incredible. I think they're shortbread but there's a hint of lemon in them." Picking up the container, I hold it toward him. "Help yourself. I planned on bringing them home for everyone."

Carefully setting down the pizza box where the container of cookies just sat, he reaches for one. "Thanks."

I stack the cookies on top of the pizza and refocus on my computer.

"Holy shit." The words come out of him like a groan, and I peek around my computer to find him with his head back and eyes closed as the cookie undoubtedly melts in his mouth. "Please tell me she's single and not out of my league."

My lips pull into a smile. "*He* is very much middle aged and married."

Lowering his head, Braden catches my eye over the monitor. "Damn. All the good ones are taken."

His tone is joking and light, but the way he's looking at me has my heart picking up speed. I know what he's implying. It's what he's been implying for months. Tilting my head slightly, I say, "Maybe you're just looking in all the wrong places."

He grins. "Yeah." Tossing the rest of the cookie into his mouth, he shrugs. "I guess I am." Perking up and rubbing his hands together, he walks around to my side of the desk. "All right. What do we have?"

His arm rests on the back of my chair as he starts to read over my shoulder. I can smell the subtle spice of his cologne and there's a lingering hint of soap like he showered recently. I can feel the warmth of his presence behind me and suppress a small shiver as I get to my feet. "Here, you take the chair."

He doesn't even look at me as I get up. His eyes stay locked on my words as he easily moves into the now empty seat. Watching him read my subpar work has my nerves on edge, and before I even realize what I'm doing, I'm pacing the small office and biting my thumbnail as I wait for him to get to the end of the piece.

It only takes minutes, but it feels like hours have passed by the time he looks up at me. "Margot."

I stop pacing, but I can't get my thumb out of my mouth. I grimace, bracing for the worst. "Yeah?"

"*Margot.*" He shakes his head, looking back at the screen. "You're an incredible writer."

"But it still needs something," I point out.

He nods. "It does, but first I need you to know this is great work."

"Thanks." I nod, but I can barely enjoy the compliment while I wait for whatever he's about to say next.

"Great work," he says again, holding my stare to make sure it sinks in. "But this doesn't read like your blog."

"You read my blog?"

"Yeah," he says absently as he shifts his attention back to the screen. "Look." He points to a few paragraphs, and I walk back around the desk to get a better view. "Like here, you talk all about the bookstore, but it doesn't feel like you're there. It sounds like you're speaking remotely. If this were your blog, you'd make the reader feel like they were standing between the shelves with you."

I frown. "I see what you mean, but the blog is so casual."

He nods. "I'm not saying you have to get rid of your professional edge here, but I think you can combine both styles a little more."

As soon as he finishes his sentence, it feels like there's a shift in my mindset. Even though I've been here for longer than I'd like, I'm suddenly excited to sit back down and take another crack at it. The idea of blending my two writing styles has me buzzing because I suddenly know exactly what I need to do. It will give the article more flare, but still envelope a style of writing that will meet the expectations of our readers.

"Braden!" I say, clapping him on the shoulder excitedly. "You're a genius."

"Yeah?" He turns to look at me, and I'm vaguely aware of how close we are.

"Yes!" I nod enthusiastically, my eyes still glued to the screen, skimming for all the places I can give the article more of a personal touch. When I do eventually look over at him with a grin, I'm taken aback by how happy *he* looks. It isn't an outward burst like the rush I'm experiencing. His happiness is subtle—quiet. It's there in the way his eyes spark and the slight lift to his lips. It comes from within, and even though it's innocent, it goes beyond the bounds of friendship.

I quickly stand up straight, removing my hand from the back of the chair. "Thank you. Really. I should be able to get those changes done and wrap things up."

He shrugs, back to looking casual. "Of course. Always happy to help." Getting to his feet, he steps around me and reaches for the pizza and cookies, keeping them neatly stacked. "Want me to leave you a cookie or two? No promise there will be much left later."

I shake my head. "No, I figured they'd be my dinner, so I already had plenty. Thanks again for the pizza."

He smiles, and the warmth that radiates from him hits me in the chest again. Nodding toward the door, he says, "Do me a favor and lock up behind me. I don't like that you're here alone this late."

I follow him to the front, and once he's outside, I stand with the door cracked. "Thanks again. I owe you one." With a laugh, I add, "Two if I count the pizza."

Braden lets out a chuckle. "I'm just glad I could help."

My lips lift. "Goodnight."

"Goodnight, Margot."

Closing the door, I turn the lock. The office feels eerie without his presence, but I make my way back to my desk and try to hold on to the spark he lit while he was here. But when I stare at the screen, I'm not thinking about the words I should be changing and rearranging. I'm thinking about the way he looked at me.

Tapping my phone screen, I see a text from Jackson a little while ago.

> JACKSON:
> Just thinking about you.

Even though I've done nothing to warrant it, guilt settles heavy in my stomach. Jackson has no idea Braden likes me because it never felt like something I can confirm. It was only a look. It's only ever a look—well, that and a subtle comment here or there. It's innocent, but I wonder if Jackson would mind. I wonder if he'd care that I was here alone with a guy who increasingly makes it clear he has feelings for me.

47
jackson

MY HEART RACES as Tarah slides her hands under my shirt. Clearing my throat, I try to get my bearings. I'm too drunk for this shit. "Uh, no. No, I don't want you to be bold. I don't think my girlfriend would want you to be bold either."

If I were still at USF, I'd be more of an asshole, but the last thing I want is to turn someone against me—it will only turn them against the band. We need a clean name. We need everyone to love us. What we don't need is this girl talking shit if she doesn't like the way I turn her down.

She pulls back so she's eye level with me again. Running her hands through my hair, she innocently asks. "Are you sure?"

With a tight-lipped smile, I nod. "Yup."

She shrugs and steps away from me. "Suit yourself."

"Thanks." It probably isn't the right thing to say, and she probably isn't expecting it to be the end of our conversation, but as soon as I'm free, I abandon my drink at the bar and head back to our booth.

I'm on such a mission to get back to the safety of the guys, that I hardly register Mya until she stops me. "Hey, where are you going? You were supposed to guard her for me."

Glancing back at the bar, I see the girl has found one of her friends. They're both looking down at their phones, neither paying us any attention. Turning back to Mya, I say, "Sorry. She uh . . ." I scratch the side of my head. "She might like you, but she likes me, too."

Mya gasps and glares in the direction of the girl. "That snake. She told me she wanted you to sign something."

"I mean, she could have."

Her eyes narrow more. "Yeah, her naked body on your bed."

I smile at that. She's probably more pissed on her own behalf than mine, but it still feels good to have her on my side. "Are you coming back to the booth?"

"I don't know." She glances at the girl again. "I'm torn between shunning her and still trying to hook up with her."

"If you see Marty in the bathroom, tell him I said, hey."

Mya whacks me in the arm with a laugh. "I'm not having sex in the bathroom, asshole. Brian got us all rooms."

My eyebrows shoot up. "Are you serious?" Looking past her, my eyes land on Brian, still wearing his suit but definitely more drunk than I've ever seen him. "What's going on with him tonight?"

Mya scoffs. "I just hope he stays this way for a little longer."

Clapping her on the shoulder, I nod toward the table. "I'm heading back."

"Yeah," Mya says slowly, her eyes drifting back to Tarah. "I may catch up with you later." Glancing at me, she shrugs apologetically. "She might be the devil, but she's a pretty one."

I shake my head with a laugh before stepping away from her. "Have fun."

"Oh, I plan to." She gives me a suggestive wiggle of her eyebrows before walking past me, and I don't bother looking back again. Let Mya be the one to find out how *bold* she supposedly is.

When I walk back to the table, the guys have clearly gotten another round. Dave is laughing hard enough to make his face pink, Brady's smile looks too big to fit on his face, and Brian's button-down is opened to the middle of his chest. Even Marty has finally decided to join the rest of us.

"You guys holding up okay over here?" I ask as I slide into the booth.

"Jackson!" Dave cheers, still laughing. "I fucking love you, man."

I let out a breath of laughter and look at Brian. "Maybe it's time to cut him off."

Brian dismisses Dave with a wave of his hand. "He's fine, but now that you're here, I want to share something with you all." He looks around at each of us to make sure he has our full attention. "We're going on tour."

I look over at Dave and Marty for their reactions. Marty furrows his brow. "We are on tour."

Brian smirks. "Your *own* tour."

My eyes widen.

"We're headlining?" Brady asks, his eyes looking almost as big as mine must be.

Brian nods. "That's right. It's been in the works for a while now, but I've just finalized everything. Six weeks, twenty stops, and we're getting a fucking bus."

Whoops and hollers erupt from the table. The guys are grabbing and shaking my shoulders, but all I can do is replay Brian's words in my head. Is this really happening? Am I actually going to play guitar for a headlining band? On stage multiple nights a week with a tour bus to call home?

The grin that takes over my face is infectious. I can feel it spreading throughout my entire body. In a matter of seconds, I'm laughing and cheering along with them.

"When is this happening?" Marty asks, but he's bouncing in his seat. I have a feeling Brian could tell him tomorrow, and he'd be ready.

Brian grimaces, but it's brief. "You may have to tell your families the holidays will be quick this year. Instead of being home for a couple of weeks, you've got a couple of days."

Brady leans forward on the table. "Our current tour will finish up in the Midwest, right? Where's the next one start?"

"California."

Brady blinks. "Shit. It may not be worth going home at all. What's six more weeks?"

Marty crosses his arms. "Hell, my family isn't on speaking terms with me anyway. I'll stay and help prep."

"Look, I know this is last minute. I had most of these cities set for a few weeks now, but the last few were giving me a headache trying to book them. I ended up having to tack them on to the beginning of the tour instead of the end, but the important thing is that we got them on the books."

All the guys agree the short break will be worth it, and I do, too. It wouldn't matter when the tour was scheduled. I'd be there. There's only one sobering thought in the back of my mind, and it's that I know this will disappoint Margot. Hell, it disappoints me—the timing of it, anyway. But I can handle letting myself down a lot better than I can handle letting her down. We've been looking forward to spending the holidays together for months, and now all that time we thought we had has dwindled to a couple of days?

She'll understand.

She always understands.

But that doesn't mean she won't be disappointed. That doesn't mean she won't be at the apartment alone for part of her winter break because I was supposed to be the one there with her. That doesn't mean I'm not letting her down.

"How are we supposed to do a toast when you don't even

have a fucking drink?" Brian points to the empty spot on the table in front of me. "Someone, get this man a drink!" he yells to no one in particular.

"Yeah, I left it at the bar." I look over my shoulder, but my drink is gone. Well, not gone exactly. I find it a moment later in Tarah's hand. She looks like she might forget she's holding it soon, though. Her free hand is deep into Mya's hair while the two make out.

Good for Mya.

Turning back to the guys, I point over my shoulder with my thumb. "I'm pretty sure that's it."

Dave leans back to get a better look and chuckles. "We'll get you a new one."

Marty cranes his neck to look at the two girls, too. "Think they'd be open to—"

"No," I say with a firm shake of my head. Then I think about what he's actually asking and backpedal. "Well, maybe. But definitely not with you."

Marty grins. "You never know."

I roll my eyes and look back at Brian. "Shouldn't Mya be here for the news?"

He glances past me to his niece with no reaction to what she's doing. "She already knows."

"She does?"

Brian huffs a laugh. "I'm impressed she didn't tell you. I needed her to start designing the new merchandise for the next tour, so I had to fill her in." He looks around at all of us. "She'll probably ask you to take new photos soon. Don't give her shit. Just do it."

"Who would give her shit about that?" Dave asks as he tosses back the last of his drink.

Brian's eyes fall on me, but he says nothing.

"I did the pictures last time, didn't I?"

There's a slight lift to his lips. "Yeah, and you only cried about it twice. You're the pretty one. We need you to cooperate."

"Dave is pretty," I say as I give a slight nod to the guy next to me.

"Yeah, what the hell? I'm pretty," Dave chimes in.

Brian sighs. "You're both pretty." Brady lets out a bark of laughter, and Brian glares at him before turning back to me. "But you're younger. Don't get me wrong, you're talented. You might even be one of the best guitarists to come out of Florida after Don Felder and Tom Petty, but you're still the pretty one."

I stare at him. "You think I'm that good?"

Brian's lips lift in amusement, but I don't care. He's never complimented me like this, and I respect his opinion. "Yes, kid. You're that good."

The words knock me right in the chest. Margot has told me I'm good. Matt and Rae have told me I'm good. And the guys in the band hired me, so they obviously don't think I suck. But no one familiar with the industry has ever dished a compliment as great as the one Brian just did, and my brain doesn't know how to process it. I've never felt this way after someone compliments me. The only thing I can compare it to is what it must feel like when your dad believes in you without a shadow of a doubt. My throat is thick with an emotion I wasn't prepared to feel.

Luckily someone comes to deliver another round of drinks, and I'm able to mutter a quick, "Thanks," before downing half the glass with one sip.

48
margot

GOLDEN MORNING LIGHT shines through the windows of Matt and Braden's apartment. Matt called Rae and told her we needed to come over now if we wanted pancakes. That's all it took for us to run here barefoot, wearing whatever we slept in.

"Braden, you need to have Friday nights off more often, so you don't sleep in. Matt never makes us pancakes on Saturday mornings."

"Does Matt ever make us anything?" I ask with a laugh.

Matt's eyes widen as he sets plates on the kitchen counter for us. "Wow, Margot. I hand you the love of your life on a silver platter, and this is how you thank me?"

Rae rolls her eyes before saying in a low voice, "If you and Jackson ever get married, I hope you're ready for his speech."

I shake my head, amused.

Matt spins around like he forgot something important. "Actually, I handed you Braden on a silver platter, too. So, you should be thanking me for the love of your life *and* the pancakes."

My eyes jump to Braden just quick enough to catch him grimace before he laughs to himself and flips another pancake.

Before I can stop myself, I open my mouth. "Aw, come on. Braden is good for more than just pancakes."

Braden looks over his shoulder at me and winks.

Rae sighs. "I'm telling you, Braden, one day you're going to make *the best* husband. I wish I had more single friends to set you up with."

He shrugs. "That's okay. I'm not really looking to date right now." He looks over his shoulder at Rae with a small smile, but his eyes quickly jump to me before he turns back to cooking.

Matt slides into the barstool next to Rae. "He means it, too. I've seen him turn down the opportunity more than once."

Braden shoots him a glare. "They weren't my type."

Matt huffs and mutters to Rae, "I'm starting to think no one is his type."

Braden shrugs. "I'm sure she's out there."

"She definitely is," I say as I look down at my phone on the counter. There's a new notification from the American Thieves account, so I tap on it to find a picture of the guys all sitting in a big, round booth together at some type of bar or restaurant. They all have huge smiles plastered on their faces, and there are plenty of empty shot and drink glasses in front of them. I read the caption.

Thanks for a great night, Lexington. You gave us more than one reason to celebrate!

They certainly look like they were celebrating something. I barely recognize Brian with his shirt unbuttoned and his hair a mess.

Braden sets a plate of pancakes in front of me, and I glance up to smile and thank him. He returns the gesture before turning back to the stove. Rae and Matt have started debating something about Thanksgiving, so I go ahead and tap on the band's tagged photos. They're usually just shots of the stage or pictures of groups of friends at the shows, but I like looking at them. It's fun to see people enjoying their music.

I pause when I look at the first thumbnail. It's not a picture from their show last night. It's a picture from what looks to be the same bar they were sitting in for the other photo. I tap on the image to make it bigger and blink. The photo is of a blonde girl in a leather jacket pressed against Jackson with his back to the bar. Her hands are in his hair, and even though they aren't kissing, her face is only inches from his. He's staring at her intently, but I can't figure out if it's because he's pissed off or turned on. Nothing in his body language is pushing her away, but he doesn't look like he's pulling her closer either.

There's a second picture with it, so I quickly swipe to see. It's just them again, almost in the same position, but now it looks like she's whispering something in his ear. Her hands have moved from his hair to his waist. I have to zoom in when my eyes land on her fingers because they're completely tucked into the waistline of his pants.

There are only the two pictures, but I keep swiping back and forth between them like I might have missed something the first five times. I'm trying not to jump to conclusions, but this doesn't look good. My heart pounds in my chest like a battle drum and sweat prickles my forehead. Then I read the caption.

I was lucky enough to score tickets to see Crooner Sins and American Thieves last night! I guess you could say I was lucky enough to score in other ways, too . . .

There's a wink emoji followed by a black heart, and the whole thing makes me feel sick.

"What do you think, Margot?" Rae asks, and I tear my eyes away from the screen.

"Think about what?"

Her eyebrows furrow slightly, but she says, "Matt coming home with us for Thanksgiving? This way he can meet my parents while we're there."

"Oh." I swallow. "Um, yeah. I think that would be great."

Rae looks back at Matt. "See, it would be great."

Slowly getting to my feet, I try to calm my racing heart. "I'm sorry. I have to call Jackson. I'll be right back."

"Everything okay?" Rae asks behind me as I hurry toward the door.

"Yeah!" I call out over my shoulder.

As soon as I'm safely in the hallway and peering eyes are all behind closed doors, I feel the hot threat of tears. It's like I've stepped into some alternate reality where Jackson might not be the person I thought he was, and I hate this heart-sinking feeling making my palms sweat.

Rushing into my apartment, I'm able to make it to my bedroom before the first tear falls. I quickly wipe it away, but I pull up the post again, screenshotting both pictures like they might disappear any minute.

Now that I'm alone, I try to study the pictures more closely. I zoom in enough to see her black nail polish poking through strands of his hair as she looks like she's thirty seconds away from kissing him. I study the set of his jaw and wonder if he's struggling to hold back because he wants her. Is he staring at her intently because he's ten seconds away from saying "fuck it" and giving in to the temptation?

I click on the girl's profile only to have the rest of her pictures feel like a punch to the chest. She's gorgeous. And not in an underrated, quiet way. She's stunning, and she poses in these pictures like she *knows* she's stunning. I bet she could seduce anyone. So, the question is . . . did she?

Part of me doesn't want to know. I'm not sure I'm ready to confirm anything. But a larger, louder part of me needs to know if something happened. Well, from the looks of things, something probably did. Now it's just a matter of how much or how little. How much am I willing to forgive?

With shaking hands, I let out a breath and press the call button next to Jackson's name.

49
jackson

I GROAN as the annoying buzz wakes me up too soon and feel around for my phone, determined not to lift my head if I don't have to. I swear to God, if Brian or Dave wants us up before checkout for whatever reason, I'm going to tell them to fuck off.

Unsuccessful, I lift my head and wince at the light shining through the crack in the curtains. It takes me a minute for my eyes to adjust, but then I see the lit-up screen in the middle of the bed.

It's only when I see Margot's name and photo that I feel more awake. Propping myself up on my elbow, I reach over for the phone and swipe to answer.

"Hey. Everything okay?" My voice is rough with sleep.

She's quiet on the other end of the phone.

"Margot? What's wrong?"

There's another pause, and then she says, "Did something happen last night?"

"Last night?" I ask, my palm rubbing against my forehead like it will somehow clear away the fog in my brain. "We played in Lexington."

"Did you do anything else?" she asks, her voice quiet.

"We went out after, but you know we do that sometimes."

"Yeah, I know." Another hesitation. "But did anything happen while you were out?"

I frown as I try to recall the night before. "Uh, Brian wanted to celebrate, so he got everyone shots. I think it's the first time I've seen Brian drunk."

"Were you drunk?"

I frown. "I was by the end of the night, but the hotel is within walking distance. What's with all the questions?"

"You're staying in a hotel?"

"Yeah, I told you, Brian wanted to—"

"Is anyone with you?"

I look around the room like she might know something I don't. "Uh, no. Why would someone be with me?"

Margot lets out a breath on the other end of the phone, and I can't tell if she's growing frustrated with me or if it was a sigh of relief. "Okay."

"Margot, can you just tell me what's on your mind? All these questions are making my head hurt."

She pauses for another beat. "You were with a girl last night. I thought she might still be there."

I let out a laugh. "What?"

Margot speaks slowly. "Do you remember doing anything with a girl last night?"

I shake my head. "No, because I didn't do anything with a girl last night."

There's a sniffle on the other end of the phone, and I sit up straight. "Are you crying?"

Ignoring my question, she takes a steadying breath. "Can you just look at the band's Instagram?"

"Yeah, hold on." What the hell could make her this upset? I put her on speaker so I can make sure she's not actually crying while I open the app. There's a picture of all of us sitting in the booth last night that I vaguely remember taking toward the end of the night. Amazingly, none of us look as sloppy as we probably were. "I see the picture of us from last night, but I don't understand why you're—"

"Go to the tagged pictures."

I do as she says, and the sinking realization hits me as soon as my eyes fall to Tarah's unmistakable blonde hair and black leather jacket. Even from a distance it looks bad, but I go ahead and tap on the image to enlarge it anyway. "Fuck."

There's another sniffle, but her voice is surprisingly steady when she says a curt, "Yup."

I zoom in. Goddamn it. She was all over me.

"Remember now?" Margot asks, snapping me out of my daze.

"I didn't forget. This was nothing, Margot. I was with her for all of five minutes, and I turned her down."

"Yeah, she looks devastated," she says flatly. "Sounds it, too. Did you read the caption?"

My eyes jump to the blatant lie under the picture, and my anger spikes. "What the fuck? The only person she might have gotten lucky with last night was Mya."

She forces a bitter laugh. "Right."

Taking the phone off speaker, I hold it to my ear. "I'm serious. You can ask Mya about it if you want to."

"I don't want to ask Mya, Jackson. I'm asking you."

The bite in her voice makes me freeze. It's the first time I've heard her anger slip through. "Wait, wait, wait," I say, shaking my head. "Do you really think I'd cheat on you?"

She sighs, and I hate the defeat in it. "I think most guys in your position might."

My jaw ticks. "That's not what I'm asking."

She lets out a huff. "I don't know! I never thought I'd see pictures of you like this either, but here we are. And you didn't even think it was worth mentioning. What else hasn't been worth mentioning?"

"Nothing!" I run a hand over my face. This can't be fucking happening. "Look, she was a fan who got too close. I was trying to let her down easy. I never know who the fuck anyone is. I don't know if they work for a label, and I don't know if they have a blog with millions of subscribers. The last thing I need is for some story getting out about what an asshole I am, but I would never cheat on you."

There's another fucking pause, and her silence is as sharp as a blade.

"Margot."

"Okay," she finally says, her voice coming out raspy and whisper-like.

"I said nothing because it *was* nothing."

"Okay," she says again.

Damn it. I wish I could see her. I wish I could look her in the eyes and see what she's feeling right now. If only I had just told her how I fucking felt when we were in New York. Maybe then she'd be more reassured. Maybe then she'd see this for what it is.

"Margot."

"I don't know what you want me to say, Jackson. I believe you. Or at the very least, I want to believe you."

"You have to believe me."

There's a faint scoff on the other end of the line.

"You have to believe me because it's the truth."

"There's truth in the pictures, too." Her voice is quiet, like admitting that fact was something she didn't want to do.

She's going to make herself miserable over this. "Stop looking at the pictures."

"How did you—"

"Because you're going to obsess over this, and it meant

nothing. Nothing happened. I'll tell Mya to remove the tag when I see her later."

"The pictures aren't the problem, Jackson. It's what you're doing in them." Her sharp tone is back, and I know I've said the wrong thing.

"I'm not doing anything in them!"

"You're not exactly doing anything to stop it either!" she throws back. "How far did it go? What did she have to do for you to stop it? Did she kiss your neck? Did she reach her hand further into your pants? How far has it gone with other fans you wanted to 'let down easy?'"

My heart drums in my chest. I don't think we've ever fought like this. We've bickered, sure. But we've never done this, and I fucking hate it. I've let her down and there's nothing I can do to fix it. My head pounds.

"Margot," I say, my voice coming out more tired than I feel. "This is the first time something like this has happened, and I promise you, the worst of it is in those photos." She's quiet on the other end, so I keep going. "You know, I don't think of you less while I'm away. I think of you more. I know touring is my dream, but it doesn't feel like my goals are just for me anymore—and it doesn't feel like my goals are just about music anymore. You've made me see the bigger picture."

Another small sniffle cracks my chest. "And where do I fit into this bigger picture?"

"Wherever you want. Take up the whole damn thing for all I care. Just be in it."

She forces a laugh.

"I'm serious. All that matters is that you're in it. But for the love of God, please don't ask me to become a fucking accountant."

She laughs again, and this one sounds more natural. "You're a rockstar, Jackson. There's no pencil pushing in your future. You'd die."

"I might." I breathe a little more easily. "But if it made you happy, I'd give it a try."

She sighs, and it sounds like she's finally lying down or getting a little more comfortable. "I'd never ask you to do that."

"I know you wouldn't." It's one of the things I love about her.

There's a pounding on the hotel door, and I wince, feeling it in my brain. Dave's voice hollers through the cracks. "Rise and shine, motherfucker!"

I let out a groan, and there's another light laugh from Margot on the other end of the phone.

"Duty calls," I say as I force myself out of bed. Holding the phone in the crook of my neck, I pull on my pants. "Are we okay?"

The beat of silence that follows has me sitting on the edge of the bed.

Finally, she says, "I don't know. I want to be, but I don't know."

"Please don't let it mess with your head. I would never do something like that."

"I'll try." Before I have the chance to say anything else, Dave bangs on my door again, and she adds, "Go. We'll talk more later."

I glare at the door wishing Dave could fuck off. "Yeah, I guess I should go before he barges in here. Text me, okay?"

"Yeah. Okay."

We exchange goodbyes, and as soon as she hangs up, I fall back on the bed and let out a breath. I feel like I just dodged a bullet. I can't believe Tarah had her friend taking pictures. Who knows, that could have been her plan all along. Maybe she just wanted to get the shot. Maybe that's why she came on to me so fast.

Dave knocks again followed by, "Jackson, wake the fuck up."

"I'm up. I'm up." I get to my feet and rub both hands over my face in a desperate attempt to shake the multiple hangovers weighing me down.

50
margot

THE DOOR to our apartment opens in the distance, and I know my moment of solitude is over. To be fair, I've been lying on my bed and staring at the ceiling since I hung up the phone almost an hour ago. I didn't trust myself to act like nothing was wrong around Matt and Braden, and I didn't want to be around either of them because they both make me think of Jackson in their own way.

Rae pokes her head into my cracked bedroom door. "Hey, you disappeared. Everything okay?"

I turn my head to look at her but don't get up. "I'm not sure how to answer that question."

She pushes open the door and takes a seat on the edge of my bed. "Is it something with Jackson? You said you needed to call him, right?"

"Yeah." The word comes out as a sigh, and I reach for my phone and unlock it. Holding it out to her, I show her the post that's still front and center on my screen because I've been staring at it every few minutes.

Her eyes widen, and she looks from the phone to me before

pulling it out of my hand to get a closer look. "What did he say?" she immediately demands, all business.

"That it was nothing."

Her eyebrows shoot up. "I wouldn't say it looks like *nothing*." She zooms in, squinting to get a closer look. "Are her hands in his pants?"

Covering my face with both hands, I let out a groan. "I'm so stupid."

"Hey, you are not stupid. This is . . . surprising."

Dragging my fingers down my face, I look over at her to find her still analyzing the evidence. "This is crazy though, right? I'm crazy to date a guy in a rock band."

Rae sets the phone down, her expression softening. "I mean, maybe a little crazy. But so is he. It's part of what makes you two great together."

I pick up the phone and investigate the two photos for the millionth time.

"He really said it was nothing?"

I frown. "Yeah."

"And you believe him?"

Letting out a sigh, I turn the phone down and set it on my stomach, clasping it in my hands like a diary. "I think I might." I shake my head. "I don't know what to think. The asshole had me laughing by the end of the call when he was supposed to be feeling my wrath."

Rae arches an eyebrow. "How did he manage that?"

I shrug. "Something about becoming an accountant."

She laughs. "He would die."

A small smile comes to my lips. "That's what I said."

She watches me carefully. "Well, if you believe him, is he forgiven?"

My brows pinch as I consider her question. With a sigh, I force myself to sit upright. "If I believe him, there's nothing to forgive."

Sitting more fully on my bed, Rae pulls her knees to her chest and rests her chin on them. "But you're still upset."

It's not a question, and something about her observation pulls my tears back to the surface. I had done so well, holding back until I was off the phone with Jackson. I let myself cry when I was lying in my room alone, but even that didn't last long. Now, having Rae look at me with concern laced in her features, I can't hold it in anymore.

It only takes half a second for her to register my crumpling face, her eyes widening. "Hey, hey, hey." She moves closer so we're side by side and wraps her arm around me. "If he said it was nothing, I'm sure it was. Jackson is crazy about you."

I itch my nose and wipe away a falling tear. "Yeah, but he wouldn't have told me about this if I never saw those photos. Now all I can think about is what else he hasn't mentioned. What else has happened that he dismissed as being nothing?"

Rae's silence makes me look over at her.

"What would you do?" I ask.

"Oh, I'd murder Matt." When I laugh, she goes on to say, "But Matt isn't in an up-and-coming band gaining more and more attention. This is kind of an occupational hazard, isn't it?"

Looking up, I wipe beneath my eyes. "Yeah. It's one of the reasons I didn't want to date him." I shake my head. "I knew I'd end up here, crying over him and feeling like an idiot. I knew long distance was a bad idea, but he can be so damn convincing."

"Because he's crazy about you."

I give her a leveling look, and she laughs.

"He is! He can be so convincing because he cares about you *so much.*"

I scoff. "He has a funny way of showing it." I gesture to my phone lying on my bed. The screen is dark, but the photos will be there as soon as I unlock it, ready for me to torture myself all over again.

Rae rubs my back. "Don't look at those pictures again. Block her if you have to. Delete whatever screenshots you have. Jackson is honest about everything. You've caught him in one small lie of omission, and if you believe him when he says nothing happened, then that's it, right?"

I nod but then turn to face her. "But what if this was a mistake? What if he has no business having a girlfriend right now? And what if I have no business dating someone with his lifestyle?"

Rae's eyes search mine, her face sobering. "Is that really how you feel?"

"It was in the beginning."

"And now?"

I grimace. "I don't know."

Rae's eyebrows shoot up, and she blows out a breath. "Well, there's no rush. This is all too fresh for you to make any big decisions based on it. Sleep on it and try to get back into your normal routine with him. See how you feel after a few days."

I nod and take a deep breath.

She watches me, those green eyes scrutinizing. "I don't think you want to break up with Jackson." Her words come out slow and careful.

Just hearing it out loud has my chest tightening. "I don't," I say quickly. "But I don't like this feeling—like I shouldn't trust him as much as I have."

Rae frowns. "I get that."

"I'm sorry I ditched breakfast."

She waves off my concern. "Don't worry about it. Are you hungry? Braden kept your pancakes on the warmer."

"He did?"

She nods and points over her shoulder with her thumb. "Yeah, I can go get them for you if you want."

I wipe my eyes again for good measure. "That would be great. Thank you."

She pats my leg before getting to her feet. "I'll be right back."

Before she leaves, I stop her. "Rae?"

She turns.

"Thank you. And tell Braden thanks, too."

She smiles softly. "I will. Try to think happy thoughts. I'll be back soon."

"I'll try," I say with a light laugh.

As soon as she's gone, I let my head fall into my hands. I don't want to let this get to me, but I can't stop thinking about it. I can't stop thinking about his night and all the other possible nights he didn't feel the need to tell me about.

51
jackson

IT'S BEEN a few days since Margot called, but we've texted. We're back into our normal routine for the most part, but it's almost impossible to read through her messages to know how she's feeling. She hasn't brought up the pictures again, and neither have I because I don't want her to dwell on it.

Mya at least removed the tag, so our band's social media is free of it. I guess she and Tarah ended up going their separate ways later that night. They didn't even exchange numbers.

Completely insignificant.

Maybe Margot can see that now. Maybe that's why she hasn't brought it up again.

We had back-to-back shows over the weekend, and then yesterday we were on the road all day. I wanted to call her then, but there's no privacy when we're moving. I'll have to wait until we pull off somewhere and have some down time where I can sit outside and try to figure out what she's actually feeling.

Pulling out my phone, I check our messages to see where we left off. She texted me goodnight around eleven, but we haven't talked yet today. I scroll up, skimming over our back and forth the past few days. Something feels off about it. Her responses are less playful—less . . . Margot. I can't tell what she needs from me. Does she need me to let this go or should I make her talk about it? If I could fucking see her, I'd know. But like this? I can't tell if she's busy and quietly trying to move on from what happened, or if she's dwelling on it and withdrawing in on herself.

Fuck, it's probably the second.

My thumb hovers over the screen as I try to figure out what to say, but then Mya plops down on the couch next to me. "Did you tell Margot about the next tour?"

Dropping my phone on the couch, I rub my hand over my face before my fingers find the strings of my guitar again. I'll have to confront her about this later. "Not yet."

She tilts her head and gives me a funny look. Mya doesn't know about my last conversation with Margot. All she knows is that I asked her to remove those pictures. Her reaction was to mutter something about Tarah's ability to make something out of nothing, and then she joked about how *not* kissing me apparently gave more bragging rights than feeling Mya up in the corner of the bar. "You haven't?"

I shake my head and keep playing. I'm not sure I want to disclose my situation with Margot. If I've learned anything about Mya, it's that she meddles, and her advice usually fucks with my head.

She turns sideways on the couch and rests her chin on her knees. "But aren't you excited?"

I nod. "Very."

Her eyes narrow slightly, and I do my best to ignore it. "But you think she won't be?"

My fingers pause, hovering over the strings. "I think she'll have mixed feelings about it." I know Margot will be happy for me, but I also know she isn't thrilled about my life on tour right now. Plus, as exciting as the tour is, it's still cutting my time with her over the holidays. Even if those pictures with Tarah never happened, Margot still would have been disappointed to some extent.

She frowns. "Trouble in paradise?"

I get back to playing. "I don't want to talk about it." The words come out with the force of a slammed door, so I quickly add, "How's the new merchandise coming along?"

There's a slight pause like she's debating pushing the topic further. I'm relieved when she settles on saying, "Good. Want to see?"

I nod and Mya moves closer, holding up her tablet to show me a new design for American Thieves. With one glance, I can tell she's changing up the vibe. Everything about the design looks vintage. The coloring has a faded hue, and the retro font and record player icon look like they could be something out of the seventies.

She grimaces. "You hate it, don't you?"

I blink and shake my head. "Not at all." Setting down my guitar, I reach for the tablet so I can get a better look. "Why such a big change?"

She takes a breath like she's rehearsed this pitch before. "Well, most of our merch gets sold to women. I have a few designs in there with the old font and logo—with some minor adjustments, of course. The guys can still buy that stuff if they'd like, but I think a lot of them will go for the newer designs, too. Anyway, women are our main demographic, and a lot of old styles are coming back in a big way. I think they'd eat this shit up."

I huff a laugh. "I mean, I think it's cool."

"Yeah?" She smiles and there's a hint of relief behind it.

"Have you showed it to the guys?"

Mya reaches for her tablet. "Before you? No way." She closes the file and opens another one. This one has the same retro feel but it's a dripping cassette tape. "What about this one?"

I nod. "I might like that one even more."

She grins. "Thanks, Lover Boy."

The nickname hits different this time, but I give her a tight-lipped smile. "Anything else?"

She swipes again. "Well, I had to bring back the floral print, but I made some slight modifications. These will be unique for the tour. Special edition."

"Right," I say with a light laugh, but my heart isn't in it.

Mya glances at me before getting back to work on her tablet. She moves a few things around and flips between different designs. Some look complete while others still look more like ideas than actual merchandise. "Are you sure you don't want to talk about what's bothering you?" She gives me a sideways glance but continues to keep herself busy.

I scratch the side of my head. "I wish I could tell you."

This time she looks over at me. "You could try."

I should keep my mouth shut, but the way she's looking at me gets past every barrier. It's because she cares. Her advice might be terrible, and she might stick her nose in things she shouldn't, but she does it because she genuinely cares and wants to help. That fact alone has my defenses waning.

"It's more of a gut feeling." I shrug. "I think something is off with her."

"With Margot?"

I nod. "You know, she didn't want to date me."

"Smart girl."

I nudge her with my shoulder, and she laughs. "She said I wouldn't want to be tied down while I was on tour. She figured I'd be too tempted."

Mya nods. "Valid concern." I shoot her a look, and she adds, "I'm not saying you'd do anything, but look in the mirror, babe. You might not be able to get every girl who walks through the door, but you could get a lot of them. A lot, a lot."

"Yeah. Thanks," I mutter.

"So, what made her change her mind?" She's turned to face me on the small couch now, giving me her undivided attention.

Blowing out a breath, I shake my head. "No idea. I didn't think she'd go for it, but she did. And ever since, I've worked hard to never give her a reason to doubt that decision."

Mya's eyes widen. "But the pictures with Tarah."

Pressing my lips together, I nod. "But the pictures with Tarah."

"Shit." The sharp word bites through the air around us. "That bitch."

Something between a huff and a laugh leaves me. I guess this is why I always end up spilling my secrets to Mya. It feels good to have someone on my side.

She gasps. "She doesn't think you cheated on her, does she?"

I weigh my head from side to side. "I don't think so, but either way, there are cracks in the foundation now. I need to call her."

"Call her."

I let out a laugh. "Not in the fucking RV."

Mya looks around like she forgot we were traveling in tight quarters with four other guys. "Where's our next stop? Austin?"

"Yup."

"Call her then."

As much as I get a kick out of Mya's urgency, I can't help feeling a sense of dread. "Yeah," I say, wiping my hand over my mouth as I try to shake the feeling. "That's the plan."

52
margot

KARAH POKES her head into my office. "You're still here?"

"Yeah." I let out a sigh, barely glancing at her from my computer screen before my fingers keep moving over the keys. "I'm still here."

"Hmm."

I have no idea what type of connotation comes with that sound, but I have a feeling her "hmm" isn't a celebration of how hard I'm working. Forcing a breath, I push back from my desk and turn my chair to look at her. "Heading home?"

"Yes," she says with a slow nod. "That's what people do after . . ." She glances down at her watch. "Almost ten hours."

"I know. I'll go home soon. I just want to finish up this piece on the farmer's market."

She arches an eyebrow. "You mean the one due next week?"

"Yeah. I really like my angle with it, but you'll have to let me know what you think."

She crosses her arms and leans against the doorway. "I can already tell you it's great. All your work has been great this week. Ahead of schedule, thorough, unique, and polished. You've barely had any revisions since the bookstore—which was phenomenal. Just . . ." She eyes me with concern. "Take care of yourself."

I nod. "Don't worry. I am."

"Okay," she says, but the tone of caution still lingers. "Lock up when you leave, okay?"

"Will do. Have a good night, Karah."

She gives me a tight-lipped smile like she'd like to say more, but I don't care. I know I've been working too much. In the span of the last week, I've become a full-blown workaholic with insomnia. Going home just means I'll be left to my own devices, and all I do is make myself miserable. Everything at my apartment—including most of the people—reminds me of Jackson. If Rae is home, it's a little easier to breathe, but I hate being there alone. I end up sitting on the couch and stalking the band's social media account and searching hashtags. Jackson has his own account, but he never posts. I think his last upload is from when he was still in high school, so the only way to get up-to-date on *anything* is through the band's page.

Well, that or I could just talk to him, but that's been painful, too. The texts that used to light up my day now add to the increasing pressure in my chest. Everything feels like a lie. Not necessarily on his end, but on mine. It feels like a lie to go back to talking the way we were before even though I'm still affected by what happened. It feels like a lie to ask him about his day when all I really care about is the night before. It feels like a lie to flirt with him when all I do is wonder who else might have whispered those things in his ear lately.

It feels like a lie to love him. A lie to laugh with him. And a lie to act like I'm not doubting everything.

This is why I didn't want to date him. I didn't want to turn into a paranoid mess, and that's exactly what I've become. I want to trust him completely. I want to listen to him talk about his day without reading between the lines I've created with my own insecurities. This isn't healthy—it can't be. It can't be right to comb through details like I'm some type of detective. But every time I try to let go of my fear, those pictures of Jackson with that girl flash in my mind like a damn neon sign. Reminding me that even when the water is calm, there will always be sharks.

I jolt when my phone starts buzzing on the desk. Seeing Jackson's name only adds to my heightened state. My heart pounds in my chest, and I actually consider not answering for a moment. We haven't talked on the phone since I confronted him a few days ago, and now it's like even this is tainted. Seeing him call always made me happy—even if I was panicking a little on the inside. Now, seeing his name just feels heavy. I've been distant lately, and he knows it. This will be him calling me out, I'm sure of it.

Forcing a breath, I make sure to smile before answering because they say you can hear a smile in someone's voice.

Another lie.

"Hey!" I say, sounding a little too excited.

He sounds like he's getting comfortable somewhere. "Hey, are you busy?" His voice melts something inside of me. I missed hearing it these past few days. His voice is grounding—it always has been. Something about the deep warmness to it relaxes my nerves and quiets my mind in a way nothing else does.

"Not really." I still scroll a little on my computer even though multitasking with Jackson on the phone is hopeless. "I was just finishing up some work."

"You're at the office?"

I nod even though he can't see me. "I am. Where are you?" I hope my voice doesn't sound accusing. Everything feels off with me lately. Just in case, I quickly add, "I know you don't usually like to talk when you're in the RV."

"Margot, it's late."

Brushing off his concern, I say, "I'm almost done."

He's quiet for a moment. "Do they make you stay this late?"

My stomach twists. For once, I wish he didn't know me as well as he does. He can tell I'm running from my feelings, staying in constant motion so they can't catch up with me. With a sigh, I slump in my chair. "They do not."

Another beat of silence. "But you're not home because?"

"Because . . ." I look up at the ceiling like there might be a teleprompter there to tell me what I should say. My lips twist because I can feel it happening. I can feel the emotions closing in, and there's nowhere left for me to run. Intentional or not, Jackson has once again backed me into a corner. I cycle through all the things he might want to hear in response to that question, but none of them are the truth—not the whole truth anyway. I could say I'm working late because I miss him, but there's more to it than that. Plus, if I know anything about Jackson, I know he wants me unfiltered. Letting out a breath, I resign and say what's on my mind. "Because I don't like being there lately."

"Do you want to tell me why?"

"Not really."

"Margot." When he says my name again, something inside me wanes. I'm no match for him. I never have been.

I groan. "I know. I'm sorry. It's just that when I'm home, I think about you more than when I'm at work."

There's a shuffle like he's sitting up. "And that's a bad thing?"

"Sort of?" I grimace as I say the words. Letting my face fall into my hand, I level with him. "I just can't get it out of my head, and I don't know how to fix it. I feel stuck, and there's no good outlet for everything I'm feeling."

"I'm a good outlet."

My chest tightens. "No, you're not. Not for this."

There's another slight pause, and my heart races faster for every beat of silence. "Because I'm the problem," he says.

It's not a question, but I jump to answer him anyway. "No, Jackson. You're not. I promise you're not. I'm just . . ." I puff out my cheeks. "I'm just angry. I know it's not your fault—not really, so all that anger just gets directed back at me."

"What are you mad at yourself for?"

My eyes burn, and I bite the inside of my cheek to help keep the tears at bay. I feel like my list has grown too long over the past week. *Falling for you* is the first thing that comes to mind, but I know I can't say that. Now isn't the time. "I'm having trouble letting go of this, and it's making me feel like an idiot. I knew you being on the road would mess with my head, but I was doing so well with it before this. Now it's all I can think about, and I feel like I should have known better than to put myself in this position."

"This position . . . as my girlfriend?"

I grimace. "Maybe."

He sucks in air through his teeth on the other end. "Ouch."

I bite my lip. "Maybe that came out wrong. See, this is why I shouldn't share what I'm feeling. I'm not good at this. I shouldn't have said that."

His voice is low on the other end. "No, it's fine. You meant it. I'm glad you said it."

My thoughts tumble out too fast for me to stop them. "It's just that I knew this would happen. I knew I'd start to feel like this eventually. You're a rockstar, Jackson. You practically have whatever you want at your fingertips. I'm trying to trust you. I'm trying so hard, but I'm miserable like this. I just feel so stupid. We're young, and maybe it was dumb to think we'd beat the odds—that we'd be different."

"We are different." The command in his voice shuts me up.

My eyes burn. "Are we?"

"I want us to be."

I can feel my heartbeat drumming throughout my entire body, and I'm starting to feel nauseous. I can feel us teetering on the edge of dangerous territory, and I hate it. I hate everything about this. Pulling my knees to my chest, I sit huddled in my office chair. My voice comes out as small as I feel when I say, "Me too, but I don't know if it's enough."

Jackson curses under his breath, and I lose it. He didn't sound angry, but I think he realized my doubts, and that thought alone breaks me.

For the past week, I've been worried this isn't working—terrified even. What if I never get over this? What if I never feel like I can trust him again? The logical part of my brain *knows* I should trust him, but the irrational, emotional part of my brain drowns out the logic until it's barely a whisper in the back of my mind, desperately trying to make me see reason.

The tears spill from my eyes, and all I can do is desperately try to control my breathing, so I don't end up sobbing into the phone. How did this conversation get here? I wanted to tell him how I'm feeling. I wanted him to understand why I've been distant. I wanted to be honest with myself and to lighten the weight that's been slowly crushing my chest a little more each day. I didn't mean for this to turn into a conversation about whether we should stay together, but that's what it feels like. It feels like I'm either prioritizing him or prioritizing me, and I don't know when we stopped being on the same side.

53
jackson

MY HEAD FALLS against my clenched fist as I sit on the edge of the bed. I should have called her sooner. Fuck privacy. She needed me, and I let her marinate with this bullshit for too long. Lifting my head, I force my hand to open. My entire body holds too much tension. I could self-combust. Since when is us wanting to be together not enough? My brain can't even comprehend that type of math.

"It's enough if you let it be enough," I finally say, and then wait with bated breath for her response.

She's quiet, and it's the loudest silence I've ever heard.

"Margot," I say, this time my voice pleading. If she wants to end this, she needs to say it. I'm not giving her the easy way out. And I'm not giving up that easily. "I only want you."

There's a sniffle on the other end of the phone, and I hate that I'm not with her. Her voice is barely a whisper when she says, "I only want you, too." I suck in a breath, finally willing to let myself breathe, but the feeling falls short when she adds, "But I can't keep feeling like this."

My heart plummets. She's already made up her mind. "Because you think I cheated on you?"

"No," she says, responding quickly. "I mean, I wasn't there, but I don't think you'd actually cheat on me—not to the extent of sleeping with someone, anyway."

My eyebrows furrow. "But you think I'd do other things?"

She takes in a shaky breath and her words come out in a rush. "No. I don't know. I just don't think I'm cut out for this. It was okay at first, but you guys keep getting bigger—which is wonderful. But it's like the bigger the band gets, the more fans you'll have, and I can't help feeling like what happened with this girl was just the beginning. It's only going to get worse."

I hate this. I hate that I can't promise her another fan will never feel like they have a right to touch me. I hate that I can't be near her *and* do what I love. I hate that I don't know how to settle her fears over the phone while I'm in fucking Texas. My hand tightens around my phone, and the words that come out of my mouth physically pain me. "I'll do anything you want me to do, you know that. But . . ." I shake my head, the disbelief of what I'm about to say crashing down on me. "For this to work, you have to trust me. If you don't trust me . . ." My words trail off, and I shake my head.

"I know."

That response might gut me more than the rest of it. Because she's not denying it, and if she doesn't trust me, there's no hope for any of this. Even if she thinks I won't cheat on her, she still doesn't trust me enough to be with me.

With a sigh, I rub my forehead to try to ease my pounding headache. It's steadily gotten worse the longer I've been on the phone with her, and part of it probably stems from the strain of keeping my emotions in check. I'm on the verge of unraveling, and I can't do that while I'm on the phone with her. I've never felt this many conflicting emotions.

My voice is thick when I finally settle on saying, "You're sure this is what you want?"

She scoffs, and there's so much sadness behind it. "No."

"Then don't do this. Just . . ." I rake my hand through my hair. "Just be with me. What do you need me to do?" Shit, this might be close to groveling.

She lets out a sigh, and she sounds tired. "Nothing. I don't want you to feel like you can't live your life with the band. I want you to jump into this with both feet. That's important to me, okay?"

"I know." She's always put my music first, but right now, I don't want to put music first. I just want her. "But I can do that and be a loyal boyfriend."

She sniffs again. "Maybe you can. But I don't think I can be the girlfriend you deserve while you do it."

"It's not you, it's me," I say dryly.

There's a light laugh on the other end, and despite everything, the corner of my mouth lifts at the sound of it. "I guess it does sound a little like that." After a pause, she adds, "I mean it, though. I love what we have," she clears her throat, "or had, I guess. I just can't keep drowning like this. I need time to figure everything out."

"How much time?"

She sniffles again but a little laugh comes with it. "Jackson."

"Days? Weeks?"

There's another laugh followed by a groan. "Can you stop being so charming while we're breaking up?" Her words stop short, and I somehow know she's crying. She has to be if saying those words hit her as hard as hearing them just hit me.

"I'll try," I say quietly, surrendering to what this is.

"Thanks." I expect her to say more, but she doesn't, and I wonder if it's because she's crying too much to talk.

My knee bounces. "I feel like I've let you down."

"You haven't." Her voice is small. "If anything, I've let you down. I'm so sorry, Jackson."

I let out a breath. "I'm sorry, too."

There's a quiet sob on the other end, and my eyes squeeze shut at the sound of it.

"Um . . ." She takes a moment to collect herself. "So, I guess that's all there is to say, right? We're breaking up?"

My jaw clenches. I don't know what to do. There's not enough time for me to figure out how I should approach this, and I can't see her to read what she's actually feeling right now. Does she want me to fight harder? Should I? Should I tell her no? Can I even do that? My head falls as my mind races. Eventually, I let out a sigh. "If you're unhappy, and you think this will make you happier, yes." I can't even bring myself to say the words *break up*. "But Margot, this isn't what I want."

Her voice is thick when she says, "I know. I'm so sorry."

We both just sit there in silence for a moment. All I can hear are her shallow breaths, and I know she's freaking out. Fuck, *I'm* freaking out, but I don't know what the fuck to do. What felt so solid a few weeks ago, somehow had cracks beneath the surface that neither of us could see. I hate it. I hate that I want to change her mind but don't know how, and even though I know she's made her decision, I can't be the one to end this call because I don't know if I'll ever get the chance to hear her voice again. So, I sit, knowing this is the closest I'll be to her for a while—maybe ever, and I can't bring myself to end it.

She doesn't say it right away, but it doesn't matter. As soon as I hear, "Bye, Jackson," I'm gutted.

"Bye, Margot." By the time her name leaves my lips, the call has already disconnected, and I wonder if she heard me at all.

Dropping my phone from my hands, I let it fall onto the floor as I flop back on the bed. What the hell just happened? Of all the ways I thought things might go with Margot, breaking up was never one of them. The thought never even crossed my mind.

There's no way this is it for us. It can't be. It feels too unfinished. If she didn't want to be with me because of me, I'd accept it. But she doesn't want to be with me because of my job. And she doesn't like my job because something happened to make her look at it differently.

Before those pictures with Tarah, Margot trusted me. Sure, the long distance sucked, but we were making it work. We had plans. She was excited to see me next month.

This *can't* be it.

I sit up straight, and an overwhelming sense of determination starts to spread through my veins. The same one I felt when I knew I needed to get her number before I left campus. It settles deep within me, and I can't explain how I know it, but I just *know* this can't be it.

I'll give her space. She asked for it, and she needs it. But I'm not ready to quit on her—not yet. I still need to give this a final shot, and she should know it.

Reaching down, I grab my phone from the floor and open my text thread with Margot. Just the sight of her name has my heart pounding in my chest. I can't imagine a world where she isn't mine. With slightly shaking hands, I text her the only thing I can think to say.

JACKSON:

I'm still yours, Margot.

Completely and totally yours.

54
margot

RAE'S VOICE carries through my closed door as she talks to me from the hallway. "Margot, you can't just stay in your room listening to 'The 1' on repeat. It's been over a week." She opens my door to find me lying in bed. It's where I've spent most of my time lately, wrapped in a blanket and questioning my decisions.

I pull the blanket up over my head, hiding from her. "To be fair, this was one of my favorite songs before we broke up. It just hits different now." I peek out from under the heavy material. "Oh, put on 'Hits Different.' That's a good breakup song, too."

Rae scoffs. "Come on," she says as she tugs at the blanket.

I grip it tighter. "I'm fine! I just don't want to do anything." It's a lie. I am definitely not fine, and the thought of doing anything at all has me on the verge of tears every time I try.

She lets out a huff and sits on the edge of the bed. "You are not fine!" I somehow know she has exasperated hands in the air without looking. "You've barely eaten, you've called out of work, and when was the last time you took a shower?" She tries to pull the blanket off me again, so this time I pull it down to glare at her. "I showered the day before yesterday."

She raises her eyebrows like she's actually impressed by that before letting out a sigh. "Look, I know this breakup is hard—really hard, but I'm worried about you. I've never seen you this miserable."

To be fair, I was almost this miserable before we broke up, too. It just feels more acceptable not to hide it now. Hugging my blanket tighter, my eyes well with tears. It's so easy for me to cry these days. You'd think my body would have run dry at some point, but nope. The waterworks are always ready and standing by. "Why am I like this?" I whisper, and Rae goes out of focus as my tears blur my vision.

She frowns, her expression softening. "You can't be with someone you don't trust."

"But why is it so hard for me to trust him?"

She takes in a breath as she considers my question. When she puffs out her cheeks and blows the air out, her shoulders drop. "I don't know. I think it's hard to trust most people in his position. I've been trying to imagine Matt in his shoes, and I honestly don't know if I could do it. I'd like to think I could, but I don't know."

"You're lucky Matt never learned how to play those drums," I say with a slight smile.

She laughs. "Could you imagine?" She shakes her head. "I can't picture Matt as a rockstar."

My smile falls slightly. "Jackson is already a rockstar."

She nods slowly. "Yeah. I think he was born to be one." Worry flashes in her expression. "Have you seen the band's recent posts?"

I shake my head. "I had to block the account. I just kept going back to it." I'll never be able to move forward if I'm hung up on every little thing he's doing.

"Well, just to warn you, they announced their first headlining tour." She watches carefully for my reaction, but all I can do is blink.

"They did?"

"Yeah. I don't know much about it, but that's pretty big news, right?"

I sit up, hugging my blanket to my chest. "Huge." My fingers grip the fabric tight enough to make it slightly painful. "Do I text him and congratulate him?"

Her eyebrows lift. "Have you two been talking?"

"No. He never texted me back." My voice is small, and I hate that I'm so affected by that fact.

She gives me a sympathetic smile, but I can't help feeling pity from it. "Then probably not."

"You're right," I say quietly. "It just feels weird not to acknowledge it. Good for them, though. They deserve to headline." I reach for my phone and quickly find my last text with Jackson. It doesn't take long to find, considering I haven't messaged anyone but Rae and Karah to let her know I couldn't come into work twice.

> JACKSON:
> I'm still yours, Margot.
>
> Completely and totally yours.
>
> MARGOT:
> I never wanted this to happen. I'm so sorry.

Hot tears threaten to fall at the sight of those words. Maybe I should have said more, but I know if he were to text me the same thing now, I'd probably answer with the same response. What else can you say when loving someone isn't enough?

I rest my chin on the tops of my knees and stare at the lit-up screen on my bed until it goes dark.

Rae moves to sit beside me and rubs a hand on my back.

Her voice is so soft when she speaks next, I almost don't hear her. "Do you regret it?"

Everything in my heart screams *yes*, but my head holds firm with a resounding *no*. I turn my head to look at her, resting my cheek on my knees and hugging my legs a little tighter because everything hurts. "I don't know."

She brushes some of my hair away from my face. "Well, I know you don't want to hear this, but if you really want to see what life is like without him, you need to start living."

She's right. She's always right.

When I don't say anything right away, her stare turns pleading. "Come out with us tonight. The guys want to check out this new arcade bar. We don't have to stay long, and I want you there." She nudges me with her shoulder. "You won't ditch me for Donkey Kong."

I force a laugh. "Definitely will never ditch you for Donkey Kong—or any other character with a vengeance from the '80s."

She gives me a wry smile. "Your loyalty warms my heart." Sobering, she puts a hand on my arm. "Come. It'll be fun."

"And what if I'm not capable of having fun?" My voice is barely a whisper.

She shrugs. "Then we'll leave."

Worry creases my brow. "You're sure?"

"Of course, I am. We'll leave, cry in the car, get ice cream—whatever we need to do."

I let out a dry laugh. "Let's hope we don't have to do any of those things."

"I think you'll surprise yourself. I think once you're outside these four walls, you'll find your world feels a little bigger."

"Probably." Admitting it is hard, but I know there's truth to her words. Since meeting him, Jackson has been like an eclipse, taking up enough space to block out everything else. The dark never got to me like it is now. Now it's swallowing me whole.

Rae gets to her feet. "Take a shower, make yourself look hot, do whatever you need to do to feel a little more *you*. It's going to be okay, okay?"

"Okay," I say with a small smile.

She's about to leave, but I call her back. "Rae?"

Stopping in the doorway, she turns.

"Thank you. I love you."

She smiles. "And I love you."

She leaves, and for the first time in over a week, I feel mildly optimistic. Maybe I can do this. Maybe there's a version of me that can thrive without Jackson. Maybe I can rediscover a piece of her.

And maybe—just *maybe*—tonight will be fun.

55
jackson

WE PULLED off the road to get some food, and now we're all sitting at an outdoor picnic table, finishing up while Brian stands off in the distance having a phone call like he always does when he can get some distance from us.

Mya catches me looking at her uncle and lowers her voice. "I know what this one is about."

"Yeah?" I pop another fry into my mouth. "Care to enlighten the rest of us?"

She looks over at the guys, but the three of them are deep into their own conversation about their plans during our shortened downtime between tours. None of them are going home. They don't think it's worth the trip for less than a day, and I can't say I disagree with them.

When I look back at Mya, she's leaning toward me across the table. "I'll tell *you*, but you have to promise not to be mad."

I stop chewing. "What did you do?"

She bites her bottom lip, her green eyes sparkling in the afternoon sun. "First, a disclaimer. You know all I care about is the success of the band, and I know all *you* care about is the success of the band. Well, that and one other thing, but I won't bring her up."

"Mya." My voice comes out as a warning.

She waves her last comment away. "I know. I know. I'm not allowed to talk about her, but she's part of it. Sort of."

"Mya," I say again. Even the indirect mention of *her* feels like a stab to the chest. It's been nine days since Margot and I broke up. Nine days since I put my cards on the table and told her I'm still hers. Nine days since she answered with an apology. The whole thing has left me feeling raw. I snapped at Mya after the breakup when she mentioned her and eventually had to come clean. The other guys don't know we broke up. I can't bring myself to explain it again.

Mya takes a moment, and it looks like she's bracing herself for how I might react, which only makes my heart beat harder in my chest. I don't think I'm ready for Margot to be a part of anything just yet. I told myself I'd give her two weeks. After two weeks I'd text her. It's been killing me to give her this space, but I know she needs it. If there's any chance of getting her back, she needs time to miss me first. I take another bite of my fry and wave my hand for her to continue.

When she does finally speak, her words come out in a rush. "So, you know that song you wrote about Margot?"

I nearly choke, but even as I cough through it and shake my head, I know the heat in my ears is a dead giveaway. "I didn't write a song about Margot." Her name feels heavy on my tongue. It's probably the first time I've said it since my conversation with Mya about everything.

Mya gives me a leveling look. "Fine. You know that song you wrote about that girl you love?"

My eyes narrow. "What's your point, Mya?"

She holds my stare before shaking her head. "You know what, I'll just show you."

"Show me wha—" I stop talking as she holds out her

phone to show a video of me sitting outside the RV, softly playing and singing the song. "You filmed me?"

"Yes, I filmed you. I always film you guys for socials, but this song is good, Jackson. Really good." She points to the screen she's still holding out toward me. "And I'm not the only one who thinks so."

I look closer, noting the numbers on the side of the screen and freeze. My eyes jump back to Mya. "Over half a million people liked that video?" I can't even wrap my head around that big of a number. And for a song I whipped together in a matter of days? To be fair, most of it was already written, but I changed a few of the verses after we broke up.

She gives me a satisfied smirk now that I'm finally catching on. "And over 2.4 million views."

I blink. "What?"

She grins. "Yeah."

I shake my head in a desperate attempt to clear it. "What does this mean?"

"It means we've gained over two hundred thousand followers in the past week, and the numbers are still climbing." She looks over at Brian. "And it means that guy's phone has been ringing off the hook with people asking when the song will be released."

I force a laugh. "Released? I don't even know if it's finished."

She steals one of my fries. "Well, you better finish it because he's going to want the band in the studio as soon as possible so he can drop this single."

Even though I can hear the words she's saying, none of it makes sense. "He wants to make it a single?"

"He'd be stupid not to. It's what the people want."

I shake my head. "The people."

She chuckles. "Yes. At least half a million of them. And that's after only hearing an acoustic segment of the song. Can you imagine how many people will love it once the guys get in on it?"

Brady looks over at us, finally pulled from whatever he was talking about with Marty and Dave. "In on what?"

"Jackson's song," Mya says. "A really good one. It's about love and heartache, and it has a grit to it that keeps the American Thieves sound. He'll play it for you. He's a viral sensation."

Dave cocks an eyebrow, amusement shaping his features. "Oh, yeah?"

It's hard for me to fight my own smile when I say, "I'll play it for you later apparently."

Dave winks. "I'm looking forward to it."

Brian hangs up the phone and heads over to us. He claps his hands together. "Okay, we need to get into the studio as soon as possible." He looks at Mya. "You filled them in?"

She bobs her head from side to side. "More or less. Jackson knows everything, and the other guys know we need to record something Jackson wrote."

Brian nods. "Good enough. So, when can we do this? We need to ride the wave, and we don't know how long this will last, so the sooner the better."

"All the days between shows for the rest of the tour will be spent traveling, so it will have to be after." Brady says.

Dave nods. "I guess we know what we're doing with our few days off between tours now. We'll find an available studio and rent it out for the day." He turns to me. "How much of this song do you have?"

My knee bounces under the table. I can't stay here between tours. I need to see Margot. "All of it. But you guys can make changes. It could probably use some help."

"No changes," Brian says with a firm shake of his head. "Everyone already loves it. We can't change it."

Brady frowns. "Who's everyone?"

Mya props her elbow on the table, looking far too pleased with herself. "Just 2.4 million viewers."

Marty balks. "I'm sorry. Did you say 2.4 *million?*"

Everyone waits for confirmation, and Mya happily nods.

The guys break out in comments I can't keep track of because all I can think about is how much I don't want to record this song using the few days we have between tours.

"Damn!" Marty leans forward to look over at me. "I knew your pretty face would come in handy."

I flip him off with a laugh.

Brian snaps his fingers to get all our attention. "Focus. Studio time. I want to reserve the hours now, so when can we do it?"

"Between tours works for me," Brady says with a shrug.

"Same," Dave agrees.

"I've got no plans," Marty chimes in.

Then they're all looking at me. My fists clench on the tabletop. I never want to be the one to let the band down, but I never want to be the one to let Margot down, either. If I don't see her during this break—if I don't even come home like I said I would, I know there will be no shot at us working things out. Saying yes to the band this time feels like saying goodbye to Margot forever, and I'm not ready for that.

I don't think I'll ever be ready for that.

But they're all fucking staring at me, and it's like I can feel the compounded pressure with each of their gazes. Especially Brian's. He's looking at me like his career hangs in the balance of how I respond to this question, and it's too much.

"I . . ." Rubbing a tense hand over my mouth, I shake my head. "I can't. I'm sorry."

Brian curses under his breath. "Why?"

I don't want to answer him because I know he'll think my reason is dumb. They all will. Well, everyone except for Mya judging by the slight lift to her lips. My knee bounces under the table, and I clasp both hands in front of my mouth. "I have to go home. I'm sorry."

The irony of my statement plummets in my stomach. Because I don't technically have a home. I wouldn't consider my parents' house home, and Margot technically isn't a home for me right now either. If I go back to the apartment, and she won't see me, I don't know where I'll go. Then losing the opportunity to record with the band will have been for nothing. I swallow at the thought.

Marty's eyebrows furrow. "To see Margot?"

My jaw tenses, and I nod.

He looks over at Dave. "I thought you said they broke up?"

His question sends a pang through my chest, and I drop my gaze. The entire table goes quiet, and when I dare to look up, I find Dave looking innocently from me to Marty. "I thought they did." When my eyebrows crease, Dave adds, "You just haven't seemed like yourself."

I guess that's fair. I haven't felt like myself either.

"He's going to win her back," Mya says with a rueful smile.

A slow grin spreads across Dave's face. "Fuck yeah, you are!"

I let out a laugh that quickly dies when Brian throws his head back. He just stares up at the sky for a moment with his fists clenched like he's trying to find it within himself not to throttle me. When he does finally bring his attention back to me, his mouth is set in a thin line. "You're serious?"

I nod.

He gives me a warning stare. "This better be worth it."

"It will be."

He shakes his head and turns away from us. After a few steps he turns back around and points at me. "I swear to God, Jackson, if you come back here with no girlfriend *and* we don't have a song, there's going to be hell to pay."

I just stare at him, holding my breath until he turns and keeps walking.

Brady crosses his arms over his chest and chuckles. "You are one brave son of a bitch."

Marty snorts. "Brave or stupid. Brian's right, we should ride the wave while it has momentum."

Dave nods. "We should, but sometimes there are things more important than work. I had to learn that the hard way with Lynn." He looks over at me with a grin. "Go win Margot back, and then we'll record the song." He looks at Mya. "For now, optimize the content you're posting as much as possible. Have Jackson record an acoustic version you can post to keep it relevant, and we'll hype up the release of the single."

Mya pulls out her phone and starts typing. "On it."

Catching Dave's eye, I say a quiet "Thanks," and he nods in response.

"All right," Dave says as he claps his hands together. "The business stuff is taken care of. Now for the real question. How are you going to get her back?"

Excitement surges through my veins. Even if this doesn't work, I'll at least know I gave it my best shot. I'll know I did everything I could. Letting out a breath of laughter, I scratch the side of my head and try to hide my panic. "I have no idea."

56
margot

THE ARCADE BAR IS FUN. I mean, it's loud and packed, and it would probably be a lot more fun if I didn't keep seeing Jackson in people who are definitely not Jackson. But I'm okay. I'm doing better than I thought I would.

I'm stable.

Coasting.

Along for the ride.

We only got here a little while ago, and Matt and Rae already started bickering about who could beat the other at Skee-Ball. Rae may have no interest in video games, but she has a competitive streak. She and Matt are now side by side, ready to face off, while Braden and I hang back to see how this unfolds.

"Who's your money on?" Braden leans in a little closer to be heard over the loud music and overlapping game sounds.

I give him my best smile. "Rae. Always Rae."

He puts his hands in his pockets and rocks back on his heels. "I don't know." He drags out the words. "I'm pretty sure Matt's chivalry dies as soon as someone keeps score. And this has points." He shakes his head. "Forget it."

I narrow my eyes at him. "And you don't think Rae can win on skill alone?"

Braden sucks in air through his teeth. "Matt plays lacrosse. If Rae beats him at this, he may need to hang it up."

My lips twist. "We'll see, I guess." I turn my attention back to our friends, but Braden leans in again.

"I heard what happened. I'm sorry."

My chest tightens. Giving him a quick glance, I offer a tight-lipped smile. "Thanks."

"Are you okay?"

My mouth opens, and I'm on the verge of creating some bullshit response, but when my eyes meet his, something shifts. There's something about the way he's looking at me that makes me feel like he really cares. He isn't asking to be polite or because it's the right thing to do. He's asking because he genuinely wants to know if I'm okay. I force a laugh that tastes bitter on my tongue and shake my head. "No."

He nods. "Breakups suck."

I blow out a breath. "Yes, they do." With a tilt of my head, I ask, "What was your longest relationship?"

Braden's eyebrows shoot up, and I'm not sure if he's surprised by my question or surprised that I'm initiating more conversation with him. While I was with Jackson, I always felt so guilty talking to Braden, especially when I started to suspect he might have feelings for me.

But I guess now it doesn't matter.

"Almost four years," he finally says, and I blink.

"*Four years?*"

He lets out a light laugh. "Almost."

"What happened?"

Braden rubs his palm over his chest like he's soothing an old wound. "Nothing really. We dated for three years in high school. Tried to make it work in college, but we got accepted to different schools." He shrugs. "The distance eventually caught up with us."

"I'm sorry." I look at him, seeing him in a different light. "Distance is such a bitch."

"Yeah." He lets out a laugh. "Yeah, she is." The song changes, and he leans a little closer. "It's okay, though. Time heals all wounds."

"I hope so."

His eyes meet mine. "It does."

I have to fight the urge to tear my eyes away, but luckily Rae bounds up to me. "I won," she says with a smug look.

Matt walks up to Braden with a cheesy grin. "I let her win."

"Oh, no you didn't. You are such a liar." She gives Braden a serious look. "He's lying."

Braden chuckles. "I know he is." Then he nods to one of the high-tops nearby. "Let's get a table. I should be able to get us some drinks if my friend Anthony is working tonight."

"Nice!" Matt walks backward toward the table and points to Rae. "What will it be?"

Rae tilts her head, considering his question as she gets onto the barstool. "I'll take a cider if they have one."

Braden looks over at me. "And for you?"

His question has me feeling like we're on a double date, and the air around me is suddenly harder to breathe. "I can get it."

He cocks an eyebrow. "You know Anthony, too?"

"Oh, right." Having him bring back a drink for me feels like too much. "Um, I'm okay."

Braden frowns. "Are you sure? I'll buy."

If only he knew how much worse that made it. I can't let him buy me a drink. Then it's way too much like a date. Heat creeps up my neck, and I shake my head again. "I'm okay."

His shoulders sag, and as if he can see what I'm thinking,

he softens. "It's just a drink, Margot. It doesn't mean anything."

My eyes search his. I already have guilt weighing on me from initiating the breakup with Jackson. I don't need more piled on for giving Braden the wrong impression. He doesn't look like he's trying to flirt with me, though. He looks sincere. He *is* sincere. Forcing a breath, I nod. "Sure. Okay. A cider sounds good."

He smiles, but I can see the sympathy behind it. I hate that he can see how broken I am. Then again, maybe it's better this way. On the off chance he actually does have a crush on me, it will be a clear indicator that I am still very much unavailable.

I watch as the guys leave us and head toward the bar, and by the time I sense Rae's eyes on me it's too late. She caught me staring.

"Braden is a great guy," she says, watching for my reaction.

I look back at the bar. Braden *is* a great guy. He's responsible, dependable, attractive, and he makes some of the best food I've ever eaten. But that's all he is. Nothing about him sets my soul on fire. Part of me wishes I had the capacity to fall for someone like Braden, but I don't think I do. Maybe one day when the wounds aren't so fresh. "Yeah," I agree. "He is."

I look back at her, and she adds, "But so is Jackson."

Hearing his name has my heart skipping a beat. The corners of my lips lift, but that's as close to a smile as I can manage. "Yeah." I glance at the bar to make sure the guys aren't coming back before saying, "I'm surprised Matt doesn't hate me."

Her eyebrows crease. "Why would he?"

"For breaking up with his best friend? If he dumped you, I'd feel a certain way about it."

Rae laughs. "Look, Matt and I talked about that as soon as you and Jackson got together. We're all friends. It might be weird for a little while, but it will balance out."

I try to imagine being Jackson's friend. Will I ever be able to be in the same room as him without the air feeling charged? What about when he moves on? Will I be able to be around his future girlfriend? Just imagining him sitting on a couch somewhere with his arm around another girl has me feeling sick. And kissing her? And I'll know they're sleeping together.

A wave of nausea hits me. What if he's sleeping with other girls *now?* I mean, he's single. He can do what he wants . . . as a rockstar . . . in a successful band.

Oh god.

Rae's eyebrows pinch. "Are you okay?"

"Yeah." I force a swallow because my mouth has gone dry. "I could just really use that drink."

She eyes me warily. "Remember, if it gets to be too much, we can go."

I shake my head, forcing myself to breathe through my nose. "It's not too much." I can't be this fragile. I can't let my self-sabotaging thoughts get to me.

Rae points over her shoulder. "I'm going to get you some water. I'll be right back."

I don't even argue with her. I'm a wreck. I don't have any business being out. I'm still in the wallowing phase. I should be somewhere that lets me wallow. Everything in me wants to unblock the American Thieves on social media so I can see what he's been up to, but I know I shouldn't. There's a very real possibility that I could be faced with more pictures like the ones that started this in the first place, and I don't have the stomach for it right now.

The song in the bar changes, and I stop breathing. I'd know that familiar tempo anywhere. It's one of American Thieves' most popular songs—usually the second to last song they play on tour. Dave's voice comes through the speakers, and the familiar sound makes me homesick. Not for a place, but for a time, for what could have been, for a feeling. Remembering how it felt to stand at the side of the stage or in the front row while the band played hits me with a force so strong, my fingers grip the table edge in front of me like I might be blown away.

I've never heard their music played out in public before. Are they being played on radio stations now? Is the bar listening to them on a Spotify playlist? Either way, it's a big deal. Between this and the headlining tour, I have to say something. Not congratulating him on something so big feels . . . wrong.

Before Rae can come back and talk me out of it, I pull out my phone and tap on Jackson's name. My hands shake as I type out my message.

MARGOT:

The bar I'm in is playing one of your songs right now. This is huge, Jackson. Congratulations.

Exclamation points felt weird, so I leave the message as is and press send.

I take a steadying breath, and my nerves immediately settle. Congratulating him was the right thing to do. I know it in my gut. And having that severed connection partially restored has the world feeling more balanced again, like it's been off its axis, but now it's shifting in the right direction.

"Here's a water," Rae says, setting a cup in front of me.

"And a cider," Braden adds as he sets a glass on my other side.

I glance between the two of them with a light smile. "Thanks."

Everyone takes their seats, and I take a sip of my water. Matt and Braden start talking about all the games they want to play while they're here, and when Matt mentions Donkey Kong, I look over at Rae and laugh.

My phone lights up on the table, and my heart jumps into

my throat. Jackson's name appears on the lock screen, and I can read the whole message without opening my phone.

> JACKSON:
> Thanks. That means a lot.

Something in me sinks. I should have known, right? I should have known he wouldn't have more to say.

I deserve it.

And it's probably for the best.

But that doesn't make it hurt any less.

I take another deep breath and turn my phone over. That's that, I guess. My cider suddenly sounds a lot more appealing than water, so I take a few not so delicate gulps.

My phone buzzes on the table again, and part of me doesn't want to know. It's probably a random notification, and I'll just be disappointed. I leave it and try to focus on the conversation at the table in front of me.

Rae catches my eye and mouths, "You okay?" She points up, and follows it with, "The song."

I nod and give her my best smile. "Thanks again for the water."

My eyes wander to my phone again, my fingers tapping against the glass bottle covered in cool condensation. Temptation gets the best of me, and I quickly flip my phone back over to see Jackson's first message, followed by a second. And as soon as I read it, I breathe a little easier.

> JACKSON:
> How have you been?

57
jackson

THIS IS the most unconventional Thanksgiving I've ever had, and considering last year my dad kicked me out of the house before we got the chance to eat, that's saying something. It's been a year since I almost kissed Margot in Emmet's old bedroom. One year since I reached my breaking point and needed to know if she felt the same.

Now I'm sitting in an RV with four other guys and a girl with pink hair, eating Chinese food and talking about all the ways we need to prepare for the next tour. It's crazy how much my life has changed in just one year. Last year, this was my dream, and now my dreams are about to get even bigger.

"Mya, how's Jackson's acoustic video doing?" Brian asks between bites of lo mein. There's something about seeing him, still dressed in a fucking suit with his tie slung over his shoulder but eating Chinese takeout from the box, that makes me like him that much more.

He was pissed at me when I postponed our studio time, but after a few days of giving me the cold shoulder, he's back to treating me the same as before. Maybe it's a Thanksgiving miracle.

Mya pulls out her phone to refresh the latest stats. "Good. We're almost up to one million views, and since I teased in the caption that the single would drop in the coming weeks, everyone is commenting and asking where they can preorder. I'm redirecting traffic there."

Mya. Mya is my Thanksgiving miracle. I'm pretty sure if it weren't for her showing Brian the benefits of dragging out the hype, he'd still be delivering death stares. He was able to work it out and found a few days early in the next tour when we can go in and record. For now, we'll play the song live at shows, and Mya will keep posting about it online.

Brian smiles at her update. He gives a curt nod of his head. "Keep it up."

"And how's operation Margot going?" Dave asks in all seriousness.

"I wouldn't call it an operation. I'm just going to show up." I shrug. "Maybe there's some hope if I can see her face-to-face. She did text me last weekend when she heard one of our songs while she was out, so that's good."

"Does she know you're coming?"

I take in a breath and shake my head. "Nope. I mean, that was the original plan, but I haven't told her I'll still be there."

Dave nods. "Would she stay if she knew you were?"

Resting my elbows on my knees, I clasp my hands in front of my mouth and shake my head. "I don't think so." It stings to admit it out loud, but deep down, I know that's why I haven't told her. Last weekend, she said she wasn't doing great. I already knew through Matt, but it was nice to hear it coming from her. I told her I missed her, she told me she misses me, too. I asked her if I could text her sometimes, and at first, she said she'd like that, but then she followed it by saying she didn't know if it was a good idea.

I get it, she's torn. But as much as I think she'd want to see me, she's always been a flight risk. She would be tempted to take the easy way out.

Dave's smile is sympathetic, and he nods like he understands everything I'm not saying. Maybe he does. He gets Margot better than the other guys in the band.

Mya is on her phone again and doesn't look up when she says, "I told him to bring her lots of flowers."

Dave scoffs. "Don't do that."

Mya stops typing whatever post she was working on and looks up with wide eyes. "What is with you guys? I swear, you wouldn't know what romance was if it slapped you in the face."

Dave sets down his takeout and leans back, eyeing Mya with amusement. "I know plenty about romance." Looking over at me, he adds, "Save the flowers for the good days. This isn't about grand gestures. This is about you and Margot figuring out which direction to go next, and you have to do it as a team. No number of flowers will sway her. You wouldn't want her to change her mind because of flowers, anyway."

My lips form a tight smile behind my clasped hands. "No, I wouldn't." Thank God for Dave because Mya had me considering it. I've never given Margot flowers. Maybe I should have. Maybe that was one of the pieces missing for her. "I'm just going to show up. We'll see if she's even willing to talk to me."

At the same time Dave and Mya both say, "She will be."

I look back and forth between the two of them, but all I can do is take another bite of my food and hope they're right.

Marty sees this as the perfect opportunity to bring up some girl he planned on hooking up with back home now that he's made it big, and I lose interest. I don't really see how a girl ignoring you until you're successful gets you bragging points, but knowing him, I wouldn't be surprised if he was looking for revenge sex.

Pulling out my phone, I text Margot before I can talk myself out of it.

JACKSON:
> Happy Thanksgiving.

I'm surprised when the three dots appear right away.

MARGOT:
> Happy Thanksgiving. Have you heard from your parents today?

I might not like talking about my parents, but the fact that she's asking me a question to keep the conversation going makes it worth it.

JACKSON:
> I spoke to my mom earlier. Still no word from my dad.

MARGOT:
> He's an asshole.

Even though there's nothing happy about that statement, the fact that she said it makes me smile. Before I can respond, a second text comes through.

MARGOT:
> Sorry. I know he's your dad. I probably don't have any right to talk about him like that.

JACKSON:
> You can shit on my dad as much as you want if it means you'll talk to me.

MARGOT:
> Jackson.

I JUST WANT TO BE YOURS

> **JACKSON:**
> Margot.

I know I'm edging too close to the line she's drawn in the sand, but I don't care. I want nothing more than to watch a fucking tsunami come and erase the line completely. I send another text before she decides to jump ship.

> **JACKSON:**
> Are you in Indiana?

> **MARGOT:**
> How bad is it that I want to answer that question with "unfortunately?"
>
> I flew in with Rae and Matt yesterday, and my mother is already making me question why I came here.

I've never met her mom, but I've picked up enough pieces along the way to know I don't like her—and to know that she *definitely* wouldn't like me.

> **JACKSON:**
> If she's trying to set you up with your ex again, tell her to back off.

> **MARGOT:**
> It's eerie how you know things sometimes.

I nearly drop the phone. I wasn't expecting to actually be right.

> **JACKSON:**
> Seriously?

My heel bounces against the floor of the RV, and I suddenly don't have an appetite.

> **MARGOT:**
>
> I think her exact words were "Chris is recently single, too. You two would have a lot in common."

My breath gets caught in my lungs. She told her parents. There has to be some finality to it if she bothered telling her parents. She wouldn't deal with the likely interrogation or make herself susceptible to her mom's matchmaking if she thought we were getting back together.

The realization slows time, and all I can do is stare at her last text. I figured she would have lied to keep her parents off her back. It's not like they've ever met me. She could have easily said we were fine. Kept it simple. But she told them we broke up?

She doesn't tell her parents anything.

It feels like a bigger blow than it should. We *did* break up.

Another message comes in.

> **MARGOT:**
>
> I'm sorry. This is weird. For the record, I am definitely not reaching out to my ex.
>
> Or anyone for that matter.

If only that was what had me worried. I know Margot doesn't date easily. Other guys aren't an issue—not yet anyway.

But she told her parents.

> **JACKSON:**
>
> Don't be sorry.
>
> But your mom is an asshole.

Her next text includes a laughing emoji, and I feel a little better.

MARGOT:
She really is.

JACKSON:
Do you still think of me?

I'm pushing my luck, but I have to know. Her response doesn't come in right away this time. The three dots appear, then disappear, only to reappear and vanish again.

JACKSON:
It's just a question, Margot.

No dots appear for a moment, but then she sends another message.

MARGOT:
Honestly?

JACKSON:
Yes.

There's another pause before her next message, and every passing second has my heart beating harder.

MARGOT:
I'm trying to cut back.

I let out a small breath of laughter and look around, remembering I'm not alone. Luckily no one notices. They're all fantasizing about this single taking off and making a music video for it. I think they're getting ahead of themselves.

Staring down at the phone, all I can do is wonder how it will be when I see her in person. Will we pick up where we left off? Will she take back the choices she made and me along with them? There's so much I want to say to her. So much I want to ask, but now isn't the time. Not when I'm surrounded by the band and she's in Indiana with her parents. My thumbs hover over the keypad, just out of reach of all they want to type. Eventually, I settle on just one word, but it somehow feels like enough.

JACKSON:
Don't.

58
margot

LIFE IS STARTING to flow into a new routine. I've done all the post-breakup things, too. Rae and I have watched every romantic comedy movie we can think of, I cut my hair to a more medium length with layers, and even though I haven't gotten a tattoo yet, I have a Pinterest board full of ideas. Jackson and I broke up six weeks ago, and every day gets a little bit easier. It might only be that I think about him a few seconds less or it takes me a shorter amount of time to stop crying, but still.

Easier.

Easier to breathe. Easier to think. Easier to rediscover a feeling that resembles happiness.

Outside of him.

Outside of us.

Outside of everything I thought dictated my happiness for a long time.

Sometimes the hardest things to do are the things you do for your own good. But it's worth it. At least, it will be worth it. That's what I keep telling myself. That eventually, it will be worth it. One day, I'll be on the other side of this, and I'll look back and know I made the smarter choice.

Hopefully.

I'm sitting with Rae in the living room while she makes final packing plans for her trip with Matt to his parents' house. My phone lights up on the counter a few feet away, and I somehow know it's Jackson before checking. He's been sending me texts every few days, and each time the progress I've built crumbles. Rae looks up from her checklist. "Is it him again?"

I step over to my phone and lightly tap the screen without picking it up—like the more distance I can keep between myself and whatever lies on the other side, the better. Sure enough, Jackson's name stares back at me in bold letters with a new message from him on the lock screen.

I nod as I slowly reach for the phone, my eyes already burning. It doesn't matter what the text says, I cry every time.

Rae lets out a sigh. "Why don't you come with us? I hate the thought of leaving you here alone."

"I'll be fine," I say, determined to keep my voice strong. I've gotten pretty good at fighting off my emotions lately, but she still sees through my mask. With shaky fingers, I unlock my phone and read the latest text.

JACKSON:

> I just found out Marty's real name is Martellus, and I feel like that explains so much.

The vice around my heart squeezes as I choke back a laugh. It comes out sounding more like a sob, and Rae puts her pen down. "What did he say?"

"Nothing." I wipe away a fallen tear. "Really, nothing. It's stupid." I let out another laugh before putting my phone face down on the counter with a shake of my head. Sometimes his texts are sweet. Sometimes he tells me he's still mine. But sometimes they're like this, and these are the ones that hit me the hardest. The texts that give me a glimpse of his day. The ones that show me what our conversations might be like if we were still together.

"You know Matt's parents would love to have you."

"I know, but—" My words cut off when Matt and Braden walk in through the front door. Quickly taking a steadying breath, I say, "I'll be fine." Then I turn to the fridge and work on pouring myself a glass of homemade lemonade to keep myself busy.

I appreciate her extending the invitation, but Jackson won't want to go see his parents. So that leaves Matt's parents' house as his best option. The last thing he needs is to walk in and see his ex-girlfriend sitting on the couch. It would be awkward, and I have no right to take his safe haven from him.

She frowns, trying to read what I'm not saying. "Do you still think he'll come here?"

I take a sip of my drink and set my glass down on the counter. The guys are talking about something unrelated, so I keep my voice low and say, "I don't know." It's the truth. I don't think Jackson will come here, but a small part of me is terrified he might. "If he does come, his flight is supposed to get in around dinner." It hurts to talk about the plans we had before everything fell apart. Between the text and this conversation, my hands grip the edge of the countertop tightly enough to turn my knuckles white.

Her eyes dart to Matt before locking back on me. In an equally low voice, she says, "I hate that we won't be here." She pauses, her lips twisting. "In case you need us."

"I won't."

She holds my stare, but I know she doesn't believe me. "I tried talking Matt into staying, but Grandma Lois really wants to go to the town's tree lighting ceremony, and she wants the whole family there."

I smile at the lighter memory. "Can't keep Grandma Lois waiting."

Rae laughs. "No, we can't." Before I can say anything, she perks up, her eyes jumping to Braden. "Hey, your parents live around here, right?"

He stops his conversation with Matt. "Yeah. Why?"

"So, you're not going out of town?"

"Rae." I try to interject, but she doesn't even look at me.

He pulls a grape from our fruit bowl. "Nope. What's up?"

Rae's eyes flicker in my direction, and I widen my own. She ignores me again and looks back at Braden. "Do you think you can get Margot out of the apartment for a few hours tonight?"

"Rae!" My eyes jump to Braden. "No. You don't have to do—"

"Yeah. I can do that." He tosses the grape in the air and catches it in his mouth. His bright blue eyes have a spark in them as they fall on me. "What do you want to do?"

"Nothing!" I try to hide the panic in my voice, but based on the lift of his lips, I think he heard it. Standing up a little straighter, I say with full conviction. "I'm actually really busy with work, so I probably shouldn't go out tonight."

Braden's eyes narrow playfully at me before he looks at Rae. "She's lying, isn't she?"

Rae happily nods, selling me out with no remorse. "Yes. Please take her somewhere."

He nods. "I can do that."

I gape at them, but they both look perfectly pleased with this outcome. Turning to Matt, I look at him with wide eyes for a last-ditch effort, but he looks like he couldn't care less. He's pulled Rae's list away from her and is checking it himself.

With a shake of my head, I let out a sigh. "You two are ridiculous."

Braden shrugs. "What good is it if we're both sitting in our apartments bored? We'll be a couple of friends, hitting the town. Nothing wrong with that."

My fight or flight instincts relax a bit at the sound of the word *friends*. He's right. We *are* friends. We can hang out somewhere other than our apartments and still be friends. "Fine." Letting out a sigh, I try to sound a bit friendlier when I look at him and add, "That would be great." Then I take a sip from my drink and shoot Rae a quick glare when Braden isn't looking.

She gives me an apologetic grin, but she doesn't look like she's sorry. She looks like she'll be able to enjoy a tree lighting ceremony without feeling guilty now—which to her, is at least one good thing about me being forced to hang out with Braden. Not that Braden is bad company. It's just that everything about hanging out with him one-on-one feels . . . wrong.

Considering it hasn't even happened yet, that's probably unfair.

I'm sure it will be fine. I'll spend some time with Braden to avoid being a riddled mess, watching the clock. Jackson won't come here because we aren't together, and by tomorrow, I'll be able to breathe a little easier again.

This day can't go by fast enough.

59
jackson

AS OF LAST NIGHT, the tour is officially over. We went out and celebrated with Crooner Sins, but the entire time all I could think about was *today*. Today is the day I'll finally get to see where Margot and I stand. All it will take is one look. One look, and I'll know how she feels. I'll know if she's moved on, or if she's just scared.

God, I hope she's scared.

I can handle scared Margot. I can handle the Margot that gets stuck in her head and wants to run. It's an indifferent Margot that terrifies me—one that can look me in the eyes and say with complete confidence that she doesn't want me. That's a version of Margot I've never seen, and that's the Margot who just might break me.

Ever since we broke up, I've held out hope, and it's made everything feel less final. Less real. Maybe that makes me delusional, but I don't care. If she still feels anything for me at all, it will be worth it.

Mya takes a seat on Brady's bunk across from mine in the RV while I toss my phone charger into my backpack. We're still parked at the hotel we all stayed in last night, but I already checked out. The plan is for everyone to drop me off at the airport an hour away. Then they'll keep heading west to California, and I'll meet up with them in a couple of days.

"Hey, Lover Boy," she says happily.

I give her a sideways glance. "You might need to come up with a new nickname."

"What do you want it to be?" she asks as she lays back on Brady's bunk and crosses her feet at her ankles. "Sad Boy just doesn't have the same ring to it." Grabbing my pillow, I toss it at her, and she laughs. "You won't need a new nickname. You'll get her back, and all will be restored."

"Maybe."

Mya sits up cross-legged. "She's not seeing anyone new, right?"

An image of Margot with someone else flashes in my mind, and I have to swallow down the thought. "Not that she's mentioned."

She smiles. "See, then you're fine. It's been six weeks. If I were single for six weeks, I'd be hooking up with whoever I wanted by then."

An entirely new image of Margot flashes in my mind, the thought of her hooking up with anyone could make me physically sick. "You suck at pep talks, you know that?"

Mya waves off my comment. "You know what I mean. If she hasn't started dating, it means she still feels some sort of loyalty to you. She hasn't moved on."

I run my hand over my hair and hope she's right. "We'll see, I guess."

Dave pokes his head into the RV. "Today's the big day!"

I flip him the bird with a laugh, and he only grins wider.

"Don't make him nervous," Mya scolds. "He's already showing up with no flowers." She gives me a sideways glance with a teasing twist to her lips.

"Here. You can have one too." I flip her off with my other hand and she smiles slowly.

Dave leans in a little more to get a better look. "Oh, good. Mya is here." Looking back to me, he adds, "Brady and Brian are in their rooms, but I haven't found Marty yet."

Mya rolls her eyes as she gets to her feet. "I don't know why Brian bothers booking him a room. He never uses it."

Dave lets out a sigh. "One can dream." He nods in my direction. "Just remember when all this goes to his head that you were the one who made us big."

I let out a breath of laughter and follow Mya toward the front. "I'm pretty sure he'd be an asshole either way."

Once we reach Dave, he moves out of the way so we can step down. Mya pops a hand on her hip, and stares at the hotel like she might be able to spot Marty from here. "Have you called him?"

I rub a hand over the back of my neck. "Yeah, because I sort of have a plane to catch."

Dave looks down at his phone, checking the time. "I've been calling him almost nonstop for twenty minutes." He lets out a sigh before pressing dial and holding the phone to his ear.

A twinge of panic ignites in the pit of my stomach, and I do my best to try to dismiss it. I'm sure Marty will get here in time. He's never gone completely missing. He'll show up with a cocky grin, wearing last night's clothes, and we'll all give him shit for almost making us late.

It will be fine.

Dave keeps calling. Brady checks all the common areas of the hotel. Brian practically bullies the front desk staff with interrogating questions. And Mya has resorted to knocking on guest's doors, even though I'm pretty sure the staff specifically told her not to do that.

And I'm by the fucking RV in case he decides to show up like he was supposed to thirty minutes ago. I've been pacing for the last ten minutes because sitting still has proven to be impossible. Pulling out my phone for what feels like the millionth time, I try to calculate how fucked I am.

If he shows up soon, I might still make my flight. I run a hand through my hair and get back to pacing. Part of me wants to text Margot to let her know I might be late, but then I remember she doesn't even think I'm coming.

"We got him!" I hear Dave's voice yell from a distance.

My head snaps up to find everyone headed my way with a tattered Marty in front. He looks like he just woke up. Dave keeps pushing him forward every few steps like he's a prisoner of war, and it's nice to see I'm not the only one frustrated.

I jump back into the RV to make room for the rest of them. There's loud arguing as soon as they're all inside, and it takes me a moment to make out what everyone's saying in the chaos.

Dave yells for Brady to drive us to the airport.

Brian lectures Marty on answering his goddamn phone when he or Dave—or anyone in the band—calls him.

Mya rattles on about what a selfish, desperate, lonely, pathetic motherfucker he is.

And Marty spews a string of insincere apologies that sound more like he's just trying to get everyone off his back.

I don't say a word. I can't. All I can do is look at the time and hope by some miracle I still make my flight. That I'm still able to see Margot tonight. That she'll even talk to me once I get there. That all of this will be worth it.

Everything calms down once we're on the highway. The yelling stops. The chaos settles. Mya comes over and tries to talk to me, but I'm only half listening. All I can do is look out the window and count the mile markers. Every time Brady lets off the gas, I look ahead for a possible traffic jam or an accident up ahead. I don't think I've ever been this fucking stressed.

"You'll make it," Mya says, sensing what I'm thinking.

I shoot a glare in Marty's direction. "I better."

He looks at me, his eyes widening to feign innocence, but it just makes him look stupid. "Hey! I said I was sorry."

"Shut the fuck up, Marty," Dave calls from somewhere in the back of the RV.

My knee bounces, and I hug my backpack to my chest. Why do we have to live in an RV? The van might have sucked in a lot of ways, but at least it could weave in and out of traffic if we needed it to.

I wish it got easier to breathe once we pulled off the highway, but then we were in city traffic. I held my breath until we turned into the airport. I could barely breathe as I said goodbye to everyone and jumped down from the RV just to run into the airport entrance. My chest was tight the entire time I had to stand in line for security. And every time TSA looked at my boarding pass and said, "Better hurry," or "You're cutting it close," my nerves only wound tighter.

As soon as I was in the clear, I ran to my gate with my backpack slung over my shoulder and my guitar case in hand. I have no idea if people told me to slow down, or if I was getting looks from other travelers. I didn't care. All I cared about was getting to her.

But the gate was empty.

And now, as I sit with nothing but vacant chairs around me, I know one thing for sure. I definitely won't get to Margot in time.

60
margot

I'VE BEEN a wreck all afternoon. How ready do you bother getting for something you're determined isn't a date? How much effort is too much? Will he read into something he shouldn't? Does my mascara say I'm putting myself out there for the taking or does it just look like mascara?

Rae and Matt left a little while ago, so I've been alone with my spiraling thoughts. I'm afraid of seeing Jackson, but the thought of him coming here to find me gone isn't exactly better. I'm sure he won't come. He'll probably either stay with the band or go to Matt's parents' house. That's what I would do if I were him. It's what makes sense. Plus, if he were coming here still, he'd tell me. Wouldn't he?

Shaking out my nerves, I stand in front of my floor-length mirror and force out a deep breath. I can do this. This is not a date. This is two friends getting out of the apartment so one friend doesn't drive herself crazy at the prospect of seeing her ex who probably won't show.

Totally normal.

There's a knock on the door, and I jump. I need to relax. I can't be this on edge all night. As I walk out of my room, my eyes dart to the time displayed on the stove. Jackson's flight isn't supposed to land for another twenty minutes. It's not him—I *know* it's not him. But that doesn't stop me from checking through the peephole.

Braden stands there, looking more or less the same as he always does. He might have recently showered, but he didn't dress any different. I let out a breath of relief and unlock the door. Before I open it, I take a steadying breath and follow it with my best smile. I can do this. I can pretend I'm okay for a few hours. I can act like this isn't making me want to bolt.

"Hey," I say with a grin as I open the door.

He smiles back at me, and I hope mine looked that effortless. "Hey. Ready?"

I nod. "Yeah." Turning and locking my apartment door, I add, "What do you want to do?"

"I want to take you somewhere."

The words give me pause. There's nothing wrong with those words, but maybe it's the way he said them? Maybe I'm just paranoid. Turning on my heels, I brace myself for what I'm about to say. "I just want to be clear that this is—"

"Definitely not a date."

I stare at him.

"Margot if this were a date, I wouldn't have shown up empty handed, and I would have told you that you look gorgeous at least once." With a smile, he adds, "Maybe twice if I felt nervous." He shrugs. "So as far as I see it, if this were a date we'd already be O for two."

I let out a light laugh, and some of the tension in my shoulders dissipates. "Okay, so where to?"

We end up at a small Italian restaurant, and the first thing I think of is the pizza shop in New York. I'm not sure why. This place may serve pizza, but they offer a lot more. I think it's just the overall Italian vibe that has me reminiscing about a time I felt truly untouchable. That was when I felt most independent. It was my first time flying alone, and it hadn't even crossed my mind. Jackson always felt so big, I think he made everything else smaller—including my fears.

"Table for two, please." Braden holds up two fingers to the hostess, and we follow her to a small booth near the back.

Once I slide into the booth, I look around. "I've never been here."

"I didn't think you had."

My defenses prickle. Did he say that because he knows I never really went on dates with Jackson? But when I look at him, it makes me think the comment was completely innocent. He's smiling at me, and heat flushes to my cheeks.

"What?" I ask, desperate to hide my blush.

"So, how was your day?" He grabs a menu and starts looking at the different options like he was never staring.

"Braden!" A woman with dark, long curls says as she walks up and playfully whacks him with her pad to take down orders. "It's been too long. What brings you in tonight?"

"Just out with a friend," Braden says with a light laugh. "Margot this is Dee. Dee, this is Margot."

Dee turns to me and does a sort of curtsy dip. "Very nice to meet you, Margot." Turning back to Braden, she holds up her notepad to block the side of her mouth. "And a very pretty friend."

"I don't disagree with you." He said it so casually. It would have been easy to miss under the shuffle of him collecting our menus and handing them to the woman. "Two pesto pastas, please."

She barks a laugh. "I see you haven't changed." She takes our drink orders and walks away. I'm left feeling like we're in the calm after a storm.

My mouth opens as I go to point in the direction I last saw her, but when I look, she's already gone. "How do you know her?"

"I used to work here when I was in high school. Dee and her husband own the place." He gives me a genuine smile. "This is where I learned how to make pesto pasta, and I promise she can make it better than me."

"Oh, so *that's* why you brought me here." I give him a teasing smile. "You just want me to have another place to get my fix."

His face falls. "Did I say hers was better? Because it's practically inedible."

I let out a laugh.

Braden's eyes dart around the restaurant. "Don't tell her I said that. I wouldn't put it past her to throw a shoe at me."

"Your secret's safe," I say, still giggling.

My smile lingers, and I realize I'm actually having fun. Rae's plan is working. I feel better than I have all day. I'm sure just getting out of the apartment is a huge part of that, but I think Braden is a part of it, too. There's something about his presence that's comforting and the fact that he knows where I stand on tonight makes it easier to accept that comfort.

For the rest of dinner, we laugh and talk. He tells me about his job as a barback and his dreams of one day owning a restaurant. Our food arrives, and I have to admit that Dee's pesto pasta is better than Braden's, but only by a small margin. Little by little, I feel my rigid, icy state softening. I start to relax and feel more like myself. Braden gives off this warm feeling that I wish I could harness and wrap around myself like a cozy blanket. I'd save it for later when I'm alone and plagued with the thoughts that turned me to ice in the first place.

We thank Dee for our meals—which we each pay for separately. He didn't even try to pay, and I'm grateful for it.

Without looking my way, he told her we'd needed two checks, and that may have eased any lingering fears I had.

As we walk out into the cool night air, Braden waves for me to follow him. Instead of walking in the direction of the car, he turns down a busy side street full of vendors. It's like an evening farmer's market I never knew existed. As we walk and carry on our conversation from dinner, I marvel over all the different tables. There's fresh honey, handcrafted jewelry, paintings, woodwork, and soaps. The energy of the market is buzzing with happy shoppers. Some look around at the market like they've stumbled upon a pleasant surprise while others look like they frequent certain tables to gather their essentials.

Without thinking, I stop in front of a cart full of bouquets. The flowers range in all varying shapes and colors, and for a moment, I find myself completely transfixed. They're stunning.

"Want one?" Braden asks, stepping up beside me.

I'm instantly brought back to the present. "No. Sorry, I was just looking." My eyes fall back to the silk-like petals, and I take one more intoxicating inhale. "Okay, I'm done," I say with a laugh as I step away.

Braden doesn't follow me, though. He takes another step toward the cart and starts muttering to himself.

I get closer and try to hear what he's saying. "What are you doing?"

He looks over at me, surprised. "Oh. I'm trying to figure out which of these is the least romantic flower. What do you think?" He pulls a bouquet from the cart. "Daisies?"

"I think dead flowers are the least romantic."

He glances back at the cart with a chuckle. "Looks like they're fresh out of dead." He shows the woman working the cart the bouquet of yellow and orange daisies before handing her his card. Once he's paid, he turns back to me with a satisfied grin.

I arch a brow at him. "Do you even know how much those cost?"

"Nope. How much could it be?"

I shake my head. "Flowers can be expensive."

He shrugs. "Well, they're a gift for a friend, so they're worth it." He hands me the bouquet, and I hold them dumbly in my hands.

I have no idea what to say or do. Eventually a confused, "Thank you?" falls from my lips, and he smiles, even more pleased.

For the rest of the night, I hold my flowers. And for the rest of the night, there are no other date-like gestures. But as Braden drives us back to the apartment, my heart rate rises a little. It's after ten, and Jackson's flight was supposed to arrive hours ago. I wonder if he lost his money when he canceled or if they gave him a voucher. Hopefully, he could just change it to fly into Orlando instead. Then he'd be closer to Matt's parents' house.

I wring my hands in my lap as we pull into the parking lot, but I don't see his car. Of course, I don't see his car. He wouldn't have come here. I don't know why I'm panicking. It's not like I'm going to open my apartment door and see him sitting there.

Braden puts the car in park, and we both step out. My hands shake as I take each step up to the second floor, but I hope holding the flowers hides it well. There's no sign of Jackson up here either, and it helps to steady my nerves. We stop in front of Braden's apartment since it's the first one we pass.

"Thanks again for tonight," I say with my best smile. "And for the flowers," I add, lifting the bouquet.

"Anytime." He nods toward the flowers. "Sorry. They do still look a little date-like. I won't tell if you won't."

I let out a weak laugh. "My lips are sealed."

As soon as I say the words, Braden's eyes drop to my mouth. And for the first time tonight, this doesn't feel like two friends getting dinner. Because friends don't look at other friends' mouths like that.

"Braden," I say, and my voice comes out a quiet plea.

He blinks. "Right. Sorry. Friends."

I give him a sad smile. Taking a step back, I say, "Goodnight."

"Goodnight," he says, but when I reach my own door he adds, "Hey, Margot?"

I stop with my hand on the door handle.

"If things were different, I'd kiss you." He rubs the back of his neck. "I just want you to know that, okay?"

I swallow, my hands gripping the flowers a little tighter. "Okay."

He gives me a tight-lipped smile before heading inside, and only then to do I feel like I can breathe again.

I should go into my apartment.

I should put these flowers in some water.

I should try to go to sleep.

But all I can do is stay here. My chest rises and falls with the realization of how fucked up this whole situation is. Jackson was supposed to be here. I was supposed to be with him tonight, not Braden. Braden is wonderful. He's kind, and smart, and considerate, but for whatever reason, I can't make myself feel anything for him.

Turning around, I let my head rest against the door and try to take a steadying breath, but it's like the more air I take in, the more I feel. Sinking to the floor, I stare at the flowers before setting them down beside me.

What is wrong with me?

61
jackson

MY UBER DROPS me off in front of Margot's apartment, and I stare up at the building in the dark. She's probably sleeping, and now her inconsiderate asshole of an ex, who didn't even tell her he was coming, is going to wake her up by knocking on the door.

I can't believe I missed my flight. We could have had all night to talk about everything. We could have smoothed things over by now. If anything, I could have found a different place to stay if she won't see me.

Maybe Braden is still here. I could always knock on his door and see if I can crash on the couch for the night. I could even wait to see Margot first thing tomorrow morning. That's probably the better decision.

But God do I want to see her.

I've waited so long to just be around her again. I probably should have thought about this while I was rebooking my flight for the next one out, but all I could think about was getting to Florida as fast as possible. I didn't think about the fact that I'd get here after eleven and have to explain myself to her this late.

With my backpack slung over my shoulder and my guitar

case in hand, I head upstairs to the second floor. It feels good to be back here after jumping from city to city. I like that nothing has changed. Thanks to the maintenance company, I doubt this place ever looks different. The grass doesn't even seem to grow.

As soon as I can see the landing of the second floor, my steps slow.

She isn't sleeping.

She isn't even in her apartment.

She's here. She's right here.

Margot sits in the hallway with her back against her door. She's holding a single flower and picking the petals off, one by one. It doesn't look like this one is her first victim either. There are petals and stems scattered around her like she's been at this for a while. Her hair is shorter now. It doesn't cascade down her arms and back the way it always has, but I like it. A few strands are tucked behind her ear, giving me a clear view of her face, and I drink her in. Her downcast eyes as she stares at the flower in her hands, her lashes casting shadows on her cheeks, the curve of her lips. It's a face I could never forget, but one I'm never fully prepared for either.

Especially when she looks this . . . hopeless.

"Margot." My voice comes out rough from lack of use.

Wide eyes snap to meet mine and she stops plucking the petals. Her lips part, her cheeks flush, and her shallow breaths make her chest rise and fall at a rapid pace.

She's panicking.

The urge to try to comfort her pulls at me, but I stay where I am. "Why are you sitting out here alone?" My eyes jump to the tattered bouquet next to her and I add, "With flowers." My chest tightens at the sight. When I didn't show up here with flowers, I never thought someone else would have already given her some.

She glances down at the one in her hand. It has one petal

still attached, and she runs her thumb over the soft petal before pulling it off with a frown. She looks even more saddened by what she's done to it. "Braden got them for me." Those words knock the wind out of my chest. Is she dating Braden? My fist clenches around my guitar case, but before I can ask, she says, "But I can't even enjoy them. I can't even be happy about a perfectly nice guy giving me flowers." Some of her sadness spikes to anger as she tosses the stem away and reaches for the next one in the bouquet.

My heart hammers as I take a hesitant step toward her. She's still a couple of doors away from me, but it feels like she might bolt any moment. "Why can't you be happy about Braden giving you flowers?"

She scoffs and shakes her head. "Because of you." She goes back to plucking petals. "Because even though you're nowhere, you're somehow everywhere." She plucks another petal. "You're always in my head, and it's infuriating." More petals. "And despite the fact that I *know* you're not good for me, I still love you."

I freeze and so does she.

I couldn't have heard her wrong. She said it. She said she loves me.

Still.

As in never stopped. As in she loved me at all in the first place. My heart feels like it might burst out of my chest. Margot Reid loves me.

Still.

Not *before*. Not *used to*. Not *did*.

She claps a hand over her mouth, her eyes going wide. She shakes her head. "I didn't mean—I was just—" She curses under her breath and jumps to her feet. "I'm sorry."

I take another step toward her. "Margot."

Her hand extends like a stop sign. "No, Jackson. I can't—I can't do this." Her eyes brim with tears, and for the first time, I see how broken she is over this. This decision hurts her just as much as it hurts me, even though she's the one making it.

The sight of her like this makes me pause, and it's just enough time for her to dart into her apartment and close the door behind her. The slam of the door jolts me from whatever trance I was in, and I rush forward and bang my fist against the wood. "Margot, open the door."

She doesn't answer, and I curse under my breath. I can't talk to her if she's on the other side of the apartment. My head hits the door with a thud, but I don't care. "Margot, please," I say a little more quietly this time. I never thought she'd actually shut me out—not like this. This can't be where our story ends. This can't be what defines us. We're better than this.

"Jackson . . . Why are you here?"

Her muffled voice is barely audible through the door, but I lift my head, hope surging through my veins. "Because I needed to see you."

"You shouldn't have come." Hearing the sadness laced in her words almost makes me think maybe she's right.

But then I remember she loves me. *Still.*

"Maybe I shouldn't have, but I needed to. I miss you. Can you please open the door?"

The door doesn't open, but she says, "Nothing has changed. There's no easy fix to this."

"Sure, there is. We work on it instead of running from it." I have no idea how to get past this, but I know the first step is not giving up. I just need her to see that. Taking a steadying breath, I try again. "Margot, you're the first person I think of when I wake up, and you're the last person I think of before I fall asleep. Every day. And every night. I know this is hard. I know being with me is hard, but if you feel even a fraction of that, we shouldn't be having this conversation through a door."

I hold my breath, afraid if I breathe, I might miss what she says.

But then the door opens. Not all the way, but it opens. After the day I've had, I don't even have the energy to take a step back. I'm practically in the door frame after leaning my head against the door to talk to her.

Margot's head tilts up to meet my stare, and I fight the urge to reach for her. Her eyes are wide and vulnerable. Her nose is a little red like she's been crying. But it's the way she looks at me that I notice the most. She still looks at me like she's mine, and I don't think I've ever been more grateful for anything. The way she's looking at me gives me so much hope, and I hope I'm not wrong to have it.

62
margot

HIS HAIR IS A TOUSLED MESS, his muscles are tense, and his eyes are wide—almost crazed looking. I've never seen him like this. I've never seen him anywhere close to this, and my chest aches knowing I made him this way.

"Did you mean it?"

My teeth sink into my bottom lip as my eyes search his. If I tell him no, I'm lying. But if I tell him yes, I'm going to lose any last bit of ground I was trying to stand on. "It's late. Maybe we should—"

"Just tell me if you meant it." The plea in his voice cracks something inside of me, and it's like whatever has been holding me together dissolves. My shoulders drop, my knees feel weak, even my hands go limp at my sides.

If I do this—if I admit my feelings for him, it will mean we aren't done. It will reopen a door I've spent the past six weeks trying to shut, and all my fears and insecurities will run rampant again. I know they're not logical. Jackson has never done anything to hurt me. He's never done anything to jeopardize our relationship, but fears aren't meant to make sense. Fears are meant to make you suffer.

Ever since I found those photos, I've made myself suffer. I felt like I was drowning that last week of our relationship, but ever since we broke up the water has only gotten deeper. Sure, there have been small bouts of air here and there. Distractions to help me forget I've been treading water for so long. But the first time I've been able to take a deep breath is now, with him here.

Jackson drops his gaze and rubs a tired hand over his face. I hate seeing him like this—I hate seeing *us* like this.

"Of course I meant it."

His storm-like eyes flick up to meet mine, and liquid heat melts my core. "You meant it?" His voice is low, steady, but his eyes give him away. Those eyes I've committed to memory search mine, and I know I have no defenses against them. He can see everything. He always can.

"I meant it." My voice is barely a whisper.

He swallows and nods, his gaze dipping to my mouth for a fraction of a second before his attention is back on me. "Say it again."

My fists clench by my sides, and I try to muster every ounce of bravery hiding deep within my bones. Heat flushes my neck, and the thought of confessing *again* with his full attention has my heart racing in my chest, like even *it* is frantically searching for an escape. "I . . ." I look at him, *really* look at him, and I wonder how I've never said this to him before. I haven't seen him in weeks, and during those weeks we've hardly talked, but it doesn't matter. He's the one who gets me better than anyone else, and he's the only one who makes me *feel*.

"I still love you." It comes out a little rushed, my riddled nerves forcing the words out in one swift kick, but they're clear enough.

He takes a step toward me, and I'm forced to look up at him. I'm completely in a trance. Having him this close again is intoxicating. I breathe him in, and the familiar scent makes me want to wrap my arms around him and bury my face in his chest, but I can't move. He gently reaches for a lock of my hair, and my eyes flutter shut when his fingertips brush the skin near my collarbone.

"You love me?"

My eyes fly open, my head tilting slightly. For someone who never made this four-letter word a big deal, he's certainly acting like it means something to him now. "Yes."

His sharp gaze stays glued on my hair before he looks at me again. "Did you love me when you broke up with me?"

My eyes burn, and a single tear falls when I nod again. "Yes."

Jackson wipes my tear with his thumb, and it's impossible not to lean into his touch. His eyebrows furrow, and I'd give anything to know what he's thinking. "You loved me when you broke up with me." He says it more like a realization than an actual question, so I wait. His hand lingers on my cheek, and the pressure in my chest builds until it feels like it might explode. He studies my face, still deep in thought, and when his thumb drags over my bottom lip, I suck in a breath. "Margot, say it again."

I'm completely frozen in place. I've said it. I've said it twice. Is he not going to say *anything* back to it? My chest rises and falls at a rapid pace as I stare into those eyes that probably don't need me to tell them anything. "I love you," I say, my voice breathless.

The corner of Jackson's mouth lifts just slightly, but he says nothing.

"Why do you keep telling me to say it again?" I finally ask.

He blinks. "Because I've loved you for months, and I never thought I'd hear you say those words." By the time he says the last word, his mouth is already on mine. I step back, my fists clenched around his shirt to pull him with me. His backpack falls off his shoulder to the floor, and he manages to set his guitar case against the wall with a little more care, but his lips never leave mine. Kicking the door shut behind us, he has me pressed up against the entryway wall within seconds.

His mouth moves over mine with no hesitation. He takes what he wants unapologetically, and for the first time in weeks, I feel awake. This kiss is the first thing that feels right after a long string of wrongs, and I lean into it. This is what he does to me. This is what he's always done to me. He makes me let go. He might have his hands on the wall behind me, caging me in, but this is when I feel most free. When I'm with him, I don't have to think about what I'm doing, I just feel.

"I love you," he murmurs against my lips. "I love you. I love you. I love you."

My hands weave into his hair, and my tongue finds his. Jackson groans, and the sound could make my knees buckle. He claims my mouth with a dizzying kiss, and that familiar ache has me desperate to be closer. It's never enough with him. One kiss, one touch, it all just leads to me frantically wanting more.

I can't stop touching him. My hands move from his hair to his face, to his chest, until I'm at the waistband of his pants. My fingers slip into the front to find him already hard, and a low guttural sound rumbles in the back of Jackson's throat. He kisses me harder, but my thoughts start racing. The girl in the pictures was doing this. Was he hard then too? Did she touch him the same way I just did? Did he make a sound like that for her?

Dazed and confused by all my conflicting emotions, I pull back. But Jackson just takes it as an opportunity to move his mouth to my neck, and my eyes flutter shut at the feeling of his hot, open-mouthed kisses against my skin.

Struggling to stay focused, I let out a breathy plea. "Jackson."

"Hmm?" he asks without stopping his slow assault.

Struggling to catch my breath, I say, "We need to figure out what we're doing." His tongue grazes my skin just below my ear, and I suck in a breath. "Before this goes further."

Pulling back, he holds my face in his hands. "I'll tell you what we're doing." He kisses me softly on the mouth. "You're mine." He kisses me again. "I'm yours." His lips brush mine. "And we'll figure the rest out."

A light chuckle leaves me. "That's not a plan, Jackson." Ducking out of his grasp, I take a few steps toward the kitchen to give myself room to think. Smoothing my hair back, I look at him, still standing near the wall where I left him. He's even more of a mess now, but he looks way too good. Just seeing him this turned on with rapt attention has me wishing I were still pressed against that wall. Blinking, I clear my throat and try to get back on track. "What about all the times we're not together? We can't go into this doing the same thing and expecting a different outcome."

He watches me intently, a small crease between his brow forming, but he doesn't say anything.

My arms drop by my sides. "Let's face it, long distance is hard. A lot harder than we thought."

He's like a statue, deep in thoughts he isn't sharing, and it's killing me. He always says what's on his mind—almost to a fault. Now isn't the time for him to hold out on me. When he finally moves, it's just to wipe his hand over his mouth.

I can't take it anymore. "Jackson, can you just say—"

"Come with me."

63
jackson

MARGOT'S EYES WIDEN, and a bewildered laugh leaves her lips. "What?"

I scratch the side of my head, barely believing the words coming out of my mouth. "Come with me," I say again.

She starts to laugh again, but her smile fades when she realizes I'm not joking. It's a big ask, and she might say no, but I don't know why it's taken me so long to think of it. I mean, I guess I do. The van was too small and things between us were too new. Then the RV wasn't much bigger, and she was excited about her internship. But I've been thinking about what it would be like to have her with me ever since Dave mentioned it. I don't think I was expecting the band to be so on board with me bringing my girlfriend, but I guess Margot has become more than that to them.

I know she's more than that to me.

She stays frozen in place. "You're serious."

It isn't a question, but I nod anyway. "Or don't," I quickly add, and her eyebrows pinch. "I'll do whatever you want. If you want to stay here, I'm fine with long distance. But if you hate that, I'm fine with you coming with us—more than fine."

She opens her mouth, but no words come out at first. I think I may have stunned her into silence until she finally asks, "In the RV?"

My lips lift. "No, we're renting a tour bus. I think the guys are picking it up tomorrow."

Her eyebrows shoot up. "Tomorrow."

Shit, she's freaking out. "I don't mean you'd have to come with me tomorrow. I just mean, there would be plenty of room . . . if you decided to come."

She doesn't look any less confused. "On tour with you."

I let out a breath of laughter. "Yes."

She blinks, her hands flying up to stop me. "Wait, you're leaving *tomorrow?*"

I grimace and pace a few steps closer. There's still a kitchen island between us, so I rest my elbows on the counter. "Didn't you see the tour announcement?"

Margot comes closer until she's up against the counter on the opposite side of the island. Her cheeks flush. "I might have blocked the band."

"Committed," I say dryly, and she gives me an apologetic look. "Well, Brian had to add dates to the beginning of the tour or something, so now we're getting thrown into it without much of a break. The other guys all stayed, but they let me come home for a day."

She frowns. "You flew across the country, just to see me? For one day?"

"Why are you saying it like you're surprised?"

"Because I am surprised."

"You shouldn't be."

"But we're not together."

I level my gaze on her. "Yes. We are."

Her cheeks flush, and she shifts her weight. I like that she still squirms when I look at her. She must register my amusement because she scoffs and turns away. "You're impossible."

The corner of my mouth twitches. She's cute when she tries to put up a front.

She spins on her heels to face me again. "So, you want me to drop my life and tour with you?"

"I want whatever you want. I'm just saying, you can."

She huffs. "What about school?"

I shrug. "Take classes online."

"And my job?" She bites her thumb.

"You'd have to quit," I say with a nod.

She frowns, and her hand falls to her side. "But I like my job."

My lips lift as I push off from the counter. Walking around the island, I stop when I'm directly in front of her. Holding her face in my hands I say, "No one is asking you to give up anything. I just want you to know you have options."

"Options." She repeats the word like it had never occurred to her.

"And I can still be an accountant if you want, but I'd make you tell Brian. He can be a real asshole when he's mad. You should have seen his face when I told him I was coming here instead of recording."

She pushes me away with a shake of her head. "Would you stop? You're not becoming an accountant." A low chuckle escapes me as she steps away, and she smiles at the sound. "Wait," she says, registering what I just said. "What were you supposed to record?"

I scratch the back of my neck. "Did you block the band on all social media?"

She nods.

Rubbing my hands over my face, I curse. "Um, we—well, I guess *I*—sort of went viral for a song we haven't recorded yet, and now Brian wants to drop the single as soon as possible. I'm delaying it a few weeks by being here, and . . . he wasn't happy with me."

"You chose me over the band?" Her voice is so small when she asks that I almost don't hear her.

"I'd choose you over everything."

She looks at me more carefully, and she looks like she might be on the verge of crying again. I want to close the space between us, but the way she's looking at me has me stuck where I am. "Jackson, you don't choose anything over the band."

"Except you."

A tear slips from her eye, and she quickly wipes it away. "Can I listen to the song?"

My eyebrows cinch. "What song?"

"The one that went viral. The one you're supposed to be recording right now."

My heart pounds in my chest. I was hoping she had already heard it. I mean over four million people have by now. It would have been nice if she were one of them. Reaching for my phone, I try to shake my nerves as I pull up the video Mya sent me weeks ago. I click on the link before sliding my phone over to Margot and bracing myself for the worst.

The song is basically a love song to a girl who has already broken my heart, and there's no mistake it's about her. All the lines I whispered against her naked body in New York are in this song, and she knows those were for her.

After the intro, my voice starts to play, and I hate listening back to it. I don't think my voice necessarily sounds good or bad, but it sounds like *my voice*, and that alone makes it weird. I was hoping Dave would be the one to do vocals. It would have been an easy way to separate myself from it, but after it went viral, that wasn't an option.

I watch her listen to it until I can't anymore. Resting my elbows on the counter, I stare at my clasped hands in front of me because it feels like a safer option. She started with a soft smile when she heard the melody, but it slowly fell the longer my words washed over her. There's nothing bad in the song. I wouldn't write anything bad about Margot, but it's a balance of love and heartache.

When it ends, I don't look at her right away. I can't. Writing the song was one of the easiest things I've ever done. Singing it in front of the band? No problem. I don't even mind singing it in front of a crowd of people. But sitting here with Margot and listening to it leaves me feeling raw.

"Jackson," she says softly, and I force myself to lift my gaze.

There are tears in her eyes again. I hate seeing her cry. Maybe I shouldn't have shown her the song.

"Jackson," she says again with a shake of her head. "That song is incredible."

Something in my ribcage relaxes, and I feel like I can finally take a breath. "Thanks."

"No," she shakes her head. "It's *incredible*. The way it sounds upbeat, but the lyrics gut you. It's the type of song people will want to sing in the car, but . . . it's heartbreaking." Her eyes lock on mine on the last word like she's finally piecing it all together.

For once, I'm the one who doesn't know what to say, so I just look at her. I just wait for whatever conclusion she'll inevitably come to. She knows I want her to come with me. She knows I love her. She knows I wrote that song about her. She has all the information, and now it's up to her to decide what she wants to do with it.

64
margot

IT TOOK everything in me not to replay the song as soon as it ended. It's devastating, but there's a beautiful longing and ache to it, too. I'm so proud of him—I'm so *impressed* by him. He never ceases to surprise me in all the best ways. The fact that he's here, the fact that he's fighting for us, the fact that he wrote a song about me at all, let alone after we broke up. They're all things I never imagined him doing, and I realize that even though I've always thought highly of him, I still wasn't giving him enough credit.

Toward the end of our relationship, I had convinced myself I was the only one sacrificing for us. He got to be on tour, have adoring fans, and when he came home, he'd get to have me, too. It felt like an imbalance I desperately wanted to right. But the distance was a sacrifice for him, too.

"Margot." His voice is soft and low, like a light nudge.

I blink, snapping out of my thoughts.

Jackson lets out a light laugh. "Take all the time you need, but if you don't say something soon, I might pass out."

His hands are wound tightly together as he leans his forearms on the kitchen counter. He's tense again.

He's afraid like I am.

We're probably fearing different things, but the feeling is the same. He's suffering because he wants this so badly, and I know exactly how that feels. Except last time, I ran from that fear. I tried to escape it only to have it catch up with me when I was vulnerable and alone in the dark.

I don't want to be scared anymore.

I don't want to run.

I don't want to hide from the possibility of getting hurt.

With Jackson, it's always felt like jumping in with both feet. Why should this be any different?

"I'm thinking . . ." Jackson lifts his head, his face neutral but his eyes clinging to hope. With a slight nod, I say, "I want to come with you."

His piercing eyes are laser-focused on me. "Really?"

I nod, and the prickling sensation behind my eyes picks up again for a completely different reason. I'm a mess. Any emotion could probably make me cry after everything that's happened tonight.

"I love you." His words come out like a breath of relief—like he's been holding them in this entire time. I don't know if I'll ever get used to hearing him say it. Those words coming from him are a dangerous combination that has the power to stop me in my tracks and make my knees buckle. Jackson holds my face in his hands and kisses me. The urgency behind his kiss ignites my core with an entirely new flame—one that's hotter and brighter than anything I've felt before.

"Say it again," I say in heated breaths against his lips.

Jackson lifts me off my feet, and my legs wrap around him as he carries me toward my room. "Trust me, Red. By tomorrow morning, this entire apartment is going to know just how much I love you."

A small smile comes to my lips, but even his humor can't shake the need building inside me. My fingers weave through his hair and my mouth finds his neck. I lick just below his ear before gently sinking my teeth into his earlobe. Jackson's grip tightens, and he pushes my bedroom door open with his foot.

Lying me down on the bed beneath him, Jackson holds himself over me. The gray-blue of his eyes are almost completely swallowed by black as he looks down at me in my oversized sweater and shorts like I might as well be wearing lingerie. "You're mine," he says with an unmistakable hunger in his eyes.

"I'm yours," I answer, already frantically reaching for his pants. It isn't until I have the button undone that I hesitate. "Um." I swallow. "Have you been with anyone since—"

He's already shaking his head before I finish speaking. "No." I only have half a second to feel relieved because the next thing I know, his mouth is on mine. I hook my leg behind him to pull him closer, and his hard length gives a delicious pressure where I need it most. I writhe against him, but too quickly he's gone. Jackson holds himself up, keeping space between us. "What about you? Did you and Braden ever . . ."

My eyes widen. "No. Nothing happened. Not with him—not with anyone." My chest rises and falls as I nudge him closer with my leg again. "Only you. I only want you."

Jackson wipes a hand over his mouth as he looks me up and down, his eyes darkening. "Sit up."

I do as he says, and with more care than I expected, he pulls my sweater up and over my head.

I reach behind, having no patience to wait for whatever he's trying to do, and unclasp my bra before tossing it on the floor a few feet away. Those eyes take me in unapologetically, lingering on my chest for a beat too long before they lift to meet my stare again.

"Lie down."

I do, and he works to unbutton my shorts. My eyes jump from his hands working them down my legs, up to the ceiling, and back again. My rapid breathing makes it impossible to think straight, but I know I've never seen him like this. My body buzzes, and when he carefully slides my underwear down too, I suck in a breath.

Jackson stands from the bed, his eyes never leaving mine. His pants are already unbuttoned, but he undoes the zipper and takes them off the rest of the way. I can clearly make out the shape of him, straining against his briefs, and the heavy heat between my legs intensifies. It's only been two months since we were together in New York. We've gone longer without being together, but with everything that's happened between us, it feels like it's been years. It feels like I've been waiting for this moment, my entire life.

"You're beautiful."

My legs shake slightly, but I let them fall open, my eyes never leaving his. Jackson stands at the foot of the bed, drinking in the sight of me. He curses under his breath and reaches into his briefs to stroke himself, and I whimper at the sight of him touching himself while he looks at me.

Jackson's dark eyes flick up to meet mine as he removes his briefs, and the sight of him hard and bare has me aching. He positions himself over me on the bed again, spreading my legs wider with his knee. "I'm going to show you how much I'm yours."

I thought he would thrust inside me right away, but he doesn't. My heart hammers in my chest as he runs his thumb over my bottom lip before taking it between his teeth, dragging across it with equal parts pleasure and pain. "But first, this," he says, his voice rough. He kisses my swollen lips softly. "Mine."

With his hand on my throat, he moves to kiss me just below my ear. He kisses my shoulder. My chest. His hand moves from my throat to my breast where he slowly palms me while he takes my other nipple into his mouth, his expert tongue teasing me exactly how he knows will get a reaction from me.

My back arches, and I can feel him smile against my skin. "And these," he says before nipping at me again. "Also, mine."

Repositioning himself, he settles between my legs, and the head of his cock teases my slick entrance. "This too," he says, his voice dragging out of him. Bringing his mouth to my ear, he moves his thick head over my clit, and I gasp. "It's all mine, Margot. Every taste, every touch, every moan that comes from that pretty mouth. Do you understand?"

I nod, but I can't take much more of this. "All of me is yours," I pant and press against him, desperate to be filled.

Jackson groans like my words physically do something to him and goes back to massaging my clit with his cock. "Good girl." His voice is low in my ear and followed by his mouth on my neck as he spreads my shaking legs further. "And I'm yours," he says as he finally presses against my opening. "I will never stop being yours."

He eases in, inch by delicious inch, stretching me in the best way. My head presses back against the pillow, and I relish in the feeling of being his again. He feels so good—*too good*. The pressure of him inside me satisfies my aching need, and once he's fully rooted, I roll my hips to feel him deeper.

Jackson curses under his breath. "Fuck, you feel good."

I nod, agreeing with him, and roll my hips again. Our chemistry has always been undeniable this way, and when we started dating, it got more intense. But now? Now that I know he loves me and he knows I love him, it's even better.

Jackson starts to move, and I feel all of him. My nails dig into his skin, and I never want this closeness between us to stop. Every time he thrusts into me, I'm desperate to pull him deeper. He moves slow and deliberate, like he wants this to last as much as I do.

In.

Out.

In.

Out.

With every thrust, he hits deep enough to make me cry out. My hands knot in his hair as he swallows the sounds I make and thrusts into me harder. My legs tighten around him, holding him to me, and he groans. "You want me to fill you up, don't you?"

"Please," I beg, my eyes rolling back as he hits deep again.

"Fuck, Margot. It's been months, you can't beg like that and expect me to last." His head falls forward like he's trying to collect himself, so I roll my hips again to grind against him deeper.

I'm so close. Everything inside my body is wound tight. All I need is for him to let go and fuck me harder. I need to feel him stiffen and pour into me. I need to feel him claim me. I need to be his. I need him to make me his again. "Jackson, fuck me like I'm yours. Please."

With a possessive hand on my throat, he picks up the pace, slamming into me harder. He doesn't swallow my cries anymore, and I know it's because he's watching. He's watching what he does to me, and I can't take how good it all feels. My walls clench around his cock, and he fucks me into oblivion. I cry out his name as I shatter around him, and with one final thrust, he comes deep inside me, finding his release.

He stays there while he brushes my hair gently out of my face and peppers kisses across my neck and throat. I think he's worried he gripped me too tight as he spilled into me, but even that felt good. Everything with Jackson feels good.

"I love you," he whispers against my skin. "I love you. I love you. I love you."

65
jackson

THE SECOND TIME I came with her was in the shower. The third was as soon as she dropped her towel after drying off. Now we're back on her bed, and she's wearing nothing but a T-shirt I left here. I want to ask her if she wore it at all during the past six weeks, or if she had hidden it away in a drawer somewhere and only pulled it out now that we've fixed things between us.

God, I hope we've fixed things.

I keep waiting for her to change her mind. Maybe she decided she'd come with me in the heat of the moment. Maybe she'll realize how crazy it all is and stay here with her best friend, her job, her *life*.

She moves to lean back on her hands, her head tilting like she can read my mind if she tries hard enough. "What's wrong?"

I shake my head. "Nothing," I lie. The last thing I want to do is plant the seed of doubt in her mind. Her eyes narrow playfully, and I grin. "Margot, I'm home with you. Nothing could be wrong."

She blushes, and it's so goddamn cute.

"You look worried."

A small smile comes to my lips. I'm busted, but the fact that she knows me well enough to see it makes me happier than it should.

"The only thing I'm worried about is getting hard again if that shirt rides up any more than it already has." I nod to her bare thighs, where the hem of my T-shirt has gradually risen higher every time she shifts.

"Yeah. We definitely wouldn't want that," she teases as she squirms to make the shirt do just that.

I cock an eyebrow, and she grins wider.

Sitting up, she crawls onto my lap, straddling me. Without thinking, my hands go straight to her bare ass, and I grip her hard against me, my cock already begging to be inside her again.

"I'll put in my two-weeks tomorrow," she says as her fingers play with my hair at the base of my neck. "And it should be easy to switch to online classes since we're between semesters. I'll call the office Monday and figure it out."

"And you're sure about this?"

Her eyes lock on mine, and there's so much clarity behind them. "I am." A slight crease between her brow forms. "Is that what you're worried about?"

I weave my hand into her hair, my thumb brushing the soft skin of her cheek. "I never want you to feel like you're giving up your dreams for mine." The corners of her mouth fall, her lips relaxing into the perfect pout, and I kiss her without thinking. I can't resist.

She puts a hand on my chest and gently pushes back to look at me. "I'm not. I'm just going about them in a different way. I'll take my classes online, and instead of working for the magazine, I'll . . . focus on my blog," she says with a self-assured nod. "Or I'll find a job writing that I can do remotely." She drapes her arms around my neck. "My dreams are more flexible than yours right now, and I'm happy to bend if it means . . ." Her fingertips absently play with my hair again. "If it means I get to keep this—us."

Hearing her talk like this feels like a dream, and imagining her on tour with me feels like an even better one. "I think you'll like touring. Sleeping on a bunk isn't bad once you get used to it, and we should be able to afford a few more hotel stays when the schedule allows for it."

Her fingers graze the back of my neck and goosebumps prickle my spine. "And you're sure the guys won't mind?"

I let my hands slip under her shirt, so my fingers can trace her lower back. "Believe it or not, Dave brought it up to me a while back, and he was all for it."

Her eyebrows shoot up in surprise. "And the others?"

I let out a laugh. "They won't mind. And you know Mya will be thrilled."

Margot's lips lift. "I do like that she'll be there, too. It takes some of the pressure off."

"No pressure. If you hate it, come home early. Either way, it's only six weeks. Then we'll figure out where to go from there. We might end up in the studio, or Brian could extend the tour. Who knows?"

She takes a deep breath and nods. "Okay. I guess the only other thing is making sure I still earn enough to pay my half of the rent."

My hands slide up, and my thumb brushes under her breast. "I'll pay it."

"Absolutely not," she says with a bewildered laugh. "I can't let you do that."

"Sure, you can," I say with all seriousness. "I've been living with minimal expenses for months. Pretty soon I'll have more money sitting in my account than I know what do with."

She gives me a leveling look. "Jackson, I don't think—"

I kiss her. "You're sacrificing so much for me. Let me do this for you," I murmur against her lips.

"We'll see." She laughs, and I can't help smiling at the sound.

I kiss her again, my smile growing. "Take my money, Red."

She laughs harder, pushing herself off me. "You're obnoxious."

Rolling onto my side, I hook an arm around her waist before she can get too far. She lies on her back, looking up at me. Her hair is splayed around her shoulders, and I love seeing her like this. "I'm serious," I say, tracing my fingertips over her collarbone where my shirt slips off her shoulder. "Don't worry about working right now. Focus on school and let me do this for us."

Her eyes search mine. But before I can figure out what she's looking for, she quietly says, "Okay." Her smile returns, and she looks up at the ceiling and lets out another small laugh. "I can't believe we're doing this."

I can't believe I have to leave her again in just a few hours. This apartment, this room, this *girl*, has felt like more of a home to me than my actual home ever did. Her room looks almost exactly the same as it did when I left for the tour, but I notice the few pictures she had of us are all missing now. I'm almost tempted to ask her if she still has them, but it doesn't matter. We'll take new ones.

My eyes fall on what's left of the tattered bouquet she put on her dresser. "Why would Braden get you flowers?" My voice is soft, and for a moment, I wonder if I even said the words out loud.

I must have, though. Margot follows my gaze to her dresser before sitting up. "We went out to dinner tonight, and he ended up getting them for me."

Tearing my attention away from the flowers, I arch an eyebrow at her. "Like a date?"

She shakes her head. "No. Like friends."

I let out a huff of what might be considered laughter. "I don't think friends do that."

"Yeah." She grimaces as she smooths her damp hair back with both hands. "They don't."

I wait for her to say more.

"I know what you're thinking, but it's not like it was with Keith. I told Braden I wasn't interested from the start."

I shake my head. "I wasn't thinking anything. Especially not about fucking Keith." I should probably just let it go, but I can't. Not when those flowers are staring me in the face. "So, nothing's going on with Braden?"

"He likes me," she blurts like it's her best kept secret.

Lying on my back, I relax my arm behind my head. "Yeah, the flowers kind of gave that away. Nothing else, though?"

"Nothing else."

I remember how much she stared at Braden the night we drove home from the party with him last year and wonder if I should believe her.

I have to believe her.

She puts her hand on mine, her fingers tracing over the lines of my palm. "Just be nice . . . whenever you see him again."

Closing my hand around hers, I pull her back onto my lap. "Why wouldn't I be nice? I can't blame the guy for liking you." My hands run up her thighs and under the hem of her shirt again. It feels so good to touch her. I can't stop. My lips find her exposed shoulder, and I press a kiss to her skin. "You're beautiful." She sucks in air and my lips move to her neck. "The way you blush with your whole body is one of my favorite things about you." I move to her other shoulder, and she squirms in my lap a little. She can probably feel me getting hard through my briefs. "You have a fierce loyalty when it comes to the people you love." Her chest rises and falls in shallow breaths, so I pull back to look at her. She's biting her bottom lip, so I pull it free with my thumb. "And you have a temper that would bring any man to his knees."

She laughs, and I take it as an invitation to kiss her again. This time, she's the one to deepen the kiss. She holds either side of my face, and when her tongue drags over mine, I groan. Margot moves to kissing my neck while she works on getting my briefs off, and I help her. With her hands on my shoulders, she holds herself above me, just out of reach.

"Mya told me to get you flowers." I don't even know why I said it, but after seeing her with flowers from another guy, I feel like I need to confess that the thought crossed my mind.

"You don't need to get me flowers." She keeps kissing my neck, not even bothered enough to look at me.

"I will. One day."

She stops kissing me but only to lower herself onto my cock. "Okay," she breathes once I'm fully inside her. "One day."

Her hips start to move, and my head falls back. Fuck, she knows exactly what she does to me. My thumb moves to her clit, circling and teasing while she rides me. She decides the pace. She decides everything. I watch as this girl uses me however she wants to make herself feel good, and it's one of the hottest things I've ever seen. I'm completely at her disposal, mind, body, and soul, and I hope she takes everything I've got and never lets go.

66
margot

WHEN MY EYES FLUTTER OPEN, my first feeling is panic. What if I dreamt it? What if none of it was real? But once my eyes adjust, and I gently roll over, I'm met with the same view I woke up with every morning during the summer. Jackson sleeps on his stomach next to me, his muscular back gently rising and falling with each breath.

He loves me.

I always thought I never needed him to say it, but looking back, I think the fact that he hadn't fed into some of my doubt. It lingered in the shadows like a taunting whisper every time I wondered if I was stupid for being with him.

But I'm not stupid.

He isn't keeping me out of convenience for when he's home. He isn't looking for a part-time relationship the way I painted it in my head. He's here, fighting—for me, for us, for the life he wants us to have.

Gently, I reach out and run my fingertips over his arm to wake him. He stirs, squinting at me, and smiles lazily.

"What time is your flight?"

Jackson groans. "Three, but we don't need to talk about

that." He reaches for me, pulling me closer so he can kiss the top of my head.

Wrapping my arms around him, my fingers graze the muscles of his back. "Are you hungry? Want coffee?"

A low hum rumbles in his throat. "Yes, and yes. My dinner last night was airport snacks."

I pull away from him. "Okay, I'll make us something."

Jackson yanks me back so that I'm underneath him in one swift movement. "I'll cook." He has me pinned against the bed and memories of last night flood through my mind. We always do this. We go so long without seeing each other and then we can't keep our hands off each other when we're finally together.

I'm not complaining.

Looking up at Jackson, I say, "Check the time."

Those steel eyes are full of mischief. "I don't want to."

I let out a laugh. "Just check. I don't want you to miss your flight."

He stares at me for another beat, and I playfully swat at his chest. "Check."

"All right. All right." Without moving off me, he reaches for his phone. He only glances at the time before setting it down and shifting his focus back to me. "It's ten."

"We need to leave in two hours to get you to the airport on time."

The corner of his mouth kicks up. "Plenty of time." Pushing up the T-shirt I slept in, he leaves a trail of hungry kisses down my stomach, and my entire body wakes up at the contact. I never would have described Jackson as timid, but ever since I told him I love him, he's different. He's different in a way that makes me think he was holding back before. He's bolder, more assertive, even his gentle moments just feel—

His tongue drags over my wet heat, and I stifle a cry.

More.

His warm tongue dips inside me, and it's almost too much. I squirm to lessen the pressure, but a commanding hand grips my thigh to keep me in place.

"Jackson," I plead, and I don't even know what I'm begging for.

"Sorry," he murmurs against me. He sucks hard on my clit, and I think my vision blacks. "I have a lot to make up for." His tongue flattens against me like he can't get enough, and my legs shake.

"Fuck." I breathe out the word.

Jackson's voice is rough when he says, "After."

In the moment it takes for me to understand what he means, he's already back to gently sucking on my clit, and it feels too good for me to speak.

I jolt at the sound of someone knocking on the apartment door.

Jackson lifts his head to look over his shoulder. "Expecting someone?"

"No." The word comes out breathy and full of need. I'm so close. Gripping his hair, I push his head back down, and he lets out a low rumble of a laugh against my center. But then he's back to bringing me close to the edge within seconds.

The knocking starts again too, and this time I hear a muffled, "Margot?"

Braden.

"Shit." I scramble out of his reach and grab the shorts I wore last night, throwing them on with nothing underneath. "I have to get that."

Jackson is still where I left him, watching me with bewilderment. "Really, Red?"

I grimace. "I know. I just—" Another soft knock on the door pulls my attention away. "I'll just be a minute."

"Who is it?" he calls over his shoulder, but I'm already running to the door.

I open the door, out of breath. "Hey."

Braden is already a few steps away but stops and turns. He looks me up and down, before checking the time on his phone. "Did I wake you?"

I can only imagine what I look like right now. I went to bed with my hair wet, and I was on the brink of an orgasm just seconds ago. My cheeks flush. "No, I've been up. Just . . . had my hands full."

He nods and grips the back of his neck as he walks toward me. "Look, I wanted to apologize for last night. I shouldn't have said I wanted to kiss you."

"Oh." My cheeks flare. "Um, that's okay. We can forget it ever happened." I give him my best smile, but he looks disappointed by my response, and my smile falls. "I'm sorry. I don't know what you want me to say."

He shakes his head. "No, you're right. We should probably do that."

The sound of the coffee maker starts somewhere behind me, and a cabinet opens as Jackson no doubt gets out two coffee cups and sets them on the counter.

Braden looks at me with a furrowed brow before realization dawns in his features. He doesn't look mad or upset. He looks embarrassed, and it's somehow so much worse. "He showed."

"He did," I say softly. He gives me a tight-lipped smile and nods. Rocking back on his heels, he looks like he's about to walk away, so I blurt, "I'm sorry," because I can't think of what else to say.

Braden frowns. "What are you sorry for?"

I flounder. "I don't know. If I ever gave you the wrong idea or led you on."

He smiles. "You didn't. I just thought . . ." He shakes his head and lets out a light laugh. "I don't know what I thought." With a shrug, he holds out his hand. "Friends."

A genuine smile pulls at my lips. "Friends," I agree, shaking his hand.

Braden leans around me. "Hey, Jackson."

In seconds, Jackson's hand is on the small of my back, and all I can think is that I hope he put pants on. "Hey, man. It's been a while," he says to Braden.

"It has." The two guys bump fists, and I finally dare to look at Jackson beside me.

Good, he's wearing pants. No shirt, but he had the common sense to put shorts on over his briefs.

"Congrats on the headlining tour."

Jackson nods. "Thanks. Next time we're in town I'll set a couple of tickets aside if you want."

Braden's eyebrows lift. "Yeah?"

Jackson puts an arm around my shoulder. "Sure. My manager already knows to set some aside for Matt and Rae. I'll tell him to save a couple more."

Braden's gaze briefly falls to Jackson's arm around me, but it only lasts a second. "I appreciate it, man." Taking a step back, he nods toward the parking lot. "I've got to get going, but I'll see you around."

We wave goodbye, and Braden heads toward the parking lot, jogging down the stairs with his usual energy. My eyes linger on him, but he doesn't look back, and I know we'll be just fine. We'll be friends.

Closing the door, I turn and Jackson presses me up against it.

"That was big of you," I say as I look up at him.

Jackson kisses me gently on the lips. "I'm in a good mood."

I lift my brow. "Oh, yeah?"

Jackson's nose skims mine, his thumb tracing the line of my jaw, and I can already feel the ache in my core again. "You've given me everything I've ever wanted, Margot—more than I ever wanted." He kisses me a little more tenderly, and it steals the breath from my lungs. "Now it's my turn to make sure you get everything you want, too."

Reaching my arms up, I drape them around his neck and kiss him deeper. I know he means my career, my friends, my own life outside of him, but I will have all those things. What I want most right now is to be happy, and I am. I'm happier than I've ever been. I kiss him deeper and say against his lips, "I already have it."

67
jackson

THIS AIRPORT GOODBYE is different than the one we shared in New York. This one isn't *see you in a matter of months*. This one is *days*. This one feels more like *see you later*, I never realized how much saying goodbye to Margot took from me, but this one leaves me still feeling whole.

Because she's coming.

I wish she were coming now, but I can wait two weeks. Two weeks is nothing compared to two months. The days will fly by, and she'll be touring with me before I know it.

Her car is still running as I hold her tight. "I'll text you when I land."

Her arms wrap around my waist tighter. "Thank you for coming back." Her voice is small, maybe a little ashamed, like she knows how different our lives would be if I hadn't.

"I'll always come back for you, Red." I kiss the top of her head, and she looks up at me. Those warm brown eyes hold so much feeling, and I hope she never stops looking at me like this. I hope she always gives away everything she's thinking with a single glance.

She smiles faintly. "I love you."

My own smile widens. Even though I could see it in her eyes, nothing beats hearing her say it.

Tilting her chin up, I kiss her. "I love you."

It feels as natural as breathing. It feels like the most mundane yet liberating thing I could possibly say to her. Loving her is so ingrained in me at this point, saying it feels like coming home. It feels like finally letting out the breath I've been holding, and no grand gesture could ever beat this feeling.

I kiss her again, and she smiles against my lips. "Go."

"I am going," I say, kissing her again.

She laughs. "Jackson, I'm serious."

"So am I." I take her bottom lip between my teeth.

She sucks in a breath and my cock twitches. After breakfast, I made her fall apart twice, and she did the same to me. I should be content, but I don't think I'll ever get enough of her.

"Jackson, you can't fuck me outside the airport terminal."

"See," I say, holding her face in my hands and kissing her deeper. "That thought never even crossed my mind until you put it there."

She puts her hands on my chest but does a poor job of actually pushing me away. Shaking her head, she says, "Two weeks," and I take a little too much pleasure in how breathy her voice sounds.

"Two weeks," I repeat.

"Go," she says again, and this time I listen. Picking up my guitar case, I dip my chin.

"Two weeks," I say again.

Her smile blossoms on her face. "Go," she mouths the word again, and I grin.

Turning, I head toward the entrance of the airport. "I love you, Red!" I call over my shoulder, and when I look, she's shaking her head at me with an adorable smile.

"I love you," she says with a laugh before blowing me a kiss even though she's definitely shaking her head at me.

As soon as I'm inside the airport, I check in, find my gate, and gradually get pulled back to my reality. I'm on my own, flying out to meet up with the band so we can finalize the set list for our first tour. It's what I've always dreamed of.

I text Dave and Margot once I've boarded my flight. It all feels unreal. I can't wrap my head around the fact that she's willing to put certain parts of her life on hold . . . for *me*. My own parents can't even manage to call and check in, but Margot can quit her job and move across the country to live with me on a bus. It doesn't compute. I don't know how I got so lucky for her to want me that much, but I'm grateful for it. I'm grateful for everything she does.

Five hours later, I touch down in California. Between the back-to-back days of heavy travel and a sleepless night with Margot, I passed out for a couple of hours on the flight. I needed it.

I turn my phone off airplane mode, and a series of texts from Matt come in all at once.

MATT:

DUDE.

Margot is going on tour with you?

I knew you wanted her back, but I wasn't expecting you to basically ask her to move in with you.

I'm kind of bummed you didn't ask me.

I'd go on tour.

Maybe don't tell Rae I said that.

Anyway, happy for you. I'm glad she came around.

It's impossible to read the messages without the corner of my mouth lifting. I didn't even think of it as asking her to move in with me. I mean, I practically lived with her over the summer anyway, so it's not like we haven't done that. But with Margot, the steps we take never really feel like official steps. We're always just adapting to whatever our situation offers us, and right now, it's her coming on the road with me.

Usually, Matt saying something like that would make me panic—especially if it's something he hasn't done yet. He and Rae are perfect. They're two of the most compatible people I've ever seen. No one who sees them together can deny what they have. If *he* hasn't asked Rae to move in with him yet, what business do I have doing it?

But I don't feel any of that right now. I like the sound of Margot moving in with me. Even if it's just onto an oversized bus with four other guys and Mya. Even if it means we won't even share a bed because the bunks are too small. Even if it means Mya might steal her away from me to help with all her design projects. None of it diminishes the fact that she'll be there.

I sent Matt back a quick text and ask him how Grandma Lois and the rest of the family are before tapping on the group chat for the band.

JACKSON:
Just landed.

MARTY:
That was today?

I roll my eyes. I hate when he tries to be funny.

DAVE:
Almost there. See you in a few minutes.

I didn't check a bag, so I step around the crowd waiting for their luggage and head for a vacant bench near the front where I can keep an eye out for the RV.

I send Margot a text letting her know I landed like I said I would.

"Excuse me," a soft voice says from somewhere behind me.

I look over my shoulder to find two girls about my age practically huddled together like they're not sure which one should approach me first.

One of the girls with short blonde hair raises her hand in a sort of wave, and I assume she's the one who spoke first. "Sorry, but um . . . are you Jackson Phillips?"

I don't think it will ever not feel weird to have a stranger already know my name. Turning to face them, I say, "Yeah, I am. What's up?"

She looks at her friend with big eyes, and it makes me think her friend doubted it was me. The other girl has brown hair with blonde at the ends, and she definitely looks like she's stopped breathing at this point.

The blonde speaks again. "We're both huge fans. I mean, especially Amy." She nudges her friend who still looks very much in shock. "She's listened to all your stuff on repeat for months."

Amy looks at her friend like she just committed the worst type of betrayal.

I look at Amy. "That's awesome. Thank you." Amy smiles but still says nothing. The two girls just stand there staring at me, and it's starting to make me uncomfortable, so I clear my throat. "Um, do you want a picture or something?"

"Could we?" The blonde grins and pushes her friend Amy toward me.

"Oh—um, okay." Amy finally speaks, and her voice is shaky.

I put my arm around her for a quick photo, and it baffles me that I could make anyone feel this nervous. I'm just me. I'm just a guy who plays guitar and has no idea what the hell he's doing outside of that.

"Thank you so much!" Amy says once we're done, her voice high pitched and squeaky.

"Are you single?" the blonde asks.

Amy looks appalled at her friend, but I just scratch the side of my head and laugh. "Uh, no. I'm not."

For a split second, Amy looks like I may have just crushed her dreams, but her friend quickly ushers her away. "Figured. Thanks for the picture!"

"No problem," I say with another laugh, and I get a text before I can sit down again.

> MARGOT:
> See you soon.

There's a heart emoji with the message. I can't wait for her to be here.

There's honking outside and I look through the windows. It isn't the RV picking me up. It's the fucking tour bus. Grabbing my stuff, I hurry outside. I don't recognize the driver, but Dave is up front with him happily honking the horn to greet me. He must have asked if he could do that—at least I hope so.

Once they slow at the curb in front of me, I hurry up the steps and say hi to the new driver. The tour bus is a huge step up from the RV. It's bright and open even though it has a lot of dark wood accents to give it a moody vibe. There's a leather couch, an eatery, a kitchenette. It's incredible.

Everyone is sitting on the couch watching something on the flat screen TV across from them, and I'm met with varying waves and head nods.

"I can't believe you guys picked me up in a fucking tour bus." I can't wipe the smile off my face. They're insane.

"Well," Dave says with all seriousness. He sits on the arm of the couch before he continues. "We are headed straight for the first stop on the tour, and I figured you might need something to make you feel better in case things with a certain redhead didn't go the way you were hoping . . ."

"Is this even allowed?" I ask, as I look past him out the window to all the much smaller cars picking up their friends and family.

"No clue," Dave says with a laugh. "I don't think so, but Mark agreed to push our luck, and no one said anything."

I look over my shoulder at our new driver. Mark wears aviator sunglasses and gives me a two-finger salute before putting both hands back on the wheel as he maneuvers out of the airport.

Turning my attention back to everyone else, I realize they're all waiting for me to say something. Mya is biting her nails, Brian looks like he might still want to kill me if this wasn't worth it, and the rest of the guys are all staring at me with their eyebrows raised.

"She'll be here in two weeks." I say as I run my hand over my hair. "She's coming with us."

I think the tour bus physically rocks with the commotion of cheers and hollers that erupts from them all. Mya jumps to her feet and gives me a hug, and Dave pats me on the shoulder. I haven't even set my stuff down yet, and my face already hurts from smiling. When I lock eyes with Brian, I'm relieved to see him shaking his head and laughing.

Everyone here is happy just because I'm happy, and I think this is what family is supposed to feel like.

68
margot

FOR THE PAST TWO WEEKS, I've been simplifying my life in Florida. It helps that I'll still be able to leave most of my stuff here in the apartment, but I have all the essentials packed into a single duffel bag. I stare at it on my bed, already zipped shut because I started packing the moment Jackson left. Today is the day I get to see him again.

Karah wasn't thrilled when I told her I'd be leaving, but when I told her why, she surprisingly got on board with it. She told me to write as much as I can because nothing beats experiencing life on the road. Part of me thinks she had a wild streak back in the day. Was she reminiscing?

I set up my online classes on my own. There were only a few spots available for the upcoming semester, so I had to sign up for a few different courses with some questionable professors, but I'm sure I'll get through it.

My phone vibrates on my bed, and I look down to see a text from my dad.

DAD:
Fly safe. Let me know when you get there.

I smile as I answer him.

> MARGOT:
> Will do. Love you.

He wasn't happy when I told him what I'll be doing for the next six weeks, but as long as I keep up with my classes, he seemed to hate it a little less. We agreed it might be best if mom just thinks I'm taking the semester to do some traveling—which is true. I'll just leave out the part about being in a tour bus with my rockstar boyfriend and his friends.

"Hey." Rae pokes her head into my doorway. "Almost ready?"

Am I? I think I am. I have to be. I bite my thumbnail as I look at my bag again. "I'm crazy for doing this, aren't I?"

Rae comes into my room. "Yes, but that doesn't mean you shouldn't do it."

I nod. She's right. She's always right. "Okay," I say as I let out a breath. "I guess, I'm ready."

"You love him," she says with a small smile.

"I know."

"And he loves you."

I nod and try to shake off some of my relentless nerves.

Rae shrugs. "Look, if you ever need to come home, you can. Even if this apartment isn't my home anymore, you'll always have a home with me."

I give her a grateful smile. "Thanks."

"It's going to be great, Margot. And I'm going to come visit you."

"You better."

She grins. "Matt is already debating which date of the tour he wants us to go to."

I let out a light laugh. "Of course he is." My smile fades because there's something I've been meaning to ask her, and I don't know how I'll feel about her answer. Running my thumb over the strap of my duffel, I hesitate before slinging it over my shoulder. "Hey, can I ask you something?"

She leans against the door frame. "Always. You know that."

I do know that, but that doesn't make asking this any easier. "Did you push me to go out with Braden that night because you thought it would make me want Jackson back, or because you were hoping I'd start liking Braden?"

"Both."

A bewildered laugh bursts from my lips. "What?"

She shrugs. "I mean, either. I just wanted you to be happy, and you were so sad, Margot." She crosses the room and takes a seat on my bed. "I figured going out with Braden would either make you realize Jackson was worth the challenges he comes with, or maybe you'd realize you could find happiness in someone new."

I glance at her before looking back down at the strap in my hand, unsure of what to say.

"Hey," she says. "I love you and Jackson together. He's good for you. But two weeks ago, you didn't want to hear that. You were trying so hard to move past him, and I had to respect that."

I can't argue with her. After one more sweep around the apartment, I'm confident I'm not forgetting anything. Rae drives me to the airport, and it's crazy to think that a whole two weeks has passed since I last stood here with Jackson. I think of how it felt to be near him—to be completely and totally loved by him—and I'm buzzing with excited anticipation my entire flight to California.

I'm just as anxious when the plane eventually lands.

My hands shake as I walk through the airport, my fingers gripping the strap of my duffel tighter than they need to.

My heart pounds in my chest with every step toward the main exit.

Then, I see him. He's alone. There's no other bandmates,

there's no Mya, he doesn't even have his guitar. It's just Jackson. He must have taken an Uber to meet me.

I stop in my tracks, and just look at him. He hasn't seen me yet. His back leans against the outside wall as he looks down at his foot as it scuffs the pavement. All the anxiety and stress I've held on to all day finally melts, and the rush of it has my eyes prickling as happy tears threaten to spill over.

Jackson looks up, and those steel-blue eyes come alive when they see me. He grins, and I hope I never forget what he looked like in this moment. I hope I never forget how the way he looks at me made me feel at this very second.

Rushing toward him, I drop my bag as soon as he's within reach so I can wrap my arms around him. He feels familiar, and safe, and exciting, and unknown all at once.

And when he kisses my hair and says, "Welcome home, Red," he feels a lot like that, too.

epilogue
One Year Later

jackson

THE VIBRATIONS from the show we just played and the energy from the crowd reverberates through me as I step inside the tour bus. Tonight, we played the amphitheater in Tampa, and it feels surreal to perform where I've paid to watch some of my favorite bands.

Pulling my sweat-soaked shirt over my head, I grab a fresh one from my bunk and slip it on before walking back to the front of the bus.

The band is all talking over each other about the show with grins on their faces.

Dave and Brady sit on the couch in front of the TV with their fiancés, Lynn and Kasey, by their sides. Kasey lives with us on the bus, but Lynn still lives here. Dave usually flies back and forth between shows to see her, and tonight he'll probably stay at her place.

Marty has already gone to a fan's hotel room nearby and told us not to expect him until morning. The girl was waiting for him at the side of the stage, so I'm starting to think he sets up his hookups in advance. We're busier now. We play bigger venues with less down time, so his usual tactics of sneaking into the crowd to pick up a fan are obsolete.

Mya and Brian left to pick up our leftover merchandise from the venue, but they'll be back soon. Mya doesn't even have to run the table anymore. Now the venue staff takes care of it, and she just picks up the inventory at the end of the night, takes count, and makes a new order.

Everything has worked out. I don't know how the hell I got this lucky, but I wouldn't change a single thing about my life on the road.

Then my eyes land on *her*. Margot sits at the small foldout table as she types on her laptop. She's wearing leggings with a lightweight pullover, one leg folded underneath her. She's comfortable here—relaxed. Hell, she's at home here, with me, and I'll never get sick of seeing her when I walk off the stage. Most nights she comes out and watches the show, but then there are nights like tonight where she works through them. Walking up to her, I place a finger under her chin to lift her face toward mine to kiss her. "Still working?"

She smiles against my lips. "Almost done."

When I release her, those bright eyes fall back to her screen where she types a few more lines before she stops and looks at me again. "Another band reached out to me to do a post on them."

"Nice. Which one?" She's had so many bands contact her. At this point, it's impossible to keep track. She writes about her life on the road, the cities she sees, the local places where we stop for lunch. She writes about everything. She wrote about a couple of the bands who have opened for us to try to get them more publicity, and it's worked. Now other bands are catching on.

"Air Trek? Heard of them?"

I try to think. "Yeah, I have actually. One of their songs

popped up on a playlist while I was working out a while back. I don't remember much about it, but I remember liking it."

The familiar spark of motivation shines in her eyes. "Okay, I'll look them up. No talk about them in the industry yet?"

It's what she always asks. I think she likes helping the small fish in the pond more than anyone else. "Not that I know of, but you'd have to ask Brian."

She looks back at her laptop and types something else. "Okay. I will." Glancing back at me, she adds, "How was the show?"

"Great." I sit across from her and prop my elbows on the table. "And did you finish your homework?"

With a tight-lipped smile, she playfully tilts her head to the side, her long hair cascading down her arm. "Yes, I did."

"Good." I lean forward across the table and kiss her again. "Because they'll be here any minute."

She blinks like she might have forgotten. "Shit, that's right. We're in Tampa."

I let out a breath of laughter and her eyes widen.

"We're in Tampa!" she says again, this time with a grin.

"I know!" I say, matching her excitement.

She laughs as she shuts her laptop and puts it away.

The two couples on the couch get to their feet, and Dave puts his arm around Lynn, holding her close. "We're headed to the Hard Rock. Want to come?"

I shake my head. "Thanks, but our friends will be here soon."

"That's right," Dave says with a nod. "Tell them all I said hey. I texted Brian but if he starts bitching, tell him where to find us."

They all wave before heading off the bus, and then it's just Margot and me. She gets to her feet, wraps her arms around me, and leans her head against my chest.

Having her here is the best feeling.

Seeing her thrive is the best feeling.

Being loved by her, is the *best* feeling.

It's not a quick hug. She doesn't pull away in a hurry to prepare for Matt and Rae. It's a hug where she relaxes into me. One that lets me inhale her strawberry shampoo.

She looks up at me, and I kiss her. The kiss is slow and sweet, and even when we break apart, she doesn't pull away. I brush my thumb across her cheek, tracing over her scattered pattern of freckles, and when I softly say, "I love you," it's nothing but a murmur against her lips.

"I love you," she says before pushing up on her toes and kissing me again.

"Jackson!" Matt's undeniable voice hollers from somewhere outside, and Margot's face breaks into a grin. She ducks around me and practically runs out of the bus. I know she's not that excited to see Matt, but where there's Matt, there's Rae.

By the time I reach the top step of the tour bus, she already has her arms flung around Rae's neck in the parking lot below, and Matt has cupped his hands around his mouth to let out another, "Jack-son!"

Our favorite couple isn't alone either. Braden walks with Matt and tosses me a wave.

The last time I saw Braden, he was knocking on Margot's door to apologize for wanting to kiss her. It's weird to think about, but I still like him. And Margot likes him. I'm glad he took me up on the free ticket.

"It's about time you showed up," I say to Matt once he lowers his damn hands.

He grins. "You've been crying yourself to sleep every night without me, haven't you?"

I cock a half-smirk. "And writing in my diary."

I step back so he can jog up the steps into the tour bus, and he crashes into me with a hug, patting me on the back before he lets go.

He looks around the place like he's considering buying it, but my attention gets pulled away when Rae wraps her arms around my waist. "The show was so good tonight!"

I lift my arms, caught off guard by the gesture, and hug her back. When she lets go, I turn to Braden and nod. "I'm glad the wristbands worked."

Matt pauses from taking in the tour bus and looks at me. "Was there a chance they wouldn't?" He holds up his arm to show the neon pink paper band that gave them all access to come back here.

I shrug. "You never know."

Matt drops his arm with a shake of his head. "Motherfucker," he mutters with a laugh and my grin widens.

The tour bus has never felt more like home.

---

margot

It doesn't take long for me to give Rae a complete tour of the bus, but by the time we make it back to the front, the guys are all sitting on the couch with beers in their hands. Just the sight of Jackson sitting with his elbows on his knees while he listens to his closest friend talk about his latest lacrosse game is enough to make me smile.

His eyes flick to me as soon as he registers our return, his hand casually lifting his bottle of beer with a raise of his eyebrow, silently asking if I want one.

I shake my head.

By the time Rae takes a seat next to Matt, the couch is starting to look a little crowded. I end up sitting on the floor in front of Jackson, my back nestled between his legs. His free hand lazily traces circles along the side of my neck while he responds to something Braden said, and I pick up my conversation with Rae, asking her how her classes have been.

A loud groan followed by, "For the love of God, Brian, I know what I'm doing," has us all looking toward the entrance of the bus. Mya bounds up the steps, holding a large box in front of her. "Can someone please tell him I know what I'm doing?"

"She knows what she's doing, Brian," Jackson calls out before taking another sip.

"Thanks, Lover Boy," she says with a huff. Then she looks around, realizing most of the people here are strangers to her. "Oh, hello." She smiles, her green eyes sparkling despite the sweat glistening on her brow.

I look back at our friends, ready to introduce Mya, but the way Braden looks at her stops me in my tracks. He may have given me some not-so-subtle glances back when he had a crush on me, but he has *never* looked at me like that.

He quickly scrambles to his feet. "Here, let me take that."

She looks up at him as he takes the box. "Holy shit, you're hot."

Braden may not know what to say back to that, but his ears are *pink*, and when he sets the box down and turns back around, he's definitely blushing.

Mya blinks like she didn't mean to say it out loud, her eyes darting to Rae. "Is he your boyfriend? I didn't mean—"

Rae shakes her head with a laugh. "No, he's very single."

That's all it takes for Mya. She goes from slightly embarrassed and nervous to letting her eyes linger on Braden as he returns to his seat.

She shakes her head and waves to the small group on the couch. "I'm Mya by the way." She steps aside as Brian comes up behind her, grumbling something about needing a damn golf cart to lug this shit back and forth. Gesturing to her uncle as he passes her, she adds, "And this grumpy asshole is Brian."

"Band manager," he corrects as he sets his box on top of the one Braden put on the table. His suit is wrinkled from the walk, and it looks like he broke a sweat, too. He glances around the room before focusing on Jackson. "Where the hell is everyone?"

"Casino. They texted you."

Brian pulls out his phone. "Ah, okay. You guys heading that way?"

"We're not sure where we'll end up yet," Jackson says with another sip of his beer. "By the way, this is Matt, Rae, and Braden."

Brian waves to our friends, but it's clear his mind is somewhere else. To be fair, I think his mind is *always* somewhere else. He could probably use a night at the casino to lighten up a little.

Mya grins and waves to Matt and Rae.

Pulling his phone out of his pocket, Brian must check the message from the guys. His eyes lift to Mya. "You coming?"

"Um . . ." Her eyes quickly dart to Braden who is trying and failing not to look like his night hangs in the balance of her answer. There's a slight lift to her lips when she says, "No. I think I'll stay here."

Brian nods. "All right," he says as he quickly sends a text, probably to Dave. "You kids have a fun night."

I expect Mya to go straight to Braden, but she doesn't. Instead, she sits next to me on the floor and gives Rae her complete attention. "I hear you want to be a teacher. What grade are you hoping for?"

Rae lights up, ready to talk about her passion, and I settle against Jackson's legs. I love this. I love that we can fall back into a sense of normalcy with the people we love. I love that everything about the scene in front of me is normal. This is exactly what we'd be doing if we still lived in the same apartment. Except this is better. It's better because now we have

Mya to add to the mix, and it's better because Braden has moved on. It's better because Jackson is happy doing what he loves, and it's better because I get to be a part of his dreams while still chasing mine.

I love our lack of a traditional home, and our hectic life.

And I love that the people around us have become our family.

Glancing up at the guy behind me, I smile. Jackson is in the middle of telling Matt and Braden about the band pranking Brian last week by changing the autocorrect settings in his phone. I smile at the story. It *was* funny. They made it so that every time he texted "no," it showed up as "yes." Then they started making all sorts of ridiculous requests.

But the story isn't even what pulls the smile from me. It's *him*. It's his messy hair and bright eyes. It's the subtle curve to his lips as he speaks. It's the way he can radiate confidence and still come across as humble.

He must feel my stare because he glances down at me mid-sentence and pecks me on the lips before finishing what he was saying. And when I turn back around, Rae is watching us with a satisfied smile.

She knows there's no questioning it anymore.

Out of all the things I love, I love my rockstar boyfriend the most.

I just wanted to be his, but he gave me so much more.

also by heather garvin

Make Your Move

Crossing The Line

Take What You Can

acknowledgments

The *Just Yours* duet is finally complete, and I couldn't have done it without help!

First, I'd like to think everyone who loves Jackson and Margot. If there weren't readers, eagerly waiting for the second half of their story, I'm not going to lie, I probably would have given up on writing it.

A special thanks to Dani Keen for reading the roughest version of this book and helping me shape it into something more defined. Your input is always appreciated!

Writing *I Just Want To Be Yours* was more challenging than I thought, so I want to thank everyone who beta read this book because they did it on a tight schedule. Tisa Matthews, Courtney Grifo, Letizia Lorini, Gabby Spiller, and Catherine Broomell, and Dawn Anderson all worked diligently to turn this story into the ending Jackson and Margot deserve.

A massive thank you to my incredible editor, Kristina Haar. You somehow know how to boost my ego while simultaneously telling me all the things I need to make better, and I can't thank you enough! I know my stories are in great hands with you, and I feel truly lucky to have had your help on this project. Your enthusiasm and love for these characters means the world to me. Thank you!

Thank you to Ava Hines for being the final set of eyes on this book! I know romance isn't your favorite, but your feedback is always so fun to read, and you're great at catching those pesky typos my eyes refuse to see.

As always, I couldn't have done this without each and every one of you.

Thank you.

about the author

Heather Garvin works as a nationally certified sign language interpreter by day and writes a variety of romances in her spare time.

Aside from working and writing, she's also a wife, mom, and a fur mama to two dogs, two cats, and Tuskan: the horse who inspired her publishing company, Tuskan Publishing LLC.

There's nothing Heather loves more than hearing from readers. Connect with her @heathergarvinbooks

www.ingramcontent.com/pod-product-compliance
Lightning Source LLC
LaVergne TN
LVHW030313070526
838199LV00069B/6464